SOUND Of Us

T.M. POLAK

Cover design by: AK Cover Designs

Developmental Editing by: Memos In The Margins

This is a work of fiction. While some real names, places, or events may appear, they are used in a purely fictitious manner. All characters, organizations, and scenarios are products of the author's imagination or are used fictitiously. Any resemblance to actual persons, living or dead, or to actual events, is entirely coincidental.

Independently published

First edition: 2026

Print ISBN: 979-8-9987943-3-9
eBook ISBN: 979-8-9987943-2-2

For inquiries or permissions, please contact:
tmpolak.author@gmail.com

CONTENT WARNING

This book discusses and includes sensitive topics such as terminal illnesses (Alzheimer's), sudden death (heart attack), stalkers, kidnapping, homicide, sexual harassment and assault, and themes involving hearing loss and assistive hearing devices.

DEDICATION

This book is a world apart from the first, shaped by new experiences and lessons, and it belongs to all the incredible mothers out there...the ones who hold families together with quiet strength and endless patience.

My mother, Maria, is the quiet force I am so much of who I am. She raised me with a patience I never seemed to possess, always there to shield me when I stumbled into trouble, and loving me fiercely even on the days I gave her every reason not to. Her unwavering support has been the steady ground beneath my feet, and her pride in me is a warmth I carry everywhere.

Wendy, my mother-in-law, left this world before she could ever hold *Code of Heart* in her hands. Still, it was her encouragement and belief in me that made that book possible. She cheered me on with the same pride as my own mother, and raised a son who became the kind of partner I once thought only existed in stories. She was the rare kind of in-law people hope for but seldom find.

I count myself unbelievably lucky to have had both a 'Delia' and a 'Denise' shaping the chapters of my life.

THE WEDDING

Estrella

Months ago, at the wedding...

The lagoon shimmered beneath the afternoon sun, its waters alive with laughter and love from the small wedding on the dock. Estrella Vale leaned back in her seat with a satisfied smile, taking a sip of the crisp passion fruit cocktail cradled in her hand.

Escaped wisps of lavender hair blowing in the gentle breeze, she watched the happy couple stand before their family and friends. She couldn't help but admire her work. That kernel of light within her—that special gift she possessed—thrummed joyfully beneath her skin.

The threads of life shimmered faintly around her, their constant presence humming with power and possibility. Estrella continued to smile, content...for now. Her work was never truly finished.

While vows of forever were spoken between the couple, her attention drifted elsewhere—to another pair among the guests. A fair beauty with hair as dark as the midnight sky and a man with sun-kissed skin and carefully styled strands of spun gold and sunlight. The moment their eyes first met, and their paths converged, she felt it: that familiar tug at the edges of her consciousness, a whisper brushing her very essence.

It was time.

A storm flickered in her azure gaze as she blinked once, those shimmering multi-colored ribbons sharpening, invisible to mortal eyes.

Before her, two luminous patterns appeared where those two stood. Patterns that were different from the others in attendance—fragile, intricate, and incomplete.

Alone, they were beautiful. Together, they would form something magnificently whole.

Something irrevocable.

A secretive feline smile crept across Estrella's face, her attention locked on the two unsuspecting guests. She leisurely emptied the glass flute, paying no mind to the small cool droplets of condensation that trickled down onto the hollow of her neck.

She had work to do.

Adelen

The wedding was a true declaration of love and commitment, and one of the most picturesque events Adelen Mazao had ever been privileged to attend.

She stood barefoot on the dock behind her friend Aurelia Douro's charming cottage, beside the small group of friends watching her marry Levi Lockwood under the small, but elaborately decorated archway at the end. They held each other's hands, devotion and contentment lining their faces, as they recited their vows.

In a nontraditional flowing turquoise dress, Aurelia reminded her more of a water sprite than a bride, and yet she couldn't picture her friend in anything else. The same could be said for Levi, standing tall and proud in tan linen pants and a brilliant white shirt. Their ease and comfort translated into the simple glamor of the event.

The expansive lagoon behind them glimmered, refracting a vibrant sunset. The streaks of light caught the small crystals embedded in the billowing cream fabric of the archway. It added an otherworldly sparkle to the beautiful couple. The dock was lined with glowing lanterns on either side, adding to the serenity of the moment.

The hem of Adelen's long pomegranate floral dress rustled in the light breeze, gently wrapping around her legs. Though the sun was setting, its warmth remained, the air comfortable and sweet. She brushed back a lock of wavy midnight hair that had blown across her face and focused on the ceremony.

She was truly happy for her friend, especially after everything she'd had to go through to reach this moment. She hadn't known Aurelia long, being the first friend Adelen made since moving to Joia City a few months ago, but there was no one more deserving of happiness.

Still, a small twinge of jealousy hit her when the ceremony ended, and Levi swept Aurelia into his arms for a passionate kiss. For a fleeting moment, Adelen wished it was her under that archway—not with Levi, of course, but as the bride.

Except she didn't have a groom.

She wasn't remotely close to getting married.

Amidst the clapping and joyful chatter, Adelen slid a sidelong glance at one guest in particular, who was staring right back at her.

The flower guy.

A towering blonde man with mischievous sapphire eyes had preceded Aurelia down the dock, carrying a delicate white basket of petals, and had thrown them down with dramatic flair. Dressed similarly to Levi, he reminded her of a Viking warrior attending his first social event, the entire ensemble at odds with his nature.

He was one of Levi's best friends—the one who'd come to Aurelia's rescue after a kidnapping and assault plot not long ago—that she hadn't met yet.

But the moment he stepped out of the cottage to begin his petal-dropping duties, her breath caught. Everything around her faded quietly into the background, hovering on the edges of her vision. Entrapped in a snare, she couldn't look away.

And the way his eyes locked on hers...

At first, he'd looked startled, eyebrows rising high, mouth slackening. The dainty basket in his hand nearly spilled to the ground when he abruptly stopped walking.

As if he felt it too.

Adelen knew his expression mirrored hers, both taken aback. She'd never experienced such an intense feeling of recognition. Like sinking into the comfort of a warm embrace. The sensation signaled that whatever her future entailed, he would play an integral role in it.

It was exciting and thrilling and sent her heart racing, but also strange and terrifying and too good to be true. She smothered the emotion, chastising herself for getting swept up in the moment.

Adelen never believed in "love at first sight," and she sure as hell wasn't about to start now. Though that didn't stop her eyes from raking over him, head to toe and back again. There was nothing wrong with appreciating eye-candy.

He was the stuff of women's dreams. The sultry lips, firm jaw, body lean and muscled—all things that made her blood sing and her heart weary. He reminded Adelen of Tommy Nunes, a boy from high school she had the displeasure of knowing.

Tommy had been the star athlete in just about everything—track, baseball, soccer—and was the class salutatorian. Meanwhile, Adelen had primarily kept to herself in high school, having learned that drawing attention never ended well.

For all parties involved.

By that point, her dating history had been disastrous, earning her a reputation for being a vicious ice queen. So when sandy-haired Tommy with the easy smile and soft blue eyes had taken an interest in her, Adelen had been hesitant.

She had avoided his advances for *months*, going so far as to turn and walk in the opposite direction when he tried to talk to her. But his gentle persistence had eventually worn her down, and she made the ill-fated decision to go on a date with him.

Just one date.

That was just the beginning of a string of disastrous dating fiascos that caused her to stop trusting men who weren't already family. In her experience, men were good for only one thing, and she preferred to keep it that way.

Adelen shook off the memory, focusing back on the present, and on the sinfully hot man still staring at her with wonder. She gritted her teeth, letting the aloof indifference she'd honed over the last decade take over, forcing her attention away from him. She needed to focus on something else—*anything* else, except for those eyes.

She wasn't willing to go down that path again. She had bigger problems to deal with.

Owen

"I want to apologize in advance for my amazing petal-throwing prowess—we both know that, as lovely as you may look, you're about to be upstaged," Owen Voss declared.

He and Aurelia were the only ones left inside her home, moments away from stepping out the glass patio doors and down to the end of the dock where Levi anxiously awaited. It was the perfect day for his friends to have their second-chance wedding.

Owen had begged to officiate (again), but given how his antics impacted their first courthouse wedding, he'd been banned from it. He was still a bit miffed at how fast both Levi and Aurelia had said no.

He did, however, manage to convince them to let him be the flower guy.

And he was going to crush it.

Aurelia giggled and patted him on the shoulder. "You keep telling yourself that. I'll be surprised if you make it down the dock without tripping and falling into the lagoon."

In mock offense, Owen's hand flew onto his chest and over his heart. "Your disbelief wounds me," he gasped.

"Yeah, yeah, yeah...are you ready to roll? Levi looks like he's going to throw up from nervousness, and I'd prefer to keep my dock clean."

Owen rolled his eyes. "Levi always looks like he's going to throw up over something. This isn't news."

Aurelia reached around him, grabbed the handle of the tall glass door separating the living area from the deck to open it, and *shoved.*

"Hey! That was rude!" Owen hissed over his shoulder, surprised by her strength. Aurelia just laughed and wiggled her fingers in goodbye. He quickly composed himself, making sure no petals had escaped the basket. He was taking this job *very* seriously.

Satisfied every petal was accounted for, he looked out at the scene, and the few close guests, and his world came to a screeching halt.

Silver eyes.

He'd never seen anything like it. Captivating and immobilizing, he could see the entire universe gleaming within them. In that short span of time, Owen memorized everything about the woman standing next to his friends—her silky obsidian hair lifting in the wind, the smattering of freckles across her cheeks and nose, the full lips, and the dangerous curves lingering beneath her dress.

He had no words, none at all, to describe the sudden urge to be near her. Owen was about to toss her a smile when her expression shifted. Whatever mutual wonder they had momentarily shared was wiped from her face, replaced by calculated disinterest.

She turned away.

And just like that, he was discarded.

For some reason, the movement cut him deeply. She was a stranger, and yet...she wasn't. The corners of his mouth dipped down.

The whole situation was strange.

Unfortunately, there was no time to dwell on it. Owen had flower petals to toss, and he wasn't going to mess up another wedding for Levi and Aurelia. He took one step towards the dock, surveying the others there, when he saw it.

Those creepy, swirling cerulean eyes from Estrella Vale, the matchmaker who brought Levi and Aurelia together. He frowned at the middle-aged woman, seeing firsthand the weird eye thing Levi had once described.

Having seen it firsthand now, Owen was more convinced than ever that she was a witch. He never believed in magic, but it was awfully coincidental that these strange feelings were suddenly hitting him while her eyes did that swirling thing.

He was going to get to the bottom of this.

But first—petals.

Squaring his shoulders, he strolled across the deck and down the dock towards Levi, sprinkling sweeping fistfuls of petals in his wake. As he drew closer to Aurelia's friend, he added a little extra razzle-dazzle to his technique, hoping to catch her eye.

Owen for sure caught her attention—too focused on her reaction to watch where he was walking. His foot caught a slightly raised plank, and he would have found himself in the lagoon had he not grabbed onto a post and righted himself.

He caught a wisp of a smirk appearing on those exquisite lips of Aurelia's friend as he careened toward the water.

This was not going well.

After the ceremony, the guests sat at the set dining table on the deck to enjoy the catered barbecue reception. He snagged a seat directly across from Adelen—thankful that his friend Ivy Blake knew her name—and tried to spark up a conversation, hoping to recreate that earlier moment between them.

Hell, he did his damnedest to flirt, but in the end, it made no difference.

All he got were basic one-word answers.

Bored stares and tight smiles.

He didn't know what to do. Because he *did* notice the slight tinge of red that would creep up her slender neck and onto her cheeks when he engaged and asked questions.

She *had* to be as affected as he was.

Right?

He snuck a glance at Estrella, and found her watching their interaction with keen interest, the corners of her mouth tipped up in amusement. Her lavender hair was pulled back in a low knot, revealing more of her face. Those eyes danced behind her dark frames. Owen scowled.

She's definitely a witch.

When the night was winding down and everyone was beginning to leave, Owen found himself at the edge of the dock staring out into the water. His sorry attempts at interacting with Adelen had set his nerves on edge. He needed a few moments to himself to regroup.

He felt Estrella's presence before she appeared at his side.

"Penny for your thoughts?" Estrella didn't look at him, but merely stood with her hands clasped together, looking out as Owen did. Her proximity scratched across his skin in an uncomfortable assessment.

"Everyone else thinks I'm crazy, but I saw your eyes do that thing that I've heard about. Be straight with me, I won't tell a soul—are you a witch?"

Estrella genuinely laughed. "What if I said I was? What would that change?" She finally turned her head to look at him. "You've been given a gift, Owen—the opportunity for happiness. What you do with that gift is completely up to you."

He met her entertained gaze with an annoyed and, albeit slightly curious, one.

"Sometimes the best things in life require hard work and sacrifice; a surrender of a piece of oneself to carve out space for something bigger. You both need to decide how much you're willing to reveal." She said cryptically, her smile widening further. "Be patient and come see me when you're ready."

"Ready for what?" The middle-aged woman wasn't making a lick of sense.

"You'll know when the time comes."

Without giving him a chance to respond, Estrella spun on her heels, leaving Owen alone on the dock with his thoughts.

She still hadn't answered his question.

CHAPTER 1

Adelen

This was a mistake, Adelen thought as her mother prattled on through her cell phone's speaker. Delia was in rare form that morning—extra shrill, overbearing, her voice hitting a pitch that drilled straight through Adelen's head. She winced and pulled the phone away from her sensitive ears, jabbing the volume down.

She owed her mother a call, but should've planned a better time. There was no such thing as a quick conversation with Delia Mazao. And calling it a conversation was generous—she hadn't managed to insert a full sentence yet.

"I don't like you living out there by yourself," her mother scolded. "Are you eating enough? You're going to waste away to nothing now that I can't bring you my food to eat." Typical European mother—raised to feed people even when they weren't hungry. Adelen had a healthy appetite; her active lifestyle required constant snacks and meals to keep her energy going. She *loved* trying new cuisines.

"Mamá—" Adelen tried, but Delia barreled right through, too entrenched in her tirade to notice.

"You're too far away from your family, all the way across the country. First, it was your brother; now, you! All my babies have left me...Have you made any friends?"

A twinge of guilt pricked like a needle beneath her skin. Adelen ignored it. Pushing a strand of onyx hair behind her ear, she stuffed her laptop into a small backpack and grabbed her keys, the movements brisk and deliberate. She refused to let this interrogation be the reason she was late for work.

Her parents hadn't taken the news of her relocation well. Her twin brother, Diogo, had been relentlessly suspicious, but mercifully hadn't pushed yet. He would, though. That nosy bastard always did.

Adelen crouched to slip on her favorite black lace-up ankle boots, the leather soft and broken-in from years of wear. By habit, she checked the small knife and pin she'd hidden inside each, and they were still secure. The scent of oil and polish clung faintly to her fingers. Satisfied, she tugged the laces tight. She was scouting their new filming location today and had no idea what kind of terrain she'd be walking into.

"Yes, I've made friends and—"

"Who are these friends? They aren't getting you to do bad things like drugs, are they? I swear to god, Adelen, I will slap the drugs out of you myself," Delia threatened.

"Oh my god," she muttered. "No one's doing drugs—"

"Do you have a boyfriend yet?" Delia pressed. "Your father and I aren't getting any younger, and your brother is a lost cause. I don't know what kind of men are out there in Joia City, but don't bring home anyone like your cousin Lucy's boyfriend..."

A flash of dirty-blonde hair, crystal blue eyes, and an infuriatingly easy smile cut through her thoughts. Adelen growled under her breath and shook her head, chasing the unwanted image away.

Thankfully, her mother wasn't able to witness the sudden flush across her cheeks. She'd never hear the end of it.

"...your aunt is *this close* to telling that boy to buy real deodorant because the organic stuff he makes himself isn't doing him any favors," Delia blathered. "Did you know he told your Tia Maria her cooking was *too spicy*? *Too salty!* Adelen, please don't bring anyone like this into my house. If you'd just come back, Fatima's son—he's your age, has a good job—"

"*Mamá, stop.*" Adelen's patience snapped, sharp as a frayed wire. "It's only been a few months, and you're worrying for nothing. I told you this was a great opportunity to set up a new POLmArK division here. No one's doing drugs, and I'm not interested in any men right now."

Lie, truth, lie. Her conscience whispered the words in rhythm. The choice to move wasn't because it was a great opportunity; she'd made maybe one friend, and someone *had* caught her attention—someone impossible to ignore.

But at least she wasn't doing drugs.

With a deep breath, she straightened and caught her reflection in the long citrine jewel-edged mirror by the apartment entrance. It was a sparkly, eclectic piece she found at a thrift store a few years ago and promptly fell in love with.

Silver-gray eyes stared back, alert and irritated, framed by thick dark lashes and the pale wash of morning light filtering through the blinds. Her gaze tracked down her freckled nose, over the curve of her lips, and to her hair. It was glossy and black as spilled ink, the long, loose waves discreetly hiding the faint gleam of the small silver studs lining her ears and her cochlear implant processors.

She wore a fitted black fleece over a slate-gray thermal and dark-blue jeggings, both practical and unassuming.

"We can talk later after work," Adelen said, her voice softening. "I'm checking out a new site today, and I need to plan the sound setup for the upcoming shoot."

Delia sighed nervously. "I know, I know. I'm proud of you, *filha*. You'll always be my baby, and I'll never stop worrying about you. I just—people can be cruel, especially when someone is different. I don't want that for you."

The quiver in her mother's voice caught Adelen off guard. She swallowed hard as memories flickered like film reels—classrooms thick with whispers, the sting of mockery, too many school yard brawls, detentions piling up, her brother's furious defense. Their home had lived in dread of the phone ringing, of another call from the principal. To their parents' dismay, neither she nor Diogo had ever been docile children.

By high school, the cruelty had shifted. The girls' mockery turned subtle, their smiles edged with exclusion. The boys grew bolder, more physical—until a few ER visits taught them caution. Her reputation bought her quiet, and quiet gave her space to dive into music and editing, into the art of control through noise.

Yeah. She knew *exactly* how cruel people could be.

"I know, Mamã," she murmured. "And I love you for that. But I can take care of myself. I'm fine, really."

"I love you too, *filha*. Call your father later too—he's been worried sick! Now go, before you're late." The line went dead, leaving her apartment abruptly still, the silence almost too loud.

Adelen rolled her eyes and huffed a quiet laugh. Only her mother could pivot from bossy to emotional in one breath.

She slung her bag over her shoulder, keys jangling from her fingers, and headed for the door. The scent of chai from the half-empty marbled navy-and-gold mug lingered on the counter, mingling with a hint of salt carried in through the cracked window.

Stepping into the corridor, the door clicked shut behind her. As a force of habit, she double checked both locks—making sure no one could waltz into her apartment. Satisfied, Adelen headed to the exit.

Instead of waiting for the elevator, she took the three flights of stairs to the lobby, giving a brief wave to Richard, the security officer, as she brushed past the desk. Stepping into the crisp morning air of downtown Joia City, guilt gnawed at the edges of her thoughts as she scanned her surroundings—the real reason she'd moved here whispering beneath her heartbeat.

That, and the ghost of a grin framed by blue eyes she couldn't seem to forget.

CHAPTER 2

Owen

Owen Voss was a mess.

He'd been staring at his computer screen for hours as emails piled up and notifications blinked like tiny, insistent alarms. Every call went to voicemail. Every instant message remained unread. The cursor pulsed in the center of the screen, a quiet accusation. People expected things from him. People depended on him.

Except for the first time in his life, he had nothing left to give. That endless well of support and protection had finally run dry.

The last several months had taken a brutal toll. Normally, Owen was the sunshine in every room, with the easy laugh and loyal hype man. Somewhere along the way, that brightness had dimmed and fractured straight down the middle. He'd been floundering ever since, unsure how to piece himself back together.

He sagged into his leather-colored chair, muscles heavy, blue eyes squeezed shut in a futile attempt to block out the world. His thoughts scattered and raced, static crackling through a blown speaker. He couldn't latch onto a single one, couldn't decide which failure deserved his attention first.

Rebuilding Neuronix.

The security breach.

Aurelia's abduction.

The public firing.

The company buyback.

The guilt.

Each one shaved years off his life, haunting him in his nightmares and waking hours alike. The aftermath pressed down on him like bricks stacked too high, the weight forcing him to his knees.

As Chief Security Officer—cofounder, protector, Levi's brother from another mother—he was supposed to *prevent* the nightmare they had lived through. Now, he froze every time he thought about how severely his friendship with Levi was tested, and how close they came to losing everything. To losing Levi, his best friend and CEO of Neuronix. To losing Aurelia, his new friend and Levi's wife.

Owen was always there to pick up the pieces of everyone else's problems...he was always there for everyone but himself. He emerged from the wreckage a different person, a piece of his soul missing.

A deep, uncomfortable ache tightened in his chest.

His eyes fluttered open and quickly readjusted to the bright lights of his office and sunlight pouring in from the large office windows. His gaze drifted to the corner of his cobalt executive desk, landing on the gold-framed photo of all of his friends—Levi, Ivy, Isaac, and his wife Grace—their arms slung around each other, and laughing on the day Neuronix launched nearly six years ago. Back when he was younger, but much more fearless. Before fear had taken up permanent residence behind his ribs.

Shifting to the matching frame beside it, his heart stuttered from the onslaught of shame and grief as he fixated on that photo...the photo of his mom.

Owen had been so preoccupied with everything else going to shit in his life that he hadn't visited her enough. Not nearly enough.

The shame intensified because, in reality, he'd been purposely avoiding visiting his mother. That admittance tasted sour on his tongue. He was nervous that the distance might have hurt her, and dreaded her reaction if he did visit.

He couldn't hide from the truth—he was terrified of being the son who failed. Ever so slowly, he was buckling under the pressure of his failures.

He shakily rubbed both hands over his unshaven face, dragging them down until they fell limp in his lap. His office was too quiet, save for the faint hum of electronics and the monotonous whisper of the HVAC vents overhead. The city outside his window glittered with winter sunlight reflecting off the colorful terracotta roofs that flooded the room with warmth and natural light, but inside, everything felt cold.

Without warning, his anxiety spiked, and the light became so unbearable his eyes snapped shut. The thin, wool pullover he wore was suddenly too tight, too constricting, and Owen struggled to breathe—

Then a memory flickered; one that had recently become his favorite intrusive thought. A shadow of a moment filled with balmy breezes, floral sweetened air, Aurelia and Levi exchanging vows on a dock, him throwing petals in the most masculine way possible, Ivy stealing food off his plate...and *her*.

Adelen.

He was truly happy his friends found their way back to one another, but that raven hair, intelligent silver eyes, and beautiful scowl had ensnared him.

He'd nearly fallen into the damn lagoon the first time he saw her. His feet forgot the concept of balance, but he managed to grab hold of a post as he teetered on the edge of the wooden dock. All it took was one glance, and suddenly he was the punchline of his own joke.

After that, every attempt to shamelessly charm her had crashed and burned spectacularly. She didn't giggle, flip her hair, or try to touch his arm casually. Instead, Adelen had delivered the most devastating deadpan glare he'd ever encountered. He was equally rattled as he was fascinated by this woman. More importantly, it made something buried deep within spark to life after months of feeling frozen and numb.

She wasn't his usual type.

She wasn't remotely interested or flirtatiously fawning over him...and he couldn't stop thinking about her.

Estrella Vale, the matchmaker who brought Levi and Aurelia together, had been watching their interaction with a sly smile on her lips that raised his hackles. Owen *saw* her cerulean eyes do that weird swirling thing that Levi had told them about, reaffirming his suspicions: she was a witch.

Though he knew witches and magic didn't exist, Owen didn't care. There was no changing his mind about this, especially after he witnessed it with his own eyes. Estrella didn't outright say or do anything, but he was aware of her attention the entire time he attempted to talk to Adelen.

Owen was in uncharted waters without a paddle or a compass and was definitely *not* a strong swimmer. The harder he tried to win Adelen over or coax a smile from her, the more annoyed she became...and the harder it became for his friend Ivy not to laugh. Instead of being a good wing woman, Ivy threw gasoline on the fire of his embarrassment by filling the awkward gaps in conversation with tales of his worst dating moments.

Owen had been raised to understand that murder was wrong, but after listening to Ivy share those godforsaken stories (blatantly ignoring the glares he sent her way), he began to understand why some people were driven to commit such a heinous act. He had silently vowed to repay Ivy tenfold for this someday.

The whole situation was unnerving and a major confidence killer.

But it did nothing to diminish his feelings. Adelen was the most beautiful woman he'd ever been privileged to behold, consuming his thoughts from that moment onward. She was different in the most exhilarating way: cool, mysterious, and had a soft edginess to her that he wanted to explore—*needed* to explore...and he had no clue how to go about it.

He pressed a fist against his sternum and exhaled deeply, as if the action could force the ache to behave.

All this after only meeting her once? *Terrifying. Absolutely terrifying.*

This obsession was the cherry atop the pile of emotional shit that kept him in perpetual exhaustion. A pile that had grown larger and more unstable with every day, every hour, and every minute that passed.

God, he hadn't slept well in *weeks*...

The high-pitched squeak of his office door cut through the quiet like nails on a chalkboard, the sound reverberating through the headache that had already begun to blossom.

Owen's eyes flew open, and he straightened fast, pulse racing. Nobody was supposed to be here. No Meeting Day meant no conversations, no surprise process mappings, no—

A head poked in from behind the door, and familiar green eyes met his, full of concern.

Owen threw his head back against his chair and groaned. He couldn't even indulge in a self-pity session in peace in his office anymore.

"God, I hope you're not here to give me a pep talk," he muttered, not bothering to mask his displeasure. "I always walk away *more* depressed afterward." It was a piss poor attempt at humor that landed just as flat as it sounded.

Taking that as an invitation, Levi stepped inside, closing the door behind him. He sported dark jeans and a gray pullover. Joia City was heading into its winter, which meant brisk weather but no snow. It never snowed here. But Levi's change of the company dress code to "business casual with jeans" was a game-changer.

Owen hated wearing suits and all suit-like elements, particularly slacks, button-down shirts, and blazers. So much so that when the policy was instituted, he burned every suit he owned in Isaac's backyard fire pit that same night. Though he hadn't anticipated how much black smoke that act would create or how the fire had briefly gotten out of control, he had no regrets.

Isaac, however, had *many* regrets, specifically the decision to give Owen a spare key to his and Grace's home. He was permanently banned from using the fire pit after that incident. Owen almost smiled at the memory.

Almost.

Levi leaned against the now closed door of his office. His dark chestnut hair was a little longer than usual, and the beard he had been trying to grow for the past few weeks was finally starting to commit. Happiness looked good on him—Aurelia had changed everything about Levi in the best ways. It made Owen's chest twist with something warm and sore all at once.

"If the threat of a pep talk is all it takes to cheer you up, then I guess my job here is done," Levi smirked. He crossed to one of the cream plush chairs in front of the desk and sat down.

Levi studied him silently, and Owen curled up inside under his scrutiny, hiding his sensitive underbelly away from his knowing eyes. No one knew Owen as well as his childhood friend did. Sometimes he hated it.

This was *definitely* one of those times.

"Please stop looking at me like that," Owen grumbled, running a hand over his face. *Damn, I'm scruffy*, he thought with a frown.

"Looking at you like what?" Levi tilted his head innocently. "Like you're going for the 'unkempt bum in designer clothes' look? Or how you're giving off the 'I can't fix everything, so I'm going to mope about it' vibe? Which one is it?" Levi's lips twitched. The bastard was trying not to laugh.

Owen leaned on his desk and pointed a stern finger at Levi's face. "How *dare* you? I'll have you know that the *unkempt bum in designer clothes* look is all the rage this season. It was the entire theme of Joia

City's Fashion Week! You've got a set of balls on you thinking you can waltz in here and tell me I'm not nailing it."

"I think you've got a set of balls on you thinking what little whispers of stubble you've been growing out the past few weeks qualify as a beard."

Owen scoffed. "You and I both know my follicle growth rate has always been slower than average. I can totally grow a beard, I never wanted to."

Levi chuckled before turning serious again. "You aren't fooling anyone, you know," he said cautiously. "I can see that you haven't been yourself lately, and I know I'm partially responsible for that."

Owen opened his mouth to argue, but shut it when Levi put a hand up to stop him and continued. "I don't want to push you into talking about anything when you're not ready to...just know that I'm here when you are. And also, I have a small favor to ask."

Suddenly nervous, Levi toyed with the zipper of his sweater, looking everywhere else but at him.

Owen's eyes narrowed at his friend. Whatever he was about to say next was going to give him a heart attack; he could *feel* it.

"I've neglected so many people over the last few years, not just my friends. I was wondering..." Owen braced himself, his knuckles white from the deadly way he gripped the armrests of his chair. Whatever the favor was, Owen instinctively wanted to decline it, but he knew he wouldn't. He could never say no to helping his friends.

Levi took a deep breath before letting the words spill out like a sudden torrential downpour.

"Can we go visit your mom?"

CHAPTER 3

Adelen

Adelen followed the directions on her GPS app to the potential new site. She was meeting the Location Manager, Director, and Production Designer for a final walkthrough before moving forward with their next movie.

The drive was serene and quiet—and the perfect time to lose herself in the memory of the day she packed up and left Vila Verde.

Months ago...

Adelen was trying to shut an overpacked suitcase by lying her body across the top, foolishly hoping her weight would help compress the contents. Instead, she unceremoniously slid off and onto the floor, landing on her ass.

The deep chuckle that echoed across the room only increased her agitation. Glaring into steel gray eyes that mirrored hers, she flashed her teeth at her twin brother.

*"Could you maybe, I don't know...*help me, *instead of just standing there being annoying?"*

*Arms crossed against his broad chest, Diogo cocked his head to the side with cool indifference, arching a single brow. "*I could, *but I* won't. Not until you tell me the real reason you decided to move for 'work' out of the blue."

The question struck a nerve, rooting Adelen to the spot on the floor. Toying with one of her silver stud earrings, she avoided his gaze, letting his words hang in the air. Her natural resting bitch face usually made it easy to mask her emotions—except when it came to him.

And the worst part? Diogo was right, though she'd never give him the satisfaction of admitting it. Moments like these were a bitter reminder of how attuned they were to one another. One of the many inconvenient gifts of being fraternal twins. It was virtually impossible to hide anything from him.

She despised it with every fiber of her being. Almost as much as the patronizing look on his stupid face.

It was true—Adelen had never seen the need to live anywhere other than Vila Verde. She was one of the most sought-after production sound engineers in the industry. And one of the most unique, considering she was deaf.

Adelen didn't need assistive technology to do her job—or to do anything really. She had the innate ability to visualize sound wave patterns. She idolized the famous composer Beethoven, who, like her, didn't let his hearing loss stand in the way of creating beautiful music.

When the opportunity to work in the sound department of POLmArK TV Romances arose, she jumped at the chance.

With multiple job offers in sound engineering lined up post-college, POLmArK TV Romances was the natural choice, as its headquarters were conveniently in her hometown. She oversaw a small team of engineers and chose which projects to pursue. They could film multiple television movies concurrently, so the options were endless.

She was really good, too; good enough to rise through the ranks and earn a respected reputation in the industry. But she didn't have dreams of grandeur and was comfortable in her role doing what she loved most, with the freedom to pick and choose her assignments.

Adelen consistently chose local Vila Verde projects, often sending a member of her team on location in her stead. She hated traveling to unfamiliar places in the field and had often expressed it throughout her career.

...Which was precisely why when she risked a glance up at him, she found Diogo glowering right back at her. The longer he waited for a response, the more his impatience seeped through, his dark brows scrunching in aggravation.

Anyone else would've been intimidated by him, but not Adelen—she could be just as menacing as Diogo; her attitude evenly matched.

He wore dark but well-loved jeans resting above his favorite pair of black boots, and a simple lightweight charcoal hoodie. His sleeves were pushed up, revealing dark, detailed artwork etched into his forearms. Wisps of ink curled out from the edge of his collar up his neck, stopping just short of his jawline.

They also shared the same onyx hair, though his was cropped close at the sides with partially tamed longer strands on top. His intelligent silver eyes revealed nothing, but a muscle in his cheek flexed, the only indication of his annoyance. With his teeth clenched so tightly, it was a wonder his tongue piercing hadn't snapped inside of his mouth...yet.

A girl could dream.

Adelen scowled right back at her brother, trying to form a believable response. Despite someone following and watching her, she refused to divulge that she no longer felt safe in her apartment or in Vila Verde. He'd consider it an invitation to insert himself into her business and boss her around.

Older than her by three minutes, he never shied away from pulling the "big brother" card. Adelen was reserved like their father, but Diogo? He had a bad habit of being overbearing and nosy—traits he no doubt inherited from their mother.

It pissed her off every single time.

Unfortunately, they were both incredibly stubborn. She knew her stubbornness would be her downfall one day, and after accepting that, she chose to deal with the problem herself.

Even as the incidents escalated.

Baffled and unnerved, Adelen often debated telling Diogo what had been happening, but stopped short every time. Not only was she unwilling to deal with his overprotective ass, but she couldn't jeopardize his career as an ethical hacker. Diogo would totally do something unethical *if it meant protecting his family.*

Thankfully, some higher power must have taken pity on her when her boss, Cary Orgura, shared that there was an opening nationwide to lead the audio engineering department at the new Joia City satellite studio. The opportunity couldn't have come at a better time.

Nor would she be completely alone there. Dax Hunter, a Director she'd worked with multiple times, and Casting Director Tessa Barnes were also relocating to Joia City. Tessa had been particularly excited, having grown up there, thrilled to be moving back home.

Cary had been shocked and disappointed to be losing his best talent and protégé, but supported her decision. Adelen quickly initiated the transfer, and her life changed overnight.

Within a month, she was settling into her new company-paid apartment and a new life in Joia City. There had been so much to do to get the new satellite studio up and running that she often forgot the reason she had uprooted her life and moved here.

Temporarily *forgot.*

She never stopped looking over her shoulder, though. That invisible presence was always there, festering in the recesses of her consciousness.

The GPS app's robotic voice blared through the car speakers, signaling her arrival at the destination, and shifting her attention back to the road. Adelen took in her surroundings, noting the affluent—no, *wealthy*—residential area as she gradually pulled forward towards a set of looming wrought-iron gates.

She gave her name and purpose for the visit distractedly over the intercom installed in the granite pillar, her attention aimed at what lay beyond the ornate gates.

Cleared by security, the gates slowly parted with a low groan and opened to a long, well-manicured drive. Tires crunched over gravel, and for a while, there was nothing but brush and sky—until the manor appeared; sudden, grandiose, and breathtaking.

White outer walls gleamed in the sun, red roof tiles warm and weathered by salty air. A fountain sparkled at the center of the courtyard ahead, water catching the light as it fell in a slow, steady cadence. Eyebrows raised high in appreciation, Adelen let out a low whistle. It felt less like arriving somewhere and more like crossing into another world.

As her car crept closer to the building, she begrudgingly realized that foregoing field work to this point was a tad shortsighted and limiting. There was so much more beauty in the world that she had been missing out on.

She pulled into the designated parking area and cut the engine once she found a spot. Bag in one hand, Adelen slid out and made her way to the small group of people already gathered by the front of the manor, the slam of the car door echoing in her wake.

Familiar coworkers' faces turned to her as Adelen neared the group. Her steps slowed when she realized her friend Aurelia stood amongst them, hands waving animatedly as she spoke, causing tendrils of rainbow-streaked brown hair to escape the messy bun piled high on her head.

Dressed comfortably in jeggings, an oversized sage-green cable-knit sweater, and pink floral rain boots, Aurelia was the picture of elegance and comfort. The moment those warm brown eyes met

Adelen's, they lit up. She separated from the group and walked excitedly to meet Adelen.

"Hey! What are you doing here?" Aurelia chirped as she pulled Adelen in for a quick—and unsanctioned—awkward hug. It's not that Adelen was opposed to hugs; she just never had friends who were so openly affectionate. She stood, arms limp at her sides, slow to react. She returned the embrace with a stiff pat on the back.

"I'm here for work. What are *you* doing here?"

"I'm the proud owner of Starhaven Manor now, remember?" Aurelia twirled, arms spread wide, and theatrically dropped into a deep curtsy. Her personality had shone brighter ever since she wed Levi, the marriage an unusual requirement for her to claim ownership of the estate she inherited from the original owner.

Socialite Eleanor Greaves had passed away with no next of kin, leaving her wealth and assets to Aurelia. While Adelen had known this, she'd never actually *seen* Starhaven Manor in person.

Until now.

"*This* is Starhaven?" Adelen exclaimed, eyes wide with awe. "I just followed the directions here—I didn't realize this was it. I don't know what I expected the site to look like, but it wasn't this."

Aurelia laughed, the sound like wind chimes in a gentle breeze. "Imagine how weird it is for me." Her eyebrows scrunched together in confusion before shooting up. "Why *are* you here? Wait—you work for POLmArK? You said you were a *deejay*," she said accusingly.

Adelen snickered. "Yup, I'm the lead Production Sound Mixer and department head for our new division out here. I mean, I *am* a deejay of sorts...but for movies. So not *really* a lie."

She had forgotten about that small fabrication of the truth, unable to trust someone so new with such personal details fully. In the past, people tended to focus on how she could hook them up with a movie role rather than on what she did there. It was simply easier to say was a deejay. Old habits die hard.

"I guess it's a day of surprises for everyone then," Aurelia murmured, glancing back at the others.

The other POLmArK representatives followed Charles Pierce, Aurelia's attorney, to the multibay garage tucked away on the side of the manor, where a pair of four-person golf carts awaited. He slipped behind the steering wheel of the first vehicle, while the others climbed into the open seats.

Though the man was in his early eighties, with neatly styled short silver hair, comfortable jeans, and a deep plum crewneck sweater, his astute brown eyes betrayed his youth.

"We should go so they don't leave us behind," Aurelia sighed. "I'm supposed to drive one of those things, and I'm not quite sure where we're going."

Adelen snorted and followed her friend. She matched Aurelia's brisk pace, their strides quickly closing the distance. Trying to ignore the curious stares from her colleagues, she jumped into the passenger seat of the second golf cart. Aurelia hopped into the driver's seat and started the vehicle.

She had barely finished fastening her seat belt when Aurelia threw the cart into drive and peeled out to catch up. The stench of burned rubber briefly assaulted her nose, but it was self-preservation that forced Adelen to grab onto a handle to keep from falling out.

She couldn't stop the small yelp that escaped her lips.

Or the glare she managed to level at Aurelia.

"I have zero plans to die in a golf cart accident today! Have you ever driven one of these before?" Adelen's heart was in her throat as they flew over a raised part of the terrain, the golf cart temporarily airborne.

"If moving it from the back utility storage to the main garage counts, then *yes*, I have experience driving them," Aurelia shouted over the roar of the engine, her eyes trained on the other cart in the distance. "Hold on, just in case, though. It seems like these could flip easily."

Adelen shot her an incredulous look that was interrupted by another wild bump—and another uncontrollable shriek.

Her ass *definitely* left the seat that time.

There was no turning back now. All she could do was hold on for dear life, make peace with her maker, and pray it would be over soon.

The ride to the wide-open expanse of land was relatively short, but residual terror still coursed through Adelen's veins. She would never look at a golf cart the same way again—not after seeing her life flash before her eyes on repeat during the last fifteen minutes. Once they arrived, Adelen had leaped out of the cart, not waiting for it to come to a complete stop.

Relief from being on steady ground again nearly had Adelen on her knees. Aurelia's hair was a disaster, her bun in disarray and leaning wildly to the left side of her head. Adelen's hands unconsciously flew to her head, fearing hers was just as bad.

No—*it was worse.*

Running her fingers through her tresses, Adelen found several twigs, leaves, and other flora tangled in it. Unsurprising, considering how, after briefly losing control of the cart over another bump, Aurelia plowed through a large bush.

She glared at Aurelia, ignoring her friend's cheeky grin and zero remorse.

Spinning on her heel, Adelen stalked towards the rest of the group and aggressively plucked out what she could from her hair, silently vowing *not* to let her drive on the way back. Inhaling the crisp air deeply, she shifted her attention to the chatter between her peers.

"Logistically, this is absolutely *perfect*," Evan Carlisle, the Production Designer, gushed, slowly spinning in assessment. Casual in jeans, sneakers, and a sienna sweatshirt, he was tall and wiry with closely cropped mahogany hair streaked with white. His simple wire-framed glasses did nothing to conceal his sharp, calculating hazel eyes. "It isn't too far from the main estate. It shouldn't be hard to get the necessary city permits to install temporary electrical poles. Generators won't be enough this far out and are too noisy." Adelen nodded in agreement. "We can get a separate metered feed from the main road."

The near-death experience all but forgotten, Adelen scanned the area to gauge its impact on production. She would normally check for traffic, airplanes, AC units, buzzing lights, echoes, or other ambient noise that could ruin clean dialogue. But it was quiet and serene this far back from the main property and road.

"This may be one of the easiest determinations I've ever made from a sound perspective," Adelen added matter-of-factly, crossing her arms. "The only interference I can see would be from nature, which is virtually nonexistent in this field. I have no objections or concerns as long as we address the power situation for our equipment."

"The crew would be able to access this easily from the back of the estate, and we could bring in portable units for offices, restrooms, costumes, etc. From a legal standpoint," Evan turned to face Charles, "as long as we can settle on the contract and rental fee, I think this is a great spot."

"The essence of this location is utterly *divine*," Director Dax Hunter breathed. What was left of his thinning, long, and unruly blonde hair flapped wildly in the wind as he absentmindedly twirled his handlebar mustache, his brown eyes alight. "It just *feels* right, as if a real legume farm has been here for generations!" He clasped his hands together excitedly against his chest.

He was an eccentric man, yet one of Adelen's favorites to work with. Despite being in a wide-open field of mostly grass, he was sporting a tan, multi-pocketed safari vest over a long-sleeved red shirt with a vivid orange-and-white hibiscus print. The bottoms of his olive-green track pants had been tucked into brown construction boots.

As he continued describing his cinematic vision to everyone, Dax reached into the left top pocket of his vest and pulled out a small handful of goldfish crackers. Aurelia's eyebrows shot up at the sight of it before sliding a questioning gaze at Adelen.

Hiding a smile, Adelen responded with an imperceptible shrug. She'd worked with Dax many times before and knew the other pockets contained more snackish delights. He claimed it helped channel his creative energy, and she was in no position to judge him or anyone else for being themselves.

The Location Manager, Lonnie Palovera, interrupted Dax's monologue, shifting the discussion to more practical topics. "Now let's talk about budget, cost, insurance, and how setting up the buildings and all that jazz impacts our production schedule for this."

Lonnie was a no-nonsense straight shooter in her mid-forties and a wizard at managing project finances. She dressed as comfortably as Aurelia, with a tightly curled auburn bob, a blanket of freckles across her face, and serious, deep blue eyes. What she lacked in height, she more than made up for during budget and fee negotiations.

"Ah, now you are speaking a language I understand," Charles teased. While they submersed themselves in the technical details to finalize the POLmArK lease, Aurelia crept closer to Adelen.

"Will there be a casting call for any local extras?" Aurelia asked casually—*too* casually—her terrible attempt at a poker face failing to hide her excitement. She didn't know why, but Adelen knew the answer wouldn't bode well for her, especially if her friend were interested in auditioning.

Aurelia's acting was *awful*, and Adelen wasn't sure how to say it. She was the worst person to deliver delicate news, usually taking a bull-in-a-china-shop approach. She'd have to tread carefully.

"Yes, there will be, but there's no way to guarantee that they will select you. Although I bet they wouldn't say no, since you own the place."

"Oh, I'm not asking for *me*," Aurelia said sweetly, picking at nonexistent lint on her sweater. "I'm asking for my friend, *Owen*." Adelen froze at that name. "You met him at our wedding, remember? It would be a great way to get to know each other since he couldn't take his eyes off you." Aurelia waggled her eyebrows suggestively as embarrassment tinged Adelen's cheeks red. "He's *obsessed* with POLmArK movies, and it's his *dream* to be an extra in one. And," she added more seriously, "he saved my life. It's the least I could do for him."

Adelen's chest tightened, remembering everything her friend went through, and Owen's role in her rescue. News outlets and tabloids covered the story for weeks. But the idea of being so close to him at work—

"Of course, your friend can be an extra!" Dax cut in. "He'll still need to audition so we can see what magic he could create, but the answer is *yes*!"

No, no, no, no, no...

Aurelia jumped up and down, squealing with delight.

Charles pressed his lips together tightly, trying his best not to laugh.

Dax smiled broadly and snuck a handful of almonds from another vest pocket as Evan and Lonnie scrunched their noses in distaste.

Adelen's mouth hung open in disbelief, trying to process what the hell just happened. When the gravity of it all settled in, she stared directly into Aurelia's eyes and said with a deceptive smile, "I'm driving the golf cart back."

CHAPTER 4

Owen

"Oh my god! Levi, you look so different, and dare I say old?"

Denise Voss was having a good day.

Levi let out a deep belly laugh, her teasing a much-needed reminder of the second mother he loved growing up. Walking through the doors of Crystal Waters Residences, the assistive care facility where she lived, Owen didn't know what state his mother would be in.

Or if she would remember him.

But today the universe decided to show him a glimmer of favor, and of the mom he knew—something he desperately needed. He missed stopping by to eat her home-cooked meals, ask for advice, and join the monthly mother-son lunches they used to have. While early-onset Alzheimer's had taken those small joys away from him, it had taken something bigger and infinitely more precious away from his mother: herself.

Forced to watch helplessly on the sidelines as pieces of her faded away each day over the last few years, he'd come to dread visiting. Not because he didn't love her, but because she had deteriorated so much that living in constant confusion caused frequent outbursts. Moments of clarity had become heartbreakingly rare.

He prayed he wouldn't be the reason behind a bad episode today. She needed round-the-clock care, and he made one of the most difficult decisions of his life to ensure she had it.

Watching her and Levi chat and joke together stirred something deep and conflicting within him: joy that she was aware enough to know her *other son* was visiting her, and panic because he knew her time was running out. Despite the laughter, she looked frailer than ever.

Retreating inward, he studied Denise, committing every detail about her to memory just as he had every other time he visited. She was sitting in her favorite navy-blue recliner, one of the few remnants of her former life, wearing a pink-floral pajama set that hung loosely on her delicate frame. A thick, knitted gray blanket she had once made lay across her lap.

Lately, she had been perpetually cold, unable to fully banish the chill.

At sixty-seven years old, she was far too thin for his liking, unsteady on her feet without assistance, and constantly tired. He inherited his golden hair and bright blue eyes from her. Except beneath the silver cap of hair, her eyes had become clouded with confusion and shadows of her former self.

He'd spent most of his youth looking after his mom after his father had unexpectedly passed away from a heart attack when Owen was ten. Daniel Voss was Owen's hero—the one who taught him how to be a man and to treat everyone with respect. He remembered it vividly: it was the middle of February, a cold, overcast Thursday, when he had been in detention for fighting, Levi sitting right beside him.

Jimmy Delmont had Levi backed up against a locker, mocking him for his struggles with reading in class...*again*. Back then, they were both young and scrawny, but Owen hadn't cared. A red haze had fallen over him before he had jumped into the mix, grabbing Jimmy by the back of the neck and pulling him to the ground. Levi had dove into the pile, and the next thing he knew, multiple teachers were separating them. Jimmy had cried as blood spilled down his face from his broken nose.

Levi had eventually been picked up, leaving Owen to sit in detention alone, waiting longer than usual for his dad to pick him up. Then the school resource officer had arrived instead of his dad. He had pulled Owen out and said he would be driving him to the hospital to meet his mom. He had followed the officer to his car, knowing something was seriously wrong, and had stopped listening after the officer said, "I have some bad news about your dad..."

After that, his mom had become a shell of herself for a long time, not so different from how she was now. She had powered through her grief to take care of Owen, and he had done the same for his mom—trying his best to fill his dad's shoes and protect her however he could. Levi had tried to do the same, since he had spent more time at Owen's house than his own over the years.

Denise had been a special education teacher and was well-versed in the challenges Levi was facing. Whenever he was over, she would help him with his schoolwork. But it went much further than that. Levi knew she loved him, too, the day she had replaced Owen's twin bed with bunk beds—cementing Levi's place in their household.

With everything upside down in his life at the moment, Owen would have given anything to talk to her, to get some advice from her. Worse, he wished he could tell his dad about Adelen, to hear his voice and wisdom once more.

Refocusing his attention on his mother's laughter, he realized this may be his only chance at that.

"I can't believe you're married! You're lucky you found someone who'll put up with you," Denise joked. Levi rolled his eyes playfully and let out an exaggerated sigh.

"You're right, I'm damn lucky, and she's made sure to remind me every day since." Lately, the way his face lit up when speaking about Aurelia had Owen feeling envious. He selfishly wanted to experience the same joy with Adelen and was stuck on what to do about it.

The loud ringing of Levi's phone startled everyone. Judging by the way his eyes softened at the screen, Owen would bet his fortune that it was Aurelia. He stood and excused himself to answer the call in the hall. Once Levi was out of earshot, Owen seized the opportunity to talk to his mom alone.

"I've missed you, Mom." The whispered words caught in his throat. These moments had become so infrequent that he worried each time they spoke would be the last.

He quickly banished the thought from his mind.

No—Not now. I'll deal with that later.

Studying him intently, Denise murmured, "I've missed you, too, Boo Bear." Owen's lips quirked up at the use of his childhood nickname. "I—I don't remember the last time I saw you," her voice faltered, her brows tightening in confusion. Owen wrung his hands and redirected the topic to something lighter.

"I'm afraid to tell you something out of fear that you'll use this knowledge against me, but...I met someone."

Her expression instantly cleared, only to shift into suspicion, and then amusement as she straightened in her chair. Tipping his head back, he concentrated on the drab, gray-white drop ceiling tiles of the room, sighing heavily.

"Her name's Adelen. She's a friend of Aurelia's, and I met her at their wedding." Dropping his head down, he rubbed the back of his neck. "I'm also pretty sure she's *the one*," he added with a grimace.

God, that sounded so weird out loud.

Contemplating his admission, she blinked slowly, a grin spreading across her face. "It's about time some lucky lady finally dared to wear you down. What a lovely surprise! Tell me more," she exclaimed, her excitement growing with every word.

Owen shut his eyes and groaned. "That's the thing—I don't *know* her. Not yet anyway. I couldn't take my eyes off her, and when I tried to strike up a conversation and flirt, she just stared at me, giving one-word answers. I don't know what to do."

Denise barked out a laugh, enjoying her son's misery. "Boo Bear, that's the biggest crock of shit I've ever heard. If she's truly *the one*, then you know what to do. *Keep trying.* That means getting to know her and what she values...which apparently isn't empty flirting."

"I hate this for me," he grumbled softly to himself, but it didn't escape Denise's ears.

"Did I raise you to throw pity parties when things got tough, or did I raise you to work your ass off when faced with an obstacle? I know the answer...*do you*?"

She hadn't taken such a stern tone with him in years. Or at least not since she found out about the secret New Year's Eve party he and Levi threw at her house in high school.

Denise had been away visiting distant family and knew nothing about the wild party—or the underage drinking—that took place that night. He had Levi to thank for blurting it out during dinner one night years ago, revealing how Owen tried to drink cooking wine after the booze was gone.

She hadn't let either of them live it down, and despite being adults at the time of the confession, she'd torn them both a new one.

"*I know*, it's just...I don't want to mess this up. I want the kind of love you and dad had, and I'm worried I'll ruin it." He let the truth and vulnerability of his words linger in the silence.

Owen was a second too late to understand his mistake as the humor and recognition fell from her face. He cursed himself for mentioning his dad. It always yielded the same result.

"Your father—My Daniel, where is he? Where is Daniel?" Her slim fingers gripped the edge of the blanket tightly, her unfocused eyes frozen in time.

"Mom, please—" Owen stood to approach his mother.

"What happened to him?" Agitated and frantic, her voice rose, filling the room with despair. "*Why am I here*? This isn't our home! Owen? Why do you look so old? *Where is your father?*"

Panicked, Denise jumped out of her chair only to tumble to the ground before Owen could catch her. His chest seized, both from crushing guilt for causing this and not preventing her fall.

"Levi!" Owen shouted towards the hallway, dropping to his knees beside his mother. Levi burst through the door, the same fear burning in his eyes as Owen's. Quickly taking in the scene, he ran back into the hallway, calling for staff to help.

Denise hadn't stopped yelling, though the shouts were interrupted by confused sobs as she lay in a crumpled heap on the floor. He reached a trembling hand out to rub her back in broad soothing strokes.

This is my fault, Owen said to himself. *I didn't think it through—I caused this.* The words echoed endlessly in his mind as he helplessly watched a team of staff members rush in to assist Denise.

She curled into herself as she sobbed, "Where is my Daniel? Is he gone? Why am I here? Where is Daniel? I want to go home! I have a class to teach tomorrow morning! *Why am I here?*"

He couldn't bear it. He couldn't handle the agony of watching his mom—his champion and biggest supporter—become trapped in her mind.

Sitting back on his heels, he shut down, empty on the inside, unable to register Levi's hand on his shoulder or the silver lining his friend's eyes.

Owen forced himself to numb every feeling, every failure, every possible thing that would cause him to fall apart in the middle of the horrible, sterile room.

So when a staff member apologized profusely after asking them to leave, it didn't bother him. Not like it should have.

Instead, he watched himself, like a prisoner in his body, nod with cool detachment before leaving the room—and his mother.

If Levi sent one more pitying glance his way, Owen was going to reach across, open the passenger car door, and push him out. It was the *perfect* time to test out Levi's ability to tuck and roll.

He couldn't shut down the sight of his mother crumpled on the floor. Or the sounds of her cries, the chilled air that prickled against his skin, the pity in the nurse's eyes...All of it was permanently carved into the walls of his memories.

Owen's foul mood marinated as he drove back to the office. The silence between them was so thick that only a chainsaw could cut through it. Levi cast him another furtive glance, loudly clearing his throat.

Teeth clenched, Owen eyed the passenger door handle again.

"If you try to push me out this door, I'm dragging you with me," Levi threatened. Owen's scowl deepened, and he refused to respond. Levi's shoulders abruptly slumped, his body sagged in the seat, and any playful energy ran out.

"Look...I know how rough that was for you." Owen stared straight ahead, attention on the road, an iron grip on the steering wheel. "There's nothing I could ever say that will make it better. If I had the power to fix everything, I wouldn't hesitate...but know that I'm here however you need me to be. We all are."

Owen drew in a sharp breath to quell the ache blossoming in his chest. There was so much he wanted to say, so many warring feelings and worries to sift through, so he shared the one thing that trumped them all.

"She's my mom," he whispered, so faintly Levi almost missed it.

"I know. She's been my mom, too," he said thickly.

They sat in contemplative silence for a few minutes. Owen's eyes temporarily blurred, and Levi angled his head to stare out the window. He blinked rapidly to clear his vision, the road ahead coming back into focus.

Levi cleared his throat again.

"For the love of god, *what now?*" Owen growled, killing the serious brotherly moment between them.

"*Wow*, okay. I actually have some *good* news to share with you," Levi retorted, offended. Owen rolled his eyes.

Nothing can cheer me up, not after that.

"Well, the call I took in the hallway was from Aurelia, and she has the biggest surprise for you." Owen slid him a sidelong glance, his attention mildly piqued. "Remember how you said that someday, somehow, you'd be in a POLmArK film—even if it was an extra?"

"Yes?" It was a lifelong dream of his that only Aurelia had come to understand and support. His heart began pounding in his chest as he waited for Levi to finish.

"Turns out that Starhaven Manor is the official filming location for their next movie." Owen whipped his head—and unfortunately the car—to Levi, eyes wide with shock.

"What?!"

The car swerved sharply to the right. Levi yelped and threw his arms out, searching for something secure to hold onto, and startling Owen enough to concentrate back on driving. He drowned out the angry horn blaring at him, quickly correcting the car. Only once his heart stopped pounding from their near-death experience did he attempt to speak.

"That was the wimpiest, most pitiful-sounding squeak I've ever heard come out of your mouth. I'm embarrassed *for* you."

"That was the dumbest, most reckless excuse for driving I've ever been subjected to. I'm embarrassed *by* you." The murderous glare Levi gave him was enough to elicit a small grin.

"Okay, but did you die?" Levi shook his head and sighed in exasperation. "Fine, let's forget about how we almost took an eternal guy's trip to hell...tell me more about what's happening at Starhaven."

Owen was practically bouncing in his seat from anticipation, knowing Levi's next words would change his life forever. Levi couldn't contain his excitement any longer either, and a sly smile spread across his lips.

He was going to throttle his friend if he didn't tell him the surprise *now*.

Levi didn't disappoint, turning Owen's entire world upside down with his next sentence.

"Next week, you have an audition to be an extra in a POLmArK film."

CHAPTER 5

Adelen

An hour had passed since Adelen arrived at the gym, still burning with rage and energy. She pounded the punching bag, but it held up, just like her anger.

It was the gym where she met Aurelia, another member who, by chance, enrolled in the same self-defense class as Adelen.

Not that she actually *needed* a self-defense class. She wasn't as skilled as her brother, who held a national title in jiu-jitsu and used her as an unwilling sparring partner, but she could take care of herself. Diogo still liked to hide behind doors and jump out at her, just to keep her reflexes sharp.

Today was just an all-around shit day, and she couldn't shake the anger. Normally, she'd go a few rounds with Diogo and let it all out. That wasn't possible, so she came to the gym and took it out on the equipment instead.

After the meeting at Starhaven, she drove the golf cart back as promised. The ride was as rocky and turbulent as her emotions. Aurelia's colorful curses and screeches were mixed with pleas to slow down.

Adelen ignored every single one of them.

The rest of the day had gone to hell.

During their site meeting, Cary emailed her, furious about the cost of new sound equipment. He even threatened to come to Joia City to fix her mistakes himself. She calmed him down with proof of her research and the lowest prices, something she'd never had to do before. Still, she had never felt so micromanaged in her entire career.

She launched into a vicious jab combination at the bag.

She still couldn't believe Dax agreed right away to let Owen audition, no matter how small the role. He basically guaranteed him a spot. The last thing she needed was to see those blue eyes more often. Owen would be a distraction she couldn't afford, especially now that Cary was watching her every move.

Owen was so flippant about everything. She usually avoided the happy, popular jock type, but it somehow made Owen even *more* attractive than he already was. He was nothing like anyone she'd dated before—if those short flings even counted as dating.

She had to be honest with herself.

He was *hot*. Molten lava hot.

Her punches, and their intensity, slowed a fraction.

Guys like him never wanted anything serious, especially not with her. She'd been fine with that, until Owen showed up.

She still didn't understand why he paid so much attention to her at the wedding. Usually, she could handle awkward situations, but this time she froze and only gave one-word answers. She didn't know if he was sincere, so she decided not to risk it.

But, oh, was she tempted to take that risk.

Adelen shook out her hands and wiped the sweat trickling down her forehead before attacking the bag again. There were so many feelings to contend with, but the only ones she wanted to deal with were the sore, tired ones.

The only men who ever tried that hard with her just wanted sex. It took more than flirting to get her attention, but she wasn't sure she could say no if Owen really tried.

None of it mattered. She couldn't act on anything. It wouldn't be professional or smart. Her heart had been broken too many times already. Just thinking about her other problem sent her into a kicking spree at the bag.

Earlier, she got a text as she walked across the parking lot to the gym.

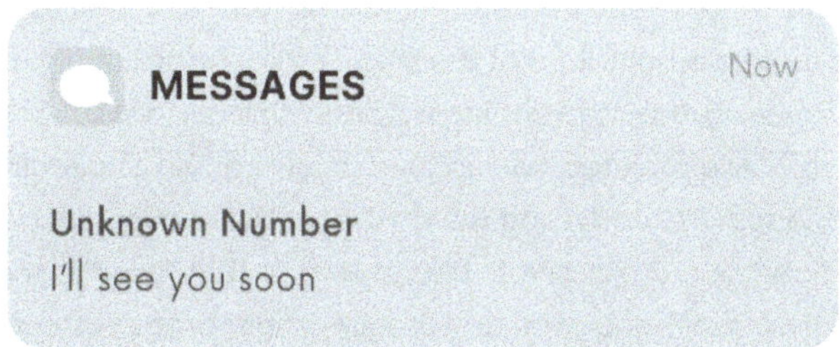

Those four words sent a jolt of fear coursing through her veins, stopping her in her tracks on the way into the gym. It lurked in the back of her mind during her workout. Things had been quiet since she moved to Joia City, but it was only a break.

Until today.

She should have known better. Should have known that moving wouldn't stop the messages.

Shit. She needed a real plan, not just hope.

"Hey, tough stuff, you've been going to town on this bag for an hour." The voice, rough as if dragged through shards of broken glass, came from a large figure looming before her. With messy brown curls, deep brown eyes that were nearly black, unnaturally large muscles, and lips curled in a cocky and self-satisfied smirk.

Another asshat, she thought. She didn't care to know his real name. To her, he was now Asshat.

These gym bros were all the same; unable to let a woman work out in peace, not bothering to care or listen when they set a boundary. Adelen chose to disregard him and refocused on the bag. She got one hook in before he stepped closer, the hair on the back of her neck rising.

"You obviously need a *real* workout with a *real* man...and lucky for you, I'm happy to help work off that energy."

Don't punch him. Violence isn't the answer. Don't punch him.

Clenching her jaw, she repeated the words over and over in her mind, a personal mantra to avoid any incidents. She liked this gym, and it was too soon to get barred from it.

Taking a silent measured breath, Adelen forced herself to ignore him and took another swipe at the bag. She kept track of him in her peripheral vision, though, keeping potential threats in sight.

For ten whole minutes, Adelen tried to ignore him. She really tried her damnedest, instead using the rhythm of her successive hits as an anchor—jab, hook, cross, pivot—channeling all that fury into the bag. Only the thump of her gloves and the hiss of her breath through gritted teeth mattered.

Then the voices grew louder, piercing her concentration.

"Maybe she can't hear us," someone snickered.

"Nah, bro, maybe her batteries died," another jeered.

"Hey, sweetheart, you need a recharge?" Asshat added, glancing over his shoulder at his pack of friends for approval.

Her body froze mid-swing. That familiar, smelted burn of humiliation and anger mixed in her gut. She knew that mocking tone too well, the kind that made her jaw clench. She'd heard it over and over in her life.

Slowly, she straightened to her full height, muscles coiled for action, her attention briefly shifting beyond him towards the three men gathered across the mat. The lot of them were unremarkable and built like they ate a bowl of steroids for breakfast.

Her attention returned to the imposing figure who had dared to breach her personal circle of space, her mind instinctively calculating. Asshat smirked, satisfied to have captured Adelen's attention, his swollen ego reflected in his posture.

Without breaking eye contact, Adelen carefully pulled off her gloves, not bothering to hide her ire, her voice low. "The next one of you manchildren to speak to me like that—" she gestured to the bag "—I'll stop taking it out on this, and start taking it out on *you.*"

They looked at each other for a moment before doubling over in condescending laughter.

Of course, they laughed. She would've been surprised if they hadn't.

Asshat, the same idiot who'd first approached her, stepped close enough to assault her nostrils with the overpowering stench of sweat. She didn't flinch, despite the violent urge to gag.

"You can work out whatever you want on me, sweetheart. *Anytime.*"

The disgust that slammed into her from his nasty proposition was coldly familiar, but no less offensive.

The others egged him on, their raucous behavior drawing the attention of other patrons. Before long, a small crowd of curious onlookers gathered. The air was electric with varying levels of tension, which only stoked the fire of her wrath.

Adelen tilted her head, lips curling into a slow, dangerous smile.

Asshat's self-assured grin faltered, and a shadow of unease passed over his face. He didn't notice the subtle adjustment in her stance, distracted by the hooting and hollering of his mediocre posse. The next time Adelen spoke, her words were deceptively sweet as she gestured to the nearby gym mat.

"Ladies first."

Pride outweighing better judgment, Asshat lunged. His attack relied more on his weight and strength than on technique or skill, leaving him unbalanced.

Just like Adelen predicted.

It wasn't even remotely a close match; it was an embarrassing display of a man attacking a woman.

Or rather, of a man *trying* to attack a woman.

In three fluid movements, Adelen deflected, pivoted, and swept his legs out from under him. Asshat hit the mat with a thud that silenced the room. When he tried to grab her ankle, she spun, caught his arm, and twisted—*hard.*

He had no time to react before she had him pinned to the mat. His initial grunt of pain morphed into a strangled yelp when her knee pressed into his ribcage—until something snapped.

The sharp intake of breath and quiet gasps audibly rippled through the crowd of spectators. Dead silence replaced the cheers and chatter, everyone paralyzed by the scene before them, the air thickening with shock.

Asshat's whimpers of pain echoed loudly in the gym.

Unable to mask her enjoyment, Adelen leaned in close enough to share breath, her voice venom-sweet. "You're lucky to walk out of here with just a bruised ego and a couple of cracked ribs. Might want to get those checked out." She applied a fraction more pressure with her knee to drive home her point.

Satisfied with his painful wail, Adelen began to back away.

When she stood and faced the crowd, they were rooted to their spots, frozen in awe...and fear.

Her gaze swept over them, cool and unflinching with remnants of her fury still trickling through.

"Remember this," she said with lethal quiet, her words both a promise and a warning, "the next time any one of you so much as *thinks* about harassing a woman."

No one moved. No one dared utter a sound. Then, Asshat started shouting in between pained gasps about pressing charges and needing an ambulance—until an unfamiliar woman's voice cut through the noise.

"What are you gonna tell them?" the woman purred, laughing as she emerged from the back of the group. Hands on her hips, dressed in a metallic gold and black zebra print athletic set, her critical hazel eyes raked over his prone body without a lick of sympathy. "That you promptly got your ass handed to you after harassing a woman half your size?" The woman shrugged, not an ounce of remorse available to spare. "She warned you, and you were too stupid to listen."

A chorus of chuckles spread through the gym. Asshat's bulky cheerleaders began to slowly shrink to the back of the crowd, leaving their friend to fend for himself, while he continued to spew profanities. Adelen silently tracked their movements.

The mystery woman did the same. "Meanwhile, your gaggle of shitty friends seems cool with leaving your sorry ass here. They're trying to slither behind the audience and out of the building." Wisps of dark maroon hair escaped her loose ponytail when she whipped her thumb towards the three hulking forms nearing the exit.

Several onlookers stepped in front of them, creating a barrier between them and the exit. Adelen couldn't help it and let out a dark chuckle as they struggled to break through. Sometimes she found it hard to believe that good people existed in the world. They hadn't always stepped up when she needed them during her childhood, but it was nice to see it now.

At that point, staff came over and took command of the situation, their tone firm and unyielding as they addressed the group. Asshat managed to get himself up from the floor, albeit slowly. They'd seen the whole thing, and the interaction—his attack in particular—was captured on their security footage. They told the men they were done and their memberships were permanently revoked. After Adelen declined to involve the police, the group left fuming, their leader slowly trailing behind.

When it was over, and everyone had returned to their workout routines, the woman who had spoken up walked over to Adelen. She had a mischievous smile and the easy confidence of someone who'd seen enough of the world to know how bad it could be yet chose to challenge it every day.

"You okay?" she asked gently. "What they said—about your hearing—that was *garbage*." There wasn't an ounce of pity in her eyes, only leashed fury...and understanding.

Adelen quirked a small smile and nodded, her adrenaline starting to ebb, her body relaxing a fraction. "Yeah. Thanks."

"I'm Kaia Fernandes, by the way. I was ready to join in and teach that asshole a lesson with you, but damn...you surprised us all with your badassery," she said, eyebrows raised high as she waited for an explanation.

Adelen huffed a small laugh.

"My twin brother holds an undefeated national title in jiu-jitsu and has dabbled in several other techniques. I, unfortunately, was forced to learn it to survive in our household. It's second nature now." She wasn't sure why, but the admission was a little embarrassing, her cheeks heating.

"Now I *definitely* want to know more. Come on," Kaia said, grinning. She flicked her chin to the entrance. "Let's get out of here and grab some drinks—on me. You earned it, and I earned hearing your superhero backstory."

Adelen hesitated, tugging at the wrap around her wrist. She was still too amped up, too volatile. Alcohol would only complicate her thoughts further. "Not tonight," she said hesitantly. "But...soon?"

Kaia's grin widened. "It's a date."

They exchanged phone numbers, and as she walked away, Adelen exhaled slowly. For the first time in weeks, she felt the faintest shift—a flicker of something resembling normalcy.

CHAPTER 6

Owen

Owen hadn't been this excited about anything in a long time.

Not since the company's early days. But when the breach happened, all that excitement vanished. Every past failure came rushing back—his security mistakes, the shame of letting his friends down, and the empty feeling of being forgotten by his mother.

The guilt never really left him, but he did what he always did—hid it behind jokes and cheeky smiles.

I'm allowed to be selfish and do something for myself once in a while, right?

He barely slept for the next few days, impatiently waiting for the details Aurelia had promised. When she finally delivered, he almost passed out from a mix of excitement and exhaustion.

The email described it as a "small on-set opportunity for staff extras," but to Owen, it felt like a reason to start planning his Oscars speech. He finally had a shot at being in a POLmArK movie, the films he loved, and more importantly, a chance to be near Adelen again.

Owen still hadn't gotten over finding out she worked for POLmArK, or how life had brought his two favorite things together, handing them to him on a silver platter.

He'd been thinking about her nonstop, like a favorite song stuck in his head. How unaffected she had been, a puzzle he was determined to figure out. She was different, and he loved that.

It was driving him crazy.

Owen kept telling himself it was just a crush, just something to distract him from everything else.

He threw himself into preparing for *Metal Love Beans*, the upcoming POLmArK romantic comedy about Dolf Ingerson, a heavy-metal frontman who falls for legume farmer Maggie Bean. Owen had already memorized every bit of the script he'd been given.

If he was going to be an extra, he'd be the best damn extra in the history of extras. He was going to be the most *extra* extra.

Unfortunately, his friend Isaac Nolan, the Neuronix CTO, got caught in the crossfire. Owen had been crashing at their big ranch more than usual. The house was tucked away in a gated community, perched on a cliff with a stunning view of the lagoon. It was bright, warm, and welcoming, with huge windows and light wood floors.

He had often visited his childhood home in Joia City's suburbs when his mother was first diagnosed and needed help. But lately, the memories there felt too heavy to handle.

He hadn't found the courage to go back for months. It wasn't his main home anymore, but he couldn't imagine ever selling it.

Instead, he kept escaping to Isaac and Grace's place, staying so often that Grace eventually turned one of their guest rooms into his own bedroom.

Isaac had only gotten more annoyed about it.

Maybe it was because of the *one time* Owen snuck into their bathroom while Isaac was showering and dumped a small bucket of ice water on him.

Or maybe it was the *one time* Owen hid under their bed and reached out to touch Isaac's leg while he was changing. Isaac shrieked so loudly that he fell over.

Isaac still hadn't forgiven him for those pranks, or a few others, and Owen had no plans to apologize for making the most of every perfect prank opportunity.

Casually dressed in various forms of loungewear, Isaac, his wife Grace, and their friend Ivy sat around the kitchen island while Owen stood across from them. The counter was about the same height as one in a hardware store, which made it perfect for his practice.

Grace and Ivy, the other Neuronix cofounders, were the Chief Marketing Officer and Chief Operations Officer, respectively. They hadn't been much help with the practice; both were more interested in watching the theatrics. Owen had been running through the same line for two hours and wasn't slowing down.

"Again," Owen declared, pointing a finger at Isaac's copy of the script for the fifteenth time that night.

Isaac flipped his glasses up, pinched the bridge of his nose, and groaned. "You have one line. *One*."

"Yeah, but it's at a critical point in the movie. It could make or break the whole thing," Owen chastised. He shook out his arms, adjusted his posture like a serious method actor, and cleared his throat...*loudly*. "Either you're looking to have a nice *lawn*, or you're looking to be added to a watch list *somewhere*. I'm *not* here to judge. That'll be $3,852.73. Cash or credit?"

"Hardware Store Guy," Isaac muttered, rubbing his temples, his deep blue eyes rimmed with exhaustion. "I swear to god, if I have to keep listening to this crap—"

"Pay attention! And this time," Owen interrupted, snapping his fingers in Isaac's face, "I'm going for *judgy but professional*." Isaac, annoyed, tried to swat Owen's hand away, but Owen jumped back before he could.

Owen took a long, deep breath, leaned over an imaginary counter, and mumbled the first two sentences.

"*Either* you're looking to have a nice lawn, or you're looking to be added to a watch list somewhere. *I'm* not here to *judge*." With a hand on his chest and a raised brow, he added, "That'll be $3,852.73. Cash or credit?"

Isaac blinked. "Was that...supposed to be under your breath? And why are you hunched like an old man?"

"Well, *yeah*, because that's how a *judgy old man* would say it," Owen said, vibrating with impatience. "You didn't catch what I said, right?"

"No, because it sounded like the worst mime in the world decided to put marbles in his mouth and introduce speech into the act!"

Ivy and Grace burst into laughter.

"Don't listen to him, you'd be the okayest mime ever," Ivy crooned. Her long sun-kissed almond hair was slicked back into a high ponytail, swishing when she laughed. Grace hadn't stopped cackling, her face turning almost as red as her curls.

"Okay, okay," Owen sighed and started pacing. Suddenly, he stopped as a new idea hit him. "What if I emphasized 'credit?' Like, make it sound *suspicious*?"

Ivy tilted her head in consideration, caramel eyes narrowing. "I don't know what that means, but do it—I want to *feel* the suspicion." Isaac sighed in exasperation.

"Either you're looking to have a nice lawn, or you're looking to be added to a watch list somewhere. I'm not here to judge. That'll be $3,852.73. Cash..." He paused, gave Isaac a distrustful look, and finished, "...or *credit*?"

"Oh, for shit's sake!" Isaac groused. "I'm tired, I'm hungry, and these chairs are hurting my back! Can we be done? You sound *exactly* the same every time!"

Grace started to reply, but Owen jumped in."Toughen up, peaches. I haven't explored all the possible delivery options yet, so take a few laps or do some stretches because it's going to be a long night!"

Much to Isaac's dismay and the ladies' delight, Owen wasn't kidding. He kept experimenting all night: sad Hardware Store Guy, existential Hardware Store Guy, flirty Hardware Store Guy. He'd studied extras in other POLmArK films to tweak his delivery, hoping to blend in just enough to be believable, but still stand out so Adelen would notice him.

Especially so Adelen would notice him. He needed her attention, just for a moment, hoping she'd give him a chance.

Aurelia wouldn't give out her number without permission, and Owen didn't want to be the weird guy who texts a woman out of nowhere. He knew he had to approach her differently and with more care than anyone he'd dated before.

He still needed to figure out a plan to do exactly that, but first he needed a reason to see her again, so he set out to make that happen. That was all.

When audition day finally came, Owen was buzzing with nerves. He had to make this moment count—not just to fulfill a lifelong dream, but maybe to start a new one.

Aurelia came along for moral support, or as she called it, "damage control." She'd seen the way he looked at Adelen at the wedding, and after Owen admitted his feelings, she never let him forget it.

Ivy decided to tag along, too, mostly for the entertainment value.

And to be a royal pain in his ass. Again.

"This is going to be gold," Ivy said excitedly from the back seat. "You're either going to land the part or go viral for all the wrong reasons. I'm hoping for the latter!"

Owen scoffed but couldn't hide his grin as he tapped the steering wheel. "Either way, I'll be famous. And you really need to take a class on how to be a supportive friend."

"I'm supportive!" Ivy exclaimed with indignation. "That's why I'm here, because I *care*...and because Aurelia has an in with her friend Adelen."

"You care about missing out on anything that makes me uncomfortable or could be used as leverage."

"Uh, *yeah*, like a good supportive friend."

Aurelia rolled her eyes, smiling as her friends argued. "Adelen's going to be there, you know. Try not to embarrass yourself."

"But that's part of my allure," Owen quipped. "It's the essence of *me*."

"Right...but maybe don't do it in front of her or her coworkers," Aurelia suggested. "She already thinks you're ridiculous."

"She thinks I'm ridiculous?!" That didn't settle well. "It'll be fine," he said, waving her concerns away. "I'll woo her with my utmost respect for professional boundaries. She won't even realize she's fallen for me until it's too late."

"Do you even know what professional boundaries are?" Ivy challenged.

"Theoretically, I do. But to be safe, I'll retract that statement. I don't trust myself to follow through on that part, but the rest still holds true," he conceded. Ivy snorted in response.

His friends weren't fooled by his false confidence, but they wisely remained quiet. In reality, he wasn't sure Adelen would participate in a conversation, let alone agree to a date. He had an uphill climb ahead of him.

Owen hated feeling unsure of himself, but humor always helped him get through those moments, the ones that almost tore him apart at the seams. Maybe he was a better actor than he thought. Or perhaps no one had ever looked closely enough to notice.

They pulled into the freshly paved studio lot, Owen's heart pounding in his chest. There was no turning back now. The parked car felt like a line he'd just crossed, and his anxiety was almost overwhelming.

This was it. His chance to be in *Metal Love Beans*, to finally do something for himself, and to stop hiding behind fake smiles and forced cheer.

A chance at the future he'd only just started to dream about.

The room was a plain conference space, not at all what Owen imagined on a movie set. There were bright fluorescent lights, freshly painted plain white walls, black folding chairs, and a handful of serious-looking folks clustered around a long folding table.

Very anticlimactic.

Yet, Owen's nerves hit immediately, a punch to the balls he didn't see coming. His stomach twisted, threatening to empty its contents. He'd never done anything remotely like this and had overanalyzed what to wear. Eventually, he settled on simple dark jeans and a deep blue Henley that brought out the color of his eyes. Now, he was second-guessing everything.

He spotted Adelen before registering anything else, the base instinct to assess his surroundings failing for the first time. Quietly in the back of the room, she sat ramrod straight, expression unreadable. Beside her was an unknown middle-aged woman, whom he assumed was also from the production team. Adelen wasn't part of the casting team, but her presence had his heart skipping a beat, knowing she was likely here because of him.

Unable to stop staring at her, he willed her to *look at him*. That's all he needed, all his heart begged for...but nothing. There was no fleeting glance. No acknowledgment of his existence.

His stomach cramped further. Maybe it was something he ate.

I shouldn't have eaten that eggplant panini.

Aurelia playfully elbowed him in the ribs, somehow sensing his inner turmoil. "You've got this, superstar."

Ready to get it over with, Owen squared his shoulders, turned on the false bravado, and waltzed to the front of the table when they called his name. He threw his signature panty-dropping smile at a strangely familiar woman roughly his age with chestnut hair pulled back into a loose ponytail, inquisitive brown eyes framed with half-moon glasses, and a clipboard that had seen better days.

"It's been a long time since we were in the same room together, Owen," the woman at the table said excitedly.

Owen's brow scrunched, trying—and failing—to piece together how they knew each other.

"It's been *ages* since I've seen you!" he exclaimed, praying she would provide a clue to her identity. "So...just how long *has* it been exactly?"

He had no idea who this woman was.

"Since our senior year of high school, we were in drama club together." She waited expectantly for him to make the connection. He paused and really studied her. Then a memory unlocked and recognition clicked into place.

"Tessa Barnes?" Owen did a brief stint in the drama club after losing a bet to Levi. He couldn't remember any direct interactions he'd had with Tessa, though, aside from one incident where other classmates were bullying her in the club, and he had stood up for her. That was the only time that came to mind, and he prayed to the heavens that any other interactions had been positive.

Joy stretched across her face, earning him a wide smile.

Thank god for small mercies.

"Yes, I'm the Casting Director deciding your future here, as will Director Dax Hunter," she gestured to a wild-looking man wearing a safari vest to her left, "and Producer Altina Pastem." The curt nod was all he got out of the stern older woman in an uncomfortably tight black turtleneck sweater on Tessa's right.

"Whenever you're ready, Mr. Voss." Schooling her expression into something more professional, Tessa pointed toward the open area before the table.

Owen discreetly wiped his sweaty palms on his jeans and positioned himself as Tessa instructed. He declined the offered copy of the script, the lines etched in his brain. With a deep inhale, he channeled every version of Hardware Store Guy he'd practiced for weeks.

It was show time.

In the best elderly voice he could muster, Owen put everything he had into those four sentences, even pretending to ring up and bag imaginary items.

"Either you're looking to have a nice lawn, or you're looking to be added to a watch list somewhere. *I'm not here to judge*. That'll be $3,852.73. Cash or credit?"

There was a long pause. Owen shifted on his feet.

Tessa cocked her head to the side. "Interesting...Could you say that again, but this time as if realizing you're in love with someone?"

Owen hesitated, unsure how to pull off Hardware Store Guy in love. It was probably the only version he hadn't rehearsed. He cut an apprehensive glance at Adelen. With her arms crossed, those silver pools locked on him.

Adelen was paying rapt attention and trying not to be obvious about it.

Instead of letting anxiety overtake him, he'd use this opportunity to his advantage. He'd do what any other sensible man would do.

Owen met Adelen's gaze and held it.

The room went silent with anticipation, the air electric as everyone waited. His voice grew soft, thickened by emotion, as he spoke only to her. No one else in the room or the world mattered in that moment except for Adelen.

"Either you're looking to have a nice lawn, or you're looking to be added to a watch list somewhere. I'm not here to judge. That'll be $3,852.73. Cash or credit?" He added a wistful sigh at the end for good measure.

Tessa's hand fluttered to her chest, and the room erupted into excited murmurs. Aurelia's eyes were wide, and even Ivy seemed to be impressed.

But Adelen—Adelen's expression shifted into something violent.

At least Owen succeeded in getting her attention.

"Now do it like you're trying to hide the fact that you did something *terrible*," Dax said emphatically as he pulled a handful of pretzel sticks from one of his pockets. A small piece of lint flurried to the ground. The action raised so many questions, but Owen didn't have time to ask what else was hidden in that vest.

He gave them exactly what they asked for and *committed*. Owen delivered it in the sketchiest way he could think of, with constant nervous glances at the casting table and subtle fidgeting, doing everything he could to sell it.

By the time they were done throwing out random directions, he'd played Hardware Store Guy as a villain, a romantic, a comedian, and even a tragic poet. He ended with a small bow and a grin that led to a smattering of polite laughter.

Owen stepped back toward the entrance where Aurelia and Ivy stood, and away from where the casting team huddled together in quiet conversation. The number of times he was forced to run through the one line seemed a bit excessive, but now he felt confident that he nailed it.

With a manicured eyebrow raised, Ivy murmured, "I'm genuinely impressed with your emotional range. Not many people are skilled enough to deliver such an absurd line twenty different ways like that."

"I wish I could attribute it to all the time Isaac spent helping me prepare, but that would be giving him *way* too much credit for my natural talent," Owen declared.

"You know he's actively changing the locks to his house right now, right?" Ivy commented, crossing her arms.

Owen waved her off, dismissing her claims. "He would never do that; he adores me. Plus, Grace would never allow it. And I'll find a way to break in anyway."

Aurelia slid Ivy a knowing glance and mischievous smile before she playfully nudged Owen in the ribs. "Let's go say hello to Adelen before we head out. Hopefully, we hear some good news within the next week or so."

The way Ivy smirked sent shivers down Owen's spine and alarm bells ringing in his head. It was the smile of a predator, utterly feline and set on its prey. He wouldn't be shocked to see a tail swishing behind her.

"What an *excellent* idea! You know, we should invite her to our girls' night this week," Ivy exclaimed. Owen began to protest, his blood pressure rising, but Aurelia jumped in.

"I see what you're trying to do here...and son of a bitch, I'm in!"

Aurelia hooked her arm through Ivy's, and they *skipped* over to Adelen, not bothering to see if Owen followed. He had no choice but to trail after them. Hands stuffed in his pockets, he assumed a steady gait and relaxed his shoulders, preparing for his next unplanned 'audition.'

His mouth went dry at the sight of her as he approached. She was dressed for comfort in an oversized beige cardigan and black leggings, her wild hair tamed into a loose side braid. All Owen could think about was undoing the braid and running his fingers through her hair.

Such a simple outfit, and yet it was the sexiest thing he'd ever seen. Adelen could wear a trash bag, and it would still take his breath away. He pulled his attention back to his friends just in time to hear Aurelia extend Adelen an invitation to hang out...and she *agreed*.

Well, those two didn't waste any time, Owen thought.

The woman sitting with Adelen quietly left the room, but not before winking at him, a smug grin tugging at her lips.

Slowly, Adelen angled her head up at Owen, and he saw the full depth of the storm that brewed within her. It seeped through and swept across her stunning face. Even standing at her full height, Adelen was about a foot shorter than he was.

He fought the urge to walk away from the tempest and instead turned the charm on full blast.

"Well?" he asked Adelen, flashing an easy smile. "You impressed? I think I really captured the emotional depth of fertilizer sales."

Adelen didn't hold back. "You captured *something*, alright."

"Is that a compliment?"

"No."

Her tone was flat, her face impassive, and he was pretty sure the silence that followed could kill a man. But it was the unmistakable flush that spread across her cheeks that gave him a small sliver of hope. Aurelia's wide eyes flitted between them as the conversation volleyed, Ivy's mouth shaped into a silent O.

Owen, however, wasn't easily discouraged. He loved nothing more than solving complex riddles.

Especially the mesmerizing one standing before him.

"Maybe I'll get lucky," he said, still grinning. "Maybe they'll need me to come back tomorrow.

"Or not," she replied without missing a beat.

Before he could think of a comeback, Tessa called his name.

"Owen?"

They all whipped their heads towards Tessa.

"Yeah?"

The casting team at the front looked oddly pleased—and slightly amused. "We'd like to offer you the role of Dolf Ingerson, the lead in *Metal Love Beans*."

Owen stared, afraid to believe the news. "The...lead?"

They all nodded excitedly.

"You mean the lead singer of *Dark Roast* who falls in love with the bean farmer?"

"Yes! If you're interested in the next step, we can discuss a contract and all that."

He glanced back at Aurelia and Ivy, whose mouths had fallen open, then at Adelen, the epitome of frozen fury.

This was his chance, the one shot at being near her and getting to know her.

"I'll take it!" he said instantly. He could deal with the consequences later.

The casting table exchanged surprised glances. "Don't you want to—"

"Nope!" Owen said, grinning widely. "I don't care what you say next, it's a dream come true. Where do I sign?"

Aurelia groaned quietly behind him while Ivy clapped her hands together in anticipation.

Adelen just exhaled through her nose, muttering something under her breath that sounded suspiciously like *unbelievable*.

But Owen didn't care. He'd just been handed the role of a lifetime and the perfect excuse to be around the one woman who refused to even look at him twice.

And had no clue what acting entailed.

CHAPTER 7

Adelen

Adelen couldn't believe what she'd just witnessed.

Owen Voss, always the flirt and the clown, the guy who couldn't go two sentences without making a joke, had just been given the lead role. Not an extra. Not a walk-on. *The lead.*

Her stomach dropped as he eagerly accepted right away, not bothering to get more details in case anyone changed their mind.

Before she could find her voice, the production coordinator and a swarm of assistants closed in, ushering him away to discuss contracts, schedules, and PR. These were the people who kept the machine running, and Adelen knew better than to get in their way.

Aurelia gave Adelen a helpless look as she followed them out. Ivy patted her shoulder in passing with a satisfied smirk. "I'll catch up with you later," Aurelia mouthed before disappearing through the door.

Rita Manos, the woman who'd sat next to her and set stylist, hadn't failed to notice how much of Owen's attention Adelen commanded during the audition. She had slipped out of the room right before her friends had approached, shooting her a knowing look on her way out. She was definitely going to interrogate Adelen about this.

Her knees gave out, dropping her back into the chair, the weight of the moment pressing her down.

She kept silent, shoulders rigid and hands balled tight in her lap. Her expression remained carefully blank, the practiced mask she wore whenever she needed to hide, but warmth crept up her neck all the same. Again. Because Owen had managed to make her blush.

Adelen did not blush.

A quiet curse slipped from her lips.

He'd managed to do the impossible with that aggravating, relentless charisma, always playing, grinning, and flirting. And he did it here, of all places, where she was just trying to keep her head down, to blend in, to feel safe.

She'd spent years being overlooked—because she was a woman, because of her quiet gravity, because she was different. And now Owen was encroaching upon her workspace, for god knows what reason. Was she some kind of challenge or conquest?

Something deep inside her recoiled at the thought, a memory of the unguarded sincerity in his eyes flickering to the surface. She slammed the door on it, refusing to let it in.

As soon as the meeting ended and the last stragglers drifted out, she gathered her things and stalked away.

Back in her office, she tried to lose herself in the technical details for the film—mapping out mics, rigging setups, plotting ways to tame the chaos of outdoor noise. But her focus kept slipping, thoughts circling back to Owen. To that damn audition. To his absurd, infectious enthusiasm.

After an hour of fighting her own distraction, she surrendered, packed up, and grabbed her gym bag.

The drive home was thick with silence, the kind that hummed in her ears and pressed in on her thoughts. When Diogo's name flashed across her phone, she hesitated, knowing he'd pick up on her mood right away. She wasn't ready for questions, but letting it go to voicemail would only make him more suspicious. She didn't have the energy for this shit.

"What now?" she barked. A deep, timbered voice poured out of the car speakers.

"Whoa. Is that any way to greet your favorite brother?" Adelen sighed impatiently. "Fine. Haven't heard from you in a few days. Figured I'd do a wellness check so I can report back to mom—you know she's been harassing me to check in on you, right?"

"Of course she is." She could feel a headache blooming behind her eyes. "I'm fine. Just...a day."

"That bad?"

"Something like that."

"Are you going to elaborate, or are you set on making this conversation painful for both of us?"

This was exactly why she debated not answering his call. She wasn't in the mood to chat, still stewing over the day's events. But...maybe she needed a little advice from the male perspective. A decision she would no doubt come to regret later. Against her better judgment, she relented.

For the rest of the drive, and as she climbed the stairs to her apartment, she let Diogo tease fragments of the story from her—the awkwardness with Owen, his new lead role, the gym fight. She glossed over the worst of it, but Diogo still laughed when she mentioned the cracked ribs.

"Come to think of it, you haven't broken anyone in a while," he quipped. "Nice to know you're out there making friends and dating again."

She groaned, shifting the weight of her bag on her shoulder, keys already in hand. "Okay, we're done. I'm hanging up."

"Oh come on, I'm kidding—"

She was halfway through an eye roll when she stepped inside and froze, a sharp breath catching in her throat—the only outward sign that something was off.

The door had been locked. But the square vase on the entry table—the one with the bouquet of fake iridescent roses, always lined up neatly against the wall—was askew.

Nestled at the front, a single fresh, blood-red rose stood out among the artificial blooms.

A rose that had *not* been there when she left that morning. Nor had a note been tucked beneath the vase.

Her heart plunged, cold and heavy.

She pressed the phone hard to her ear, pulse thundering in her veins.

"Addy?" Diogo's voice sharpened at the brief intake of breath. "What's going on? You went quiet."

She couldn't answer—not yet. Shock hollowed her out, leaving her mind blank and her body trembling. Her stomach twisted. The warmth of the apartment vanished, replaced by a chill that seeped into her bones.

Her hand shook as she picked up the note, eyes tracing the single line again and again.

The fragile sense of safety she'd begun to rebuild splintered in an instant.

She was such a naive fool.

“Addy,” Diogo pressed, his tone laced with concern and protectiveness. “You’ve been totally off lately. Weird. Avoiding everyone’s calls. What the fuck is happening?”

“Nothing,” she lied. It sounded rushed and unconvincing even to her. She forced her voice to steady. “I’m fine. Just tired. Honestly, I’m still adjusting to the move and new city.”

“*Bullshit.*”

“I’ll call you later.”

“Do *not* hang up—”

But she ended the call anyway. She couldn’t have that conversation right now—not with that *thing* sitting in her apartment, a silent message that *they* had found her again.

The silence that enveloped her felt suffocating, a sharp contrast to the roaring in her head. She locked the door more vigorously than necessary, her breathing ragged. Her back pressed against the door, and a violent shudder racked through her body. She slid down against it and sat there on the floor, knees pulled to her chest, the reality of the situation sinking in.

For a moment, she couldn’t even think—couldn’t plan, couldn’t breathe past the rush of panic. The safety she’d clung to had vanished, leaving her exposed all over again.

Adelen pressed her face into her hands as the first sob broke free. "What am I supposed to do now?"

CHAPTER 8

Diogo

Diogo's hands trembled, knuckles white around his phone. He didn't buy a word of it. Not from Adelen. Not for a fucking second.

His twin sister had always been a terrible liar, especially when she was scared. She'd learned to dodge and weave, acting like everything was fine until it all splintered open and she fell apart. That stubborn streak—they both had it—never made things easier.

He knew her too well. They'd shared everything, even before they were born. He couldn't ignore the clipped tone, the tightness in her voice, the way she hung up before he could press her. Every bit of it screamed at him: *something was wrong.*

He stared at his phone long after the call ended, replaying every word. The fear in his gut morphed into something sharper, something darker. He wasn't just worried anymore. He was ready to do something about it.

Fine, she said.

Fine, my ass. He knew exactly what he had to do, and he didn't care whose rules he broke to get it done. Sometimes you have to cross a line. It wouldn't be the first time he did that, nor would it be the last.

With renewed energy, he headed straight for his office, the one place that always felt like his. His gear waited for him, silent and ready. He dropped into his chair, pried open his laptop, and let his fingers fly. Muscle memory took over.

Within minutes, he was back in his digital element. Screens flickered on, dashboards came alive, and his focus narrowed to a point. Officially, he was an ethical hacker—the kind companies threw money at just to see how he'd break in and show them where they'd screwed up.

Online, he was known as the *Silver Shadow*. Nobody knew his real name. Nobody knew what he'd done in the past to get here.

He was *that* good, and he liked it that way.

Unofficially, he never slept well when his sister sounded like that. He could *feel* her fear, even through the phone. He'd never admit it, though, preferring not to give her that kind of ammo to blackmail him with.

He'd been going back and forth with a big tech firm in Joia City, trying to decide if he wanted to take them on as a client. They'd been chasing him for weeks, but he'd had a few other projects to wrap up. The timing had been inconvenient before, but now it was perfect.

He fired off an email, officially accepting the job and locking in the contract. His fingers moved faster than he realized.

As soon as he hit send, Diogo leaned back and dragged a hand over his face. He didn't know what he'd find when he got there. Maybe nothing. But the way Adelen's voice had sounded told him enough. The way she ended the call told him the rest.

Something was very wrong.

Whatever it was, he was going to find out. Whether she liked it or not.

New Message

From: **Silver Shadow Consulting**

Subject: **Neuronix Engagement Acceptance**

Mr. Voss,

I have great news: I was able to rework my schedule and can take on this project, with an anticipated start date within the next few weeks. I am currently wrapping up another engagement and will have a more definitive timeline within the next week or so.

Attached is my standard draft of the service and non-disclosure agreement for your review and signature.

Let's set up an in-person kickoff as soon as possible to discuss the process and finalize the project scope.

Thanks,

— Silver Shadow

CHAPTER 9

Owen

Owen stared out the floor-to-ceiling windows of his penthouse, clutching his favorite mug—navy blue, a little chipped, and still sporting the world's most judgmental llama. His mom gave it to him years ago, and he'd used it so much that the handle was threatening to give up. The sunrise was just starting to creep over the city, painting everything gold. He took a sip, hoping the coffee would work some kind of miracle.

Llamas had been his thing as a kid—something Levi often asked about—so the mug was their inside joke. Proof that his mom actually remembered the little things about him. Now it was one of the last real pieces of her he had left.

His reflection in the glass looked about as wrecked as he felt. Hair sticking up everywhere, last night's sleep lines still creasing his face, and the usual uniform of a wrinkled white undershirt and gray flannel pants. Classic morning disaster.

But the hollow, tired eyes? That was new. He didn't like it.

He'd slept like shit. Again. Probably because he hated being here by himself. Most nights, he'd rather crash at Grace and Isaac's place, but with Levi off living his best life at Aurelia's cottage, he was running out of backup homes. Even he knew his friends deserved a break from him sometimes.

He hated being alone.

The penthouse was the ultimate bachelor pad—close to Neuronix, all glass and steel, and so clean it looked like no one actually lived there. He'd let some designer go wild with the budget, resulting in sleek furniture, a bar that could supply a frat party, and not a single thing out of place. He almost never brought anyone over. It was impressive, sure, but it didn't feel like home.

It was the kind of place that screamed success but forgot about people. Nothing like the house he grew up in.

The only thing the penthouse really had going for it was the view. Twentieth floor, all of Joia City spread out below, sunrise on one side, sunset on the other. Sometimes it almost made up for everything else.

The other miracle was finding anything edible in the kitchen. The coffee he was drinking was probably older than some of his houseplants...well, the plants that were barely clinging to life. Lately, he wasn't good at remembering to water them. He really needed to get his act together on that front. His mother's garden beds had thrived because of his green thumb.

Apparently, he was still feeling risky.

He still couldn't wrap his head around how fast everything had changed. An impulsive decision later, and suddenly his whole life was on a different track.

One minute, he was auditioning for a one-line extra role. The next, he'd somehow agreed to play Dolf Ingerson, world-famous heavy metal frontman. The lead. In a freaking POLmArK movie.

It hadn't felt real.

A week later, and it still didn't feel real.

The meeting after was a total blur. Contracts, schedules, NDAs, wardrobe fittings, media training, script readings—he barely kept up. By the time he stumbled out of the production office, his head was spinning, and his stomach was doing somersaults. Anticipation, disbelief, and a little guilt all tangled together. After everything with Neuronix and his mom, it felt weird to do something just for himself.

But maybe it was time. Maybe he'd earned it.

Or maybe it was the wrong time. Maybe he'd been selfish.

Owen sighed, rubbing the back of his neck like that would magically fix the knots in his shoulders. He took another gulp of coffee, letting the burn jolt him awake.

Wrong or right, there was no turning back. He made a very real and *very* legally binding commitment when he signed those documents with POLmArK. Now he had to figure out what the hell he was doing next.

The room brightened as the sun climbed higher, warm light spilling across the floor and over his skin. It made him think of Adelen—her face, the way she looked at him after the audition.

Complete disinterest when he spoke to her after the audition.

The delicious red flush that splayed across her cheeks.

Shock and horror when they offered him the lead role.

The way her lips parted in disbelief when he quickly accepted. He hadn't been able to stop thinking about those lips...

He tore himself away from the window, shaking his head to clear out the images. Just thinking about her sent his pulse racing like fire through his veins. It had been like that for weeks.

He set his mug down on the kitchen island and marched to the master bathroom, stripping off his clothes with brutal efficiency. He took the fastest, coldest shower of his life. He had too much to do before tomorrow showed up and ruined everything. No time to waste.

With a brief detour in his room for a fresh undershirt and black track pants, Owen was as ready as he'd ever be.

Ready to fulfill a lifelong dream.

Ready to be a part-time movie star.

Ready to win Adelen's heart.

He started another pot of questionable coffee and ordered groceries before he could forget. Time to hunker down, strategize, and make a plan.

Operation Make Shit Happen has commenced.

For the past week, every spare minute had gone into prepping for this. He did it the only way he knew how: obsessively. The weekend was no different.

He started with acting techniques, interviews, and every "*How to Be an Actor*" article the internet could cough up. Now his apartment was a graveyard of sticky notes and printouts with titles like "*Find Your Motivation*," "*Acting 101: Tips to Being Okayish*," and "*Act Like You Belong Here*."

He wasn't half bad. Or at least, that's what he kept telling himself.

With a little confidence (or a lot of delusion), he started plotting how to get Adelen to agree to one date. Valentine's Day was coming up—no one wanted to be alone on that day. He'd even settle for a pity date at this point.

By the time his sushi arrived, he'd spiraled into a black hole of possible romantic gestures. The problem? He barely knew anything about her. He'd tried grilling Aurelia, but she didn't know much either—just a few scraps from their girls' night out.

Owen couldn't help but smile as he read and reread the text she'd sent after doing some reconnaissance.

AURELIA Details

Message
(Thursday) PM 4:16

Hey…so random question: What does Adelen like? Interests? Asking for a friend of course

Hmmm…I feel like I should know that but I can ask during girls night tomorrow?

You're the best!

I know

Okay, SO chai tea is her go-to, and unfortunately she loves heavy metal and EDM like you and Levi

She works out a lot and is always down for a cheeseburger and milkshake. That's all I got

Not much information to go on, but he'd make it work. At least being in the same studio meant he'd have plenty of chances to get to know her—and maybe figure out what made her tick.

Feeling pretty pleased with himself, Owen wrapped up the night by slogging through work emails. The day he nailed the audition, his luck kept rolling—he got an email from the cybersecurity expert he'd been chasing for Neuronix. He nearly fell out of his chair when he saw that *the* fabled *Silver Shadow* had agreed to take them on.

It stung a little that even he couldn't figure out the guy's real identity, and Owen could hack almost anything. Or so he thought. The *Silver Shadow* was on another level. The name fit because it was earned.

He'd only talked to the guy once, just to confirm travel plans for their kickoff. But even that one call convinced Owen this was the start of a beautiful bromance. The mysterious *Silver Shadow* would be in town in a few weeks.

He signed and sent the contracts in record time. Project officially locked in. Owen was practically buzzing, hoping his lucky streak hadn't run out yet.

Still, he knew he had to talk to Levi and Isaac. Not just about the project, but about stepping back from Neuronix for a while. Just a temporary sabbatical.

He was absolutely dreading that conversation.

They met in Owen's office at Neuronix the next morning. Because obviously, nothing says 'happy Monday' like a tough conversation before coffee.

Owen woke up with a pit in his stomach, and it only worsened as the morning dragged on. By the time Levi and Isaac walked in and sat down, both staring at him like he was about to confess to murder, he was ready to bolt.

Outside, the sky was turning darker by the hour, thunder rumbling in the distance. They needed the rain, but it felt like a bad omen anyway.

Owen had handled way worse than this, but somehow talking to his best friends was harder than any boardroom showdown. Had he always been this avoidant?

He frowned at the realization and leaned forward, elbows on the desk, hands clasped. No point in dragging it out. He just went for it.

"We are gathered here today for a very serious and life-changing discussion. One that's going to rattle your bones and shock you to your core, but will heavily benefit me in the end."

Isaac pinched the bridge of his nose, with a slight shake of his head. Levi softly muttered, "Christ," and shot Owen a withering look.

Owen pressed on. He was already in too deep to back out now.

"I'll hit you with the bad news first and rip the metaphorical bandaid off. I'm going to need to take an intermittent leave of absence for an unknown period of time. I'll check in with my team regularly, but otherwise I think Martin Strasburg can take over most of my job in the interim."

Both Levi and Isaac's eyebrows shot up, but neither appeared alarmed or surprised.

"Martin makes sense," Levi mused. "We wouldn't be back at Neuronix having this conversation if it weren't for him."

"So then the good news, for me at least, is that I'm going to be a POLAmArK movie star!" Levi stifled a laugh behind a hand when Owen stared at Isaac, full arrogance on display, and added, "Just. Like. I. Told. You."

"Oh my god, here we go—"

"Some people are naturally skilled at recognizing good talent. So instead of nabbing the small role of Hardware Store Guy, they made me an offer I couldn't refuse...and then I remembered I had a real, and woefully conflicting, full-time job."

Owen leaned back, trying to look smug while his heart hammered loud enough to wake the dead. The truth was out, delivered Owen-style. Waiting for their reaction was pure torture.

"Let me get this straight," Isaac said thoughtfully, leaning back in his chair, one hand absently stroking his beard. "You auditioned as a hardware store clerk, and in a surprise plot twist, they offered you the lead role on the spot...and now you're the star of a romantic comedy?"

"*Metal Love Beans*," Owen corrected. "And *yes*. Apparently, they saw something in me."

"Delusion?" Isaac offered.

Owen's nostrils flared. "This is just like *Climbing into Love.* Ron, the big city marketing guy, gets a shot at a cave spelunking challenge. His friends think he's doomed. *Guess what happened, Isaac?*"

"The directors did the audience a favor and ended the film with him trapped in a cave forever?" Owen scoffed at Isaac's misplaced hopefulness.

"In your dreams, bruh. He crushed it, fell for Sharon, the event organizer and fellow spelunker, and landed the biggest account ever." Owen stood, leaning over his desk and pointing at Isaac. "It's a *sign* from the universe, I'm telling you."

Isaac bristled. "Yeah, a *sign* that the only thing climbing around here is your ego!"

Levi openly laughed this time, cutting them both off. "Isaac, ignore him. Owen, it's too early for movie references." Levi paused, all traces of humor gone. "Seriously, though, this is incredible, man. Of course, Aurelia told me all about it last week. I'm surprised it took you this long to bring it up to us, though."

Owen dropped back into his chair, grinning as guilt and relief crashed together. "I didn't want to disappear on you guys, not without a plan. I can work remotely if needed—or take a leave for the shoot. Whatever's best for the team."

"Surely this has nothing to do with working alongside your new girlfriend, right?" Isaac snickered.

"She's *not* my girlfriend—*yet*. I don't want to know what Ivy's told you, it'll ruin my mood."

"We'll make it work," Levi cut in, Isaac nodding in agreement, though his eyes still danced with laughter. "You've earned a break. Besides, you're still tied into our next big win."

"Despite how I feel about these movies, I'm honestly happy for you. It's been a dream—albeit a weird one—of yours for so long. You'd be a fool to pass it up," Isaac said with a genuine smile.

"Right," Owen said, his throat thickened with emotion. "Speaking of our next big win—I finalized the contract with that consultant. We landed one of the top ethical hackers in the world to assess Neuronix's vulnerabilities."

Isaac's eyebrows rose. "No kidding. What's his name?"

"Silver Shadow," Owen said, glancing at his notes. "He's supposed to be a genius—big on data privacy, does deep security audits. I think he's consulting from Joia City for a while, and he'll be here in the next few weeks. We are still nailing down the date."

"Wait, I've heard of him! He seriously agreed to sign on with us? He's a *legend* and virtually impossible to book!" Isaac bounced in his seat with excitement.

"Perfect," Levi laughed. "Couldn't ask for better timing."

"I'll keep you both updated, but I have to go to the studio in a couple of hours to pick up my script, review the filming schedule, and have my first wardrobe fitting. The next time I see you, I'll be Dolf Ingerson!"

Owen let himself smile, letting the excitement finally win. They spent the rest of the morning hashing out the plan for his absence, totally clueless about what was coming next.

CHAPTER 10

Adelen

Adelen had been wandering *Pins n' Needles* for over an hour, and her basket was still empty. Usually, she'd be hauling around a cart stuffed with yarn and accessories, barely able to steer. Today, she just drifted, eyes sliding over the shelves without really seeing anything. She was moving, but her mind was somewhere else entirely.

The gym was her haven for releasing pent-up anger and frustration, but knitting sweaters and blankets was a way to soothe, a way to relax by creating something physically comforting. Except neither seemed to be the solution to ease her edginess today.

She needed a strategy. Desperately. Anything to stop her mind from spinning in circles. She was no closer to a solution now than the moment she first laid eyes on Owen.

The week after the audition disaster should have been enough time to get a handle on working in the same space as Owen without falling all over him. But every time she even thought about it, her focus shattered. It was starting to mess with her work

Instead of making a plan, she kept imagining what it would feel like to ignore that pesky voice of reason and just give in, to let him explore every inch of her body—and let her return the favor. Every time her thoughts wandered into that territory, her body lit up, craving something she couldn't even name, let alone satisfy.

Every. Single. Time.

Aurelia and Ivy, plus their friend Grace, had made good on their promise and hauled her out for a girls' night at a paint bar. Normally, Adelen would have loved it—listening to the instructor talk about painting a vase of multi-colored roses, sipping wine, and pretending she was the next great artist. A few glasses in, paint everywhere, and she'd usually be relaxed.

Those sneaky bitches, however, had other plans. A girl's night with Owen's inner circle was never just a girl's night. By the time she realized what was happening, they were already firing questions at her like it was an Olympic sport.

She replayed the whole night in her head all weekend, trying to figure out exactly when she'd walked into their trap. It was probably when they were all huddled around the paint-splattered table, her second glass of Moscato almost empty, when Ivy's voice cut through the noise.

The inquisition had begun.

"You know what, ladies? Now that our little shrew crew has grown so quickly, this is the perfect opportunity for us to get to know one another better. And what better way to do that while creating our masterpieces than to rapid-fire questions at each other?"

"Oh, I love that!" Grace exclaimed. She somehow managed to have a myriad of paint droplets mixed in with her freckles. "We can take turns asking questions, but you have to answer fast with the first thing that comes to mind!"

"I'll go first!" Aurelia quickly chimed in, effectively blocking any objections. "Addy, what's your favorite drink? Besides pink Moscato, of course."

Adelen hadn't agreed to this, but the Moscato was already infiltrating her senses. Though their eyes remained fixed on their canvases, she felt the subtle shift in attention as three sets of ears strained to hear her response.

"Chai tea," she blurted, swiping her brush to fill in the white space of the outlined blue vase. "Doesn't matter what time of year it is, I always start the morning with it and will switch to coffee later in the day if I'm dragging."

"Ooh, that's a good one! I love that around the holidays," Ivy commented as she dipped her brush into black paint and aggressively attacked her canvas with it. Adelen frowned, wondering what the hell Ivy was actually painting. Her movements and color choices didn't match what everyone else had been instructed to do.

She brushed the irregularity aside, preparing to ask a question when Grace beat her to the punch.

"What kind of music do you listen to, Addy?" She asked sweetly while not-so-secretly flashing Adelen the biggest shit-eating grin she'd ever seen.

"Heavy metal and EDM." Exaggerated gagging noises from her left had Adelen side-eying Aurelia as she continued. "The beat of both helps to regulate my thoughts and settle my nerves so I can focus."

"Ugh, you listen to the same crap as the boys!" Ivy whined.

"I can play some of it too," Adelen smirked at the unabashed curiosity on her friends' faces. She took an intentional and quite leisurely sip of her wine, draining the glass before adding, "I can play the guitar, and so can my brother."

After that, the Shrew Crew went in for the kill, questions flying at her from every direction. Her defenses didn't stand a chance. Before she knew it, she was spilling everything, words tumbling out like water from a busted dam.

For once, she didn't mind the interrogation. Even stranger, she didn't mind sharing. Not at all.

Adelen had never really had female friends like this before. She'd always been stuck in the doorway—never a total outsider, but never really inside the circle either.

She just didn't fit. Simple as that.

Meeting Aurelia had changed everything, and it was a small turning point in her life. For once, her resting bitch face hadn't scared someone off. Aurelia just showed up, offered friendship without a second thought, and stuck around. Adelen never said it out loud, but she was grateful.

Until their paintings were finished, and they all shared their completed works.

Of the four of them, three had painted a terrible variation of the vase of roses the instructor had displayed, while Ivy had gone *utterly* rogue.

While the skill level was a step above that of a kindergartner, it was still painfully clear that Ivy had painted Adelen and Owen in quite the compromising position. It was hard to tell exactly *what* the position was, but the little hearts bordering the image and the fact that she clearly labeled "Adelen and Owen" at the top were enough.

Grace had sprayed a mouthful of wine all over her painting when she first saw it. Aurelia howled so hard that she almost couldn't breathe, her gasps for air causing a severe case of hiccups. And Ivy...she was damn well pleased with herself, grinning like a cat who just ate the canary.

"Valentine's Day is upon us," Ivy cackled, "You can give this to Owen as a gift for him to hang in his dressing room!"

At the time, despite being mortified, Adelen couldn't help but laugh along with them. The painting was the most ridiculous thing she'd ever seen, and it was no secret that Owen had a little crush on her—his outlandish personality didn't waste time on subtleties.

Once the alcohol wore off, she knew she'd been bamboozled. All those questions? Definitely going to be used against her. And probably shared with the one person she was trying to protect her heart from.

Adelen had busted her ass to get this far in her career, and she loved her job. She was a professional, no question. Getting involved with coworkers? Not her thing. Sure, sometimes it worked out, but most of the time it just got messy and awkward for everyone.

Her biggest fear was being the subject of office gossip, losing respect, and credibility in the process. She'd spent enough of her life as the topic of whispers. She wasn't about to let it happen again.

She needed to stay alert, keep her head down, and stay busy behind the scenes. Valentine's Day was coming up fast, which meant she had to be extra careful. She hated the holiday—overpriced flowers, chocolates, everyone showing off their love like it was a competition. The irony wasn't lost on her, working on romantic movies for a living. But she was a realist. These films were fiction. Valentine's Day was just a commercial circus, and she wanted nothing to do with it.

Pulling herself out of her thoughts, she found herself staring at the rows of yarn, realizing this was just another lie she'd been telling herself. Or maybe one she'd never bothered to question until now.

It wouldn't stay buried anymore. The truth was, she didn't really hate Valentine's Day. She hated what it had turned into, sure, but not the idea behind it.

What she really hated was never having celebrated it. Every year, Valentine's Day came and went, and she was always on the sidelines—never anyone's valentine, never had one herself. This year, though, it felt different. It felt lonely. She wanted *more.*

How did I get here?

She shook her head and body out, bringing herself back to reality, and accepting that she had other things to worry about than some silly made-up holiday.

On autopilot, she started tossing yarn into her basket—yellows, tans, deep blues—anything that caught her eye. All she could think about was getting through the next few weeks with her heart and sanity still in one piece.

Monday crept in quietly, and Adelen found herself unexpectedly grateful for the chance to escape the confines of her apartment.

She tried to lose herself in the familiar rhythm of knitting, surrounded by a mountain of new yarn, but her hands moved with a mind of their own. By the time she was done, a massive crew neck sweater had taken shape—far too large for her father or brother. Her heart, it seemed, had quietly hijacked her brain.

It would never fit either of them, but she knew precisely whose broad shoulders would fill it out.

With a frustrated growl, she shoved the sweater deep into the black velvet ottoman, as if she could bury the inspiration along with it. The idea of unraveling the whole damn thing flickered through her mind, but the prospect only darkened her mood further.

She had exhausted every distraction her apartment could offer, so returning to the studio the next morning felt like a lifeline. Tessa had offered to carpool since they lived in the same building (along with other staff transplants), but Adelen wanted to get out of there as early as possible. She didn't like waiting on others or holding them up if she chose to stay later, either.

The new sound equipment for her department had finally arrived, and anticipation thrummed beneath her skin as she imagined the unopened boxes, wondering what small treasures waited inside. She loved staying up to date on new technology and practically ran across the parking lot and into the studio.

Filming started next week, which meant she had to make sure nothing was missing—especially since she'd be splitting her time between the studio and the Starhaven Manor set soon. Being prepared was *everything.*

The day unfolded with a quiet productivity that surprised her, then Owen appeared, moving through the space with an ease that bordered on arrogance. Against her better judgment, she found herself watching him navigate the room.

Damn, he looked just as good coming as he did going.

He'd only been around for a couple of days, yet the crew seemed attracted to him. He spoke to everyone—from maintenance person to executive—with the same easy warmth, making each person feel seen. There was an unexpected allure in that genuine kindness. Even the treats he brought in were chosen with care, every allergy and preference quietly accounted for.

Adelen found herself unsettled by the slow, reluctant affection growing toward him, despite every promise she'd made to herself. Just that morning, Tessa had been nearly breathless with excitement, sharing news that a mystery donor had quietly erased the crushing medical debt of a sanitation worker whose child had just survived a major organ transplant.

Adelen suspected she knew exactly who was responsible. The knowledge further chipped away at her defenses.

She tried to disappear into the sound editing room abutting her office with as much equipment as she could carry, but it was too late.

Owen's gaze found her instantly, as if he'd been searching for her all along, and he crossed the room with determined purpose. She bit back a groan, silently berating herself for lingering too long with the equipment. Her eagerness over the packages had betrayed her, and now she stood face-to-face before the one person she'd hoped to avoid.

He stopped at her side, close enough that she could feel the heat radiating from him, his height casting a shadow over her. He nodded toward the stack of boxes, hands tucked carelessly into his pockets.

"Good afternoon, my fair lady." The deep timber of his voice vibrated over her skin, a siren's call that could lure the female population into a frenzy, ensnaring them in his thrall. He grinned, and her eyes zeroed in on the small dimple on the right side of his cheek—she hadn't noticed it before. She hadn't stood this close to him before, either, the scent of citrus and toasted almonds mixed with the heady scent that was uniquely Owen caressing her senses.

Her traitorous body reacted as heat pooled between her thighs, and her nipples chafed against the confines of her bra. Adelen stiffened, arms folding tightly across her chest to cover up the evidence of her desire—and to give her time to summon the practiced chill she'd honed over the years. Her reply was flat, almost bored. "Hi."

"What are you up to?" Owen shifted his feet. Adelen blinked and raised a single brow, the only acknowledgment of his question.

"Working. The same thing you'd be doing if you actually took this seriously," she replied, each word edged with dry sarcasm while she tried to regain control of her senses.

Owen bristled. "I *am* taking this seriously. Being in a POLmArK movie is a dream come true. But that's not why I came over here..." He trailed off, swallowing once and averting his gaze, shoulders curling in as he stared at the boxed equipment. With a deep breath, he flicked his eyes back to her. "What are your plans for Saturday?" The words rushed out, clumsy and hesitant.

Her brows knit together, unsettled by the gravity in his voice, the flicker of vulnerability that was so out of place. She didn't recognize this version of him. It was almost as if—

"Owen!" A raspy yet authoritative voice shouted from behind them. They both whipped their heads towards the source, the clumsy small talk effectively over. Adelen's shoulders relaxed, filled with gratitude for the reprieve. "You're fifteen minutes late for hair and makeup!"

Rita Manos, the stylist, wedged her petite frame between them, her finger wagging up accusingly at Owen's startled face. He winced, chastened by her scolding. Rita had sat beside Adelen during Owen's audition and hadn't let her forget his obvious crush on her since.

Grinning down at Rita, he held his hands up in mock surrender and earnestly apologized to the fiery woman.

"I'm so sorry, Rita. I couldn't stop myself from shamelessly flirting with Adelen for a few minutes first."

"*What?*"

Adelen's arms fell to her sides, her cheeks burning.

He did not just say that.

She stared at him, stunned, but his smile only widened, feeding off her disbelief. How quickly he'd switched from bashful to brazen.

"It's okay, Addy. You shot me down today, but I'm not giving up on us. This is just the beginning of our courtship." He bowed deeply at the waist, his devilish gaze meeting hers as he slowly rose to full height.

Her glower promised retribution. She was going to strangle him.

Rita watched their silent exchange with open delight, her gaze flicking between them. She seemed to settle, tossing Adelen a conspiratorial wink before turning back to Owen.

"You are forgiven, *this time*, you rascal. Get your ass in there!" She caught the edge of his sleeve and nudged him toward the studio salon, cutting off any chance for further conversation. Owen glanced back, half-apologetic, and had the audacity to blow her a kiss.

She stood rooted in place for several seconds, watching them disappear, wondering what the hell just happened. One thing was abundantly clear, though: ignoring Owen would likely be impossible.

She exhaled sharply, squared her shoulders, and forced her attention back to the boxes. The distraction lasted all of four minutes before all hell broke loose.

Anyone within earshot of the hair and makeup room heard Owen's alarmed voice shout, "*What* hair extensions?"

Rita hurriedly shut the door, muffling their argument.

A snicker escaped her, quickly morphing into a satisfied laugh. Apparently, no one had warned Owen that Dolf Ingerson wore his hair *long* and blonde.

Serves him right.

She continued to chuckle under her breath as she sorted through the last box, the stifled argument between Rita and Owen drifting through the closed door.

A couple of hours later, Rita emerged from her space, flushed from exertion and a smug smirk tugging on her lips. She stepped to the side and leaned against the wall, arms crossed, her eyes filled with wicked delight, locking with Adelen's.

"You can come out now, *Dolf*," Rita cooed.

Owen emerged, irritation etched across his face, golden hair tumbling past his shoulders with every step. The entire crew, Adelen included, fell silent, transfixed by the transformation.

The long hair actually looked *good* on him. Too good. Dangerously good. Like she needed to run her fingers through it, kind of good.

He drew the attention of nearly everyone in the vicinity of the room, women and men alike, their admiration buzzing around him. Tessa's delighted squeals rose above the rest, insisting it had turned out even better than she'd hoped.

And Dax—Dax was so pleased with the outcome that he offered Owen a fruit roll-up treat from his back pocket. Adelen was stunned. Dax *never* shared his snacks. *Ever*. Owen, to his credit, politely declined and tried to ease his way out of the small crowd.

The commotion drew the attention of his co-star, Henrietta Lacroix, who emerged from her self-imposed isolation to mingle with the rest of the crew. Adelen had hoped someone else would be cast as *Maggie Bean*, but fate seemed determined to test her patience and make her suffer.

Henrietta was POLmArK's top-billed actress, her reputation for talent matched only by her snobby attitude. At first glance, she seemed almost angelic—cherubic features, luminous skin, and striking aquamarine eyes—until she opened her mouth to speak.

The crew, Adelen among them, kept their distance, speaking to Henrietta only when absolutely necessary, lest they provoke the wails of that banshee. Her words were intentionally cutting and cruel; she delighted in tearing others down, but her gift for acting kept audiences enthralled and her position secure.

POLmArK might not have the luxury of replacing her, but Adelen was under no such obligation to cater to her whims. She watched Henrietta's every move, every breath, unable to look away.

Henrietta's delicate hand settled on Owen's chest, her other hand weaving slowly through his hair, both gestures feeling both invasive and far too intimate.

A cold stillness settled over Adelen as she watched, the urge to claw Henrietta's eyes out intensifying with every heartbeat. Despite her attempts to keep him at arm's length, Adelen knew that Owen didn't deserve the likes of Henrietta either. No one deserved that kind of punishment if the rumors about her were true.

Henrietta brushed a lock of hair aside and leaned in, whispering something into Owen's ear. He recoiled, eyebrows shooting up, making no effort to hide his discomfort as he gently removed her hands.

Maybe the rumors are *true.*

His panicked gaze swept the crowd until he found Adelen. Relief washed over his features, the anxiety replaced by something far more intense. The look he gave her nearly melted her where she stood. Only her.

Shit shit shit.

The air thickened, the temperature rising in the space, that slow-burning fire from a few hours prior reigniting deep within her core. Adelen couldn't tear her gaze away. Owen's expression was both a challenge and an invitation, and every part of her ached to respond.

A small, satisfied smirk curved his lips, dousing her in cold reality.

That asshole *knew* exactly the effect he had on her.

Henrietta watched the exchange in silence, annoyance flashing across her face before it vanished. She smoothed her expression into a brittle smile, tossing her strawberry-blonde curls over her shoulder.

But her attention had shifted. It was no longer Owen she watched—it was Adelen.

Fantastic.

CHAPTER 11

Owen

The sun was shining brightly, the sky stretched wide and cobalt, and not a single cloud dared to intrude. The songs of canaries and blackbirds chirping joyfully in the trees filled the air, weaving a soundtrack that matched the lightness in Owen's chest. Even the parking lot, with its faded lines and oil stains, felt almost welcoming as he strolled toward the squat, unremarkable concrete building that housed the studio.

Clifford, the ever-stoic guard stationed at the security booth, also seemed to have caught the good mood bug. Instead of his usual silent scowl, he offered Owen a curt nod—practically a parade wave by Clifford standards.

Carrying a piping hot chai tea in one hand, and Ivy's hideous excuse for artwork tucked under his other arm, he was a man on a mission. The first time he saw the monstrosity—her so-called masterpiece—Owen blanched, unsure of exactly *what* it was. The lopsided heart border, with his and Adelen's name scribbled across the top offered a clue, but no amount of squinting could make sense of it.

"I don't know what kid you paid to make this...*thing*, but you overpaid. Big time. I'm not a fan of taking things away from children, but you should demand a refund," Owen had advised, rotating the canvas multiple times to inspect it from all angles.

"*What?* I made it during our paint night! It's a masterpiece and Adelen *loved* it," Ivy hissed, hands on her hips, her glare angry enough to melt his skin off. "I'm being helpful by giving it to you. It's an accurate representation of your feelings for her."

They'd argued about it for a solid thirty minutes before Ivy's stubbornness finally wore him down. Owen surrendered, agreeing to play courier for her questionable creation. He'd stashed it in the trunk of his car, out of sight and out of mind, until this morning. Just looking at it felt like an assault on his senses, but if Adelen loved it, well—he'd take one for the team.

A rogue chunk of hair whipped across his face as a sharp gust of wind cut through the parking lot, a chilly reminder of the new lifestyle he'd signed up for. When Rita first explained what becoming Dolf would entail, he balked. The dark eyeliner was fine—it made him feel dangerous and occult.

But the hair extensions? They crossed the line. He *loved* his hair. Took real pride in those luscious locks. The idea of gluing or sewing anything into them was almost a dealbreaker.

Then Rita insisted it would knock Adelen off her feet.

Rita had watched Owen fumble his way through the entire conversation, her expression shifting from amusement to secondhand embarrassment before she finally stepped in to save him. He hadn't even been late for his session—she just couldn't stand to watch the train wreck any longer, swooping in to put *both* him and Adelen out of their misery

Rightfully so. Approaching Adelen had been the easy part; actually talking to her was a full-blown disaster. His anxiety had hijacked the moment, tossing his brain out the window.

But he couldn't pass up a shot at redemption. He stopped fighting Rita on the hair extensions, and instead peppered her with questions about life on set, eager for any tips and tricks she could share.

And anything she could possibly tell him about Adelen, of course.

Rita was happy to oblige, blabbing about everyone and everything, including a stern warning about his co-star, Henrietta Lacroix, and how she was "the antichrist in angelic clothing" and to make sure he didn't "look into her eyes for too long or he would turn to stone." That was the moment the stylist became his second-favorite person on set.

Unfortunately, she didn't have much dirt on Adelen. She was very private, quiet, and kept mostly to herself. She described her as private, quiet, the type who kept to herself. Rita herself had only just moved to Joia City for the new studio launch, though she'd worked with Adelen for years.

"She's a gifted sound engineer who knows how to maximize a scene. Consistently offered promotions, even once to replace her boss—except that's a secret and he doesn't know that—she only ever told me...and now you know. *Shit.*" Owen laughed and mimed zipping his lips. Relieved from his promise of secrecy, Rita continued sharing what she knew about Adelen. "She always turned down the offers because Cary, her boss, is her mentor. And because she just wants to focus on what she loves. Never rude, always respectful, she just...doesn't let anyone in." Rita had carefully applied another clip of hair, pensive as she had waited for the adhesive to set. "But I've never seen that poor girl so off balance until you showed up."

His heart had raced the entire time, desperate for Rita's words to be true. He needed them to be true, because honestly, he didn't have a backup plan. Owen knew without a shadow of a doubt that beautiful dark thunder cloud out there was it for him.

And he was pretty damn sure she knew it too. The way she'd looked at him after he left Rita's salon yesterday—lips parted, eyes hungry, like she was considering *him* for dessert—left no room for doubt. Still, she was fighting whatever this was between them.

The question was *why*.

There had to be a reason she kept herself so tightly guarded, living behind those carefully built walls of steel and stone. Luckily, if there was one thing Owen was good at, it was digging through people's self-imposed defenses, like a persistent, slightly unwelcome gopher in someone's vegetable patch.

This time, though, he'd have to be less intrusive, and a lot more charming, if he wanted to break through. He wasn't afraid of a little sweat equity; Adelen was worth every ounce of effort and then some.

Henrietta, however, was shaping up to be a problem though. He'd been genuinely excited to meet her, having seen all of her films. What he did *not* expect was to be groped by her wraith-like hands in front of half the crew.

And then there was the moment she leaned in and whispered, low and sultry, "I'd drink your bath water." He nearly dropped the chai right then and there, shuddering violently at the memory of her alcohol-infused breath scraping across his skin, how close he'd come to throwing up in his mouth. Turns out, Henrietta was disappointingly a day drinker. And into some weird shit.

Owen scanned his new security badge and nudged the building door open, the automatic lock releasing with a soft click. He made sure to arrive a little early to surprise her with the tea and the sorry excuse for a painting.

He breezed through the entrance, striding down the halls with a little extra bounce in his step. The sight of the big steel office door, already unlocked, felt like another small victory.

Another stroke of luck, though he planned to talk to Adelen about keeping her space locked and secure after hours.

He'd already spotted a handful of other weak spots in the building's security. As he set the tea on Adelen's desk and rid himself of the abomination masquerading as art, by placing it on her chair. He made a note to corner the head of security later.

I should do the world a favor and burn that godforsaken thing.

Shaking his head, he took a moment to inspect the small but drab room. A u-shaped oak desk dominated the space, cluttered with monitors and various audio gear. Another hulking gray steel door connected the office to the sound studio beyond.

It was a smart design—the main entrance to the sound studio accessible from the hallway, could remain locked while providing Adelen a direct connection from the inside.

Other than the big glass window looking into the studio, her office was about as remarkable as a waiting room. The walls were a sterile, hospital white, stripped of any hint of personality. She probably hadn't had a spare second to jazz it up.

Maybe I can help with that, he mused, spinning on his heel and locking the door behind him. He could already anticipate Adelen's reaction to at least one of the gifts. He'd gone to her favorite coffee shop to get it—or at least the one Rita swore by.

As he slipped through the doorway of the actor's lounge to run through his lines while he waited for Adelen, Owen heard a voice he never expected to hear again in a million years.

"You lost, boyo? This room is for *actors*, not *snitches*."

For a split second, Owen considered turning on his heel and making a run for it. Instead, he took a deep breath and spun around to face the voice. Beady little eyes sunken deep into a shriveled face glared at him. The old man hunched over his cane, waving it like he was ready to go twelve rounds right there in the lounge.

"This can't be happening," Owen muttered under his breath. Was this punishment for something he'd done in a past life?

"Speak up, son! I'm not getting any younger!"

Owen planted his hands on his hips and stared up at the ceiling, trying to summon the patience to deal with the living mummy in front of him. He remembered all too well how unhinged conversations with this man could be.

"Mr. Dallingford, I'm glad to see you survived your short stint in jail. Clearly you didn't let your time in the clink put a damper on your usual cheery self."

The last time Owen crossed Bertrand Dallingford, the man had been handing out ecstasy tablets to his fellow retirees and soaring higher than a kite. He even tried to gut Owen with a butter knife in the middle of Aurelia's charity gala, somehow finding the energy to flip a dining table in the process.

That had been the same night Aurelia was abducted, and Bertrand's antics had cost them precious time. The police took hours to secure the scene, and Owen had been stuck there as an official witness, replaying every chaotic moment in his head.

If ever there was an omen, Bertrand's presence was it.

And for some reason, the surly old man was there, glaring at him with the wrath of a thousand suns, as he said, "Now you listen here—go find someone else's fun to ruin or I swear on my soul that—"

"Oh no no *no*, you can't swear anything on something you don't have."

Bertrand gasped. "How *dare* you—"

"How did you get in here? You looking to add breaking and entering to your rap sheet too, old man?"

"I'm going to be in the latest POLmArK film," Bertrand bellowed, loud enough to rattle the ceiling fixtures.

"*What?!*" Impossible. Owen refused to believe it. No one in their right mind would cast this surly creature in a beloved POLmArK romance. But Bertrand's next words sent a shiver down Owen's spine.

"I'm the Hardware Store Guy, you overgrown baboon!"

CHAPTER 12

Adelen

Adelen had overslept. The realization hit her like a bucket of ice water dumped over her head.

Flustered and upset, she scrambled through her morning routine at a breakneck pace, barely registering the blur of clothes, keys, and half-brushed hair before she was out the door in under twenty minutes.

Unfortunately, that meant no time for breakfast. She'd have to scavenge for whatever sad excuse for food was available at the studio. This was so unlike her. She lived to savor her mornings, not sprint through them.

Despite every attempt to slow the racing thoughts, to succumb to the overwhelming exhaustion from pushing her body to its limits at the gym, and to satisfy her body's demand for release that lingered long after yesterday's encounter with Owen, sleep remained elusive.

She was plagued by images of Henrietta's talons on him, whispering in his ear like a gold prospector staking their claim. Many men had fallen into her clutches under similar circumstances, unable to resist her charm. But Owen...Owen had been disgusted by her advances.

It was none of her business whether or not Owen was interested in Henrietta, but on the inside, she had basked in the glory of his rejection of her. Henrietta was just the *worst*.

After their confusing interaction yesterday, she was more unsure than ever about his interest being genuine. And Adelen had been the butt of too many pranks and gossip growing up to risk it. There was no desire to willingly subject herself to it again, and definitely not with Owen.

Because she'd never recover if he hurt her like that.

Too bad her heart and mind refused to listen to logic and reason. She was still pissed at how her body continued to react at the thought of him. Just hearing his name set her skin aflame. She tried to take the edge off last night, but it didn't help. She needed the real thing.

Against her inner protests, the fortress around her heart had fractured the second he'd unceremoniously plucked Henrietta's hands from his body. It grew into a small fissure when he'd sought her out over the crowd of office fans.

Nothing could have prepared her for what she saw next, the moment catching her off guard and leaving her breathless.

His eyes glittered with unadulterated hunger, his stare holding nothing back, intentions fully on display. He wanted to *devour* her. Had he tried right then and there, she would've given zero fucks about dragging him into the nearest broom closet. But Adelen was confident that it was all a hallucination, her mind's manifestation of what she *wanted* to see.

Real or not, something primal within her had awakened, a predator uncoiling and stretching itself out with animalistic grace. The feeling lingered, prowling beneath her skin as she sped through the streets of Joia City towards the studio.

It was thrilling. Exhilarating. And ill-timed.

During her mad dash out to her car, her phone chimed with two new messages. Once out of the parking lot and nearing a red light, Adelen scanned the screen.

Instant regret washed over her, a cold wave that made her wish she'd never glanced at the screen.

It wasn't the message from her new Boom Operator, Rodney, calling out sick (for the fourth day in a row) that caused her hands to tremble. No, it was quite the opposite of what she expected, its existence a digital blemish.

Another anonymous text.

Her chest tightened, breath catching as her focus shattered. The world narrowed to a single point of panic, and she barely registered the car looming ahead before her foot slammed the brakes. Tires screamed in protest, the acrid scent of burning rubber curling up into her nostrils, sharp and immediate.

God, what was happening to her? She *never* texted and drove.

Normally confident and self-assured, she was suddenly questioning everything—her judgment, job proficiency, whether moving was a mistake, and even her feelings. Adelen had never been on such uneven ground before.

Every worry and fear bubbled to the surface, a whirlpool of stress that slowly dragged her mood further and further down into its icy depths. Deeply entrenched in those thoughts, Adelen wouldn't remember reaching her destination or crossing the parking lot to the studio building.

The world blurred around her as she scanned her badge at the entrance, her mind too tangled to register much of anything. Even Henrietta's venomous glare as Adelen brushed past in the corridor barely registered, nothing more than a background hiss in the static of her thoughts

Not even the loud, escalating debate from the actor's lounge as she marched past it could penetrate the thundercloud she found herself trapped in.

But the moment she shoved open the heavy door to her *locked* office, a wave of nausea rolled through her. There, perched on her desk, was a tall cup of chai, steam curling up from the lid. Her favorite order from the new cafe she'd be frequenting. Her bag slid off her shoulder and crashed to the floor with a dull thud.

Every thought evaporated as she stared at the cup, her mind going eerily silent. In that hush, a tsunami of fear surged in that left her rooted to the spot, trembling, lungs aching for air that suddenly felt scarce.

It was a visceral reminder of why she left Vila Verde, the memory of unwanted intrusions haunting her. Adelen edged backwards towards the threshold, eyes furtively scanning the room for any other foreign objects, anything else out of place. Each shallow breath echoed in the stillness.

The thing on her black office chair captured her attention.

Recognizing Ivy's horrendous painting from the other night eased her nerves a fraction, but it wasn't enough to slow the erratic drumming of her heart. The fear dug its claws deeper, harsh and paralyzing.

For several moments she lingered in the doorway, gulping air like she'd just surfaced from deep water. Slowly, understanding seeped in, threading through the panic.

The unknown person that lurked in the shadows wasn't behind this—this was all Owen.

The Shrew Crew had committed high treason by giving the painting to Owen, but the tea was meant to win her over. His good intentions had clashed with her stalker's malicious ones.

With the anonymous texts resurfacing, the unwanted flowers showing up in her apartment, and now the unnerving sight of a stranger's hand in her office...it hammered home just how easily her boundaries could be crossed, how fragile her sense of safety really was.

Adrenaline shot through her body, splintering the illusion of safety and acceptance she'd tried so hard to build when she moved to Joia City.

Adelen needed to figure out who was behind the messages, *fast* and—

"Hopefully, the tea is better than that painting." A voice sounded from behind her, close enough to startle her and send her over the edge.

Instinct zipped through her like a live wire. She drove her elbow back hard, the motion sharp and automatic, already pivoting on her heel as she spun to face the threat.

Her breath tore from her chest as reality rushed in, pulse hammering, hands half-raised and ready even after she recognized who she struck. It was too late; the damage had been done.

The figure was doubled over, strong muscled arms encased in a simple burnt orange tee wrapped around his midsection. Owen let out a painful groan from behind the curtain of long tawny hair hiding his face.

"If this is your way of saying that we need to burn that abhorrent painting out in the back lot, then I deserve that."

Straightening to his full height, Owen winced as he prodded his ribcage where Adelen delivered the blow.

A flicker of guilt twisted in her gut at the pain she'd caused him, but it vanished almost as quickly as it came. She wasn't about to apologize, and honestly, she didn't give a shit. That prick deserved it.

She needed space, fast, so she stalked over to her chair, every muscle still buzzing with leftover adrenaline. She didn't trust herself not to take another swing at him, and this time, it wouldn't be an accident.

"How did you get into my office?" Adelen ground out. Her body was tightly coiled, and she needed to do something with her hands. Clocking an actor after they snuck up on her like a creep, would likely violate some human resource policies.

The idea was *very* appealing, consequences be damned.

Instead of risking her job by decking an actor, Adelen channeled her restless energy into moving the painting to lean against the wall, then dropped into her chair. The chai sat untouched, and she eyed it with the same suspicion she reserved for Owen himself.

He lounged against the door frame, arms crossed, studying her with a focus that made the fabric of his shirt stretch tight across his chest. Adelen's glare was unwavering, a silent dare for him to say something.

"I stared at the door and used my mystical powers to unlock it for me." Adelen rolled her eyes at the absurd non-answer, her irritation rising further. "Fine, the truth is that I turned the doorknob and hoped it was unlocked. To my surprise, it was." A small, secretive smile tugged at his lips.

Adelen didn't miss a beat, fingertips tapping on the desktop as she lashed out. "Are you ever serious, or is life one big perpetual joke?" Owen stiffened, and all traces of humor went up in flames, now ash on the wind. "My door *was* locked when I left last night. I have expensive equipment in there, and it's irresponsible not to."

She hadn't forgotten; locking up was muscle memory by now. A cold trickle of fear slid down her spine.

Someone else had been in her office.

Judging by Owen's stormy expression, he reached the same conclusion, but before he could utter a word, Adelen impatiently waved the situation—and Owen—off with a single hand. Both were dismissed.

"Not a big deal, I probably forgot. I had a lot on my mind." *Not a lie.* The forced casual tone sounded half-assed even to her own ears. "Why are *you* here?"

His jaw tightened as he pushed off the wall, agitation emanating from him in thick, invisible waves. He closed the distance to her desk with a predator's precision, all sharp edges and intent. Sitting down suddenly felt like a tactical error as she was forced to tilt her head back to meet his eyes, painfully aware of how much he loomed over her.

He was incredibly pissed, that much was obvious, but beneath the anger, she caught a flash of hurt in his eyes. It was a fleeting, unguarded glimmer that quickly disappeared.

"I'm here because I wanted to say hello and because Ivy talked me into bringing that godforsaken thing," he pointed an aggravated finger at the painting, "claiming you loved it, and figured I'd brighten your day with a nice hot beverage."

Adelen's mouth was suddenly bone dry. Words had always been her sharpest weapon, and today she'd used them to slice right through Owen. It felt wrong.

I guess he does *know how to be serious.*

"I'm also here because I wanted to see if you had plans for Valentine's Day this weekend, but instead, you assaulted and insulted me. We seem to have gotten off on the wrong foot, and I'd like a chance to start over—unless you have incredibly salacious plans already scheduled," he paused, allowing his words to hit their mark. He crossed his arms and added sarcastically, "...though *highly* unlikely given your violent disposition."

He had yet to properly experience my "violent disposition."

The word *no* hovered on the tip of her tongue, her temper simmering hotter with every heartbeat, but she kept her mouth shut. A small, unwelcome prickle of shame tried to worm its way in, but

Adelen shoved it aside. She knew she'd hurt him, but he hadn't exactly cared about her boundaries when he barged into her space.

So she did the most mature thing she could possibly think of and served him with the most scathing glower she could muster, settling into the staring contest, refusing to back down. Anyone else on the receiving end of it would have turned on their heels and scattered.

Except Owen. He did the opposite.

With an evenly matched attitude, the glare he volleyed was a pig-headed, silent challenge that demanded surrender.

He was about to learn the hard way that Adelen didn't submit to *anyone.*

The silence between them stretched on, the invisible tether connecting them charged with energy, neither willing to yield first. Adelen had to admit, this side of Owen—the one she'd managed to rattle—was unexpectedly hot. They'd been locked in this standoff so long, she almost forgot what started it.

Without thinking, she caught her lower lip between her teeth, a lazy, absentminded gesture. That tiny slip was all it took—Owen's composure disintegrated, and he tore his gaze away with a sharp inhale, eyes lingering on her mouth.

The spell broke when Dax's head popped into the room, waving at Adelen with a mouthful of beef jerky and hair sticking out in every direction like he'd just rolled out of bed.

"Owen! I've been searching everywhere for you!"

Owen's attention snapped to Dax, and just like that, he slipped into performance mode, conjuring up a broad, easy smile out of his ass. Even Adelen would've believed it was genuine had she not just spent the past five minutes purposely pissing him off.

"I could never hide from you, Dax. What's up?"

Dax actually beamed at Owen.

Does everyone around here have a crush on him?

"We'll be shooting our first scene tomorrow and must run through the schedule. Then we need to develop your on-screen chemistry with Henrietta." Dax took another excited bite of his jerky. "We have also hired a new Hardware Store Guy, and I'd like to introduce you both."

Owen's smile faltered, just a hair, and a ripple of tension passed over him, tightening the lines of his face.

Adelen couldn't tell if Owen's jaw clenched at the thought of more introductions or at the sight of Dax's half-chewed jerky threatening to make a break for it mid-sentence.

"Oh, you mean my pal Bertrand? No introductions needed—we go *way* back. We just spent the last 30 minutes catching up in the actor's lounge. Loudly, may I add," Owen said evenly. "Is there any chance we could reallocate him somewhere else? Perhaps a nursing home?"

Dax laughed and playfully slapped Owen on the back. "I do enjoy your sense of humor! Come along now, we need to ensure you're ready to shoot these scenes tomorrow."

Eyes finding hers again, Owen took a slow step backward to follow Dax, grim determination settling over his features, and promised, "This conversation isn't over."

It was a wonder the office wasn't rimed with frost from the chill of Adelen's glare. Beneath that icy surface, though, a volcano simmered, heat licking at her insides. She'd seriously underestimated how attractive Owen could be when he got stern.

Even after he was gone, Adelen found herself staring at the empty doorway, grudgingly admitting that, attraction aside, she missed having him around. The scent of chai drifted up from the cup, curling through the air and tempting her closer.

Her resolve, and whatever plan she thought she had, took another hit as she let herself savor that first, perfect sip. And realized she hadn't turned Owen down for a date.

CHAPTER 13

Owen

Henrietta was a fucking problem.

Owen usually avoided saying anything bad about people. Even Bertrand hadn't made him this angry, which was impressive given the whole stabbing incident in the past and today's antics during the script read-through.

The whole point was to get cozy with each other as costars, because apparently, there were some semi-intimate scenes coming up. On paper, that sounded like no big deal. In reality, it was one of the most ridiculous, soul-sucking days he'd ever survived.

He'd finally escaped to his dressing room.

It was modest, with a layout closer to a compact studio apartment than anything glamorous, designed for comfort rather than show. One wall was dominated by a sleek black-veneer vanity lined with soft golden bulbs and a matching salon chair, stocked with every hair and makeup product he could need.

The rest of the space was filled with warm lamps, muted earth tones, and soundproofed quiet. A small couch, a low table crowded with scripts, and the faint scent of cedar made it feel less like a set and more like somewhere you could actually breathe. Right after signing the contract on audition day, Tessa had asked his preference, and he'd only said to make it private but warm and calming.

Holy balls did she deliver on that promise. When he stepped into the room the first time, it felt like a living room disguised as a dressing room. The kind of place built to hide in.

Which was exactly what he was doing. Hiding like a total coward. He slammed the lock shut because trusting Henrietta with a closed door was like handing a raccoon a bag of chips and expecting it to behave. He collapsed onto the couch, head thrown back, fingers digging into his temples while a headache started to ooze out of the shadows and set up shop behind his eyes.

The second he set foot in the conference room, the read-through just detonated into chaos. Honestly, that was his life now. Chaos lurking in every shadow, waiting to leap out and pants him in front of everyone, just for the hell of it.

Bertrand, for god knows what reason, was already perched in the corner of the clinical, white room when Owen arrived. His time was spent providing running commentary from the sidelines like a sports announcer no one had asked for, heckling Owen every time he stumbled or cleared his throat. He came very close to tossing that human relic out on his ass.

Normally, he'd let that kind of crap slide or just lighten the mood and keep it moving. But after the morning's disaster with Adelen, his mood had done a full Olympic swan dive straight into the flaming pits of hell.

And Henrietta, bless her shriveled little heart, made sure the rest of his day packed its bags and followed his mood straight into the inferno. She was a wolf in sheep's clothing, but only if the wolf had rabies and the sheep costume was falling apart with mange.

Mere minutes after Owen's arrival, she waltzed through the conference room door with an exaggerated sashay, her long curls bouncing as she moved. She wore a crimson floor-length floral dress with an obscenely deep plunging neckline, and the two slits on either side of her thighs reached dangerously high.

To the general male population, she was as seductive as forbidden fruit, an embodiment of a wet dream. To Owen, she was little more than a gremlin. Of course, the only person who was brave enough to acknowledge it was Bertrand, his eagle eyes zeroed in on her half-exposed breasts.

"How about you come back to my place after this and change my diaper while I get better acquainted with those knockers?"

An uncomfortable shroud of silence blanketed the room, save for the cracking of necks as appalled faces snapped to the old man.

Henrietta merely placed a spindly hand over her unconcealed chest and chuckled. Owen's blood ran cold when her serpentine smile was aimed in his direction instead of Bertrand's. Alarm bells clanged in his mind as she slinked down into the open seat next to him, absently trailing her hand up and down her chest.

The scent of perfume and vodka warring for dominance nearly suffocated him. Heavy talc and dying roses were layered over the sour, medicinal bite of cheap liquor. Like mothballs soaked in alcohol. It clawed straight up his nose.

He sneezed twice, his body jerking back reflexively. Henrietta's eyes narrowed slightly, ultimately deciding to grab a copy of the script from the pile before her instead. Angling her body closer to Owen, she made a show of reaching for a script with one hand, while the other unobtrusively reached beneath the table and grabbed his crotch.

He stifled a yelp of horror and pain, his knee slamming up into the table. Henrietta capitalized on his temporary distraction and leaned in to whisper, "If we were alone, I'd use my other hand to slather you in lard."

In the blink of an eye, her hands were back in front of her, holding a highlighter to a page in the script...as if nothing had happened.

Owen had been on edge from that point forward, afraid of what other weird shit she'd whisper at him—and rightfully so. That incident was just the tip of the iceberg.

What was supposed to be a clean table read turned into people talking over each other, chairs scraping, scripts getting marked up, and passed around. Lines were repeated, reworked, half-acted, and in many cases completely improvised.

When Owen had read his first line, that shriveled raisin in the corner fired his opening shot.

"I lost a bet to myself that you could even read, son!" Bertrand cackled wildly, slamming his cane repeatedly against the floor, pleased with his joke.

"Bold move betting with yourself. You look like the type that *still* wouldn't pay up."

"Oh-ho! Big feelings, Owen. You should try acting sometime," he called back lazily, kicking his feet up on another chair. The rest of the room had erupted into laughter.

Except for Henrietta, who had turned an ugly shade of red, her face contorted in anger—anger directed squarely at Bertrand.

"Put a sock in it!" Henrietta screeched. "You're lucky to even be in my presence, and so help me god I will have you permanently banned from ever being in a POLmArK film ever again!"

Owen was surprised his ears weren't bleeding from the high-pitched shriek that came out of her mouth. He looked around the room and was met with several faces wincing in pain from her voice.

Bertrand didn't bat an eye; instead, he lifted his chin defiantly and said, "I'll still let you come over, but just for that, I'll be sure to shit in my diaper for you first."

Everyone just sat there, stunned and speechless, like their brains had blue-screened trying to process that exchange. As much as Bertrand got on his nerves, even he didn't deserve that level of snobbery. Still, Owen couldn't help but snort at the sheer audacity of that comeback.

Thankfully, Dax recovered quickly enough to steer them back to the task at hand. At that point, Henrietta had run out of patience and demanded they rehearse one of the final scenes and lines.

Owen tried and failed miserably to conceal a grimace as he rose from his seat and followed Henrietta to the middle of the room. He pulled out a small container of breath mints from his pocket and popped one in his mouth.

Naturally, Henrietta didn't wait for any kind of cue and couldn't be bothered to ease into anything. She crowded him, hands on his chest, breath hot and way too close, steamrolling right past professional and straight into his personal bubble. The sharp reek of vodka hit him so hard his eyes watered. His whole body jerked back on pure survival instinct.

"Whoa—" he muttered, turning his face away.

Bertrand howled. "Romance is alive and well, folks."

Trying not to gag, Owen fished another mint from the container still in his hand and, without thinking, plunked it straight into her open mouth like she was a toddler. "Please," he said, deadpan. "For all that is holy."

The room lost it. Laughter, whistles, someone nearly choked to death on their coffee. Dax pinched the bridge of his nose. Even Tessa was shaking with laughter.

Henrietta just smiled like none of it was weird, though her eyes belied her true feelings. She leaned in close again and whispered, "You can put other things in my mouth. I'd like to sample the coffee from *your* beans."

Owen seriously considered just walking straight off set right then and there. But there were too many expectant eyes glued to him, waiting for the trainwreck of a kiss. He let out a heavy sigh, looked down at Henrietta's way-too-excited face, and delivered his final line with every ounce of fake romance he could scrape together.

"There's nothing more metal than the love beans we grew together."

Henrietta's eyelashes fluttered shut, a small gasp caught in her throat, followed by a simpering smile. Then she launched herself at

Owen, her claws wrapping tightly around his neck, the force of it sending him rocking back into the wall.

"Oh, Dolf! I'd climb the tallest beanstalk for you!" Henrietta cried, adoring eyes shining.

She pressed herself against him and slid up on her toes, face inching closer, lips parting like she was about to devour him whole. Owen stared in horror at the gaping maw in front of him, his stomach violently flipping, and reluctantly lowered his lips to meet hers.

Thank god I had mints.

Henrietta went for it with the wild enthusiasm of someone licking an envelope for the first time. It was all lips, way too much moisture, and absolutely zero aim.

Her mouth mashed against his, damp and overeager, that cloud of perfume and vodka breath wrapping around his face like a chemical weapon. He could actually *hear* this awful little smacking sound, her teeth clacking against his.

He pulled back fast, scrubbing his sleeve across his mouth and not giving a single damn about how it looked. That mint he'd tossed in her mouth didn't stand a chance. Only something industrial strength could survive that.

Another set of powerful sneezes plowed through him.

"I remember my first time kissing a woman, but it sure as hell wasn't that embarrassing," Bertrand howled.

Owen shot Bertrand a murderous look, and for once, the man got the hint and wisely shut his mouth, his weathered frame shaking with laughter.

Henrietta's fingernails trailed across Owen's chest. "Let's take it from the top," she purred.

"Absolutely not." Owen took several large steps back to distance himself from Henrietta. "It's just about dinner time. I'm tired, I'm hungry, and I don't have the mental capacity to think through this anymore today." Gaze never leaving hers, he pointed an arm and finger in

Bertrand's direction and added, "Not a single word out of you. *Not. A. Single. One.*"

A derisive snort from the corner was all he got. He absolutely did not want to hear any jokes about his mental capacity after surviving that facial assault.

Wordlessly, Owen marched back to his seat, packed up his materials, and strode to the door. Looking over his shoulder at Dax, he said, "I'll see you all tomorrow, prepped and ready to go," and just about ran out of the room.

To where he was now hiding in his dressing room.

The soft hum of the little beverage cooler mixed with the warm air drifting from the vents, trying its best to soothe his frazzled nerves. He peered into the fridge and sized up his options like a man on the edge.

Sweet merciful hell, did he need a drink.

There was a variety of waters, juices, soft drinks, and alcoholic drinks to choose from.

The second he spotted the vodka, Owen shuddered so hard he nearly rattled the fridge door. Disgust steamrolled right over his craving. That scent was now permanently branded in his brain as Henrietta's signature stench.

He grabbed a can of ginger ale and flopped back onto the couch, letting his brain wander while he took a long, desperate sip. Even after all the chaos and effort, Adelen's words from that morning still hovered in the back of his mind.

"Are you ever serious, or is life one big perpetual joke?"

A slight ache stabbed him right in the chest at those words. Adelen had formed an opinion of him without even trying to get to know him, which, honestly, was probably his own damn fault. Being the class clown was second nature. It was like muscle memory at this point—he couldn't turn it off if he tried.

But what if he used it to his advantage? To convince her to give him *one* chance to see her the real Owen?

Suddenly, the mental fog that had been clinging to his brain all day just lifted. The answer was so obvious it practically slapped him in the face. It had been right there the whole time.

A mischievous grin took control of his mouth, his entire face alight as the gears in his head began turning.

He might not be able to woo her directly at work or on set, but he could be his usual self until she either caved or snapped. Laughing to himself, Owen leaped off the couch and bolted out of his dressing room. So much to do, and so little time.

Adelen was going to be very surprised to learn just how persistent Owen could be.

CHAPTER 14

Adelen

Wednesday started normally: traffic on the way in was light, and there was no immediate sign of Owen lurking anywhere. When she reached her office, a fuchsia sequined tablecloth draped over a rolling cart was stationed directly in front of her door, which she had ensured was locked the night before.

She approached it hesitantly, already knowing who put it there, but unwilling to let her guard down. There was another tall chai tea and...fresh raspberries still attached to their thorny branch?

Adelen was confused by the raspberries. They weren't her favorite fruit, though she liked them well enough, and hadn't the faintest idea where one could clip a branch of them. She inspected the branch more closely and found a small note tucked beneath it.

She peeled the note open and snorted when she read the message.

My sweetest Adelen,

Most girls are made from "sugar and spice,"
And that's why you got another chai tea.
But the part about "and everything nice"
Is somehow missing from the Adelen recipe.
So here is a full branch of raspberries,
Red, lucious, juicy, and still a bit tart.
The thorns as prickly as you sometimes are,
But you still pierced through my heart.

With a burning pit of love,
Owen ♡

P.S. You can eat them as a snack.

P.P.S. I may or may not have stolen them from Grace's neighbor's yard.

P.P.P.S. I'm pretty sure I have rabies now because the neighbor has a Great Dane I was unaware of...who doesn't like backyard intruders.

The entire setup was absolutely ridiculous, yet she couldn't help the small tug at the corner of her lips. She refused to acknowledge or thank him either; his ego was overinflated as it was. Adelen hurriedly opened her office door and pulled the cart inside.

The last thing she wanted was for other people to see the glittering display and start asking questions.

That hope dissolved midday when lunch arrived… along with three towering caution-tape-wrapped vases of multicolored roses, thorns still viciously attached to the stems. The botanical weapons weren't even remotely trimmed, just like the raspberries from that morning.

And because the gigantic floral displays themselves weren't enough of a public statement, the delivery guy hadn't just left them either. No, the universe hated Adelen, hated her so much that he had wheeled them straight through the bullpen, escorted by a security officer, like a goddamn parade float.

Past the lighting department.

Right past makeup and wardrobe.

He pushed those monstrosities directly into the employee lounge, where a curious crowd gathered.

She should've packed a lunch that day.

"Whoa," someone muttered. "Someone in the dog house?"

"Engagement?" another guessed.

Both Owen and Bertrand had already claimed their seats at a nearby table, each with a large plate of food. Owen stopped eating and smiled innocently when she walked in. Her presence was more interesting to him than the food.

Bertrand also stopped eating, his hawkish eyes alert, darting between her and Owen in suspicion.

She could pinpoint the moment that awareness struck him. With a shit-eating grin, Bertrand leaned back in his chair as the procession passed. "Those thorns aren't the only thing that may be poking someone tonight—I wonder whose pants they're trying to get into," he snorted, side-eyeing Owen.

Owen miraculously ignored the obvious jab, too invested in Adelen's reaction.

Adelen pinched the bridge of her nose so hard she saw stars, but it did nothing to stop her discomfort. She hoped a sinkhole would open up beneath her, swallowing her whole.

She wasn't that lucky.

But she *was* petty.

After noticing the unlabeled card attached, a new idea took shape. Owen had been so sure she would know the flowers were for her that he did not bother to address the envelope on the center vase.

By then, the staff fully congregated around the cart of flowers, their nosiness taking precedence over anything else. Adelen's walk towards the arrangements was measured but brisk, and the crowd parted as she approached.

Tessa stood before the flowers, debating whether to open the envelope. Adelen reached around her and grabbed it, making Tessa jump back a step.

Adelen tore it open and scanned the scribbled poem.

It confirmed what she already knew.

Adelen,

I can be super serious, so here's the deal.
I'm going to keep doing things to show you how I feel.
Say yes to Saturday night, and I'll stop here and now,
Or I'll just keep trying, this I vow.

Your future baby daddy—**Owen** ♡

P.S. But seriously, be careful with the thorns. If you injure yourself, then HR says it could be considered a Workman's Compensation claim, and that's highly discouraged.

"Your future baby daddy."

Her eyes widened and her cheeks flushed as she read those words. For a moment, she thought about setting the entire cart on fire.

Then her lips curled upward as a new idea formed.

Two can play this game, she thought.

She fought back a wicked grin as she stuffed the note back into its envelope. Then she looked up and announced to the room that Owen had sent flowers for Henrietta.

A wild hoot of laughter filled the room, followed by the sound of someone sputtering mid-drink at the tables. Adelen used all her willpower not to turn and see Owen's reaction.

A real smile appeared when Henrietta squealed with glee and pushed through the crowd to claim her prize. Tessa tried to hide her surprise and amusement with a hand over her mouth. That was the only sign she had not believed Adelen.

"Oh my god, Owen! These are gorgeous!" Henrietta circled the display, hand fluttering to her ever-exposed chest, her critical eyes taking in every detail. "How did you know these were my favorite? Though I do wish they had removed the thorns."

Adelen peeked over her shoulder at Owen. His expression was stormy, the smirk gone from his face. He crossed his arms tightly, and his right knee bounced with annoyance. Her smile grew wider. She was quite pleased with herself.

"You would make *such* a cute couple," Adelen gushed. "Go on and thank your man!"

A chair crashed to the floor as Owen leaped out of it, no doubt to escape Henrietta's clutches.

"*No*, don't thank me for *anything*, this was—"

"—the most romantic grand gesture a woman could ask for!" A speed walking Henrietta rounded the side of the table in record time, leaving Owen very little time to get away. She managed to ensnare him in a tight embrace, once again leaning in to whisper in his ear.

Adelen waltzed out of the room feeling lighter, chuckling to herself as Owen's frantic attempts to escape faded behind her.

The victory didn't last long.

By the next morning, Owen had apparently decided that subtlety was dead and Thursday's theme was *Public Humiliation: The Musical*.

She had been minding her own business on Stage C, checking a plant mic placement Rita had done, when four elderly men in candy-striped vests materialized out of nowhere.

An actual fucking Barbershop Quartet. Adelen didn't know they even existed anymore, yet they formed a semicircle around her.

Before they could begin, she pointed at Henrietta, sitting in her labeled chair on the other side of the set, reading a script, and said, "Oh, you have the wrong person! *That's* Adelen!"

"Our deepest apologies, ma'am," the tallest one apologized. He looked to be about her age with rust-colored curls and a light beard to match. Gathering the rest of the members, they descended upon Henrietta. She shrieked with joy when they began singing, clapping along to the tune.

♫ We hear you're a really sweet gaaaaaaal
The kind that can make a man fall-to-his-knees
Owen wants to be more than your paaaaaaal
Now won't you take a chance-on-him-please
He can't stand the heartbreak
(He really hates the heartbreak)
So say yes and be his Valentiiiiiiiine ♫

The entire grip team erupted. Someone dropped a C-stand laughing. Adelen stood there, relaxed but holding a coil of XLR audio cables, as it might double as a weapon. Just in case.

From across the stage, Owen glared at her, betrayed by her quick thinking and forced to fight off Henrietta's advances. Again. She didn't stick around to watch the aftermath; she just...left.

Adelen wasn't used to this much attention and human interaction.

She was emotionally exhausted. Immediately upon entering her office, she fell into her chair and removed her processors, needing space and for the sounds of chaos to disappear.

She pulled out her phone and sent the Shrew Crew group chat a scathing text about what Owen had pulled in the last few days. Naturally, those bitches were unhelpful, instead pushing her to go on one date, or Owen wouldn't stop. Then they started bickering over whether their couple name should be *Owelen* or *Adelwen*.

Both options sucked. And so did their advice.

Growing up, she'd always been the quiet one—not because she had nothing to say, but because people rarely listened. Teachers assumed she was fragile. Classmates treated her like she was strange or broken, often harassing and making fun of her for being different, rather than trying to be more understanding. She learned early on that silence was safer than trying to explain herself...and when that failed, her fists spoke for her.

So she retreated into herself and focused on what she could control: sound. Adele had her dream job doing what she loved most: mixing and editing audio. And when she didn't want to hear them, she didn't.

Where others listened by default, she watched. She could read sound waves the way others read sheet music. She could spot a pattern seconds before feedback hit. That skill had built her career. She didn't need anyone to succeed—least of all someone like Owen Voss, whose mere presence commanded attention whenever he walked into a room.

It was still a mystery he'd chosen to pursue *her*...yet, he made her feel seen in a way that was infuriating. Dangerous.

He wasn't supposed to get under her skin. He wasn't supposed to make her wonder if she was making the wrong choice by ignoring him.

But he did.

The more he pursued her, the harder it was to pull away—because she couldn't afford to let someone like him close enough to see the parts of herself she'd worked so hard to protect. Or the part of her past she was hiding from. That had been the whole point of moving out here.

She'd spent an hour alone letting her mind run rampant before shifting back into work. The solitude was exactly what she needed to get some things done—like sort through the short list of job applicants.

By the time the stars blanketed the evening sky, she was running on fumes. She put her assistive technology back in place and glanced at the time. It was well past dinner time.

Adelen groaned and rubbed her neck, stiff from sitting in that chair for hours on end. Her legs protested as she stood and peeked out the door to her office. She was the only one still there.

The crew had packed up. The lights were dimmed. The only sounds left were the hum of equipment cooling down and the distant rhythm of the late-night cleaning crew sweeping the main areas.

Adelen hadn't lingered any longer and was out the door in record time.

Any hope of ending the day on a high note had been shattered when she saw the crisp white sheet of paper tucked under her windshield wiper. With trembling hands, she removed it, reading the words scribed within before crumpling it into a ball.

WE'LL BE
TOGETHER
SOON

As if burned by the paper, she threw it as far away as possible, an abysmal hope that distance could erase the words from her memory.

It didn't. She had barely slept. By the time she was back at the studio before sunrise, exhaustion and rage were doing laps in her skull.

how to commit murder and get away with it

Sequestered in her office, Adelen's fingers hovered over the keyboard, itching to hit the Enter key, hoping the internet search terms wouldn't flag her on a government watch list somewhere. Serving any kind of jail time was never something she'd dreamt of, but after the shit Owen pulled this week, it was tempting.

Very fucking tempting.

A frustrated growl rumbled in her throat.

Three days. It had only been *three days* since her showdown with Owen in her office, yet plenty of time for him to wreak havoc on set and with her colleagues.

God, she was so fucking tired. The note from the night before had haunted her for the remainder of the evening, into the late hours of the night when she should've been sleeping, and when she barreled through the studio very early in the morning. So early that no one else was there yet.

Or so she thought.

Already on a rampage, Adelen hadn't been in the right headspace to find both doors to her office *and* sound studio under siege.

By paper.

Pink and red paper.

Everywhere.

Bordering around the door frame.

Taped to the doors themselves.

Hanging from the drop ceiling above.

So many tiny origami hearts.

She plucked one from the massive pile and unfolded it, somehow equally surprised and not surprised to see ***Still serious about you*** scrawled across it in black ink.

She yanked another: ***Incredibly serious for you***

Another: ***Extremely serious about dinner***

And another: ***Professionally serious about being your Valentine***

"...I'm going to kill him," she whispered between clenched teeth, fishing for her keys. After unlocking her door, Adelen dragged her trash can out and, in one fell swoop, swept half of them into the bin. She made quick work of removing all traces of the pink and red paper from the vicinity, praying no one had seen it.

With the trash can out of sight under her desk, she sat back and stared at its bright contents, unable to hold back anymore. A lone tear escaped and slowly descended down her cheek, the heaviness of her despair bearing down with it.

Adelen was at a complete loss, struggling to know how to handle *everything.*

The mysteriously ominous messages, adapting to a new city and routine, missing her family, feeling homesick, fitting in with her first group of real girlfriends...Owen's embarrassing public antics at work. Perhaps if the circumstances were different, it wouldn't bother her so much. Maybe she'd even be flattered.

Instead, she felt stuck in a never-ending loop of worry and stress, and the sight of those obnoxious paper hearts had further shredded her defenses.

Wiping her cheeks with her palm, she took a few big gulps of air and fanned her face dry. She needed to get herself together before heading back to Stage C to finish the sound setup.

They were setting up the green screen for some computer-generated backgrounds, and she was so close to finishing the connections. It was taking much longer than usual to get everything wired because she was short-staffed.

Once she was calm, and her eyes no longer looked like they were about to pop a blood vessel, Adelen stood. Casting one last parting glance at the trash can, she hadn't let herself dwell too much on why she fished a few of those hearts back out, convinced she should keep a record of their existence.

For evidence.

Not sentiment.

Obviously.

Trash can shoved under the desk again, eyes dry, she headed straight for Stage C.

The hallway was already buzzing with whispers and secretive glances, stiff greetings and barely concealed snickers. By the time Adelen reached her destination, the walls had begun to close in on her. It felt eerily similar to walking through the halls in high school, when her classmates had been talking about her.

Silently slipping through the doorway, Adelen overheard the tail end of a hushed conversation between Tessa and Gerald Croswell, the Assistant Director, that made her heart sink.

Gerald Croswell had always reminded her of a bird of prey that had somehow learned to wear khakis. All sharp angles and restless energy. His sandy hair was thinning in the front but aggressively gelled back like he thought no one would notice, his wireframe glasses perpetually sliding down a long, narrow nose he kept pushing up with one irritated finger. Everything about him felt beady and watchful—small eyes that missed nothing, a mouth that curled like he already knew the punchline to a joke at someone else's expense. The kind of man who thrived on set gossip and "just checking in" conversations that were really interrogations.

He was one of Adelen's least favorite people.

"It's all the crew is talking about. No one believes any of these gifts are for Henrietta," Tessa whispered, leaning in close to Gerald, pretending to review the clipboard in her hand.

"It's the most entertaining thing that has happened all shoot! Marge in Craft Services has a pool going, and the pot is just under a thousand dollars so far," he replied. Tessa's eyebrows shot up. "Odds are five to one Adelen will mace him. Ten to one she caves by next weekend. Twenty-five to one, Henrietta realizes he's not even remotely interested in her and tries to embarrass her in front of Owen—there's a whole list of betting options available."

Adelen saw red. On silent feet, she crept up behind the pair and clamped a forceful hand down on each shoulder. Both Tessa and Gerald nearly jumped a mile at the contact, the clipboard clattering to the floor.

"What are the odds that I get pissed when I find out about this bullshit gambling ring and take it to HR?"

"Eavesdropping on a private conversation is inappropriate," Gerald snapped.

"Talking about a coworker like she's a piece of chattel is inappropriate, yet here you are, doing it anyway."

"Oh, look! It's time for me to fetch Owen from wardrobe!" Tessa wouldn't look Adelen in the eyes as she hastily made her exit, pausing only to pick up her clipboard on her way out. Adelen watched her cowardly retreat with a glare.

"Well, aren't we testy this morning?" Gerald huffed.

"Well, aren't we confident that we won't walk out here with a black eye?" Adelen hotly countered.

Gerald blanched, then spun on his heel and stalked off.

Adelen also walked away, ignoring the curious stares from the quiet audience that had gathered in Stage C. The tornado roiling within her lost a little steam when she noticed the fresh chai tea sitting on her AV cart. Though this time there was no note.

Because fate had a twisted sense of humor, she'd realized that Owen had somehow nailed down her exact tea order.

Correct amount of milk, three teaspoons of sugar, tea steeped for at least 5 minutes, and the perfect temperature to still be hot but not scald her mouth with the first sip.

And like clockwork, they magically appeared whenever she needed one. Which rattled her more than the public serenades, not used to such small and deliberate gestures.

The door to the studio burst open, and the devil himself paraded through it with Rita hot on his heels. His hair was perfectly styled for a rock star having an existential crisis, his outfit low-key and comfortable.

Today, they were shooting the scene where Dolf decides he needs a break from the limelight, makes the long drive to the small town of "Pinto Hills," and meets Maggie Bean for the first time. It was an effort to tear her eyes away from him.

Owen looked *delectable*. Adelen wasn't the only one who noticed. Every woman in the tricounty area surrounded him, along with Dax, Gerald, and a few other men. Everyone except Rita, who had made a beeline right to her side.

Instead of a greeting, Adelen gestured to the tea with one hand and scowled.

"How does he know that?" she demanded.

Rita shrugged. "A while back, he asked what you grab every morning and wrote it down." A wistful smile graced her lips. "I think he's got a crush on you."

"Did you deduce that on your own, or did you put a wager into the gambling ring about my life?" She knew Rita didn't deserve the level of disdain that dripped from her mouth, but Adelen couldn't help herself.

"I put up two hundred dollars that you'd find out about the pool and raise hell about it in three days," Rita quipped. "Looks like I'm a winner!"

The sarcasm mollified Adelen...a little bit. Rolling her eyes, Adelen refocused her energy on her actual job and tuned out the rest of the crew.

Unfortunately, that was the moment everything actually fell apart. It wasn't an explosion or spectacle, but a quiet yet brutal unraveling when Adelen reached into her primary case for the new trunk cable...and it was empty.

She frowned and checked the secondary, but that was empty too. She looked in her backup kit—nothing. Her pulse ticked up, and panic began to swell.

"Rita," she called behind her. "Did you move the new XLR bundle?"

"Nope."

In desperation, Adelen even checked the equipment truck in case it had been moved prematurely, but it was empty too. She tore the building apart looking for them. Every storage area, drawer, crate, or crevice had been turned upside down, and yet....nothing.

They were gone, disappeared into thin air.

Adelen's stomach dropped into her boots. Those weren't generic cables—they were custom-length sound snakes that she had special-ordered and labeled. Without them, the mixer couldn't feed, the booms couldn't route, and the lav receivers couldn't run.

Which meant no sound. Without sound, they couldn't film. Having forgotten their earlier argument, Adelen went to notify Gerald of the issue, his face going gray as she explained. Dax swore when he found out.

There were no other productions nearby to call and borrow gear from, so Adelen focused on ordering expedited replacements while she continued to search for them.

Except it was Friday, and the earliest replacement shipment wasn't until next week.

Just like that, the day collapsed. The studio lights were shut down, all the actors released for the day, and several crew members were left milling around with nothing to do.

All Adelen could think about was how she had *one* job and somehow screwed it up.

Her throat burned. This situation was very different from Owen's chaos, and it was no laughing matter. It was her department. Her responsibility. And she somehow fucked it up.

She didn't know how long she stood mired in self-loathing, but it was long enough not to notice the hunched figure that had shuffled up to her.

Bertrand was the last person she expected to encounter. He poked her shin with his cane, shaking her out of her stupor. He was uncharacteristically gentle when he tapped his head and murmured, "Hey, sugar lips. I may be old, but I can still see. This smells like theft. I wouldn't give up looking if I were you."

Adelen nodded robotically. His words registered, but it wasn't enough. Part of her job was overseeing and accounting for all of the sound equipment. Unless she could prove someone stole the missing equipment, she would be held accountable for it.

She briefly considered leaving early, since they were dead in the water from a sound perspective, but she couldn't do so without resolving the equipment issue.

Unfortunately, she was doing the majority of the work herself. Rodney had been fired after being a no-show too many times. A third person had accepted the open Utility Sound Technician position but had ghosted her. Now she needed another Boom Operator after Rodney's departure.

Surprisingly, Rita had stepped up to wire the actors with their mics, change batteries on the transmitters, and lay out plant mics within the spaces. She was a godsend, but without a Boom Operator, they would be forced to restructure the film schedule...*again*.

On top of everything else that had happened, she had a new problem to contend with: how the hell was she going to find additional staff members before Monday, when Cary was set to arrive. Her technical mishaps, coupled with Owen's bullshit, had made it up the chain of command, leaving Cary very pissed off.

Her boss flipped out when he got the news and cut his vacation short. Instead of heading back home to the Vila Verde headquarters, he adjusted his travel plans to fly straight to Joia City and "fix her mess."

He'd screamed a lot of other things over the phone thirty minutes ago, too, but she tried to block most of it out. She got the gist of it. Cary had never spoken to her with such condescension and fury.

The call from Cary had pushed her close to the edge. She was ready to snap and—

A sharp rap on the door interrupted her thoughts.

"*What?!*" She didn't bother to hide her frustration. The handle twisted gently, the high-pitched creaking of the hinges drilling a hole in the center of her consciousness. Adelen gritted her teeth as a head of golden hair poked through.

Owen crowded the doorway, concern shining in his eyes. That was all it took for Adelen to come undone, allowing her pent-up fury to rain down upon him.

And Adelen would never forget—or forgive herself—for the look on his face when she finished.

CHAPTER 15

Owen

At the age of thirty-six, Owen didn't consider himself old—at least not physically. But on the inside, where it counted, he *felt* old. Because he'd seen too much and been subjected to countless experiences in his life to know how one second could flip the world on its axis.

Tragically, this was one of those times.

He heard about her heated exchange earlier that morning while Tessa escorted him and Rita to Stage C. Learning about the illegal gambling had tested the leash of his temper, and normally it was a pretty long one.

It was inconsequential compared to discovering the missing AV cables. Adelen had been a wreck when he walked in, frantically searching for them, the tendrils of her anxiety snaking around him. For a second, Owen could've sworn he *felt* her panic, and his chest constricted.

Then she just stopped—frozen in place with such a hopeless look on her face...

Owen had taken a total of two steps before Tessa stepped in his path and tugged his sleeve towards the backstage area for prep. Gerald had taken up the rear, following to ensure he complied. His heart roared at the thought of walking away from her.

To his surprise, Bertrand had approached, gently poking her with his cane to get her attention. That wild geezer was *always* here, regardless of whether he was needed or not...and *always* had shit to say.

Bertrand murmured something for only Adelen's ears. Whatever it was snapped her out of her daze, and she calmly left without acknowledging anyone.

Instinct—and a deep-seated knowledge he couldn't quite place—screamed to follow her, but not only did he have Tessa and Gerald to combat, but Henrietta and Dax had joined them. Owen had zero patience for this shit and lasted just under an hour before trying to leave again.

Tessa and Henrietta had tried to guilt him into staying longer and running through lines, but Gerald...guy must've had a death wish that day.

"Don't bother going after that ice queen," Gerald sneered. "She threw a tantrum when she found out no one believed your dramatic efforts were for that one—" he hooked a finger over his shoulder at Henrietta, who had stiffened at the jab, oblivious to the shadow that fell over Owen's face, "—and the crew placed a few friendly wagers about it. Not to mention losing her equipment. She clearly isn't cut out to lead her department. Don't worry, I've already escalated it and told her boss what was going on."

Gerald had prattled on, but Owen had stopped listening to whatever shit he was spewing. Enveloped by a white-hot rage, he took a large step closer to the sniveling Assistant Director, thrusting into his personal space, close enough to share the same breath.

"Talk about Adelen the way you just did again, and I'll make sure you won't be able to wipe your own ass for *weeks*," Owen softly threatened. "The only reason I'm here is because of that amazing woman. I don't need the fame, money, or the job—I already have all that. But you? You're replaceable."

A startled Gerald wisely clamped his mouth shut, weakly nodding in agreement.

Owen turned to the rest of the toxic clique, hands clenching and unclenching at his sides. "We are *done* for today."

He instantly sought Adelen out, starting with her office. He pressed his ear against the door, but was met with eerie silence on the other side. Despite no indication that she was even in there, he lightly knocked on the door anyway and flinched at the answering bellow.

"*What?!*"

With a deep breath, Owen carefully eased the door open and slipped into the doorway.

He was woefully unprepared to face the wrath of the woman seated behind the desk, her beautiful face contorted into something bitter and violent. Adelen looked as if she was a moment away from buckling from the weight of the world she carried atop her delicate shoulders.

All he wanted to do was apologize for everything—for embarrassing her at work, for being the inadvertent reason the crew was placing bets on them, and for causing her any kind of pain. This was not what he intended.

The anguish written all over Adelen's face pushed his mind into utter silence, all thought sucked into a black hole, his previous goal of apologizing forgotten.

Only her words registered, the underlying bitterness cleaving his soul in two.

"*You.* This is all *your* fault. You are the *last* person I want to see right now. It only took *three days* for you to completely embarrass me in front of my colleagues and undermine the credibility I've worked so hard to establish at POLmArK and in this industry. Take a fucking hint, Owen. *I. Am. Not. Interested.* You can leave the same way you came in."

Dismissed.

Adelen reiterated that message when she removed her processors and resumed working, focused only on her computer screen, and no longer acknowledged Owen's existence.

Whether it had been a few seconds or an eternity, Owen couldn't tell, but found himself at a crossroads. He saw the familiar sunny and well-traveled winding path of using humor and silliness to deal with difficult situations, but it didn't look as safe as he remembered.

Had those sharp, jutting branches been there the whole time? When had the gaping sink holes formed?

The other path, the one he generally avoided at all costs, was dark, cold, and overcast with tall twisting trees devoid of leaves...but for the first time, he looked at it—really looked at it—and noticed the visibility between the branches was better, and it was a smooth and direct trail. There was an uncomfortable wind howling, but that's all it was: uncomfortable.

When had it stopped looking so scary?

Like a rock to the face, Owen realized what he had to do, even if it felt wrong.

So he remained silent and stealthily retreated, taking great care to noiselessly shut the door behind him, not wanting to interrupt Adelen any further.

His body went through the motions, mechanically navigating him through the building, out the exit, and into his car. With no destination in mind, Owen just drove around aimlessly for the next hour, playing Adelen's words on repeat.

She was right. It was all his fault. He mistook her rigid indifference for playing hard to get when, in reality, she was trying to set boundaries, and he selfishly disregarded them.

He was an asshole.

"She hasn't spoken since your last visit, and getting her to eat or drink anything has been a challenge," the head orderly on duty at Clear Waters Residences reported.

Owen had taken a position leaning against the wall of his mother's room, arms crossed, studying the frail woman in the navy blue recliner. He was listening to Jared—or was it Jeff? John?—though his eyes remained fixed on his mother.

Earlier, feeling lost and directionless, he had felt an insistent tug in his soul to visit her. Owen stopped by his mother's local florist and walked out with a tall arrangement of her favorites: sunflowers, daisies, and blue asters.

He was glad he did, because in the very essence of his being, Owen knew this was another one of those moments that would change him forever. He couldn't explain why, but he just knew.

The arrangement was carefully laid on a small table, but the multi-colored flowers did nothing to brighten the room—or the mood.

Denise had been sitting in the same spot in her favorite chair, engulfed by the thick gray blanket she'd once made, staring out the window. Staring but not really seeing, held captive by her progressive disease.

She had yet to acknowledge their presence. After arriving, he had placed himself between her and the window, gazing into her vacant cobalt eyes.

That was the moment, the one precious moment, when Owen knew—their borrowed time was running out. Though he'd been preparing himself for this exact situation, it didn't hurt any less.

Jackson—Jamie?—was still talking quietly when Owen interrupted him. "Please make her as comfortable as possible," he whispered brokenly, lips beginning to tremble.

The orderly nodded, then left Owen alone with his mother.

With a sharp intake of breath, he pulled the spare chair up next to her and reached a hesitant hand out for hers. Denise didn't react, not even so much as a blink in awareness, but Owen felt the slight squeeze of her hand.

He spent the rest of the evening talking to her, telling her everything he had done to Adelen, how he'd messed up, and, more importantly, how much he missed Denise. She remained unmoved, a statue frozen in time, for the entirety of the visit...

Except for the occasional gentle squeeze of her hand.

CHAPTER 16

Adelen

Diamante Cavern was packed, the laughter and raucous shouts from patrons meandering off the dance floor, rising above the deep bass of the current dance track.

It wasn't like any nightclub Adelen had ever seen—*nothing* about it was typical. The bar felt like a secret you weren't supposed to know.

Hidden below street level, the venue had been carved straight into the black volcanic stone, wrapping around them like the inside of a mountain. The walls were rough in places, smooth in others, warm from the low amber lights that lined the shelves of liquor like firelight in a cave.

But the ceiling—

God.

The ceiling *glittered* like stars burning overhead in slow, lazy constellations, a whole night sky trapped underground. Blues and purples rippled faintly like a distant nebula, reflected in the polished bar top and in the glasses lined up like soldiers.

It made everything feel softer and closer, as if the regular world above didn't exist anymore. Like anything could happen down here, and no one would ever know. Several candles flickered against the stone in time with the low, steady beat of the music. Dancing shadows clung to the corners.

Diamante Cavern wasn't just a club, it was the kind of place people disappeared into—and sometimes didn't want to come back out.

Not normally Adelen's scene, but she felt herself seduced by its magic, her hips swaying as she strutted towards the bar, her head bobbing to the hypnotic EDM track.

She didn't look dressed for a club, opting to just dress in her favorite color palette: black on black, head to toe.

Her favorite worn band tee—cropped just enough to show a sliver of skin when she moved—hung loose over her frame, the fabric soft and faded from endless laundry cycles and too many late nights at the studio. The graphic was lined with age, the ink peeling at the edges.

More importantly, it was comfortable, broken in, and *hers*.

After validating the dress code online earlier that evening, Adelen forewent her usual jeans in favor of a pleated black skirt that skimmed mid-thigh, with sharp lines against the slouch of the shirt, and sheer tights underneath that blurred the pale length of her legs into shadow.

And of course her boots. They were non-negotiable and well-loved, the leather scuffed and creased from use, not fashion distressing. They made a solid, unapologetic sound against the floor when she walked...and made her feel *safe*.

Adelen had texted that eccentric woman Kaia from the gym earlier that evening, finally conceding and asking to cash in her offer to grab a drink. Kaia had replied immediately and invited her to *Diamante Cavern,* since she was working a late-night shift at the bar anyway.

The idea of a tightly packed space filled with sweaty, writhing bodies was totally unappealing, but she desperately needed someone to talk to about everything that happened. She couldn't go to the Shrew Crew because while they welcomed her into their group, they were still Owen's friends first.

She'd been too ashamed to text them.

Adelen needed an unbiased opinion. It had been hours since Owen had knocked on her office door, but the shame from the words she said had been eating her alive. This was hardly the first time she'd put a man in his place, but it *was* the first time she'd felt bad about it.

Lord, did she feel *guilty*.

So despite the location, Adelen had readily agreed to meet her here tonight and spent extra time getting ready. Judging by the reviews online, this wasn't a place someone could just waltz into off the street. So she had been somewhat deliberate in the selection of accessories.

As she neared the mob of people surrounding the bar, silver caught the low light when she moved from the thin chains at her throat, a couple of rings, and a tiny ear cuff climbing the edge of her ears. It was nothing overly flashy, just metal and edges.

Her dark hair fell loose and messy like she'd tied it up all day and finally let it down (which was technically true). Smudged black eyeliner and lightly glossed lips completed the look.

Adelen didn't want to look like every other girl dressed for attention. She dressed to blend in—which backfired. She ignored the number of appreciative looks sent her way by the opposite sex and focused on slipping through an opening among customers surrounding the bar.

Kaia was easy to spot because she didn't look like a bartender. The rest of the staff dressed like stardust. Similar to Adelen, they were entirely in black, but not matte black.

Their fabric caught the light and twinkled when they moved, the material threaded with the faintest shimmer like a celestial dusting of light. Every shift of their shoulders flashed silver, the mesh sleeves spilling against bare skin.

Under the galaxy ceiling, they looked less like employees and more like constellations drifting through the cave. Kaia was the golden sun in the center, and the others were the night flitting around her.

Adelen knew virtually nothing about Kaia; coming to this kind of place was in itself a risk. Judging by how she carried herself and the subtle glances of deference the staff threw her, Adelen could only assume she was in charge at some level of management.

Solid metallic gold flashed when she moved, black zebra stripes catching the low light like something wild pacing behind glass. Adelen laughed at the animal print, remembering Kaia's similarly patterned attire at the gym.

The athletic set hugged her frame. It was sleek, functional, and exuded confidence. The long, comfortable-looking tunic was paired with leggings. A cropped black bomber hung open over it, sleeves shoved to her elbows like she was ready for a fist fight or to throw someone out herself. Which, to be fair, she likely had to do.

Adelen peered over the counter, curious to see her footwear, and wasn't disappointed.

Heavy black boots hit the floor with authority behind the bar instead of the traditional delicate shuffle of service industry shoes. No, those were definitely heavy-duty drag-a-drunk-by-the-collar-and-out-on-their-ass boots.

Her ponytail had half-escaped, dark maroon strands framing sharp hazel eyes that missed nothing, no bartender smile. Kaia looked like the kind of woman who could mix your drink, run your tab, and bench-press you if you got stupid.

Despite her mood, Adelen smiled.

Kaia was *exactly* the person to talk to; she would offer a direct opinion.

She waited patiently for Kaia to finish serving the crowd huddled at the counter. As soon as Kaia spotted Adelen, her entire face changed.

Quickly wiping her hands on a towel, Kaia leaned in to say something in the ear of the closest bartender, who nodded in confirmation. Beckoning Adelen to follow her to the opening at the end of the bar. With one hand, Kaia yanked her into a quick bear hug.

Kaia was surprisingly strong, and the hug knocked some of the wind out of her. Once the greetings were out of the way, Kaia led Adelen to a special, reserved VIP booth. The clear glass privacy pane was set right into the rock,, creating a surprisingly quiet spot to hang out. One where they didn't have to shout over the music.

"Are you going to get in trouble for stealing a reserved booth like this?"

Adelen was marveling at the plush midnight blue velvet chair she had sunk into. It wrapped around her like a warm embrace, the soft material caressing her skin.

A fresh bottle of champagne was chilled in a bucket of ice on top of the sparkling black quartz table, with a pair of crystal glasses resting beside it.

Kaia raised an eyebrow and snorted, reaching over to grab the bottle. "The only one who can yell at me is me—and sometimes my sister Mena—but that's about it," she said, pouring champagne into the glasses. "Biggest perk of self-employment there is."

"Oh shit, you're the *owner*?" Adelen hadn't expected that.

"Half owner, though Mena is more administrative and handles the finances...you know, the boring stuff. I'm management," she laughed and handed Adelen a glass.

The savory tartness exploded across Adelen's tongue; the underlying notes of mango, papaya, and passion fruit perked through. She'd never tasted anything like it before—it was surprisingly refreshing.

"So what happened today that required my sage counsel? You look hot tonight, but like walking on a tightrope that's also a live wire, you know?"

"That's an oddly specific description," Adelen huffed.

"But accurate, right?" Kaia flashed a cheeky smile and swirled her drink.

"Yeah, yeah, yeah, it's accurate." Adelen wasn't sure where to begin, so she just jumped into it, going as far back as Aurelia's wedding. She explained the reluctant attraction she felt to Owen, how she's been actively avoiding him, trying to lay low at work. All of the crazy and embarrassing antics that culminated in her epic meltdown that day.

To her credit, Kaia patiently listened without interruption, only moving to refill their glasses and signal to a passing cocktail waitress to bring another bottle.

By the time Adelen was done recounting the events, she felt lighter. Not from opening up about her feelings or anything like that. It was obviously from the booze.

Eyes squinted, Kaia studied her like a bug under a microscope, a never-before-seen specimen. Sober Adelen would've been uncomfortable with the scrutiny and thrown a strongly worded barb out by now. But tipsy Adelen? Well, she was a traitorous bitch.

"What do I *dooooo*?" Adelen whined.

"I'm going to ask you a bunch of questions, and I don't want you to think about them for too long. Just answer with the first thing that comes to mind, really fast. Capisce?"

"This is exactly what the Shrew Crew did to me!" Adelen grumbled. She took another sip of her delicious drink, knowing she was trapped.

"Super duper! Okay, let's start with the painfully obvious one first. Confirm or deny: you think he's hot."

"Fuck yeah." *Whoa.*

Kaia snickered. "And you like him."

"Who wouldn't?" *Damn it.*

"And he keeps asking you out?"

Exasperated, Adelen threw her hands up in the air. "*Yes!* He won't take no for an answer either!"

"Uh huh...so he's gotten your favorite hot beverage memorized, has showered you with flowers, written love notes and poems, *and* serenaded you—by proxy—and you're mad because...?" Kaia trailed off and waved a hand in the air expectantly.

"*Because* he embarrassed me at work. I'm the laughing stock right now. People are *betting on me.*"

"Sweetie, put your villain hat on. What's the best way to fuck with their bets?"

Adelen stared blankly, not sure where she was going with this. Kaia sighed and took a long sip of her champagne.

"Nothing terrifies gamblers more than an outcome they didn't price in. Torch the entire pool by asking him out instead. Tonight. *Right now.*"

"What? No. *No.* That is the opposite of a good idea! You didn't see his face after I said those awful things to him." Adelen put her head in her hands, trying to stop the memory from taking over.

The light in those gorgeous baby blues winked out before her eyes, and then she just ignored him. While there was truth in what she had said to him, that wasn't the right way to communicate her feelings. Owen hadn't deserved that. Adelen's mother would be so disappointed.

She felt like such a bitch. No—she *was* a bitch.

"You know what this is, right?" Kaia said.

"What?"

"Schrödinger's Date."

Adelen paused mid-sip and frowned.

"You're convinced that if you never show up, nothing changes. The date both happens and doesn't happen. Total quantum nonsense if you ask me."

"That's not—"

"Open the box," Kaia urged. "Worst case, it's awkward. Best case...it's him."

Adelen was stunned that her illogical argument made any kind of sense. Maybe it was time to slow up on the drinks because that was *not* at all how Schrödinger's theory worked.

"Listen, Addy—I'm going to call you Addy from now on because we just became best friends for life—you're not wrong for feeling frustrated, even with him," Kaia said gently. Adelen slowly raised her head to look her in the eye as she continued. "How you lashed out at him was wrong. It sounds like he came to check on you, and dare I say perhaps apologize?"

She really hated how right Kaia was.

"I don't even have his number!"

"But you sure have a shit ton of excuses! Ask your friend Aurelia...*Now*," Kaia snapped. Her new best friend sure was intimidating when she wanted to be, with an attitude that rivaled Adelen's.

"Ugh, *fine*." Adelen whipped out her phone and shot a fast text to Aurelia asking for Owen's number. "She may not even get it tonight. For all we know—"

Her phone screen lit up with a reply from Aurelia. There was no message, just Owen's contact card to download. She swallowed hard, having run out of excuses.

Suddenly, her phone was yanked out of her hands. She barely had time to react to what just happened when Kaia finished tapping on the screen and tossed her phone back into her lap.

A smug smile on her lips, Kaia settled back down into her seat and said, "And now we wait for confirmation of your Valentine's Day plans tomorrow night. You're welcome."

Adelen's mouth hung open in disbelief.

Shit.

CHAPTER 17

Owen

Owen had been parked on the couch in his apartment, staring out at the skyline since visiting his mother at Clear Waters Residences. The city lights blinked and flickered, as if trying to keep him company. Traffic hummed, sirens wailed somewhere far off, and the sidewalks were filled with people beginning their night out.

He let out a deep sigh and took a long pull of his beer. His thoughts were his own worst enemy. There was too much room for his brain to start replaying things he didn't want revisited.

It was why he practically lived at Isaac and Grace's house. Why he lingered after hours at work, and now on set long after wrap. It was the need to fill every second with noise, people, and dumb commentary.

Lately, finding the humor in everything felt less like a defense mechanism and more like a self-imposed cage.

God, he was a mess.

That realization was loud and inescapable, the sound amplified by the hollow silence of his apartment. It didn't give him anywhere to hide.

Tonight, the silence was winning.

But maybe...for once, he should surrender to it.

Owen's shoulders slumped in defeat. The whole situation with Adelen had blown up in his face spectacularly. What was supposed to be a series of grand gestures had fallen flat. The concept was solid, but the execution was humiliating.

But Adelen wasn't just anyone—and Owen hadn't paid the right kind of attention to her. Instead, his attempts at wooing her came off like a circus act. Like she was a joke.

In that respect, Adelen hadn't been wrong. When he reviewed the events of the last three days in his head, he was mortified to see that it came off more like annoying desperation than real interest.

In the end, Owen was the punchline. The irony wasn't lost on him.

After every failed attempt to capture her attention, he would plaster on a smile he didn't feel so that other people didn't have to feel uncomfortable or ask any prying questions. It was how he handled all the difficult moments in his life.

He pretended nothing ever really hurt by focusing on the safety and comfort of others—by ignoring his mental health like it was optional maintenance. Unfortunately, he was learning that neglect has a way of collecting interest.

It was slowly killing him.

He didn't know when being the comic relief had stopped being an act and when it started being the only version of himself people recognized. Owen didn't want to be the guy everyone expected to make their bad days easier while his own quietly rotted out from the inside.

Adelen had easily seen through that layer of bullshit with no qualms about calling him out. And it stung. Because if she could see through the outer layer...what was left to see underneath?

He wasn't sure he even knew how to put the real, thoughtful version of himself forward. Hell, he wasn't sure that guy existed. Even worse, he wasn't sure who to talk to about it. Well, he had one option, but wasn't ready to go down that path yet.

Owen slowly exhaled, a sharp pang striking deeply in his chest.

Watching the bustling nightlife below, he'd never felt more alone.

He missed his dad, their time together cut short too soon. Even though she was still physically here, he missed his mom too. They used to have daily chats before her diagnosis began to strip her sense of self away. Denise was his sounding board—the only person who truly saw him. *All* of him.

Maybe he was feeling extra low tonight because Valentine's Day was tomorrow. The holiday never really bothered him before because there had never been anyone he really wanted to celebrate it with.

He usually spent the evening with Ivy and Levi, wallowing in singledom together. With Levi forever off the market, that left him and Ivy as the unpaired oddballs. But even she had a mystery date lined up for tomorrow night.

Owen foolishly banked on convincing Adelen to go on one date, meticulously planning out the perfect evening. He'd also gotten Adelen a special custom gift, but now...now it was nothing more than a wistful dream.

Taking another long pull of his beer, he slid a glance at the open pizza box occupying the coffee table. All but two slices of the large pizza were gone, but it tasted like ash. Even his favorite food let him down tonight. It was par for the course.

He threw his head back against the back of the couch with a heavy sigh, focusing on an invisible spot on the ceiling. He had to sort himself and his life out—but first, he needed to start making cancellation calls.

Tomorrow. He could make those calls tomorrow, when his mind was more awake and fresh, instead deciding to end the night early and—

From the corner of his eye, his phone screen lit up with a new text message. Owen glanced down at it, lying haphazardly on the cushion next to him, and frowned.

Unlocking the screen, he did a double-take, reading the text from an unknown number:

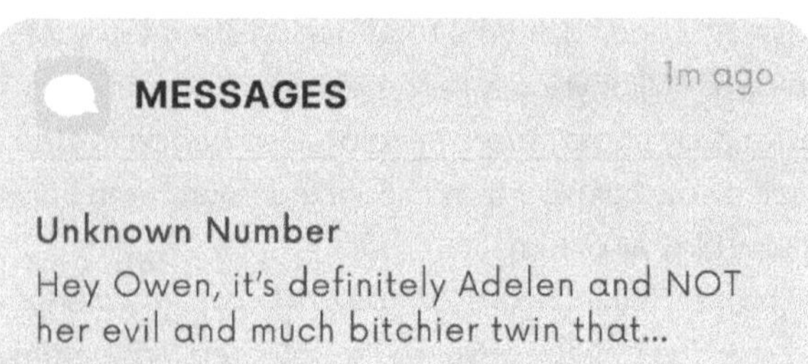

A text from *Adelen.*

His entire world stilled as Owen stared at the screen, frozen and afraid to read the rest of the message, his mind playing tricks on him.

Maybe he was turning into a lightweight if two beers were enough to cause hallucinations. Or maybe the pizza he'd ordered for dinner had shrooms and not regular mushrooms.

Honestly, either option was easier to deal with than the alternative of falsely raising his hopes.

Though the possibility of finding shrooms on his pizza wasn't all that far-fetched either. It was exactly the level of bullshit Bertrand would stoop to and call it a "prank." He'd already pulled several small on-set pranks on Owen...like the day he went to use his hairspray only to find it was really a well-masked can of aerosol auto lubricant. Rita was *furious* and had to replace his hair extensions. But the way Bertrand howled when he heard the commotion, barely grasping his cane enough to steady himself, had become a core memory.

At first, Owen was pissed off—and was still a little annoyed about it. Except most of his anger had faded into begrudging respect. Even he had to admit it was a damn good joke. The old man had a pair of steel balls on him that was kind of impressive.

Admiration aside, someone like Bertrand having too much time and money on their hands was never a good combination, which was precisely what worried him. Bertrand paying some young kid at a pizza shop handsomely to do something like that was very plausible.

Was he being overly paranoid?

Yes.

Did he have a good reason to be?

Also yes.

Despite their sordid history, the crotchety old man had been warming up to him lately...in a strange, co-dependent way where insults passed for affection and minor crimes counted as bonding. He wasn't playing pranks on anyone else besides Owen, nor did he seek anyone else's company as often as he did Owen's.

There were moments when Bertrand would sit with him on a lunch break or shuffle to his side while observing a scene, silent and thoughtful. It unnerved Owen more than the fear of whatever bullshit he was plotting next.

He recognized it for what it was: the man was lonely. And unfortunately, he decided to entertain himself by harassing Owen, though he preferred Bertrand's level of attention over Henrietta's.

That woman was truly making Owen uncomfortable on set. He'd heard stories of men being the subject of sexual harassment, but never dealt with it himself. The constant groping, suggestive whispers that made him want to vomit, and the obscene amount of that hideous perfume she wore...he was at his wits' end.

Any time Henrietta was near, he practically clung to Bertrand's side whenever they weren't actively filming, just to avoid her unwanted advances. Even Bertrand began to develop an obvious distaste for her, which was wild. On more than one occasion, Tessa would intervene to guide Henrietta away or give her some bogus assignment. She had become a godsend in those situations, stepping in whenever Owen was being accosted.

But it all came to a head after being cornered in his dressing room one evening—those spindly fingers of hers traveling too far south of the border—Owen had taken matters into his own hands by installing cameras throughout the space.

He'd also begun to do what he did best: investigate the situation. Being such a big fan of POLmArK movies meant knowing enough of her past co-stars to start making contact about her past conduct. The fact that this behavior was allowed to continue for so long infuriated him. No one should be forced to deal with that level of harassment.

Henrietta was entitled, self-absorbed, and an absolute monster when she didn't get her way: basically a lawsuit waiting to happen. Owen had no intention of being the subject of one without proof.

The only hands he craved all over his body were Adelen's.

Every drop of blood in his body surged downward and swelled at the detailed image of Adelen's hands exploring his skin. A single thought of her was all it took—and he was instantly hard.

He hissed a breath through gritted teeth, willing himself to calm down, and unlocked the phone screen. Eyes wide as saucers, he read and then reread the text message, making sure it wasn't a figment of his imagination, that it was real.

Not that he'd be too upset if it was a cruel joke—he deserved it after the level of embarrassment he'd caused Adelen.

Just to be safe, he shot Aurelia a quick text to confirm Adelen's phone number. Owen hadn't told anyone except his mother what had happened earlier that day, so the only chance of her knowing about it would be because Adelen told her. Part of him was worried his friends would be disappointed in him and his behavior if they found out. So he hadn't said a peep.

A minute later, shock rippled through him when Aurelia validated it was, in fact, Adelen's number.

He huffed a laugh at the unhinged request as he saved her number and fired off a response.

Excitement took over, and no longer tired, he got to work finalizing everything.

"Holy balls...this is really happening," he voiced aloud to no one but himself, as if hearing the words solidified it. Heart racing, he jumped off the couch, re-energized and refocused on planning their date.

This time, he would deliver a *real* grand gesture.

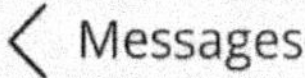

FUTURE WIFE Details

Message
(Today) PM 8:47

Hey Owen, it's definitely Adelen and NOT her evil and much bitchier twin that yelled at you earlier today. I'd love to go out tomorrow night if you're still interested in being my "future baby daddy."

Reply with YES to confirm our date, or STOP to unsubscribe from future messages from this number.

(Today) PM 9:01

YES
YES
YES

I don't know who you are or what you've done with the REAL Adelen, but I'm not complaining!

I'll send you the specifics of what, where, and when in the morning after some beauty rest

Typing...

CHAPTER 18

Adelen

Adelen was usually an early riser, but at 10:14 AM, she was still in bed. She opened her eyes just enough to see the mid-morning sunlight sneaking through a gap in the blinds, landing right in her eyes.

A splitting headache throbbed behind her eyes. The bright light from the window only made it worse.

Fucking Kaia and that delicious, never-ending flow of booze.

Adelen grumbled obscenities under her breath and turned away from the light, pulling the blankets tighter around herself. Some people hated too many covers, but she was the type to crank the air conditioning during a heatwave just to stay wrapped up.

When she was younger, her parents called her an "Addy Burrito" whenever she rolled herself into a ball. Diogo was the opposite and couldn't sleep with more than a thin blanket at night. Their father, Fausto, had designed and built their family's raised ranch when they were five.

Adelen's front-facing room and the master bedroom were set over the garage, making their bedrooms naturally colder than the rest of the house. Diogo's room was next to hers and at the front of the house, but his room was generally much warmer.

Their two bedrooms shared one thermostat, and it was in Adelen's room. When it got cold, she turned up the heat and wrapped herself in blankets, needing the room to feel cozy. Diogo, who slept in just shorts with no covers, always complained about it being a sauna, even after closing all his vents.

Moments like these made her appreciate living on her own, being the master of the apartment's temperature.

Buried under layers of blankets, Adelen tried to piece together what had happened the night before.

She winced, both from the headache and embarrassment. Owen had probably told everyone about their argument *and* the wild text Kaia sent for her. Most of the night was a blur, but she knew she needed to thank Kaia.

First, for getting her and her car home safely. She remembered getting into the back seat of a taxi with Kaia while a sober bartender drove her car. Once Adelen made it inside her building, the bartender joined Kaia in the taxi.

A small smile tugged at her lips. Kaia was wild, but she was a good friend—the kind Adelen wished she'd had growing up. Someone who cared enough to make sure she and her car got home safely.

And a friend who had offered to sign on as the newest member of the POLmArK sound department.

Kaia didn't have much going on during the day and wanted a change. Even better, one of *Diamante Cavern*'s DJs was also looking for a new job and already had the experience needed to be a Utility Sound Technician.

Adelen had a video interview with her scheduled after lunch. If it went well, her staffing issue would be handled by Monday.

One problem solved.

She crawled out from her blanket cocoon just long enough to take some ibuprofen. Then her phone buzzed with a text.

From *Owen's Cell.*

Her confusion faded as her memory snapped back into place. She unlocked her phone and scrolled up to see what the hell Kaia had sent Owen. Adelen groaned. She would never have sent something like that herself.

It got the job done, though.

Her dread faded, replaced by anticipation. With her stomach fluttering, she sent a quick reply and tossed the phone onto the bed.

Running her hands through her unruly hair, Adelen analyzed the whole exchange. There was no offer to pick her up, and the message lacked the usual persistence she'd become accustomed to. And the idea of sweatpants was *very* appealing.

What stood out most was that she could drive herself. He'd given her a choice so she wouldn't feel trapped. That made her heart skip, or maybe it was just the hangover.

Either way, it made her trust him a little more, which was something she desperately needed.

OWEN'S CELL Details

Message
(Yesterday) PM 9:01

YES
YES
YES

I don't know who you are or what you've done with the REAL Adelen, but I'm not complaining!

I'll send you the specifics of what, where, and when in the morning after some beauty rest

(Today) AM 10:22

Meet me at the King's Miradouro for 4:30 PM. Dress warm with comfortable shoes. Promise it's low key, and sweatpants are totally fine. Don't need to bring anything other than yourself (leave your weapons at home pls)

And you can bail anytime if I'm being too weird.

10-4

She spent the last thirty minutes trying to calm down and wondering what the hell she had gotten herself into.

The "plan" Adelen had—the one where she was supposed to avoid Owen at all costs? Flushed down the toilet. She wasn't a quitter by nature, but after realizing how badly she wanted to trust Owen, the plan went to shit.

Her stomach churned. She couldn't tell if it was nerves or the questionable steak-and-cheese sub from lunch. Alcohol was definitely off the table tonight. She needed a clear head with the hangover still hanging on.

A calendar alarm sounded from herHer phone chimed with a calendar reminder. She didn't need it—she'd been thinking about the date since Owen's message—but putting everything in her calendar was a habit she couldn't break. This was happening.

The date.

There was no backing out now, no matter how much she freaked out.

Once she pulled herself out of her blanket fortress, the rest of the day went by quickly. Adelen thought the interview went well, but she was so distracted she barely remembered it. She hoped this candidate would work out, since she'd already offered her the job.

Choosing an outfit shouldn't have been stressful, but Owen hadn't given her much to go on. She'd driven past the mountain viewpoint before, but never stopped. With all the rain lately, the path could be muddy, extra windy at the top, or even require climbing over rocks. Not exactly date-friendly logistics.

Adelen dressed for a hike, not a date. Treating it like nothing special made it easier to handle. Hard to be disappointed when expectations were low, the bar nearly on the ground.

Especially on Valentine's Day.

She chose practical layers: black skinny jeans she could move in, thick enough to block the wind, and a charcoal thermal tucked in at the waist. Over that, her favorite oversized cardigan, the heavy knit one with sleeves that covered her hands. Wool socks she knit herself went into her usual boots.

Her makeup was minimal, just a bit of smoky liner and mascara. Rose-tinted chapstick finished the look and kept her lips from getting chapped.

No one likes chapped lips. Not that she was expecting anything like that, of course.

Hair loose and dark against her shoulders, she knew it would be wind-tangled in minutes once out of the car. It would end up under a wool hat she knit from the same yarn as her socks. Hat hair was unavoidable.

There were no other accessories aside from thin rings, tiny studs, and a delicate chain at her throat; the small silver jewelry she always wore out of habit. The processors rested behind her ears, hidden by her hair and hat. Everything was mostly functional and completely unapologetic.

She needed to stop stressing and leave, or she'd be late.

"You look great, it's not a big deal, you're not trying to impress him."

Good thing she never wanted to be a motivational speaker, because her pep talk was useless. She glanced in the mirror, left her bedroom, and grabbed her bag. Just as she was about to leave, she remembered something.

She ran to the ottoman in her living room, threw the lid open, and stuffed the large men's sweater she had made into her bag.

Just in case.

Pulling out her phone, Adelen reread Owen's message and instructions. Her brows knit together in confusion as she stared at the

"Closed for Maintenance per the Joia City Department of Forestry and Conservation" sign hanging from a rope chain in front of the overlook trail entrance. A police SUV was parked next to it, likely tasked with enforcing the closure.

The road up the caldera curled in tight, familiar bends, with the hydrangeas crowding the shoulders turning into sleepy blue ghosts as the light faded. Fog clung low in the valleys, but the sky above was clear, deep blue, with streaks of orange and pink beginning to appear, as if someone had dragged watercolor across the horizon.

By the time she parked, the air had that sharp, clean chill that only came right before sunset. She had a little time to spare, so she double-checked the address, then, frustrated, got out and walked over to the police car for help. They would know the city better than she did.

There was no doubt its occupants had been watching her, the feeling confirmed when an enormous officer emerged from the driver's side door. Roughly a few years older, he was imposingly tall with dark eyes and close-cropped hair the same shade as hers...definitely not someone she'd want to piss off.

"Adelen Mazao?" he asked by way of greeting, meeting her halfway across the lot.

"Um, yes?" She was unsure why it came out as a question, but it wasn't often that Adelen was taken by surprise. Especially when a hulking law enforcement officer already knew who she was.

"I'm Sergeant Pacheco. I'll be escorting you up to the overlook."

"Oh! Okay, so I *am* in the right place. I was just walking over to ask because it looked shut down."

"No ma'am, you're in the right spot. Mr. Voss went to great lengths to secure this location tonight and requested our assistance." The corners of his mouth twitched upwards. "He clearly thinks you're special," he added drily.

Adelen stiffened and put her hands on her hips. "What's *that* supposed to mean?" she demanded, then quickly slapped a hand over her mouth, eyes wide. Getting snippy with a huge police officer was not smart.

A low chuckle was his only response. "Follow me right this way." He strode toward the blocked-off path entrance and glanced back only once to check that Adelen followed.

Of all the scenarios that had played out in her mind, this wasn't one of them. She expected Owen to meet her here, not a police officer. Still, his presence made her feel safer, especially since she'd never been here before and wasn't a hiker. If a bear showed up, she just had to run faster than him.

They walked in companionable silence up the well-traveled path, the crisp wind whipping against her cheeks. It was technically winter, but in Joia City, it felt like a chilly fall day. The temperature would drop a bit more in the evening, but no more than a few degrees.

Adelen couldn't help but notice the solar-powered black iron lanterns lining the trail. Though the sun was still out, she could only imagine the soft lighting that would pour out later that evening on the way back.

Adelen guessed Owen was behind the lanterns, but doubted her escort would say anything. She'd have to find out for herself. She hated surprises almost as much as waiting.

The walk itself was a different kind of torture; every second seemed to drag on for an eternity. It gave her time to wonder how Owen managed to get the city to close a public trail and arrange a police escort. It made her pause. Examining the lanterns more closely as they passed, Adelen realized that he must have gone to great lengths—and cost—to plan this date.

Finally reaching the top, anticipation rippled through her. She spotted him before he saw her, selfishly taking a few moments to drink in the sight of him, looking like a woodland god. Adelen had tried to ignore her attraction, but now the full force of it hit her like a brick to the face.

Owen sat with his back to her on what looked like a big convertible sofa, folded down into a mat, and covered with oversized blankets and pillows. The setup was on an outdoor rug, at a safe distance from the overlook's edge, with a large cooler nearby.

He wore a simple long-sleeve Henley that hugged his broad shoulders, sleeves pushed up like he'd gotten too warm. Over it, a soft gray-blue flannel, and dark jeans faded at the knees. His brown boots had real dirt on them, proof he'd touched grass recently.

Altogether, it was the kind of outfit that felt more "boy next door" than "billionaire chaos gremlin." It made him look approachable and safe. Like he'd actively tried to sand down anything flashy about himself.

His long hair wasn't styled, just pulled back in a low knot, already coming loose in the wind. Adelen's hands hung at her sides, fingers twitching with the urge to run them through his hair. The feeling had only grown stronger since the day Rita installed the extensions.

Seeing Owen like this, unguarded and looking out at the horizon, meant more than any grand gesture he'd attempted so far. Adelen was sure she was seeing the real Owen for the first time. Like an optometrist flipping through lenses—*better or worse, better or worse*—while everything sharpened with each quiet click, the world snapping into clear view piece by piece.

Looking around, there wasn't anything extravagant spread out, no ridiculous charcuterie tower or catered nonsense like she half expected, considering how outlandish his antics had been so far. Instead, two white ceramic mugs rested on a mahogany wicker outdoor storage ottoman situated in front of the makeshift sofa bed.

A large, portable fire pit had been lit in front of the seating area, with a neatly stacked pile of firewood off to the side. The number of logs were enough to last a couple of days, but from what she's observed so far, Owen was a master of preparedness.

It was simple, plain, and almost laughably understated. And *perfect*, as if he knew her better than she knew herself.

He fussed with the blanket corners, like they had personally offended him, then pulled a small black gift box from his pocket. He frowned at it, checked his watch, and quickly stuffed it back, as if deciding it was a bad idea.

Adelen bit back a smile.

He finally heard their footsteps on the gravel and stood up. And for a split second, before the trademark grin slid into place, she saw it.

Nerves.

Actual, honest-to-god nerves. The smirk didn't quite reach his eyes, but it did underscore the quiet hope in his eyes.

"Hi," he said, softer than she'd ever heard him, afraid that if he spoke too loud, the moment might break.

"Hey."

They both stared at each other, frozen in place, neither ready to make a move.

Sergeant Pacheco loudly cleared his throat, an overt reminder that he was still there. The officer had ceased to exist the second she spotted Owen.

"I'll be in my vehicle by the path entrance should you need any assistance," he gave Owen and Adelen a curt nod before making his way back down the trail.

Once they were alone, Owen gestured awkwardly at the setup. "I, uh...brought food that doesn't quite require utensils because I didn't want this to be such a formal situation. I was thinking we could make paninis over the fire. There's other stuff in there, too, for you to choose from."

She huffed out a laugh. Such a different side of him—one that she really liked and wished she'd glimpsed sooner. There was no pressure to be anything but themselves while enjoying a beautiful sunset, some fire-roasted sandwiches, and fluffy blankets.

It was the most considerate thing anyone had ever done for her...and also the most romantic.

Adelen felt a slow, genuine smile roll across her face. She took a steady step forward and said, "What woman could ever say no to a man willing to make her dinner?"

CHAPTER 19

Owen

That smile.

The sight of it stunned Owen into silence, awed that it was for him.

Maybe this idea wasn't as stupid as he'd originally thought.

For a second, the wind, the water, the whole stupidly gorgeous valley behind him ceased to exist. The only thing that mattered was her, smiling at *him*.

It was the first real smile she'd ever given him. It was different from the tight, polite one she gave coworkers. But it definitely wasn't the same as the flat "I tolerate you" version he'd become accustomed to.

This one was wide, slightly crooked, and sincere. It made her eyes softer, like the expression had started somewhere deeper and worked its way out.

It hit him square in the chest.

Owen didn't know where to look first. Dressed in layers of edgy comfort, Adelen looked amazing. All he could think about was peeling away each article of clothing until there was nothing left but *her*. He had plenty of ways to keep her warm...and not one of them was appropriate.

He'd done a lot of elaborate, borderline unhinged things trying to impress this woman. Owen wasn't sure what had changed her mind, but he thanked every god that would listen for the second chance. And for any help ensuring he didn't fuck it up.

"Okay," he said, clearing his throat like a teenager whose voice had yet to fully deepen. "First things first...I owe you a massive apology for being so disruptive at work. I've always wanted to be an extra in a POLmArK movie, but I only accepted the lead role so I could spend more time with you."

Adelen's arms slackened at her sides, his directness catching her off balance. Owen didn't care; he needed to get it off his chest.

"I couldn't think of any other way to get your attention, and I didn't consider the optics of that, especially with your coworkers. You tried to set boundaries, and I ignored them. And I'm so incredibly sorry for overstepping...multiple times." Owen let the earnestness in his words hang between them, allowing Adelen to recover from her initial shock.

"I owe you an apology, too. The things I said yesterday, that wasn't—you didn't deserve to be treated like that, no matter how frustrated I was. And for that, I'm sorry," she said softly, the words feeling foreign on her tongue.

They didn't need to drag it out further than they already had.

"Truce?" Owen asked hesitantly. "We start from scratch right now, like nothing ever happened?

Adelen dipped her head in agreement.

"Truce."

Owen heaved a sigh of relief.

"Okay, so, full disclosure...I brought an activity."

Her eyes narrowed immediately. "That's not comforting."

"It's not absurd," he promised quickly. Then paused. "Okay, it's only a tiny bit absurd."

"*Owen*."

Hearing his name roll off her tongue like that sent a jolt right to his groin. If she only knew how much power she had over him.

Calm down. I need to calm the hell down. He inhaled slowly, silently negotiating with his hormones like they were misbehaving toddlers.

Desperate for a distraction, Owen held up a small stack of dog-eared cards like he was surrendering a weapon. "Relationship icebreakers. I figured we could either stare silently at the lagoon like Victorian ghosts, or ask each other mildly invasive questions while I make paninis."

Her brows furrowed together in confusion. "You brought *flashcards* to a date?"

"They are *not* flashcards. They're highly rated relationship builders, and Ann from Lakeville gave it five stars for saving her marriage. I even laminated the cards so we don't get panini bits all over them."

"...You laminated *homework* you brought on a date," she said incredulously, lifting her arms up animatedly. "Doesn't this sound crazy when you hear it out loud?"

"It's not homework, and even if it was—*which it's not*—they're heat-resistant," he added defensively. "For the fire situation."

For a beat, Aden stared in disbelief. Then she *snorted*. He would absolutely die on this hill, confident that laugh might've been the most amazing sound he'd ever heard.

"Fine," she conceded, closing the distance between them and dropping down onto the blanket next to him. "But if one of those cards asks about our five-year plan, this date is over."

"Totally valid boundary."

Owen quickly flipped through the deck to make sure such a card didn't exist. He nearly shit his pants when he came across the '*Where do you see us in five years*' card. Hastily, he yanked it out and threw it in the fire with zero regrets.

Adelen raised her eyebrows. "Already testing the heat resistance of your laminating efforts?"

"Just eliminating any potential reasons for the night ending prematurely." Owen handed her the rest of the stack with a tentative smile. "You pick first. Dealer's choice."

The small camping grate crackled softly over the fire pit while Owen worked, his movements practiced and efficient as he buttered bread and stacked cheese and pesto.

He felt oddly domestic and loved every second of it. There was something mildly erotic about preparing a meal for this woman, imagining what it'd be like to spend the rest of his days in this realm taking care of her like this.

Heat spread across his skin—and it wasn't from the fire. Out of the corner of his eye, Owen could've sworn he caught Adelen watching his hands for a second longer than necessary, but she averted her gaze to the pile of flash cards so fast it made him question his sanity. He needed to keep his wits about him and his body in check.

"Alrighty," she said, curled under a blanket, reading the first card. "What's the most unhinged thing you've done this year?"

He didn't even look up. "Emotionally or legally?"

"Come on."

"Kidding. Mostly." He flipped the sandwich. "Probably officiate Levi and Aurelia's first courthouse wedding.'"

"Oh god, I heard about that."

Owen cringed. "I was trying to make it less awkward. If I acted like a fool, it would distract them both from the high-stress situation. Now they have a great story to tell future generations."

She hummed. "That's actually pretty unhinged."

"Your turn."

She glanced at the lagoon as if it might judge her. "I sent a guy to the ER a couple of weeks ago with a few cracked ribs."

The metal grate—and the panini within it—almost fell into the fire, Owen's surprise nearly causing it to slip from his hands.

"You what now?!" He scrambled to salvage the sandwich.

"He deserved it, *and* he got banned from the gym."

He slowly looked up at her again. "*Adelen*."

"What? It's not that big of a deal. If that asshat was going to press charges, then he would've done it by now."

He swore under his breath as he removed the grate from the fire. "Remind me never to really piss you off, though I'd be lying if I said I didn't find this oddly endearing."

Adelen stifled a laugh, yanking Owen's attention to her mouth. With a slight shake of his head, he tore his eyes away from those lips and refocused his attention on the task at hand.

He slid the panini onto a plate and handed it to her like an offering, their gazes locking. Their fingers brushed, long enough to imprint the warmth he felt at the slightest of touches. Owen pretended that didn't short-circuit half his brain.

"Next card," he said, voice softer now.

She read it, voice a bit more hoarse. "What's the worst condiment?"

He didn't hesitate. "Mayonnaise."

Her eyes snapped up. "Correct answer."

"It's egg glue with an expired aftertaste."

"It's edible regret."

"It ruins sandwiches *and* friendships," he stated solemnly.

They stared at each other for a second, then both burst out laughing at the same time. It felt ridiculously easy, like this was what talking to her was *supposed* to have felt like all along. He hoped this was enough for a fresh start.

Still laughing, she picked another. "What's something you're legitimately bad at?"

He sighed dramatically. "Slow dancing."

She tilted her head. "That's very specific."

Owen rubbed the back of his neck, somewhat embarrassed. "I move like a confused golden retriever. You may find it hard to believe that someone with my natural grace struggles to find the rhythm when it's that slow. It's tragic."

"...I would pay money to see that."

"Nope, hard pass."

"Ooh, maybe we could work it into the script! Henrietta would have a coronary if she had the chance to be in your arms like that," Adelen quipped.

"Listen, I'm a pretty easygoing guy, and I think my affections for you are fairly obvious," Adelen blushed at his admission, "but I will straight up murder you if you betray me like that. She's become the star of my nightmares, and thanks to *you*, she thinks I'm in love with her. I can't carry the amount of breath mints needed to survive a close-up scene with that poltergeist, and my pockets aren't that deep."

Adelen nearly choked on her sandwich with laughter. *"Poltergeist?!"*

Owen sat back and crossed his arms defiantly. "I said what I said. She said she wanted to drink my bathwater. She whispered it *in my ear*. I cannot work under these conditions."

Wiping her mouth with a napkin, Adelen giggled. "She really is the worst, and you're not her first victim. I've heard rumors of her harassing costars like that, but it's never been confirmed...or rather, there have never been any complaints filed against her. No one knows exactly what she's done. This is the first direct account I've heard of."

"She's *always* trying to touch my junk when no one's looking. I wish I were kidding, but I'm being dead serious. She's a problem, and you egged her on. I'd rather have mayonnaise on every sandwich for the rest of my life than have her anywhere near me."

"Maybe I wouldn't have had to do that if my peace at work hadn't been consistently disrupted by someone's embarrassing antics," Adelen countered, the glare she shot at him full of hurt.

Hanging his head in shame, Owen whispered, "I know...and I'm really sorry." The cushion shifted a moment later as Adelen sidled closer.

She whispered back, "I'm sorry too—both for how I acted yesterday and for throwing that back at you again just now." Waving the flashcard still in her hand, she added, "Let's forget it and instead talk about how horrendous I am at making coffee."

Owen chuckled, and she bumped his shoulder with hers. Not hard, but just enough to knock into him. He waited for her to shift away after, but she didn't. His head shot up to meet those glittering steel eyes.

"But—but making coffee is so *easy*. How the hell do you mess that up? Like even the pre-measured K-Cups?"

A ghost of a smile appeared as Adelen looked up at the darkening sky. "I don't know how, but it's offensively bad. It doesn't matter if I follow the instructions to the letter and measure out the appropriate amount of scoops and equal ounces of water. It comes out awful. K-cups are okay, but they're terrible for the environment, so I avoid them. But yeah...I've tried every method out there, and it always tastes like burnt sadness."

Owen considered her for a minute. Another puzzle piece fell into place. "Ah, so that explains the chai tea addiction."

"I'm feeling personally attacked on our first date," she said wryly.

"I would *never*...although it makes sense. It's really hard to screw up throwing a premeasured bag of tea into a scalding cup of boiled water—you *do* know how to boil water, though, right?"

"Ugh, *yes*, I know how to boil water. Next question!" She reached into the deck and pulled another card.

Watching her laugh in the firelight, hair glowing copper at the edges, her shoulders were relaxed for possibly the first time since they'd met. Owen wished he could keep her just like this forever.

The questions kept coming, light and ridiculous and dangerously easy.

"Aliens or robots?" he asked, sliding another panini onto the grate.

"Aliens," she said immediately, popping a red grape into her mouth. "Robots feel too personal, like we caused that."

"Yeah, I don't want to get murdered by my own Wi-Fi."

"Exactly."

"If I get abducted, tell people I went heroically," Owen begged.

Popping another grape, her eyes twinkled with mischief. "I'm absolutely telling them you followed a glowing rock."

"Saying it like that teeters on the edge of defamation because, *of course,* I'd investigate a moving glowing rock—that's the nature of my work in security." He looked down his nose at her in mock disdain, flipping the grate over. "Plus, capturing a floating glowing rock would be so cool."

"You're proving my point," she laughed.

Once he removed his panini from the fire, he wolfed it down in record time. Adelen's mouth hung open as she watched, her face a mix of abject horror and concern.

With the last bite in his mouth, Owen dusted his hands off, reached into the ottoman, and pulled out a campfire kettle. It took a few minutes to fill it with the ingredients for hot chocolate—and some extra spices—from the cooler and heat it over the fire.

"Did you even *taste* that sandwich before unhinging your jaw like that?"

Owen scoffed, swallowing the last bite. "My jaw stayed right where it's supposed to be. It's not my fault, I'm a growing boy, and my mandible evolved accordingly."

Adelen simply shook her head, at a loss for words. After a few minutes, Owen interrupted the silence by pouring hot chocolate into the pair of mugs, handing one over carefully so he wouldn't spill on her sleeves.

"Cinnamon and a little cayenne," he warned. "Don't panic."

She eyed the beverage skeptically, fighting some private inner war before taking a cautious sip. Adelen paused and peered into her mug.

"...Okay. That's annoyingly good."

He grinned, preening. "I accept your reluctant admiration."

"Yeah, yeah...Don't push it," she said defeatedly, rolling her eyes.

But she took another sip. And a third. Then she adjusted herself on the blanket and scooted a bit closer. Just a tiny scoot.

Owen's heart nearly stopped right then.

Probably for the fire.

She inched a fraction closer.

Totally for the fire.

Except her knee pressed lightly against his thigh when she settled, and the contact stayed there. A blaze burned hotter and brighter than the fire before them, where their bodies connected. He was on the verge of spontaneous combustion.

Owen risked a glance at her, needing to see if she was as affected as he was. Her attention was on the kaleidoscope of colors splashed across the horizon, like she hadn't noticed.

Or maybe she had and was trying to distract herself?

He couldn't tell.

Instead, Owen went very still, not daring to move, like she was a skittish animal that might bolt if he breathed wrong.

Don't react. Don't make it weird. This is normal on a real date. Humans sit near each other all the time. Sometimes they brush against each other in a totally casual and super chill way. It's fine. You're fine.

Unfortunately, his heart did not get that memo. It was a small miracle that its thunderous claps didn't echo through the valley of the caldera.

As the sun continued to make its descent into night, they worked through the cards, trading answers like volleys.

They talked about everything from petty crimes to bad haircuts, and even middle school disasters. Her deadpan delivery killed him and was fast becoming one of the many things he loved about her.

"My worst haircut was bangs," she said flatly. "I looked like a haunted porcelain doll who got into a fight with craft scissors and lost. Unfortunately, it was more recent than you'd think. They're still growing out."

He barked out a belly laugh and gasped for air. "I had a bowl cut thanks to Levi. He used an actual bowl from my parents' kitchen. I looked amazing, but my mother was *furious*."

Adelen's musical laugh carried on the wind.

"My dad didn't say a word, though," Owen continued, reminiscing about the memory fondly. "He walked away and then came back with a ruler and silently handed it to Levi."

She laughed low in her throat. "That explains so much. You've come a long way now, upgraded to hair extensions."

"I'm telling you, I could be bald and I'd still look amazing," Owen joked.

Their knees knocked again when they laughed. She didn't even glance down and simply stayed there, shoulder brushing his arm, cardigan sleeve grazing his wrist whenever she reached for the cards.

Each touch was small, incidental, and constant. It felt like gravity had quietly shifted, and he was no longer tethered to the ground. Every subtle connection had his pulse racing. The slightest movement had her intoxicating scent overwhelming his senses.

She was like the rain-heavy air before a storm, and just as cool, mineral, and electric. Petrichor and damp cedar clung to her clothes, but were softened by something quieter underneath.

Hints of wild jasmine, crushed lavender, and the green snap of fresh stems. It wasn't perfume, but something more intimate, like fresh flowers that felt like they grew there naturally, blooming after a fresh cloud burst.

It had driven him insane in the brief moments he'd been close enough to experience it at work, but out here in the wide open expanse of nature, the tantalizing source of it so close...

Owen was hanging on by a thread, every second that passed steadily ripping through his self-control. It had been several minutes of silence between them, and he was thankful for a reprieve, needing a moment to get his shit together.

The lagoon below darkened from blue to ink, the last streaks of sunset fading out slowly and syrupy. The fire popped softly between them.

Sitting this close should've felt awkward, but it didn't. It was the most natural thing in the world, and he felt oddly at peace for the first time in god knows how long.

She tugged her sleeves over her hands against the cold and inched a little closer to the fire. Or maybe—

No. Not towards the fire, definitely closer to him. Her hip brushed his and stayed, another symbol of comfort and trust.

All the stupid, elaborate stuff he pulled off in this past week suddenly felt loud and desperate compared to this inscrutable moment. The small act of *choosing* to sit next to him was bigger and more personal than all those previous attempts combined.

Is this it? Is this what it's supposed to feel like?

No, he wasn't quite ready to put a name to that feeling, but he knew it wasn't some elaborate spectacle or fireworks lighting up the sky. It was gentler. It was finding one person you could really be yourself with, picking them every day, flaws and all, and instinctively reaching for them first to share the good and to survive the bad.

He'd known from the first second he laid eyes on Adelen that she was endgame for him—no one else would ever compare. But even he knew it was way too soon to say anything. They'd both need time, and there was no guarantee that his feelings would ever be reciprocated.

But they were here together.

Owen wasn't about to waste the gift given to him. He stole a glance at her, meaning to ask another question, but his gaze snagged on the small processor tucked behind her ear instead, barely visible beneath her hair.

Firelight caught the edge of it when she pulled her hat off and shook out her hair, tucking a strand behind her ear.

He'd noticed them before, obviously. But sitting this close, seeing the tiny details like the way her hair curved around it, or the way her fingers absently brushed near it when she was nervous...They were a part of her, and it didn't feel like a thing to politely ignore anymore.

It was something he wanted to understand—he wanted to know everything about her.

He rubbed his thumb against the edge of his mug, hesitating as he mulled over how to ask the question sitting on the tip of his tongue without sounding like an idiot. The last thing he wanted to do was break whatever this soft, fragile bubble was.

"...Hey," he said gently.

She hummed, still looking out over the water.

"If it's okay to ask..." He swallowed hard, a man standing at the edge of a glacier wearing nothing but a Speedo, preparing to plunge into the icy depths.

It's now or never.

"Can I ask you something about your hearing impairment? I want to understand you better."

CHAPTER 20

Adelen

"Can I ask you something about your hearing impairment?"

The question crept over her skin, slick and unwelcome, like the slow drip of oil down glass. She'd known it was coming—Owen was bound to ask eventually—but that didn't stop the prickle of irritation that slithered up her spine at use of the phrase 'hearing impairment.' Sometimes it felt like the whole world was fumbling in the dark, clueless and clumsy when it came to things like this.

Old habits were indeed hard to break.

The entire night had gone spectacularly better than she ever expected. He'd let his guard down a bit and allowed her the privilege of seeing a side of him others rarely did.

But her body had its own agenda, inching toward him like a plant desperate for sunlight, hungry for every scrap of warmth he offered. Even the lightest brush of his hand sent sparks racing beneath her skin, igniting nerves she'd almost forgotten she had.

No one had ever had a fraction of this effect on her.

Every inch between them felt charged, and she wanted to drown in his warmth. If she moved even a breath closer, she'd be in his lap—and the thought of it grew more tempting with every heartbeat.

Her bra chafed against her skin, the fabric suddenly too rough, her nipples tight and aching for reasons that had nothing to do with the chill in the air. The real source of her discomfort and temptation sat right beside her.

Adelen angled herself toward him, unable to stop her gaze from drifting to his hands—strong, capable, and resting so innocently in his lap.

God, she could almost feel those broad hands sliding beneath her shirt, cupping her breasts, teasing her until she was nothing but sensation. The thought alone made her breath hitch, her nipples pebbling harder, heat pooling low in her belly. She pressed her knees together, trying to contain the ache.

Owen stared into the deepest part of her, earnestly awaiting an answer.

Right. He asked a question.

Reality crashed over her like a bucket of ice water, shocking her out of her reverie. She'd always loathed when people treated her processors like some kind of party trick, something to gawk at or prod with questions.

Most people went wide-eyed and curious. *Can you hear everything? Do they hurt? Can you turn them off?* Like she was some kind of Bluetooth device with legs, unaware of how sometimes semantics actually matter.

Except Owen hadn't asked like that. Or at least, he'd tried not to.

He'd asked gently, each word chosen with care, and that effort alone eased the tightness in her chest. Still, it didn't stop the blush from creeping up her neck, coloring her cheeks.

Her fingers found the processor behind her ear, tracing its curve without thinking, a habit so ingrained she'd only noticed it when someone else pointed it out years ago. The plastic was warm, molded to her like a favorite ring or a well-worn watch, a part of her she barely noticed until moments like this.

"Before I get into my backstory, using the phrase 'hearing impairment' or even 'mute' is a sure-fire way to piss off anyone in the Deaf community. Many of us—though not all— don't consider it to be a disability. I can do the same things anyone else can do just fine, if not better, except for hearing. And making coffee, apparently."

Owen gazed at her intently. "I wish conversations like these happened more often in society. I wouldn't have known this had you not explained it, and we both know that I'd end up offending someone unintentionally." With a small smile, he added, "Your directness is one of your best qualities."

She shrugged off the compliment, thankful for the golden light of the fire to conceal her blush. "I just tell it like it is."

"Don't ever stop."

Good lord, this man was going to be the death of her.

"I was born with progressive loss," she continued. "By the time I was three, most of it was gone. My parents had the surgery scheduled before I even understood what 'hearing' really meant."

She lifted one shoulder in a half-shrug, a tiny gesture that somehow said everything she couldn't. Owen watched her with an intensity that made her feel like the only person in the universe, every word she spoke precious.

Maybe, in that moment, she was. The realization sent a ripple of confidence through her, urging her to keep going.

"It wasn't exactly a family meeting situation. I was too young to have a say, and don't remember much aside from getting lots of stickers and apple juice from a very enthusiastic surgeon."

A ghost of a smile flickered at her lips, but it faded before it could settle in.

"There's...a lot of debate about it now, in the Deaf community. Whether it's right to implant kids. Some think it takes away the chance to grow up fully immersed in Deaf culture. That it's more for the parents' comfort than the child's."

Her thumb circled the edge of the magnet, lost in thought, grounding herself with the familiar shape.

"And truthfully?" she admitted, much quieter and more open than she'd ever allowed herself to be with anyone, "if you handed me the decision today, as an adult...I don't know what I'd choose."

The confession was heavier than she anticipated, but she felt better having finally voiced it.

"These things helped me navigate a hearing world. There were days when I hated them and refused to wear them, but they made getting through school and work a lot easier. I can mix sound for films, for fuck's sake. But they're not magic, and it's astounding how little people understand still. It's exhausting, and sometimes I wonder who I would've been if I'd grown up without them. If silence had just been...normal."

She risked a glance at him, her vulnerability leaving her uncomfortably exposed. The look on his face wasn't of pity, but something deeper and protective. As if he would have carried the burden for her even back then.

"My parents weren't trying to change me. They were scared and wanted me to have every door open. They made the best choice they could with the information they had."

She let out a soft, fond huff, the sound barely more than a breath of old affection.

"They showed up to *every* appointment. Learned everything they possibly could about my condition. Fought with health insurance when they tried to deny any coverage. When I had the surgery, my dad slept on my bedroom floor beside my bed that night."

Her shoulders lifted again, an act of self-preservation.

"I can't fault them for their choice. Even if I'm still figuring out how I feel about it." Her hand dropped back into her lap. She lifted her eyes to his and held nothing back.

"They don't define me," she added softly, but more firmly. "They're tools. Like glasses or contact lenses. They aren't perfect, and I don't need them to do my job or exist in this world."

Owen's gaze burned into her, kindling a fire that had nothing to do with embarrassment. She broke away, letting her eyes drift to the lagoon, its surface catching the firelight and scattering it in a thousand directions—anything to escape the heat of his attention.

"Growing up and going through school wasn't sunshine and rainbows. I was already awkward and introverted—not much different from the sunny and chipper Adelen you've been lucky enough to meet."

She chanced a quick glance at Owen and found him smiling back.

"What do you mean? The Adelen I've had the pleasure of getting to know has been an utter delight," he teased.

She rolled her eyes, but couldn't quite smother the smile tugging at her lips. It slipped away as quickly as it came, replaced by something more serious as she turned to face Owen directly.

"Kids are mean. Some grow out of it, but many grow up to be meaner teenagers and even meaner adults. The mocking, whispers behind my back, and cruel pranks were constant. I'm an adult, and it hasn't quite stopped yet either."

Owen's features twisted into a dark scowl, but his hand found hers, fingers weaving through hers with a gentleness that belied his anger. The warmth of his palm wrapped around her, sending a jolt straight through her body. She couldn't pretend it didn't send a rush of heat between her thighs.

A slow, wicked smirk curled her lips as she traced lazy circles over the back of his hand with her thumb. Owen's eyes went hazy, his throat working as he swallowed, but he stayed silent, letting her take the lead.

"But so was the amount of time my twin brother Diogo and I spent in the principal's office after kicking anyone's ass who dared to bully me over it. I spent quite a bit of time learning both sign language and lip-reading. My whole family learned sign language, but my brother and I liked to use it as a secret language in school." Half her mouth curved up in a sinful smile. "We still use it in public situations when we need to have a private conversation."

"Good," he said thickly. "I have so many twin-related questions I want to circle back to, but yeah, I know how your brother feels having grown up with Levi. I'm well acquainted with the principal's office. It wasn't just him, though—I didn't like anyone being bullied. One of the fights I was involved in was because Tessa was being bullied in high school. My tolerance was exceptionally low if it was because they were different."

That confession broke down the last of her walls. She reached up, fingers curling around the back of his neck, and pulled him in, crashing her lips to his in a kiss that left no room for doubt or hesitation.

His groan rumbled up from deep in his chest, vibrating through her like the bassline of a song she couldn't get out of her head, settling low and hot between her thighs. One arm banded around her waist, hauling her tight against him, while his other hand tangled in her hair, anchoring her to him.

She swung a leg over his lap, straddling him, and deepened the kiss, her tongue tracing the seam of his lips in a wordless plea. He opened for her, and she tasted him—sweet, a little wild, a delicacy she wanted to linger on her tongue forever.

He matched her hunger, the kiss shifting from gentle exploration to something primal and urgent. When a soft whimper slipped from her lips, it was like a spark to dry tinder—he let go, giving in to the need simmering between them.

His hands locked around her waist, holding her close as they moved together, bodies desperate and perfectly in tune. She could feel every inch of him, hard and insistent through the denim, and the thought of nothing separating them almost pushed her over the edge.

The question burned through her, stoking her desire until it was almost unbearable. She'd been so intent on taking it slow tonight, but now she couldn't believe what a stupid idea that was. Every part of her screamed to stop holding back. All she wanted was Owen, all of him, right now.

She'd never been shy about going after what she wanted, never hesitated to take the lead when it came to sex. But this was different. This was instinct, something deeper than simple desire, pulling her forward.

It felt *right.*

She broke the kiss, leaning back just enough to meet his gaze, holding it steady as she shrugged off her cardigan. Her hand drifted down his chest, tracing the lines of muscle, lower and lower until her palm pressed against him through his jeans, claiming him.

Owen hissed, his hips jerking beneath her touch. When she took his other hand and slid it under her shirt, guiding him to her bare skin while still stroking him, the sound he made was pure, unfiltered need—it sent a shiver straight to her toes.

Adelen wanted him *unchained.*

His palm settled over her breast, hot and heavy, but he didn't move, some invisible line holding him in check. His eyes—deep, endless blue—searched hers, asking a question without a single word.

"You don't have to do anything, Addy," Owen ground out through clenched teeth, his chest rising and falling erratically. "This wasn't part of the plan tonight."

The sound of her name—Addy—on his lips sent a jolt through her, almost as much as the way he handed her the reins, letting her set the pace. It was the biggest gift he'd given her yet, melting something frozen inside her and daring her to see just how far she could push him.

She wanted to see just how far she could push Owen. How much he'd let her take.

Flicking the button of his jeans open, she leaned in as close as humanly possible without their lips touching and whispered, "Let's not worry about tomorrow, Owen. I want this moment with you tonight."

A tremor tore through him, so intense it seemed to shake the air between them.

The next words tangled in her throat, more honest than anything she'd ever said.

"I just want you—*all* of you."

CHAPTER 21

Owen

When those soft, supple lips pressed against his, all coherent thoughts ceased to exist.

Feeling her hand around his neck had him harder than he'd ever been in his life. Completely driven by instinct, Owen had dragged her flush against his chest.

But when those long legs straddled him right when that tongue began its thorough exploration of his mouth, he almost exploded on the spot. *That* was the effect she had on him.

No one was more gobsmacked than Owen had been when Adelen closed the gap between them. His goal for tonight had been to get to know her better and apologize for everything he'd done.

Never in his wildest dreams did he think the evening would take a turn in this direction. Had he fantasized about it? Every damn day. Instead, the goddess he daydreamed about was in his lap, one hand stroking him through his jeans, the other showing him exactly what she needed him to do.

Maybe he was an idiot or a foolish gentleman, but he made himself stop long enough to make sure this was what she wanted. He was raised by the two best people he knew, and they taught him to be respectful.

So he gave Adelen the choice to decide how fast or slow they went.

Didn't mean he wasn't silently praying to keep going. It turns out he was a selfish, selfish man when Adelen's hands were all over him. So when she uttered the most beautiful words he'd ever heard in his life—words that were laced with something more, he let go.

Owen kissed her with a ferocity he didn't know he was capable of. Everything he gave, she gave right back. His thumb grazed over the sensitive tip beneath the flimsy lace barrier covering her, swirling in light circles before teasing it between his fingers.

Holy shit, the moan that escaped those parted lips almost undid him. Having found one spot that elicited that sound, Owen was determined to learn what else made her come alive.

He wasted no time relieving Adelen of the rest of her shirt in record time. Face to face with the most supple tits he'd ever seen in his life, he didn't know what to touch or taste first.

Calling the lingerie she wore a bra was generous at best, for the delicate material was completely transparent. It served no purpose; it was only there to be ripped off.

Licking his lips, Owen took a sensitive peek in his mouth, fabric and all, while his hand lavished the other with attention. He gently bit down while he used his hand to tease her other nipple. Adelen cried out, her body convulsing against his.

"Owen, *please*," Adelen begged.

"You're lucky I'm such a stickler for manners," he murmured against her skin, dipping a hand beneath the waistband of her jeans, not needing to go any further to feel how wet she was. She was soaked.

That was all the confirmation he needed. In a matter of seconds, they had stripped down, both burning so hot that the cold evening air hadn't registered. Adelen pushed Owen back down and resumed her place in his lap.

His hands were everywhere, trying to memorize every dip and curve of her body, when she slowly sank down, taking him inch by inch. Owen's eyes nearly rolled into the back of his head. She hadn't even begun to move yet, and it was already the best moment of his life.

Following her cues, Owen let Adelen set the pace, giving the entirety of his being over to her. She rode him fast and mercilessly, her shouts echoing through the woods. The shadows from the firelight danced across her skin, giving her the appearance of a woodland nymph.

The sight was exquisite. Owen knew tasting her once wouldn't be enough. Not nearly enough.

With one final cry, Adelen gave in to her release. Owen's own release followed shortly after, climaxing harder than he ever had before with a roar that was more animal than man. It echoed through the trees, scattering various wildlife.

She collapsed against Owen's chest, panting hard, their bodies slick with sweat. Neither said a word, content to just lie tangled together for a little while. Eventually, Adelen peered up at him, a hint of embarrassment fluttering across her features.

In no way would he allow her to feel embarrassed about what just happened between them. As they quietly dressed, Owen broke the silence the only way he knew how.

"So tonight I learned what 'becoming one with nature' actually means."

He didn't have time to dodge the boot aimed directly at his chest.

CHAPTER 22

Adelen

"What was *that* for?" Owen bellowed, rubbing the center of his chest where the boot Adelen hummed at him landed. A large red mark was forming.

Arms crossed, Adelen glared at him. She should probably feel bad about marring that gorgeous golden skin, but she didn't. The *thwack* of it hitting his chest was incredibly satisfying.

"We had a serious intimate moment, and you went and made a joke about it," she yelled back as she wrestled her jeans back on. Their voices carried across the open space. If there were people at the bottom of the caldera, she wouldn't be surprised if they heard every word of their argument.

"And you started to act embarrassed! I watched the regret slip onto your face," he fired back. He needed to put a shirt on, so she could argue with him properly. "Are you embarrassed by me—by what we just did?"

It wasn't the question that had her whipping around to face him, but the quiet hurt and simmering anger in his voice.

"No, it was the fact that you turned it into another joke!"

Adelen was incensed. It was as if he hadn't listened to a word she'd said about his inability to take things seriously. He apologized for it earlier, so she held his stare and waited for another apology.

Except it never came. Instead, Owen grew angrier, turned his back on her, and finished getting dressed. She'd seen him wear several emotions to this point, but anger was new.

It was unexpected...and she was unsure why, but it made her uncomfortable. The answer came a few minutes later, when Owen spun back around and erupted.

"Do you even know what a joke is, Adelen?" he challenged.

Good god—angry Owen was terrifying and sharp, like a pressure cooker having reached its limit. Adelen swallowed hard, her mouth having gone dry.

"I've already apologized for the dumb over-the-top shit from earlier this week," he fumed. He dragged a hand through his hair, pacing like he didn't know where to put himself. "I saw your face. I *watched* you pull away. Like what we just did was something you regretted. Like it was...*dirty*."

The last word scraped out of him.

"So yeah," he said, quieter now, rougher, but no less irate. "I made a joke. Because if I didn't, that silence was going to swallow me whole.

Adelen opened her mouth, but Owen held up a hand. She clamped it shut and crossed her arms defensively.

"*No*. Yesterday was yours. You tore into me in your office, and I sat back and took it like a good boy. So just—just let me have my time."

Adelen was bewildered, bolted down to her spot, his words hitting far too close to home. A reminder of how shitty she had treated him. His chest rose hard with every breath.

"Not every joke is me screwing around or disrespecting you," he rasped. "Sometimes it's the only way I know how to stay standing."

He shook his head; his laugh hollow and humorless.

"You think I'm trying to make everything smaller. I'm not. I'm trying to make it survivable."

Survivable. The word lingered in her mind. He turned away, yanking his shirt over his head in jerky movements, voice muffled for a second before he faced her again.

"You hide behind this tough-girl, don't-need-anyone thing façade like it's armor," he countered. "Like if you glare hard enough, nothing can touch you." His anguished eyes met hers.

"Don't act like I'm the only one pretending here." His words weren't cruel, but laced with exhaustion, a tiredness felt deep within his soul.

"You think I like being the comic relief all the time?" he pressed. "You think I wake up every day excited to be the punchline?"

Owen's throat worked, briefly glancing out at the vista, collecting himself before he addressed her again.

"When everyone else falls apart, I'm the guy who fixes it. I make a joke so they don't cry. I make the joke so they don't feel out of place or left behind. I make the joke so nobody looks too closely at me," he confessed, his voice trailing off on the last word.

"And you looked at me tonight like I ruined something beautiful just by being...*me*."

Fragile silence stretched between them.

"Tell me what I'm supposed to do with that," he quietly pleaded. "Because if I'm not allowed to be funny...I don't know who the hell I'm supposed to be. But in the end, whatever version you get of me is still real."

Adelen swallowed hard. Tears began to brim, but she held them back, refusing to break in front of him.

Damn him.

"You think this is armor?" she asked finally, voice hard. She gestured vaguely at herself. At the crossed arms, the glare, the stiff posture she'd perfected over the years.

"You think I wake up and *choose* this?" Now it was her turn to laugh, the sound cutting and brittle.

"I didn't build this so people wouldn't get close. I built it so they wouldn't even think to try and hurt me."

This time, he didn't interrupt or try to be funny; he just simply watched. His unflinching gaze somehow made it worse.

"You make jokes so people don't cry, well, I make people uncomfortable so they look away. Because the second they start staring, the questions start."

Her jaw clenched.

"Why do you talk like that?"

"Can you hear me if I whisper?"

"Does it hurt?"

"Can you turn them off?"

Each one landed like she'd heard them yesterday.

"Kids used to snap their fingers next to my ears to 'test' me. Adults talked to me like I was five. Boys thought it was hilarious to imitate how I pronounced things when I was little."

Her mouth twisted.

"One of them used to call me 'robot girl.' Followed me around making beeping noises."

She said it flatly, as if it were as common as a weather report. Like it hadn't mattered when it clearly had.

"So *yeah*. I stopped smiling and being friendly. Turns out when you look like you might stab someone with a pencil, people leave you alone."

Adelen paused for a breath.

"That guy at the gym a couple of weeks ago? The one who ended up in the ER and was banned from the gym?"

Owen's shoulders stiffened.

"He got up in my personal space during my workout, and was rudely hitting on me. I tried to ignore him, but he wasn't taking no for an answer. Then his little gaggle of friends started to taunt me, saying that my batteries must be dead because I wouldn't acknowledge him."

She shrugged her shoulders nonchalantly, but it didn't hide her fury.

"He wanted me to work off my energy on a real man. I obliged him. Turns out he wasn't a real man, but he learned a lesson about consequences," she said evenly.

Owen read between the lines and understood that she'd handled it with brutal efficiency.

"I excelled at being unapproachable," she finished. "Because it's safer than the alternative. Being different isn't always a gift...at least not for me." The admission slipped out unintentionally, but she refused to take it back.

"If I look tough, people hesitate. If they hesitate, they leave me alone. And if they leave me alone..." Her voice thinned. "They can't hurt me." Her hands shook, and she shoved them into her sleeves so he wouldn't see.

"And tonight—" she faltered, just for a second, before regaining her strength, "—tonight was the first time in a long time I didn't feel like I had to be on guard. I felt comfortable enough to let myself just...exist next to someone."

Her eyes lifted to meet his, open and clear.

"So when you joked, it felt like you were laughing at me. Like maybe it didn't mean as much to you as it did to me." The confession cost her something, but she didn't have the chance to examine what it was too deeply at that moment.

"I wasn't embarrassed by you," she spoke so softly, Owen almost missed it. "I was scared it didn't matter as much to you as it did to me. Don't act like you're the only one hiding," she whispered. "You wear a mask so everyone loves you."

Adelen's voice broke, and the first of many tears broke free.

"I wear one so they don't get the chance to try."

CHAPTER 23

Owen

Valentine's Day had gone completely off the rails. Stars dotted the night sky, and the fire danced in the background.

It didn't feel like an argument anymore. They stood across from each other, both worn out from the fight, looking at the mess their words had made.

Owen watched Adelen, her hands tucked into her sleeves and wrapped around her middle, trying to make herself smaller. Her guarded expression told him she'd just handed him something fragile and expected him to drop it.

His chest tightened, the feeling heavy. She should never feel the need to shrink herself, especially around him.

"Addy," he breathed. "I didn't..." His voice snagged. He tried again. "I didn't know it was that bad."

He scrubbed a hand down his face hard onough to hurt.

Of course it was that bad, idiot.

Owen had spent his whole life making things lighter, yet in the short time they'd known each other, he'd never stopped to imagine how heavy hers must've been.

He stepped closer without thinking, his legs understanding what needed to be done long before his brain caught up. Each step was slow and cautious, not wanting to overstep any more boundaries.

"I wasn't laughing at you," he said quietly. "I swear to God, Adelen...that moment scared the shit out of me."

She blinked a few times rapidly, confusion settling over her face, as she looked up at him.

"What?"

"I don't joke because things are meaningless," he said. "I joke because when something means too much, it feels like it's going to rip me open." Owen let out a shaky sigh. "I don't actually know how to sit in something good without trying to defuse it."

There it was—the honest, unpolished truth.

He rubbed the back of his neck, eyes fixed somewhere over her shoulder, his thoughts turning inward to a different decade.

"My dad died unexpectedly from a heart attack when I was young. One minute he was fine, and the next minute he was gone. I was sitting in the principal's office with Levi after another fight when I found out. I had a hard time dealing with it. I'm not sure I've fully dealt with it. I had to grow up fast since it was just my mom and me...After that, every time things got too quiet or too serious, my brain just..." He snapped his fingers. "Worst-case scenario."

His throat bobbed as he shoved his hands into his pockets, eyes dropping to the ground.

"So I started making jokes. All the time. At school. In hospitals. It didn't matter. If everyone laughed, it meant they were still breathing. Still there."

Owen's voice caught. He tried again, this time managing a broken whisper, "And now my mom doesn't even know who I am anymore."

Saying it out loud tore him apart, a truth he never wanted to admit.

"She's in a care facility. Early-onset Alzheimer's. Some days she calls me by my dad's name. Some days she thinks I'm the nurse. Most days, she says nothing and gazes emptily out the window. But her tether to this world is fading quickly...I have no other family left but her."

He cleared his throat and rubbed the back of his neck.

"So yeah. Humor's kind of my...duct tape solution to navigating the shit life throws at me."

Owen kept his gaze low, afraid of what Adelen's reaction would be if he looked at her. The silence woven in between the roaring fire was almost unbearable. It wasn't surprising that he somehow messed this up, his one chance to get her to take a risk on them.

Unsure of where to go from here, Owen debated whether he should call the Sergeant to come back and escort her to her car or—

Something heavy and bright landed on his shoulders. He looked up, confused, and pulled down the soft material. It was a thick sweater, knit in uneven stripes of blue, yellow, brown, and gold. It was clearly made by hand, not bought.

He dared a glance at her, unsure of what to say. God knows his communication skills had been shit all night.

"I didn't know what size you wore," she muttered, shifting on her feet and tucking her hands further into her sweater. "So I guessed. If it's wrong, don't say anything and just...suffer quietly."

His throat closed, all the air whooshing out of his lungs.

"You made this?"

She shrugged as if making a precious gift was an everyday occurrence. "Keeps my hands busy when I need a reset from the world."

Just when he thought Adelen couldn't surprise him, she did. Owen hugged the sweater close, afraid it might disappear. No one had made him something since—

Jesus. Since he was a kid. His mom used to knit. He wanted to tell Adelen this was the best gift he'd ever gotten, but he didn't want to ruin the moment.

"Hold on," he said suddenly, fumbling for his bag. He needed to even the scales before he did something embarrassing like cry in front of her.

"Okay, this is way less emotionally devastating, but—"

He handed her a small black box, his palms sweating and trembling. Adelen cocked her head and frowned. As she opened it.

Inside were two sleek cochlear skins. Matte black with subtle silver linework etched through them, offering a clean, modern interpretation of soundwaves. It wasn't the everyday medical gear; it was intentionally designed to take it to the next level as an accessory. Something to show off with pride.

"I had them custom printed," he blurted quickly. "Figured you're already wearing cool tech, but it can always kick it up a notch and make it look badass. Thought you deserved something that reflected how cool I think you are."

Adelen didn't say anything, nor did she move as she simply stared at them. Then she touched one, afraid it might vanish.

"They're waterproof too," he added, softer. "So you don't have to baby them." Her silence was driving him insane, and the worry about how much they sucked was following closely behind. "Say something—*anything*. Even if you hate them, I won't be mad."

When she finally lifted her head, her eyes were glassy.

"Wow," she whispered.

Oxygen raced back He let out a breath, some of the tightness in his chest easing. is the best gift ever' or 'wow, you're really shitty at gift giving' because there's been a lot of emotions tonight and I can't tell."

Instead of answering, she stepped forward and kissed him, one hand tenderly cupping his cheek as the other held the box. It was gentle and said so much more than words ever could, the complete opposite of their earlier kiss.

He wrapped his arms around her waist and pulled her closer. The firelight warmed them both.

"My family, especially my brother, would like you," she said quietly.

He blinked. "Yeah?"

"We're twins, remember? He used to beat up anyone who made fun of me. Got suspended so many times in middle and high school."

A faint smile appeared on her lips.

"He's nationally recognized in various martial arts and taught me, so I wouldn't need him. Usually, I was his unwilling sparring partner. You two would get into so much crap together."

"That explains...*so much*," Owen muttered.

She rolled her eyes and huffed.

"He still checks in like I'm twelve by saying my parents are interrogating him for details of my life, but I talk to them regularly. Pretends he doesn't...but he does."

"Sounds like a good brother. I always wished I had another sibling, but the universe sent me Levi. We got into the same shit brothers would have."

"He really is a good brother. Never lets me forget he's 'older and wiser' though the wise part is debatable." Something in her face softened. "Guess it's not a bad thing to have someone wanting to protect us."

"Yeah," he said. Then, Owen added more quietly, "Guess we're allowed to protect each other now, too."

The words slipped out before he could stop them. Neither of them laughed. It was a quiet step forward.

Later, when the fire died down and the cold crept in, they packed up their things in comfortable silence.

For once, there was no tension between them. Owen knew they had reached some kind of unspoken milestone. He just wasn't sure what to do next.

Adelen had been skeptical about leaving everything at the site, worrying that the furniture and other supplies would be damaged or stolen. He had reassured her that it would be fine and he'd hired a crew specifically to handle it.

Walking down the lit path to the parking lot, Adelen didn't shy away from his touch when he'd reached for her hand. They were both acting a bit shy now, which was strange considering they had just slept together.

Owen was still reeling from the taste and feel of her. Nothing and no one would ever compare to her...except for maybe having Adelen in a different position. The thought alone had his blood heating and his pants feeling tight again.

Finally, outside her car, neither of them reached for the door right away, both lingering.

"Hopefully you had fun, footwear assault aside?" he asked cheekily.

"What do you mean? That was the highlight of my evening. Hearing the loud smack it made when it hit you was music to my ears." The innocent sarcasm made her even sexier.

"Calm down now, let's not make that a habit. I can't imagine Dax will be too thrilled to see me covered in bruises as we film."

That earned a true belly laugh from Adelen.

"It's kind of funny how taken he is with you, though. He never shares his snacks—*never*. The fact that he even offered you any is a tremendous honor."

"At least one of us thinks so," he grumbled. "He keeps loose fruit snack pieces in those pockets, which can't be sanitary. They come out covered in fuzz!"

She shook her head and laughed again, her expression softening. Adelen stepped forward and placed a hand on his chest, right over his heart. Owen's breath caught, afraid to move, but wanting to kiss her again.

"Thank you for giving me a second chance," she whispered, her mouth dangerously close to his. "I've never been someone's Valentine, so if this is what I have to look forward to, I'm afraid you've just set the bar outrageously high."

Her quiet confession caught him off guard.

"You've never had a Valentine?" He didn't believe that for a second, not from such a beautiful woman.

Her lips quirked upwards, eyes twinkling mischievously as she asked, "You think I'm a beautiful woman?"

"Oh my god, did I say that out loud?"

Her laughter filled the space between them and remained as her lips met his. The kiss was slow and unhurried, promising more to come.

She gripped his shirt while his hands slid into her hair. When his thumbs grazed the new cochlear skins he'd given her, Owen almost purred with content, his inner alpha male pleased that she had put them on.

They stood outside, wrapped in each other's arms, and Owen didn't care how long it lasted. When they finally broke apart, foreheads touching and both a little breathless, he missed her warmth right away.

"Happy Valentine's Day, Owen," she whispered.

"Happy Valentine's Day, Addy," he murmured, before adding, "What time should I pick you up tomorrow?"

"What? What's tomorrow?" Adelen asked, alarmed, as if worried she had forgotten about an important appointment.

"Hopefully another date, if you're up for it."

She blew out a relieved sigh.

"Text me in the morning," she said shyly. With one last quick peck on the lips, Adelen slipped into her car.

Owen waited to make sure she was safely in her car, not moving from his spot in the lot until she pulled out onto the main road.

Tonight felt like the first of many more to come.

CHAPTER 24

Unknown

The woods grew colder after sunset, quiet except for the wind scraping through the trees and the faint crackle of the fire. Two silhouettes moved in the glow, distant and small.

It had been this way for hours.

Standing out of view for this long had caused their legs to ache. Watching and waiting.

It didn't matter how much time had passed; it was impossible to look away.

The easy laughter between Owen and Adelen was the hardest part to watch. It felt like whatever was between them had always been there, leaving no room for anyone else.

With clenched fists, their eyes fixed on the two of them.

It wasn't right. It wasn't supposed to look like that.

Every touch lingered too long.

Hands intertwined. Knees brushing. Heads tipping close like shared secrets.

It was too comfortable, too *intimate.*

Then the unthinkable happened.

They kissed.

Something hot and sour twisted in their chest. The noise in their head went quiet.

Time slowed to a stop. The temperature dropped.

Fine.

If they wanted to play, then it was time to kick it up a notch.

Both of them would learn soon enough just how high the stakes had risen.

CHAPTER 25

Adelen

Sunday morning started with a text. It was early, even for her, considering how late they were out last night. Still, Adelen couldn't help but smile like a schoolgirl with her first crush.

Whatever he'd planned, it involved physical activity. There were other activities they could engage in...damn, she needed to get her head out of the gutter.

Last night was all she could think about. She'd slept like the dead, completely worn out from the best Valentine's Day ever. The only thing that could top that was if she'd woken up next to Owen this morning for round two.

After one ride with Owen, she was suddenly sex deprived. Or maybe it was a testament to how terrible her past partners were. The act itself had always been fine, but Adelen had never wanted more than to satisfy her needs.

Everything that happened last night was so unexpected.

OWEN'S CELL

Details

Message
(Today) AM 6:36

Meet me at the Joia City Athletic Multiplex at 10:00 AM sharp. Wear socks you don't love but that aren't gross with holes in them. Trust me.

I expect a tall chai tea (you know how I like it) heated to exactly 87 degrees waiting for me when I get there. What are the chances this activity is clothing optional

The tea I can definitely do. I always keep a thermometer handy

As for our scheduled activity, it would be frowned upon by society and facility staff if it were performed without clothes...

But that doesn't mean we can't squeeze in a more hands-on activity afterward

Unless that *was* her real character, and it took finding the right person to reveal it. Didn't matter; she regretted nothing and would do it all over again in a heartbeat. Once was in no way enough. She always went after what she wanted.

And she wanted Owen Voss. Badly.

The ache between her legs that had been there when she awoke intensified. Frustrated, she threw a pillow over her face and yelled into it. Sexual tantrum now over with, she replied to Owen's message.

Adelen watched the dots appear and disappear on her screen a few times as Owen figured out how to respond to her request. She didn't really know how to flirt, considering the goal was usually to scare people away, but how hard could it be?

His response sent a delicious shiver running down Adelen's spine. Jumping out of bed to get ready, she was determined to make damn sure they had time to fit *that* in.

The ice rink smelled like rubber mats, stale popcorn, and aggressively burnt coffee.

Adelen stopped just inside the entrance of the expansive facility and looked around with a frown. She scowled at Owen like he'd double-crossed her.

"This," she said slowly, "is not what I pictured when you said 'fun winter activity.'"

"What do you expect? It's classy, it's wintery, and you're going to love it," Owen insisted, spinning in a circle with arms spread wide, "Look at this place!"

She stared at the uncomfortable metal folding chairs. The flickering fluorescent lights. The vending machine that wheezed like it had asthma.

"...You brought me to a middle school gym with ice," she said flatly. Owen crossed his arms and doubled down.

"It has *character.*"

"It has *tetanus.*"

Adelen was underwhelmed. She could do a lot of things, but successfully staying upright on any kind of slippery surface was not one of them. "I'm going to break my ass, Owen!"

"Then we'll break our asses together, because that's what real couples do. Come on, the class is starting." He reached for her hand, but she pulled it back.

"I'm sorry—*what* class?"

Instead of answering, Owen shot her a roguish grin, flicked his chin in the opposite direction, and started to walk away.

Adelen had no choice but to follow him towards whatever fresh hell he signed them up for.

CHAPTER 26

Owen

Owen's ingenious idea was meant to push them out of their comfort zone by offering a brand-new experience together. When he came across a drop-in adult instructional curling course at the ice rink, he signed them up.

Having actually been in the class for five minutes now, Owen learned something important about curling.

The shoes were a *lie*.

One step onto the ice and his feet shot out from under him. He landed flat on his back, the sound echoing through the rink.

The alleged gripper sole didn't do *shit*.

Adelen leaned over him, inky hair spilling out from beneath her hat, and a sarcastic smirk on her face.

"Aw, my sweet little love muffin! You good?"

"*No*."

"Did you hurt your bum?"

Owen glared at her. "Stop it."

"Did you get a little boo-boo?"

"Are you going to kiss it better?"

She clicked her tongue. "Hmm, I suppose that depends on how long you continue to subject me to this punishment."

"Oh, so *now* you have jokes?"

Glenn, a seventy-year-old classmate with a beer belly, glided past them with inexplicable grace. He didn't even look down or offer any assistance.

Owen whispered, "That guy must be a cyborg...but if he can do it, then so can we."

Adelen stared after the man with a malevolent glint in her eyes. "Fucking Glenn is a show off."

"Yeah...fuck Glenn," he echoed, trying to ignore the pain radiating up his spine.

CHAPTER 27

Adelen

Once Owen finished crawling away from the curling zone, it was Adelen's turn.

He managed to get back up on his feet and could stand, as long as he remained as still as a statue and ignored the searing ache in his back.

Adelen, however, made it exactly three steps onto the extra-slick lane before she slid sideways, windmilling her arms and crashing directly into his chest.

"Nooooooooo!" Owen's shout was amplified by the cavernous building, making their collision that much more epic. They both went down in a heap. It was the least graceful thing she'd ever experienced in her life.

For a second, they just lay there, a tangled mess of limbs, staring into the oblivion of the bright stadium-quality lights.

"I'm not an expert, but I think my boobs are misaligned now," Adelen whispered.

"I'd still love them anyway," Owen whispered back. "My boobs are fine though, thanks for asking, but I can't say the same about my knees."

Laughter bubbled up in her throat. She slapped a hand over her mouth to stop it, but it was no use. Owen joined in as they both lay prone on the ice, in no hurry to move. Laughing so hard they couldn't breathe.

"I hate this," Adelen wheezed.

"We're so bad at this," Owen agreed. "Why did I let you talk me into this awful idea?"

"Don't you dare blame this on me," Adelen threatened. "I swear to god I'll ask Deborah to come and give you suggestions on how to improve your technique again."

Across the rink, a stern elderly woman in an orange snowsuit narrowed her eyes at them, disapproval permanently etched into her wrinkles.

Owen turned his head towards her in abject horror. "That punishment does *not* fit the crime!" He paused for a moment before asking, "But seriously, is Deborah judging us again?"

Adelen nodded ruefully. "She's giving us the stink eye right now. That woman absolutely runs this place."

"She's the final boss...We obviously need to defeat her."

Adelen snorted, the action sending pain shooting down her hip. "Yes, *obviously*."

CHAPTER 28

Owen

Somehow, against all logic, Adelen figured it out.

Owen didn't know why he was amazed by this, because *of course* she did. Adelen was immensely intelligent and talented. She could learn to do anything she wanted; her potential was limitless.

Her first real throw slid straight down the ice and knocked another stone clean out of the center like a sniper shot.

Owen's mouth hung open in disbelief as he tried to process what the hell he just witnessed.

"...Did—Did you just hustle me?"

She shrugged. "No, I've never played this before, but honestly, it's just physics."

"No one randomly knows physics, Addy."

"Okay, except I'm not 'no one' and I actually do?"

Owen looked at her in a new light. "You're formidably competent at everything."

Adelen laughed, the sound joyful and adorable. "My brother used to make me practice balance drills in the yard."

"Wait—*Why?*"

"So he could throw me at people if needed." She said it so casually, as if it were the most common extracurricular activity to sign up for after school.

Owen stared at her. He found himself doing that a lot lately for a myriad of reasons.

"...I'm choosing to believe that's a joke."

She shrugged and, with a small smile, said, "You do you, but someday you'll learn that I'm telling you the truth." Adelen gestured towards the ice, enjoying the situation way too much. "Your turn, sunshine."

By the time they left, both their socks were soaked through, and Owen had fallen four more times. Well, fallen was a generous description of what happened. It was more like an epic wipeout, each one increasingly worse than the last.

One of which involved taking out two cones and a broom like a human bowling ball. A small child clapped enthusiastically, thinking it was a performance instead of a grown man being conquered by a sport.

To Adelen's delight, she successfully recorded the last fall on her phone "for legal reasons." When he asked her to clarify what that meant exactly, Adelen didn't hesitate to reply with, "Blackmail. I definitely mean Blackmail."

This was the second date Owen had planned that went off the rails. Anyone else would have walked away by now. Not Adelen.

She was the dream, the final chapter he wanted. It scared him how deeply he already felt for her. It terrified him how quickly she had become important.

As they put on their regular shoes, Owen grew quiet, lost in thought. Adelen noticed. She scooted closer, sliding down the cold bleacher bench until they were shoulder to shoulder.

"Hey," she said quietly.

Owen glanced over. "Yeah?"

"You went from complaining about needing a hip replacement to radio silence. What's going on up there?" She tapped his head gently with one finger.

His shoulders felt heavy, as if he didn't say something now, he'd regret it.

Blowing out a breath, Owen said, "This is going to sound...insane."

"Your track record thus far would suggest that, yes."

He huffed a laugh, but it died on his lips.

"My mom's care facility is about twenty minutes away." Her posture changed immediately, her expression growing softer and more attentive.

"She's good some days," he said. "Most days are not so good."

Owen braced his hands on the bench.

"She keeps asking where my dad is."

The words burned like acid on his tongue.

"And I keep having to tell her he's gone. Over and over, because it's brand new every time. So is the pain she feels each time she finds out."

He stared at the floor.

"I don't usually bring people there, aside from Levi. *Ever*," he trailed off, needing a second to form the question burning deep within him. He hadn't risked looking at Adelen yet, though she'd been completely silent.

"I know it's weird to ask someone to meet your mom on the second date. That's objectively unhinged behavior. I'd..." He swallowed hard. "I'd regret it for the rest of my life if she didn't meet you at least once."

Adelen's breath caught.

"Not because I'm assuming anything. Not because I'm rushing anything. I just—"

His voice was quiet but full of everything he felt.

"You're important to me already. And if something happens, or we don't work out someday, or life does what life does...I don't want to look back and realize she never got to know you."

God. He hadn't meant to say it like that.

"She'd like you," he whispered. "You're honest and brilliant. You love to knit like she used to. She notices stuff like that."

Adelen hadn't said a word up until this point, but she didn't have to. Her warm hand slid into his and gripped it firmly, with certainty.

"I'd love to," she said simply, like it wasn't even a question.

Those three words sealed it for Owen. His heart belonged to her now.

CHAPTER 29

Owen

"Dinner?" Owen asked later, following the visit with his mother.

Adelen had held his hand from the moment they walked through the entrance of Crystal Waters Residences, a quiet reassurance he wouldn't be alone.

The visit was just like the last, except his mother seemed even thinner and more fragile. She sat in her recliner, staring out the window with empty eyes. It broke his heart to see her like that. Witnessing the regression was something he wouldn't wish on his worst enemy.

Adelen was patient, talking to her as if she could still join in. She told Denise about all the things Owen did to get her attention, their first date, and how bad he was at curling.

His mother barely moved, but sometimes she squeezed Adelen's hand. It was the only sign she was still there. After a while, they left so she could rest.

Before leaving, Adelen gently tucked the thick knit blanket around her. Owen turned away, his eyes stinging.

Now they were in the parking lot, standing outside the driver's side of Adelen's car.

She eyed him suspiciously. "Define dinner."

Dropping her hand, he slipped his arms around her waist, slowly backing her up until she was pressed against the car, enveloped by Owen's massive body. He nuzzled her neck and whispered, "You come to my place. I cook. We engage in another activity—clothing is highly discouraged."

Adelen arched into him. Running both hands up his back and through his hair, she scraped her teeth along his throat and up to his ear.

"Counteroffer," she said. Owen rocked against her, gloriously hard, and Adelen let out a small whimper. "I come to your place, I take you for another ride, *then* you cook, and we stay naked for the rest of the night."

He captured her mouth in a searing kiss, and Owen whispered, "Deal."

They sped back to Owen's apartment, barely slowing for the lights.

Once both cars were parked, they practically ran inside the building, unable to keep their hands off one another. As soon as the elevator doors shut behind them, Adelen was topless, on her knees, and taking him in her mouth.

It happened so fast he barely had time to react. Her tongue wrapped around him and his mind went blank. The ride to the thirty-fourth floor was short, but Adelen made every second count.

He fisted a hand in her hair as she worked him into a frenzy, watching her pert breasts bounce as she sucked and licked. Owen was getting *so* close when the elevator doors opened to his penthouse.

Adelen's hand quickly replaced where her mouth had been, with long, deliberate strokes as they stepped off the elevator. She was about to drop down and finish the job when Owen crushed his lips to hers.

Kissing her deeply, he used that time to push her back towards the tall glass windows overlooking the city. He made quick work stripping the remaining clothes off of her—and himself.

He spun her to face the skyline, one hand around her throat, tipping her head back to his shoulder. His other hand slid down, slipping a finger inside her, his thumb circling that sensitive spot.

Adelen moaned, her body arching from the sensation. He held her steady, slipping in a second finger and teasing her. He pressed kisses down her throat, rolling a nipple between his fingers.

She cried out, and Owen chuckled darkly.

"A sensitive spot?"

"*Yes*," Adelen breathed. "I had gotten them pierced once, but haven't had them since college."

The thought of Adelen with pierced nipples nearly undid him. He pressed her against the window, hooked her leg over his arm, and thrust into her.

She hissed as the cold glass met her hot skin. He moved slowly at first, his body pressed tight against hers.

Owen whispered, "I want to show you off to the world." He moved faster, deeper. "Let everyone see how beautiful you are. Let them see how much I want you." He kissed her shoulder and set a hard, steady pace.

It was his name she cried out when she fell over the edge. But it was her name he whispered when he followed.

CHAPTER 30

Adelen

His penthouse kitchen looked like it belonged on a cooking show.

What happened inside it felt like an insult to the architecture.

So much smoke.

"Why is it screaming?" Owen demanded through the mist, frantically fanning the pan with a hand towel.

"That's the smoke alarm," Adelen said flatly, trying to find a lid in the millions of useless cabinetry. "It's begging you to stop. Ugh—you live in this fancy apartment, but you can't open a damn window because it's the 34th floor!"

"First off, I followed the recipe—"

"You put olive oil in a cold pan and walked away!"

"I was preheating emotionally!"

Adelen threw her hands up. "That's not a thing!" she yelled, exasperated.

"Second, no one ever buys a penthouse apartment in a prime downtown high-rise thinking 'Oh, I better make sure I can pop a window open *just in case I briefly walk away from a pan of steak,*'" he retorted.

Owen filled a glass of water and tipped it toward the pan. Adelen couldn't believe what she was seeing. She caught his wrist, pivoted, and redirected the motion as if she were guiding a dance step. The glass slipped neatly from his fingers and shattered against the tile.

He snapped his head to her, outrage written across his face. "Hey, Mr. Miyagi—*What the hell was that for*?"

"Are you *insane*? You *never* pour water on a grease fire! Do you *want* to burn this place down?"

How the hell has he survived this long?

She resumed her search, rifling through cabinets, while continuing to chastise him. "Put a lid on it or baking soda, but never *ever* water."

Finally, Adelen found one and quickly covered the pan and the flames within it. The immediate danger abated, she spun around and asked, "What kind of security expert doesn't know basic kitchen safety?"

He opened and closed his mouth, trying—and failing—to come up with an answer. After a solid minute, Owen straightened. "Maybe I was just testing *your* knowledge of kitchen safety and was so committed to it that I sacrificed a drinking glass in the process."

Such an Owen response.

Adelen shook her head in disbelief and peered under the lid. The charred lump of meat formerly known as steak had turned black. Literally solid black like a charcoal briquette.

They both stared at it. Adelen sighed.

"Do we bury it or apologize?" Owen asked.

"I don't even know what state of matter its become."

Owen's eyes lit up. "Did we just create a new element?"

"*We* didn't do anything. *You* defiled what used to be a prime piece of meat." She confiscated the spatula. "Step away from the stove, you just lost fire privileges."

Owen had the nerve to look affronted. "You're overreacting."

"You cremated our dinner."

"Okay, but in my defense—"

"No—No defense. What happened here was a criminal act."

"Fine," he pouted.

A pouting Owen was hot, hotter than the incinerated steak.

"What else do we have to work with in here?" Adelen asked as she opened the freezer.

The empty freezer. She shut the door and rubbed at her temples in defeat. After the piercing wail of the fire alarm and smoke inhalation, a headache was forming.

"I only bought the ingredients needed for the recipe," he said sheepishly. "I never really keep this place stocked. I tend to stay over at Isaac and Grace's more often than not."

That kernel of information took her aback.

"Why? Isn't this place close to work? The views are gorgeous," she admitted.

His shoulder lifted in a small imperceptible shrug.

"I don't like being alone with my thoughts. A lot has happened over the last couple of years, and the silence gets too loud."

Wasn't that the truth?

Understanding exactly what he meant, especially after meeting his sweet mother earlier that afternoon, she let it go.

"Alrighty, takeout it is."

CHAPTER 31

Owen

They ended up parked on the living room floor with cartons everywhere, city lights glowing through the windows like a movie backdrop.

The electric fireplace insert under the television was on, emitting a cozy warmth. In all the time he'd lived there, Owen couldn't recall a time he actually used it. Adelen's eyes had lit up when she saw it.

Shoes and socks were off. Her knee pressed against his, and neither of them said a word. Sitting next to her felt natural. With her there, his apartment felt like home.

Adelen was home to him.

The kitchen fire was mostly forgotten now, and they talked about anything and everything as they worked through their Asian culinary feast.

She told him more about her twin brother between bites. How they used to—and very often still do—fight about the stupidest things.

Like how he once punched a kid in third grade for making fun of her speech. It resulted in his first suspension because he refused to apologize to the boy and said he'd do it again if he could.

And how they were still arguing about "the rake incident."

Owen paused mid-bite when Adelen casually mentioned it. "The what?"

She pointed a dumpling at him. "Ah, yes, the rake incident that happened about a decade ago. It comes up every Thanksgiving, the wounds still fresh as if it happened yesterday."

"Why am I imagining something extremely violent?"

Adelen chuckled, "Because it kind of was."

Owen stared at her expectantly. Now that she said it, he *had* to know what could have possibly happened for it to keep resurfacing each year. Adelen took one more bite before setting her container and chopsticks down, readying herself for a ghost story.

"Okay, so it was when we were in college. I had moved out into my own apartment off campus and he still lived at home with my parents because he thought it was dumb to pay rent when he could come and go as he pleased.

I stopped by one Saturday in the spring, and my parents were outside doing yard work—planting new flowers, weeding, and all that. My mom and I were inside the kitchen when Diogo walked in. I don't remember why he came in or what prompted him to sternly say 'don't go in my room,' but whatever, I didn't care. I had no desire to go into his gross room."

Owen snickered and popped a piece of teriyaki chicken in his mouth.

"Then he went outside again. My mom then looked inside the basket they kept in the family room, which usually had candy—my dad has quite the sweet tooth—and found it empty. That was when *she* told *me* that Diogo had a wholesale-sized bag of those orange-and-green tiger-striped lollipops in his room. My mom handed me the basket and told me to get some to fill it."

He was really enjoying Adelen the storyteller. She was so animated, with her hands everywhere.

"...I said, 'Mom, did you not just hear him? He's going to be pissed if I go in there,' and she got mad at *me* and said, 'It's not his house. His room is my room and I paid for those lollipops. Now go get some for your father's basket.' I really didn't feel good about this, but my mom is kind of terrifying when she's mad."

Owen interrupted with a quick clarifying question. "To be clear, the root cause of this whole thing so far is lollipops?"

Her eyes shone with mischief. "And alleged trespassing."

"And alleged trespassing, got it."

"Now, it's important to note that we lived in a raised ranch. His room was over the garage, and mine was next to it. It used to be my room, but we had to switch because we fought over the shared thermostat—but whatever, that's a different story."

Owen shook his head and laughed.

"*Anyway*, so I'm in his room trying to find these damn things, and I'm coming up short. I really didn't want to risk stumbling upon his underwear drawer or something weird, so my dumbass self gave up and decided to just ask him. I went to one of the long, narrow casement windows, cranked it open, and shouted down at him to tell me where the lollipops were."

Adelen paused dramatically, her face turning fearful as she looked Owen in the eyes and said, "I thought I was going to die that day."

Noodles almost flew everywhere when Owen choked on a laugh. Adelen kept going.

"Diogo was in the driveway below and was *furious* I was in his room after he specifically said not to go in there. He started angrily marching up the driveway, where a heavy metal garden rake lay on the ground. In that moment, I *knew* what was going to happen, and I tried to warn him, but it was too late. I swear, it was like the next few seconds happened in slow motion. I yelled 'raaaaaaaaaaake' but it was too late—"

"He stepped on the rake?"

"He stepped on the rake! Right on the teeth, and I shit you not, Owen, the second I heard the smack of the wooden handle smack against his forehead, I knew my life was over. He stood there stunned for a second before looking up at me and yelling 'You're going to die today!"

Owen burst out into uncontrollable laughter.

"Remember how it's a raised ranch? *Well*, Diogo came in through the garage, past the family room, and up the bi-level stairs. Meanwhile, I booked it and ran down the hall past the stairs, sliding on the hardwood floor, aiming for the side door to the upstairs deck. I threw the door open and flew down those stairs with my brother hot on my heels. I sprinted for my dad and hid behind him, clutching his shirt, peeking out from the side to make sure Diogo couldn't get me."

"You used your dad as a human shield?"

"Fight or flight, Owen. Diogo was so pissed. When we told my dad what happened, I swear to god, he *struggled* to keep a straight face and not laugh. He said I shouldn't have been in his room, and told Diogo he needs to be more diligent about his surroundings."

Her eyes danced wildly as she said, "He had an egg on his forehead for *two weeks* and refused to talk to me until it was completely gone."

Owen's sides hurt from laughing so hard at the absurd story. He wiped his mouth with a napkin and asked, "Why is this such a hotly contested incident that it keeps coming up?"

"Ugh, because my mom apparently doesn't remember telling me to go into his room, when she most certainly did! I wouldn't have gone in there if she hadn't. Diogo believes I just did it to piss him off and that my actions nearly caused him brain damage, when it was my mom who instructed me to go in there."

"Jesus, that was a wild ride of a story. I'm an only child, so I never experienced such shenanigans. Levi is the closest person I have to a sibling, though I did lock him in my trundle bed once during a sleepover."

Her eyebrows shot up. "Why did you do that?"

Owen scowled at the memory. "He ate the last package of fruit snacks."

Aghast, Adelen asked, "So you stuffed him in a trundle bed?"

"All is fair in love and war—I loved those fruit snacks, and shots were fired. I responded accordingly." Owen smirked as he added, "To this day, Levi is a little claustrophobic."

Adelen threw her head back and laughed.

This.

This moment, this *woman*, was everything Owen wanted.

Later, they stood by her car, neither one opening the door. The work week would start tomorrow, but neither wanted the night to end.

"You're a disaster in the kitchen," Adelen said.

"I know—probably my only flaw."

She laughed lightly.

"...Today was really good though."

He smiled. "Yeah?"

"Yeah."

She stepped closer, so close he forgot how to speak or breathe.

When he kissed her this time, it wasn't careful or tentative. It was slow and warm and certain.

Her hands splayed against his chest.

He traced lazy circles across her back.

There were no masks, jokes, or pretense.

Just them.

They broke apart only when they were both breathless, foreheads resting together, her laugh warm against his mouth.

"Text me when you get home," he murmured.

"Only if you promise never to cook again."

"No promises."

She rolled her eyes, smiling, and slipped into the driver's seat.

He waited until her headlights disappeared, then turned back to the building. His hands were in his pockets, his heart pounding like a teenager's.

Behind him, somewhere across the street, a car door clicked softly shut.

Neither of them noticed.

CHAPTER 32

Adelen

Her body still hummed after the best and most refreshing weekend of her life. Unfortunately, all good things must come to an end. Monday morning came fast and unforgiving.

The next week on set was chaos. Crew members everywhere, cables snaking across the ground, directors shouting, actors rehearsing. Adelen stayed in her lane, quietly trying to train both Kaia and the other new girl, Lizzie, while still doing her job—monitoring levels, adjusting mics, running interference when things went wrong.

She didn't know what she had done to deserve an amazing coworker and friend like Rita. That wonderful woman hadn't abandoned her either. Whenever she was finished with hair and makeup, Rita was right where Adelen needed her to be, stepping up to help with getting her two new team members up to speed.

The replacement cables arrived overnight Sunday, and she thanked the universe for that one small mercy, praying that it was the last incident she would have to deal with. It seemed like that request had fallen to the bottom of the gods' priority list if the screaming match between Kaia and Henrietta during their first meeting was any indication.

The bold pink leopard-print leggings Kaia showed up in were certainly a *choice*, and Henrietta took it as an invitation to critique her while Kaia wired her mic. Then she "accidentally" spilled coffee down Henrietta's blouse, and the set erupted. Henrietta's shrieking bounced off the studio walls; Kaia answered with equally dramatic (and loud) tearful wails, forcing Tessa to jump in and pull them apart. Adelen might've believed the meltdown—if Kaia hadn't shot her a quick, satisfied smirk.

Adelen had sent a bonus prayer asking for divine intervention should Kaia and Henrietta ever be caught in a room together alone...otherwise, there would be bloodshed. Her new friend was shaping up to be a handful, though her money was on Kaia in a fight.

She might've had a smidge of regret for hiring her, but it was too late now. And Henrietta deserved it.

Cary, her boss, showed up before lunch that Monday and immediately began hovering. He'd become a huge pain in her ass in a very short span of time.

Picking apart her process. Questioning her reports. Circling like a vulture waiting for her to slip. He barely let her settle at her station before leaning over her shoulder to ask what she was doing, why she was doing it that way, and whether she'd double-checked something she'd already checked twice.

He'd been more than just her boss—Cary was her mentor. He was a decade her senior, average build, with graying, curly, charcoal hair. Since her first day at POLmArK, Cary had taken her under his wing and taught her everything he knew, his analytical brown eyes capturing the slightest of details. She had looked up to him ever since.

When she'd been approached by network executives to take her career to the next level by sliding into Cary's role, Adelen had balked. She loved her job and had no interest in ousting him. The executives were disappointed but understood, and had left the door open for the opportunity should she change her mind.

Adelen had never uttered a word to anyone about it.

Things were otherwise fine, but ever since she accepted this new position, his attitude changed. He'd never treated her like this before. It set her teeth on edge.

They were at the barn constructed at Starhaven, shooting Owen's grand arrival scene that morning, and squeezed in the Hardware Store Guy scene at the end of the day back at the studio. Aurelia, Grace, and Ivy popped in to watch, excited to witness a real movie being filmed.

But also because the nosy bitches were tired of Adelen's evasive answers to their texts. The three of them instantly hit it off with Kaia, who filled them in on how she "helped" coordinate her first date with Owen. To Adelen's surprise (or dismay), Kaia was formally inducted into the Shrew Crew.

She could've lied or played dumb about what was happening between her and Owen, but she was also astonished that she wasn't ashamed about it either. It actually felt *good* to have girlfriends to confide in. The downside was that they all watched her like a hawk on set, scrutinizing every interaction she had with him.

And then there was Owen himself.

Every time she turned around, he was there—smiling, chatting with other crew members, avoiding Henrietta at all costs, trading barbs with Bertrand—nothing out of the ordinary.

There was a shift between them. Owen stopped trying to get her attention with wild acts. Now it was small glances and private smiles. She blushed and felt butterflies, just like the lead in one of these films. Those small things meant more than any public display. The butterflies in her stomach were real this time, not just nerves.

The first time he needed his mic fixed, she did it herself, even though Rita or Kaia could have. She just wanted to be close to him, to breathe him in. Owen smelled like sunlight on fabric, warm cotton, clean soap, sandalwood, and a hint of coffee and brown sugar. It was comforting, like fresh laundry or late afternoon grass.

It was the kind of scent that someone could lean into, and that was precisely what Adelen wanted to do—lean into him. Her face burned the whole time, and his knowing smile made it hard to focus.

As did the giggles and commentary from her friends.

"He looks like he joined a biker boy band," Ivy had at one point quipped before Aurelia elbowed her with a stern shush.

Adelen forced herself to focus on the mic wire, the transmitter, the small clip at his collar. But when her fingers brushed his warm neck, her mind went short-circuited.

He, of course, had to say something.

"Careful," he teased lightly. "Our pal Henrietta might get jealous and try to grope me again. You'll have to make a scene to defend my honor."

Adelen said nothing as she stifled a smile, struggling to keep a straight face as she taped the wire in place. Once satisfied, she gave him a pointed look and walked away, the low rumble of his laughter echoing behind her. She didn't mean to linger at the monitors. She was only supposed to check the sound levels, make sure the dialogue was clear, adjust for wind, and flag any peaks. That was it.

But somewhere between Scene 5 and Scene 8, she stopped listening for quality's sake. Adelen was genuinely following the story, so engaged that she didn't notice her phone vibrating in her pocket.

Owen was...actually not bad.

She watched him stumble through Dolf's arrival scene. Owen looked ridiculous in leather, windblown extensions framing his face as he wrestled the motorcycle into place. He had torn up Maggie Bean's prized pinto crop with the motorcycle and was dealing with the fallout as Maggie/Henrietta wailed about the damage he'd done.

Dolf's adlibbed line about doing the world a favor by reducing methane emissions made the crew laugh. Henrietta was caught off guard and managed to hide her agitation well.

Adelen snickered quietly as her phone buzzed again. This time, she pulled it out to check.

Her stomach tightened in fear as she scanned the set for any hint of who had sent it.

But no one was out of place or acting out of character. Everyone seemed to be going about their work, nothing obviously unusual.

With shaking hands, she locked the screen, shoved the phone away, and forced her attention back to the mixer. She told herself it was probably nothing. They were just toying with her. They had to be. Because if it wasn't, it meant someone in the building.

But when she checked her phone again later, the message was gone.

What started as a strange moment on set didn't stay that way. Adelen felt herself unraveling as the week went on.

A text here, a strange feeling of being watched there. Her bag moved a few inches from where she'd left it. A zipper she hadn't opened. Odd patterns of static feedback over the headset. The rational part of her brain said coincidence. The rest of her wasn't so sure.

She tried to shake it off and focus on work. With Henrietta and Bertrand, the set was chaotic enough to hide her nerves. Owen in leather, swearing at bees, lip-syncing to heavy metal, and knocking over a bean display at the legume festival kept the crew laughing.

Watching the shenanigans unfold helped her temporarily forget about it, at least until her radio crackled with a faint, unfamiliar, distorted whisper. It was so quiet she nearly missed it.

I see you.

Static swallowed the words, but she could've sworn someone said it. Her hand trembled on the volume knob. She cast a quick glance at Kaia, whose brows scrunched together in confusion for a fleeting moment before relaxing again. If Kaia had heard it too, she gave no indication.

Feedback, she told herself. *Just interference. That's it.*

Through her headphones, Owen's voice filtered in, rough and sincere. He started to soften and get the hang of it all, leaning into the character, letting a sliver of his true self show through. He even managed to look at Henrietta as if she hung the moon, despite her bizarre sexual advances.

Which had grown bolder and more depraved. Owen had been diligently documenting every incident, cleverly creating a paper trail. The dressing room footage he captured weeks ago would be the nail in her coffin.

It didn't stop Adelen from wanting to bury Henrietta under the fake legume field. But that would be the first place the police would look.

Knowing it was all an act was one thing, but the desire to claw Henrietta's eyes out was very real. She told herself it was simply professional irritation—he was the actor, she was the crew, and that was a boundary they needed to keep in place. But jealousy was a bitter taste, and it burned going down.

When the rain machine thundered on the roof and they huddled close in the barn, she found herself leaning forward. Watching, listening, reading him through the monitors as if she could hear his heartbeat.

Her phone buzzed.

Her breath stalled. She set it face down, pretending not to see, pretending her hands weren't shaking.

Later that day, she saw someone in the shadows beyond the barn doors. The silhouette was too still to be crew. Kaia noticed too. She tilted her head and asked, "You ever get the creepy crawly feeling that someone is watching you?"

Adelen quickly brushed off with a nervous laugh. "That's what being on set is all about: everyone is watching someone."

Just to be safe, she'd asked security to check it out, but the space was empty.

By midweek, she got a message with a photo attached—a clear picture of her taken from behind, on set. For a moment, the world tilted and her knees went weak. It could be anyone. There were too many people around to tell.

Adelen didn't tell anyone. She didn't know *how* to explain it without proof. In her panic, she hadn't saved the notes, and the messages kept disappearing. Every time she tried to document it, she second-guessed herself.

Diogo knew something was wrong, but she was too proud to ask for help. If she said it out loud and it wasn't real, she'd sound paranoid. Now she was starting to question her own sanity. She focused on work instead.

But she wasn't doing a good job hiding her unease. Adelen could do many things, but acting wasn't one of them. Kaia watched her more closely, but Adelen pretended not to notice. Even Rita saw she was off kilter.

"You okay?" Rita had quietly asked once, watching her fumble a cable. Adelen had forced a smile, assuring her she was fine.

She buried her fear under work, staying busy so she wouldn't think about it. Aurelia kept suggesting a girls' night out, Kaia included. After putting it off a few times, she finally said yes. Any more excuses would look suspicious.

It was exactly what she needed. Laughter, drinks, gooey cheese pizza, and fun stories. For the first time in weeks, she felt almost a sense of normalcy, until the conversation inevitably turned toward Owen.

"He's obsessed with you," Ivy said with a knowing grin, plucking a large, offensive-looking mushroom off her slice. "It's like watching a golden retriever patiently waiting for a belly rub."

Aurelia nodded. "He's never like this. Usually, women chase him to the point that he will sometimes retreat inward, being more of a homebody."

"You're lucky. It's so romantic, having someone that determined," Kaia added wistfully. "He's a fine specimen of male perfection...objectively speaking, of course."

Lucky. The word made her laugh, but it sounded brittle. None of them knew what it was like to look over your shoulder every few minutes, to second-guess every shadow and every text.

Still, they were right, and Adelen couldn't deny the way her pulse jumped when she thought of him—the warmth that cut through all the unease. He was frustrating, infuriating, and loud, but he was also incredibly sexy, thoughtful, and attentive. When he smiled at her across the set, it felt like the noise in her head quieted for a moment.

"Admit it," Grace said, waggling her eyebrows suggestively. "You've got it just as bad for him."

"Oh, come on, no more inquisition," Adelen begged.

"Sweetie, is that why you've been so off the last few weeks?" Kaia looked down her nose at Adelen. "You've been dropping stuff, spacing out, and talking to yourself once in a while. That man has you hooked!"

Adelen nearly choked on her pizza. Aurelia started whacking her on the back as everyone cackled about their "blossoming love." It was a nice distraction from the real reason she was coughing, Kaia's observation hitting the mark.

"Or is it Henrietta again?" Ivy inquired innocently. "We've all heard how...*direct* she's been in making her affections for your man known."

"Last week she told him he could 'sow his fava seeds in her fertile field anytime' and I've never seen anyone turn the shade of green that Owen did," Kaia exclaimed, more wildly entertained about it than she should be.

"Ugh, please let's talk about something else—*anything else*. That troll makes me violent," Adelen groused.

"Everything makes you violent," Aurelia laughed as the others, and Adelen herself, joined in.

Long after Adelen made it home from girls' night, she lay in bed, staring at the ceiling, listening to the hum of her building. Outside, a car passed. Somewhere down the hall, a door clicked. She wasn't ready to take off her processors yet, her mind still very much awake.

Her phone sat face-down on the nightstand, the screen dark.

She didn't want to look at it. Didn't want to risk being awake to see another message.

But she couldn't stop thinking about Owen—about the way his laugh filled a room, how he looked at her like he saw through every wall she'd ever built. The way his lips felt, trailing across her skin...

She let out a frustrated growl. Something was finally going right in her life, but she couldn't enjoy it. Someone out there was watching her.

The only person she wanted watching her was the one man she was starting to trust.

CHAPTER 33

Owen

Owen was starting to think acting might've been a terrible idea.

At first, the energy and chaos on set had been fun. The cameras, the noise, the rush of it all. But the novelty faded quickly. Acting was harder than Owen expected. The hot lights made him sweat, and repeating the same line over and over wore him down. Pretending to be someone else sometimes felt natural, but most of the time it just felt forced.

Despite the hectic filming schedule, Owen kept thinking about his work at Neuronix. He set aside an afternoon at the end of the week to meet the *Silver Shadow* and start their security engagement. He may have bitten off more than he could chew.

Owen knew he could handle the technical work, the cues, and the schedule, even with his other job. What he couldn't handle was Henrietta.

His co-star had decided she was in love with him, and while he wasn't one to normally blame shift, Owen couldn't lie and say that Adelen hadn't played a role in this situation. Henrietta's antics were steadily escalating. On-screen, off-screen, didn't seem to matter. The overtly sexual looks lingered, the scripted touches lasted much too long.

The first few times, he tried to brush it off and ignore the strong smell of vodka, hoping she was just acting. But then she tried to grab his junk not once, but several times, persistently finding reasons to hang around between takes. She leaned in too close, whispered borderline deviant comments under her breath, sometimes right in his ear.

Baffled that no one had spoken out against it yet, he began documenting the incidents. In the meantime, he channeled all the discomfort into his acting—which, unfortunately, the director loved.

But lord almighty did he hate being near this woman. Mainly because she wasn't Adelen, but also because she was just absolutely off her rocker.

Owen was completely gone. He wasn't just a little smitten. He had fallen head over heels for Adelen.

He kept thinking about the past weekend, wishing for more. More time with her, more easy conversation, more playful arguments. He missed the sounds she made when he was deep inside her. It was hard to believe only a few days had passed. It already felt like a lifetime ago.

Every time Adelen gave orders to her team, moved equipment, or put on her headphones, Owen thought it was the hottest thing he had ever seen.

She tried to avoid talking to him on set, and he understood why. If they hadn't talked about boundaries on their last date, her distant attitude would have made him worry.

When he saw her across the set, adjusting sound levels and giving orders, it hit him again.

God, he was screwed.

When Adelen did talk to him, it was usually to wire him with a mic or give him quick, professional directions. Her words were clipped and polite, but her eyes said something else. Her lips always seemed to fight a smile, and it drove him crazy. It felt like a secret game between them, the closeness making it more intense.

The stolen glances and unspoken words became the highlight of his days.

Unfortunately, Henrietta wasn't his only problem. Owen also had the costumer to contend with; the man was determined to test his patience.

Larry, a loud, eccentric man with a flair for tight tailoring, had been the latest trial. During one fitting at the beginning of the week, he got way too close for comfort while making adjustments to Owen's inseam, humming like he was fine-tuning a violin.

"Larry, buddy," Owen said through a forced grin, his jaw clenched so tightly it could crack walnuts, "you're a little close to the—uh—danger zone."

Larry just winked, his hands traveling higher and higher up Owen's inner thigh. "Relax, sweetheart. I'm a professional."

"Yeah, except I'm pretty sure that's *not* how you're supposed to do pants."

Paying his concerns no mind, Larry kept measuring—and double-checking his measurements—over and over again. Owen wasn't sure if he wanted to laugh or file a complaint.

He needed to focus and get ready for the next scene. They had already filmed his arrival earlier, so there was time for another. It was supposed to be a short scene, but it ended up with the Hardware Store Guy. That meant his new bestie, Bertrand, would be the challenge today.

To make matters worse, Ivy and Grace had shown up with Aurelia, all pretending to be "supportive" but really there to watch him squirm.

They had been holed up in his dressing room with him, their nonstop chatter making it impossible to concentrate. Eventually, he simply gave up and decided to wing it. If he had to make shit up on the fly, then so be it. God only knew what bullshit Bertrand was going to pull anyway, so trying this hard to stick to the script was likely a waste of time.

When it was time to shoot the scene, Owen led his friends to Stage B, where a makeshift hardware store set had been constructed. Wardrobe had outfitted him in black leather pants, a black band t-shirt with the sleeves cut off, and some fierce combat boots. Long-wearing temporary tattoo sleeves had been applied to his arms, and a fake lip ring completed the look.

It was exactly what any normal, everyday lead singer of a heavy metal band would wear on a regular trip to the hardware store. The fake tattoos were the only redeeming part of the ensemble. It was weird not having sleeves on a t-shirt, his pants squeaked when he walked, and he was sweating his balls off in them. While they *did* make his ass look good, it wasn't worth the trouble.

He deposited his friends to the side of the space designated for guests and other crew members, where they wouldn't be able to interfere with any filming.

"Don't screw up," Grace whispered with a grin as she handed him a water bottle.

"No pressure," Owen muttered, accepting the beverage and heading to the set.

He'd been trying to focus on the script and his cues when he spotted Adelen, checking sound levels and chatting with her team. As if sensing his eyes on her, Adelen nonchalantly peered over her shoulder.

The look she gave him was both a summons and an invitation. Owen decided he would find her after work. She blushed, and he loved seeing her like that.

Suddenly, Owen felt another set of eyes on him, or rather, multiple eyes. Aurelia, Ivy, and Grace were watching the entire interaction with rapt attention. Scowling, he decided right then that they would never again be allowed on set, not after the kissy faces they started making at him. Adelen had also taken notice, and from the deadly glare directed at the ladies, she shared his sentiments.

The heavy metal door to Stage B flew open, hard enough to slam against the wall, loud enough to startle nearly everyone in there. An agitated Dax burst through the entryway, with Gerald and Tessa hot on his heels. Owen could almost see the thundercloud following the director, who normally had the creative attention span of a caffeinated squirrel.

Tessa and Gerald shared nervous looks as they hurried to keep up. Dax still wore his safari vest full of snack pockets. He went to the snack cart, glanced at the options, and threw a handful of cashews at the wall when he saw they were unsalted.

Christ, Dax was in rare form today.

This was a clear foreshadowing of the bad things to come. He'd never seen Dax behave like this. From the shocked and concerned expression on Adelen's face, neither had she.

Then, like the receding tide in advance of a tsunami, Bertrand Dalingford shuffled in, the red flannel shirt hanging loose on his thin frame and half tucked into ill-fitting denim overalls—he was the epitome of the prophetic omen. He tried to shake the bad feeling off but knew in his soul that this simple scene would not go as planned today.

After they had gotten into their positions on the set and Dax finally stopped criticizing everyone, they were ready to start filming. It hadn't taken more than five minutes before chaos erupted.

Bertrand pulled a red handkerchief from his back pocket and tied it around his head, making him look like some western barmaid. Dax was appalled and demanded that he remove it, claiming it was ruining the whole look. Bertrand told him to go eat glass.

Tense negotiations ensued, resulting in a concession from Dax: he could wear it only if it was tied around his neck instead of on his head. Bertrand miraculously agreed to his terms.

At long last, they were ready to start rolling. Bertrand was situated behind the checkout counter, perched on a stool with his nose buried in a copy of the local newspaper.

Dax settled into his chair, eyes glued to the small screen displaying the live video feed, and yelled, "Places, everyone! Cameras start rolling in three, two, one—Action!"

The Hardware Store Guy/cashier was catching up on the local news when a customer approached the counter. On cue, Owen/Dolf Ingerson stepped into the frame, carting several stacks of fertilizer up to checkout.

The cashier didn't look up from his newspaper, too engulfed in an article to acknowledge anyone else's existence.

Dolf waited patiently for the cashier to assist him for a few extra moments before loudly clearing his throat in an attempt to capture his attention.

With a loud, exaggerated sigh, the cashier made a production of putting the newspaper away, highly inconvenienced by the interruption. He looked down his nose at Dolf and snorted derisively.

"Well, well, well, what do we have here?" the cashier said in quite possibly the worst Southern accent Owen had ever had the misfortune of hearing. "You must be the fancy rockstar from the big city everybody has been jabbering about."

That's not in the fucking script.

Alarm bells went off in Owen's head, but he adapted quickly and improvised.

"Yes, sir, just taking an extended leave of absence in this quaint little town. Unfortunately, my motorcycle had a tragic encounter with Miss Maggie's garbanzo field. I have to do right by her and make amends. Since that entails purchasing a whole lot of fertilizer, I figured I'd go right to the expert. I hear you're number one in the business of number two." Dolf flashed the most charming smile in his arsenal.

The cashier narrowed his eyes at Dolf and studied him for a moment.

Say your line, god damn it, Owen yelled silently in his head.

Bertrand did not recite his line as originally written. Instead, he went in a completely different and unscripted direction.

The cashier flexed a crooked finger in Dolf's direction, beckoning him closer. Dolf briefly hesitated, then indulged the man and leaned over the counter.

"Where did you find those bags of fertilizer?" The near whisper of a question caught Dolf off guard.

Owen realized it wouldn't matter what he said or did at this point. Bertrand had no intention of following the script today. So, Owen did what any professional would—he rolled with it.

"In the back near the electric fireplaces?"

"Oh, you poor, poor boy...There's a legend around these parts—" the cashier whispered conspiratorially, "—of cursed silverware scattering themselves about, looking for new souls to steal. Did you see it?"

"See *what*?"

"The fork, you fool!" The unexpected bellow nearly sent Dolf crashing to the floor in surprise, but he caught the edge of the counter with his hand, managing to keep himself upright. "Beware of the haunted fork for its curse is tied to the electric fireplaces!"

Why do these situations always happen to me? Owen asked himself.

"Sir, it looked like it was just minding its own business, trying to warm up before a cozy fire," Dolf said matter-of-factly.

"Haunted, I tell you!" The cashier slammed a weathered fist on the countertop. "You can't just leave cursed silverware in a hardware store! You saw it, now you need to let it steal your soul!"

"Sir, I don't think the fork's cursed. It's stainless steel."

The cashier gasped dramatically. "That's what it wants you to think!"

"I'll make you a deal," Dolf offered. "If you can cash me out right now, I'll go back there and retrieve the fork myself. After the damage I did to Miss Maggie's crop, it's the least I can do."

Mollified, the cashier nodded in agreement. He rang up the large stack of fertilizer, cast suspicious eyes at Dolf, and said, "I don't know if

I believe you. You don't look like the type Miss Maggie would associate her sweet self with." Turning back to the register, the cashier mumbled, "You're fixin' to get yourself added to a watch list somewhere with all that crap, but *I'm* not here to *judge*." He held out a hand for payment, loudly stating, "That'll be $3,852.73. Cash or credit?"

Dolf dutifully handed over a credit card and casually wheeled the cart out of frame once his payment was processed.

"And cut!"

"*What the fuck was that about, old man?*" Gerald's question reverberated off the walls of Stage B.

"It's called fixing your shit script, you pompous twerp. How about saying 'thank you for making it better' instead of crying about a little change?" Bertrand yelled back.

Gerald looked ready to explode, his face an unnatural shade of purple. Owen was confident he could fry an egg on his forehead from the amount of steam coming out of his ears. But Dax—Dax was doubled over laughing. Between mouthfuls of trail mix, he waved his hand. "Keep it! Keep the fork! It's art!"

And just like that, the haunted fork scene became part of *Metal Love Beans*.

Despite the madness, Owen begrudgingly agreed that the haunted fork elevated the scene. That spindly fruitcake was right.

His little improv session let them shoot the scene in one take, which was the silver lining. Owen sauntered over to his friends to escort them from the building. On his way out, he searched for Adelen again, only to find that she'd found him first, her face alight with laughter. Waggling his eyebrows at her suggestively, he waved goodbye, silently promising to see her later.

He still had prep to finish for *Silver Shadow* before Thursday and had some extra time before Adelen finished work. Work didn't stop just because his heart had decided to.

Back in his dressing room, he opened his laptop and pulled up the security brief, forcing himself into professional mode.

If anything weird was happening around the set...

If anything touched her...He'd be ready.

Because protecting people? That part came naturally.

CHAPTER 34

Owen

Despite all the chaos on set—the long days, the complicated feelings, and the nuance of his budding relationship with Adelen—Owen still had a day job to juggle.

Neuronix didn't exactly stop running just because he'd decided to chase his dream of being a wannabe movie star whose first role is playing a rock star with limited emotional depth and lackluster motorcycle coordination.

Between filming days, he still checked in with Levi and Isaac, managed a few remote security reviews, and prepped for one meeting in particular—the upcoming consultation with their newly contracted ethical hacker, the *Silver Shadow*.

Levi had been digging deeper into this guy's background and professional successes. It was on the verge of being obsessive, and he'd been hyping the guy up for weeks. "He's one of the best in the world. Does deep-dive threat analysis, breaks into systems to test resilience. Thinks like a criminal but works like a saint."

When Thursday morning finally arrived, Owen sat in the Executive Conference Room down the hall from Levi's office, expecting some reclusive tech genius who lived on energy drinks and wore sunglasses indoors.

What he got instead was...cool.

Like, unreasonably cool.

So cool that Owen was confident that he was developing a man-crush. Which could potentially be a problem if he couldn't maintain any level of professionalism.

Try as he did to be professional, Owen couldn't help himself. The meeting was supposed to be an hour. It lasted almost three.

The *Silver Shadow* walked in with raven-black hair, cropped close on the sides and longer on top. A smattering of piercings lined his earlobes—and if Owen's eyes weren't deceiving him, one on his tongue. A feral sort of confidence lived in his silver gray eyes that said he'd seen everything twice.

That must be where his moniker came from.

Though he was dressed professionally in business casual attire, his shirt sleeves did little to hide the intricate tattoos that began at his fingertips and climbed up his neck in clean, deliberate lines. His handshake was firm, his smile sharp.

"Do you have a name you like to go by, or are you as cool as I think you are and prefer *Shadow*?" Owen knew he sounded ridiculous, but he had to ask.

The man smiled, revealing what Owen had accurately assumed to be a tongue piercing. "You can call me Lou."

"That's a bit anticlimactic, Lou," Owen said dejectedly as Lou laughed. They went around the room making introductions before getting down to business.

He caught Isaac's slight headshake of embarrassment and the look he gave Levi, out of the corner of his eye.

Within minutes, Owen decided the man was *fascinating*. He looked oddly familiar, like he'd met him before, but couldn't place where. Didn't matter, he decided. They were going to be best friends.

"Most people hire me when it's already too late," Lou said, scrolling through Neuronix's data security map with the kind of focus that made everyone else in the room nervous. "You did the right thing bringing me in, though the best time was before the breach happened." Owen winced. "There's a lot to fix, but nothing's unfixable."

He talked about vulnerabilities as if they were discussing an art form, his descriptions and explanations clean, methodical, and precise. Owen couldn't help but admire that kind of confidence.

"Dude," Owen wistfully said at one point, leaning back in his chair, "you're like...a hacker superhero. Minus the cape. Or maybe the cape's just invisible."

"Owen, please don't hit on Lou, it's weird...for all of us," Isaac pleaded.

Lou's mouth twitched in amusement. "Trust me, no cape. It's excess baggage when I'm sneaking through the shadows at night."

And just like that, they clicked. Those three hours had passed by effortlessly, as if their tight-knit trio had taken on a fourth member. He almost forgot that Lou was a paid contractor.

At some point, Levi and Isaac had excused themselves, both having other meetings scheduled for the afternoon. Owen and Lou ended up staying a little longer after the meeting, trading stories and half-serious jokes about the weirdest things they'd seen in tech security.

Owen learned that Lou had a dry sense of humor and an obsession with motorcycles.

"You ride?" Lou asked when Owen shared that it had been months since his last ride.

Owen grinned. "Own three. It's an old Triumph Bonneville. You?"

"Two," Lou said, his eyes lighting up for the first time. "Built one from scratch last year."

If he had to pick a moment in time when their bromance began, that was it.

"You're kidding," Owen said excitedly. "I have a storage space only minutes away from here. Next time you're in town, we'll ride."

Lou smirked. "You sure you can keep up?"

"Oh, I will keep up. I'll race you to prove it."

"Then it's a date."

They shook on it—two men who couldn't possibly know the irony of what that handshake would mean later.

Once Lou packed up his laptop and other belongings, Owen escorted him to the main entrance, where a car waited to take him back to the airport. Sadly, this consultation was only a brief one-day drop-in event. The next time he was in town would be for an extended stay.

While Owen was unknowingly bonding with Adelen's brother, planning future motorcycle rides, and nerding out about firewalls, he still couldn't stop thinking about her.

He didn't realize that the man he had just hired and scheduled a bro date with was the one person in the world who could ruin his chances with her faster than any bad love note ever could.

By the time Owen got back to set later that afternoon, the easy camaraderie of the morning had faded beneath the familiar hum of production chaos.

He didn't know someone else had been watching that same set with a very different kind of interest.

CHAPTER 35

Unknown

They'd gotten comfortable. *Too* comfortable.

From behind the row of lighting rigs, the same routine unfolded every morning: Owen arriving first, Adelen trailing a few minutes later with her clipboard, tablet, and that smug air of observance she wore like armor.

They didn't touch. They didn't flirt.

But they didn't need to.

It was in the small things.

The way Owen looked for her before every take.

The way Adelen tilted her head slightly when she was listening. Not with her ears, but with that freakish, mechanical focus of hers.

The way his smile softened whenever she was near.

Everyone else might've missed it, but they didn't.

On set, she'd crouch near the monitors, checking audio levels while Owen stood just off camera. He'd lean down to ask something stupid, whisper in her ear, brush tendrils of hair away from her face. Always some pathetic excuse to touch her...

Every day, she lingered a little longer, unable to hide the flash of heat and longing from her face.

Finding a reason to check his mic or adjust levels. Pretending it was about work.

Those moments repeated in their mind again and again every time she walked away, every movement measured and self-important.

Everyone saw her as the miracle sound engineer. But they knew what she really was—manipulative and calculating.

She'd made herself indispensable.

Wrapped herself into every part of his routine.

No one ever asked what she'd done to get there—what she'd done to deserve it.

She was taking what wasn't hers.

It was time someone reminded her of her place.

That night, long after the crew wrapped, they kept to the shadows watching as Adelen locked up the sound equipment. She lingered, checking her notes, humming softly under her breath.

A sickening smile slithered across their face.

Every pattern could be learned.

Every habit could be exploited.

And soon, she'd learn that some things weren't hers to take.

CHAPTER 36

Adelen

For the first time in months, Adelen felt good about herself, light.

She'd begun to smile again, without forcing it. And she'd somehow found Owen...or rather Owen had found her. It had been a relatively short amount of time, but perhaps they found each other. Two lost souls that found the missing part of themselves in each other.

She and Owen weren't perfect by any stretch of the imagination, but what they built so far lifted the constant heaviness she felt bearing down on her. She'd even caught herself humming on the way home, something she hadn't done since before she had taken this position in Joia City.

This made the uptick in anonymous messages and mysterious happenings at work all the worse. Just when things were looking up, when she was feeling good about herself and the future, an impenetrable wall emerged in her path. As if a malevolent being was working to ensure her misery.

Does someone have an Adelen voodoo doll? She couldn't think of any other explanation as she strolled across the parking garage and up the stairs to her floor.

But the second she opened her apartment door, the rug was pulled out from underneath her feet again, giving credence to her cursed thoughts.

Her keys slipped from her hand and hit the floor with a sharp clang.

Something was *wrong*. The entire space felt wrong, the walls beginning to close in on her, trapping her in a pit of fear.

The lights were off when they were tied to a motion sensor, designed to turn on when the door opened. She didn't need to flip the switch to *feel* the wrongness. It was the faint shift of air, the open living room window she had left shut, the scent of something sickly sweet she couldn't quite place. Her heartbeat thundered in her ears.

She cautiously stepped farther in, her eyes darting across the space. A shattered, unused coffee mug lay in pieces on the kitchen floor. The living room rug was slightly off-center, as if someone tripped over it. Pillows ripped open, the stuffing strewn about as if its assailant had been enraged. And on the ottoman table, lying perfectly aligned with the edge, was a single flower, its message frighteningly clear.

A black dahlia.

Her phone buzzed.

She snatched it up, hands trembling.

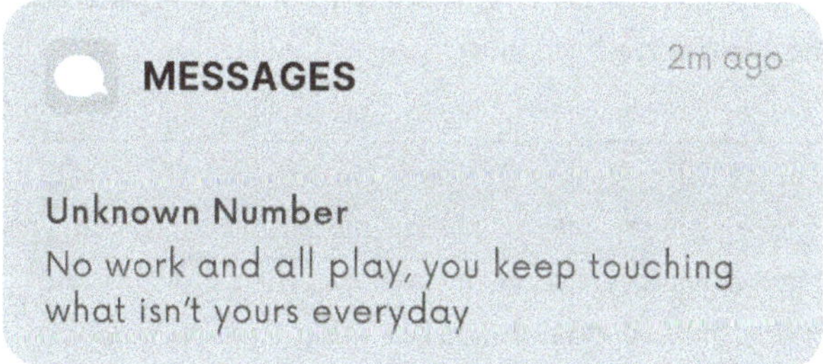

The phone shook as she opened the attachment—a photo of her checking Owen's mic, head bent and mid-laugh.

Her knees gave out before she realized she was falling. She hit the floor hard, the crunch of bone against the tile echoing in her skull. Scooting back, Adelen curled against the door as if she could hold herself together by force.

Silent tears came fast, a violent stream rushing down her cheeks.

Every ounce of joy and excitement she was just celebrating, the small amount of peace she'd managed to claw back disintegrated in seconds.

She stayed coiled against the door for most of the night, bathing in the never-ending stream of tears, wondering how she could possibly climb out of this abyss without endangering any of the people she had come to care about so deeply.

Only when the faint rays of dawn slipped through the living room blinds did she realize how fucked she was. There was no way she would be able to sleep now—morning had already arrived.

Throughout the night, she had debated telling someone, going so far as to type out messages only to delete them as a fresh cycle of tears began.

So she told no one.

Not Owen. Not Aurelia. Not even Diogo, who knew everything about her. She had never kept a secret this big from him. She couldn't.

But as the dawn filled the sky, and the sunlight grew brighter, so did her resolve. She needed to stop crying and rally.

Adelen wouldn't go down without a fight, but until she knew her opponent, she'd have to lie low.

The next few days didn't settle. If anything, the air around her grew more constrictive, pulled tight, as if waiting to snap. Each day was the same and she moved through it like a zombie. Figuring out who was behind this was her new obsession.

Even though she had begun to pull back from everyone, little things continued to happen over the next week anyway.

She made sure to change the locks on her door *again*, yet she found it slightly ajar one evening. She *knew* she'd locked it. There were only so many excuses she could come up with for needing a new lock before building management would start to get suspicious.

None of it made sense. She racked her brain, trying to piece the puzzle together, but kept coming up short, knowing a critical clue was missing, mentally running through the list of everything she *did* know. Yet there was no glaringly obvious missing piece.

Installing cameras around her apartment did nothing; the WiFi kept going down, rendering them useless. She'd changed the locks multiple times, only for the perpetrator to get in anyway. After speaking to Richard at the security desk, he had nothing on his surveillance footage that captured any clues about who was accessing her apartment, either.

Adelen felt hunted by a phantom.

Then the little things escalated into bigger things.

A package arrived at work with no sender information—inside were a pair of broken earbuds, and one of the original missing cables was shredded. Another piece of her equipment had gone missing despite restricted access to her space.

And nothing was caught on security footage.

Every time she started to relax, something else chipped away at her sanity.

Sleep became impossible. Every shadow stretched too long; every sound felt wrong. The exhaustion was taking a severe toll, and her paranoia was growing.

She had started showing up to work early and leaving earlier, always making sure someone else was nearby when she walked to the parking lot, editing at home and away from everyone when she could.

Crew members began to walk on eggshells as her temper and patience had grown noticeably short. She forced herself to speak only when necessary, avoiding eye contact with everyone, including Kaia and Lizzie. Kaia was growing increasingly suspicious and aggravated and had tried to corner her in a supply closet one afternoon, but her efforts were interrupted by Cary, who was on another rampage.

Her days became a perpetual blur of work notes, sound checks, and equipment status reviews. Nothing personal remained; the career she loved so much was reduced to administrative shit.

But she hadn't prepared for the crushing agony every time she saw Owen's name appear on her phone, and she forced herself to mute the notification or reply with some half-assed excuse.

Or how every time he walked into the room, she straightened her posture, kept her eyes down, and pretended she didn't notice how his smile faltered.

It was a slow death by tiny papercuts, each slice growing a little bigger and never knitting itself back together. It killed a piece of her each day, but it was safer this way.

Owen couldn't be pulled into this. He didn't deserve it.

Whoever was watching her had made that much clear.

So she slowly built the walls back up—brick by brick, lie by lie—and tried not to flinch every time he looked at her like she was breaking his heart.

Because Adelen *knew* she was, and was demolishing her own in the process.

She was doing a shit job of hiding her exhaustion. She became an empty husk of a human being, unable to concentrate on even the most basic of tasks at work.

Then she fucked up.

One afternoon, Adelen had holed up in the sound room to finish editing the files for a handful of final scenes. But when she tried to open one of the more intimate scenes from the network shared drive—one between Owen and Henrietta she'd been avoiding—it was corrupted.

Usually, they could film one of these movies in a matter of weeks. But that scene had taken a couple of days to film because of what she assumed to be Henrietta once again overstepping Owen's boundaries...except she couldn't be sure since she hadn't answered any of Owen's calls. A deep sense of foreboding settled into her stomach.

She opened another file and found it was scrambled. Another folder where work she had already completed should have been was empty.

Panic had begun to set in. Files missing, others scrambled. All her work *gone.*

If that hadn't been bad enough, Cary had chosen that moment to storm into the studio, demanding to know when the Pinto Hills Bean Festival file was going to be finished. She tried to explain what she'd discovered, to finally tell someone what had been happening to her on set, but the look on his face made it clear he'd already formed his opinion—and it wasn't in her favor.

He looked at her with disgust, as if reconsidering ever trusting her to handle this department on her own. "Maybe if you spent less time making eyes at our leading man, this wouldn't have happened," Cary barked, his voice sharp enough to cut.

The words were a slap in the face, the anger and humiliation burning deep.

Adelen almost broke down right then and there, coming dangerously close to throwing a monitor from the overwhelming need to destroy something. Like the way someone was destroying her life.

When Owen stopped by her office later, worry etched across his face, one look at him had her casting her eyes downward in shame. After watching some of the video footage, it was obvious that Rita was piling on extra makeup to cover the dark circles under his eyes and contouring to hide the weight he had lost.

"Hey, stranger, do you have a few minutes to talk?" he asked, his forced nonchalance and strained smile giving away his true feelings. Hands in the pockets of his leather pants, Owen leaned a shoulder against the open doorway, still in his wardrobe. He likely came searching for her the second he was done for the day.

"I can't, I have to finish these edits as soon as possible. I—I'm just a little busy right now."

"You mean busy avoiding me? Like you've been for over a week now?" The words were soft and unguarded. Yelling at her would've been preferable.

Sucking in a sharp breath, she made the mistake of peering up at him. His lips had settled into a grim line, his eyes dull and almost lifeless. It gutted her to know this was her fault.

But she stuck to the same playbook of excuses, playing the greatest hits on repeat: *I'm busy. I have a deadline. It's just work stress.*

He merely nodded, undoubtedly seeing right through her, but still giving her the space she needed to work through her problems. Fulfilling his promise to respect her boundaries, as they discussed on their first date. Except she found herself *wanting* him to push, to shake her until she spilled the beans about what she was going through.

The irony wasn't lost on her. She got what she asked for, right?

No, she hadn't asked for *this*.

Each lie carved a little more space between them, and Owen, the collateral damage, who hadn't done anything wrong aside from falling for the wrong girl.

Every text he sent—every painfully sweet, persistent attempt to see her or to check in on her—tightened the knot of fear in her stomach and widened the chasm that had formed between them. Even the simple memes that let her know he was thinking about her made the pit grow deeper.

If she stayed close, he'd be next.

If she pushed him away, maybe she could buy time to protect *him*. Owen gave so much of himself to protect others and deserved nothing less in return.

So she continued to ignore his calls. Left his messages unread. Pretended she didn't see him waiting outside the studio one night, bouquet in hand, looking lost and confused and making herself leave through a different exit so she didn't have to face him. Face what she was doing.

That night, Adelen went home and cried until her throat was sore.

It wasn't just his calls and messages that went ignored, but also those from Ivy, Aurelia, Grace, Kaia...even Diogo. Because this was what survival looked like now, though deep down, she wasn't sure she could keep it up much longer.

At some point, she had fallen asleep from sheer exhaustion. By morning, she'd managed to convince herself that the way she was feeling was nothing—nothing worth naming at least—just something she needed to endure for a little while longer.

Across Joia City, however, Owen had realized it wasn't nothing. For every piece of herself that she willingly sacrificed, a matching piece of Owen died with it.

CHAPTER 37

Owen

Owen couldn't remember the last time Adelen had laughed at one of his jokes. Hell, he couldn't remember the last time she acknowledged his existence. The days blurred together and stretched to infinity.

At first, he thought she was just tired from all of the chaos on set. Everyone was running on fumes as the production schedule had been brutal lately.

She had two new team members who needed to be trained while simultaneously doing their job. It hadn't helped that the audacious one named Kaia had made a mortal enemy of Henrietta. The initial screaming match between the two of them had swiftly become legendary. A headache threatened merely from the memory of it.

There was a series of equipment issues that plagued her team as well. The information was secondhand, of course, since he hadn't had a full conversation with her in god knows how long now, but Tessa and Rita had filled him in here and there.

Despite all that, it was the way she carried herself lately. The exhaustion. The jumpiness and how easily startled she'd become. And her silent retreat inward.

It became clear pretty quickly that it was more than just work stress. But he promised to respect her boundaries, so he wouldn't push her to talk if she wasn't ready. Agreeing to that may have been one of the stupidest things he'd ever done—and the list was *long*.

And so the distance between them started to stretch. It stretched until they were virtually strangers again. Not only did he not recognize who Adelen had become, but he didn't recognize himself either.

And now, Adelen only talked to him when she had to.

It had turned cold and impersonal. Just the variations of the same phrases:

"Mic check."

"Your battery pack's fine."

"Scene starts in five."

It felt exactly like the beginning all over again, where she again barely tolerated his existence, but this time it hurt a hell of a lot more.

He replayed every interaction in his head, trying to pinpoint the exact moment he'd screwed up. Had he said something insensitive? Pushed too hard? Not enough? Made another inappropriate joke?

He didn't know what he'd done wrong. What he could do to fix it. Or how to convince her to talk to him, to just look at him and see that he was still here. Because not knowing was killing him.

How could he try to fix things if he didn't know what he did wrong? She was so disgusted with him that she wouldn't even look at him, eyes always downcast or focused on something else. Staring through him like he was invisible.

And, of course, the worse he felt, the worse his acting got.

Dax naturally loved it, calling it "tortured realism."

Owen called it capturing his flailing love life and subsequent downward spiral on camera.

By the end of the week, he couldn't take it anymore.

He found himself standing outside Isaac and Grace's house one night, despite having a key, clutching a six-pack like it was a peace offering. He didn't remember texting them—just that Isaac had responded with, "This better not be about your hair extensions again," which was a fair statement. He *had* tormented Isaac with a tirade about them the first day Rita installed them.

When Grace opened the door and saw the condition he was in, her expression faltered. "Oh no. You've got the sad eyes. Come in."

Inside, Isaac was lounging on the couch, looking annoyingly smug, but, like Grace, his face turned serious as he really looked at Owen. Ivy was plopped on the couch, eating popcorn, attention zeroed in on whatever movie they were watching.

Owen groaned, realizing he had miscalculated the Ivy factor. "Did I accidentally book a panel of critics?"

"Too bad," Ivy said through a mouth full of popcorn, eyes glinting. "You're my entertainment."

Usually, remarks like these didn't bother him, often letting them roll off his back or outright ignoring them. Not this time.

In a voice his friends had never heard him use, Owen said, "I've spent a good chunk of my time on earth being the comic relief. But my life is falling apart, and I'm not fucking laughing. So if you're not interested in actually being a friend when I need one, then say so."

His voice wavered towards the end, an appropriate metaphor for how his heart was faring. Shoulders slumping, the pack of beer in his hand suddenly felt like a sack of rocks dragging him down.

Ivy shot up into a sitting position, upending her bowl of popcorn in the process, eyes wide with concern. "Oh my god, Owen! What happened?"

He dropped onto the couch unbothered by the popcorn everywhere, rubbing the back of his neck, trying to stop the sting of tears already beginning to form. Fucking hell, he *never* cried.

Clearing his throat, he finally asked, "Okay, so hypothetically—if someone you were close to and had *potentially* fallen madly in love with suddenly started acting cold and distant, what would you do?"

Isaac didn't even hesitate. "Apologize."

"But what if I didn't do anything?"

"Are you sure you didn't?" Isaac asked, a skeptical eyebrow raised high. "You're a walking disaster of charm and insecurity. More often than not, you can't read a room to save your life. Odds are good you said something dumb and didn't notice."

Grace glared at her husband and smacked him upside the head. "Isaac, can you for once stop shitting on Owen? You can go back to using him as your personal punching bag tomorrow, but right now, *you're* the one who can't read the room."

Isaac had the decency to wince—not at the pain his wife inflicted, but her admonishment. He massaged the back of his neck and shot Owen an apologetic look.

Grace turned back to Owen and gently suggested, "Maybe she's going through something, and it's not about you."

"I thought about that," Owen admitted. "But she won't talk to me. *At all.* She won't look at me or acknowledge my existence. She's shutting me out—just like when I first met her."

Ivy shrugged her shoulders helplessly. "I haven't spoken to her much lately, so I don't know. Maybe she's just over you."

The glare he directed at Ivy had her reconsidering exactly how bad things were between him and Adelen. "Helpful as always," Owen ground out.

Isaac leaned back, studying him with a thoughtful frown that Owen usually hated.

Now he understood how Adelen had felt about his jokes in the beginning, because if Isaac made a joke right now, one of his best friends was going to end up with a broken jaw.

"Remember when Levi thought Aurelia hated him?"

Owen impatiently bounced a knee. "Yeah."

"Turns out there was another person involved, and you're the only one who figured it out," Isaac mused. "She didn't hate him, but there were other factors in play that we weren't aware of. You sure this isn't the same thing? Something more than meets the eye?"

Owen hesitated, tossing the idea around in his head. It was a possibility he hadn't considered. "Like what?"

Isaac shrugged, his analytical mind at work. "You tell me. Anything weird lately? Any behavior that doesn't add up?"

He thought about it, replaying every conversation and situation again, but through a different lens. This time, he removed the emotion and evaluated it with an objective inner eye. The instinct that made him so good at his job.

The late nights Adelen spent alone in the sound booth...and left earlier than usual.

The way she flinched when someone approached from behind.

She gave her phone a guarded look whenever a message came through.

Fucking hell.

"Actually, yeah. There have been a few things," he murmured, dragging a hand over his face.

"Then maybe stop assuming it's about you," Grace said softly. "And start paying more attention to her."

The possibility that it had nothing to do with him was a momentary relief, because that meant there was someone else in the picture. It had the same bad vibes as Aurelia's horrifying incident. He ardently prayed that he was wrong.

This was exactly what he needed, the support of his friends helping to ease some of his anxiety. Owen had stayed a while, of course agreeing to dinner (Grace's cooking was the *best*), but that night, he barely slept.

He kept hearing Isaac's question: *Anything that doesn't add up?*

And Grace's suggestion: *Start paying more attention to her.*

By morning, he decided to do something he never thought he'd ever do—visit Levi and Aurelia's matchmaker, Estrella Vale.

Estrella had been waiting for him, opening the front door before he had a chance to knock. "Come in, come in," she said, ushering him through the front sitting room and into the kitchen.

It smelled like freshly baked apple pie, vanilla ice cream, and secrets. Candles burned at odd intervals, and the air shimmered faintly in the corners like it was alive. He sat down at a large wooden farmer's table facing the backyard windows, the various plants and flowers beyond it reminding him of his mother's garden beds at the house.

His heart squeezed.

"You've been carrying too much on your back, Owen," Estrella said, frowning as she poured him a cup of fresh coffee. Moments later, a hearty slice of delicious-looking homemade apple danish slid next to it.

"Why do you always say such creepy stuff?" Owen sighed heavily, digging into the pastry. He wasn't raised to be a rude guest. And holy balls did it taste amazing. He inhaled it within seconds, before Estrella had a chance to join him at the table.

"You came here for answers, not comfort." She said, slipping into the seat across from him and smiling behind her cup of tea.

Owen leveled a dubious glance at her, flitting a finger between them. "I take it this is what you meant by the whole 'You'll know when the time comes' thing you said to me at the wedding?"

"You tell me," she snorted, settling back and taking another long sip, patiently waiting for Owen to reveal the reason for the visit.

Estrella's foretelling of this moment didn't sit well with him, nor did it diminish his suspicions about her, but he needed advice. He wished there weren't such slim pickings, though he had the distinct feeling she wouldn't lead him astray.

He set his fork down on the plate, restless. "I think I messed something up with Adelen. She's been distant—cold and reclusive—and I don't know why. Everyone says maybe it's not about me, and objectively I could agree with that...but I can't help feeling like it's my fault anyway."

Estrella tilted her head, eyes glinting in that unsettling way that made him think she could read his mind.

"You've always wanted to protect the people you care about," she stated. "But sometimes, that protection blinds you to what they're protecting *you* from."

Protecting him?

He blinked. "Okay, see, this is exactly why people think you're a witch."

Her knowing smile didn't fade. "Maybe she's fighting a battle you can't see."

He frowned, trying to dissect her riddles. "You're saying she's in trouble?"

"I'm saying," Estrella replied gently, "you might need to stop seeing her as something to save, and start seeing her as someone who's surviving."

The epiphany of truth struck him soundly in the gut. Such few words, but a profound impact. For all his security experience, the one thing he was supposed to be an expert in, he'd blatantly missed the signs that had been there all along. The most obvious clues had been staring right in his face this entire time.

God, he really was a fool.

Re-energized by the conversation—and the third-party perspective—Owen had hastily thanked the strange woman for her insight and ran out the door.

Later, on the drive to set, Owen couldn't stop thinking about his conversation with Estrella.

"Protection blinds you to what they're protecting you *from."*

The Adelen he'd come to cherish was a fighter, not a coward. What could she possibly be trying to protect him from?

He began a mental deep dive into every incident from the past month, treating it like a security audit rather than a heartbreak. If he was going to figure this out, then he needed to stop moping. Things started to fall into place the moment he flipped the switch on his emotions.

What he hadn't factored in were the whispered rumors around the set or the little pieces of information shared with him from Tessa and Rita. Far more had happened than the behavior he'd directly witnessed, but he'd been so compulsively focused on Adelen that his mind hadn't logged any of that data correctly. Now the keys to unraveling this mystery were slipping into the right locks, the whole picture coming together.

The tampered audio files. Cary had made several comments about it to other crew members during a break session. Tessa had been shocked, and Henrietta pleased. Even Bertrand had been bothered by the news, going so far as to tell Cary to "Shut his gossiping pie hole and be a better boss." Cary had stalked away, fuming about the old coot's reprimand. Owen wasn't sure where Adelen stood with fixing the files.

The missing equipment that had yet to be found. The optics around delayed production weren't great, nor was the added cost to overnight replacements. He'd heard comments about Adelen not being cut out to lead the new division.

The way her face paled when she received that mystery package. Rita had witnessed her reaction, but Adelen had spun on her heel and disappeared into her office with it. She hadn't been able to catch a glimpse of the contents, and Adelen was evasive when she inquired further.

How she froze whenever her boss raised his voice—or when someone walked behind her. He'd noticed the subtle behavior on more than one occasion. So had Kaia, if he was interpreting the openly suspicious glances she shot Adelen's way each time it happened.

Owen had brushed it all off before, thinking it was stress, bad luck, or just another rough production cycle. Her boss was definitely an asshole; Owen had debated taking him out back for a couple of rounds a few times, but otherwise chalked her newfound jumpiness up to that.

But now...now it didn't seem random at all.

There was a very clear pattern.

And if there was one thing Owen Voss knew how to do, it was follow a pattern.

That familiar focus and determination to investigate a problem blanketed his senses. He was all in, whether Adelen wanted it or not.

Even if it meant blasting a hole in every wall she'd built to keep him out.

CHAPTER 38

Adelen

Adelen hadn't slept in two nights.

She was petrified to sleep without wearing her processors, afraid she wouldn't be able to hear an intruder. At a time when the lack of alertness could literally mean the difference between her life and death. But wearing them came with a price.

Every noise in her apartment had sounded like a threat. Every shadow that moved made her heart jump into her throat.

Adelen was going through the motions, not remembering getting out of bed that morning, or the drive to work, or if she had bothered to eat breakfast...or was it lunchtime now?

Last night she'd spent an hour staring at job postings for companies in different cities, different countries, anywhere else—when she finally shut her laptop and tried to sleep, but she continued to entertain the idea.

Maybe she could just...*leave*. Pack up and start over again somewhere else. Simply disappear before all this swallowed her whole. Or worse.

The thought stayed with her well into the night and was still with her as she walked down the corridor toward her sound studio, the familiar hum of fluorescent lights and the faint echo of voices grounding her just enough to keep moving, but leaving her oblivious to her surroundings.

When she reached for the doorknob, metal met skin and then—*pain*.

Adelen cried out as a sharp, violent snap of static electricity snapped through her hand, racing up her arm and into the processors that hooked over her ears. It was similar to the twinge she'd get after stepping out of a warm car interior and shutting the door in the dead of winter...but *more*.

There was a pop that sounded a lot like feedback through a speaker, and then nothing. Her ears filled with warbling distortion, a flicker of sound that collapsed in on itself until everything went quiet.

Her heart dropped into her stomach.

She tore the processors off her ears, the magnet coils snapping free from her scalp, and stared at them in disbelief, like they might explain what the fuck had just happened. The tiny status light that should've glowed steadily was erratic—flickering like it couldn't hold a connection.

When she tried to reset the coil and power it back on, nothing.

"Come on," she whispered, fumbling through the settings, her fingers shaking so badly she kept missing the buttons. "Please...not like this..."

But her efforts were in vain.

The silence was absolute.

Her chest tightened. She sank against the wall, clutching the useless equipment in one trembling hand as the first sob broke loose. It wasn't about the damaged equipment—she didn't need them. It was deliberateness behind it that struck her, the intentionality...*the malice*. Coupled with the months of tension and questioning *everything*, whoever was behind all this had finally won.

"Adelen!"

She didn't hear him, but she saw the blur of motion in her peripheral vision after Owen burst into her office, his expression changing from confusion to alarm as he saw her leaning against the wall for support. He must've heard her shout.

He gripped her shoulders, giving her body a cursory scan before worried eyes met hers, asking her if she was alright. She couldn't hear him but had focused on his lips instead. But Adelen was still in shock, mired in a bog of fear and disbelief.

When she didn't respond to his question, his brow furrowed—and when he noticed what was clutched in her hand. He reached out, hesitated, then gently tucked a lock that escaped from her ponytail behind her ear. She looked up at him, tears streaming down her face, trying to form the words.

"I—" she started, voice breaking. "I got a huge static shock. It—it's not working. I don't know how this happened—" Her hand moved to her ear in frustration. "I can't hear you. I can't hear anything."

The panic returned in full force. She didn't even try to hide it this time. "I don't have a local audiologist yet. I—I can't—"

Her words dissolved into silent sobs.

Owen didn't think. He just moved, gathering her against him, pulling her close until her forehead rested against his chest. She was shaking so hard it felt like her bones might splinter.

He tipped her chin up and pressed his forehead to hers. Her eyes fell to his lips.

"I'm going to fix this. Right now. You don't have to worry about anything, okay? Just breathe."

Her hands fisted in his shirt, her breath uneven against his mouth.

He wanted to promise her the world. Wanted to murder whoever dared to hurt her, but taking care of her first was the priority. There was plenty of time to hunt them down later. For now, he just held her tighter.

Slowly, her breathing began to slow and match his. The trembling eased, her body softening against him. She looked up, eyes red and wet, searching his face for something—anything—to hold onto.

He smiled faintly, brushing her tears away with his thumbs. "You're not alone, okay?" he murmured, still knowing she couldn't hear him. "Not anymore."

Owen leaned in, resting his chin on her head, and stealing a moment to breathe her in. When he pulled back, her eyes had softened, though the confusion and fear still lingered there.

Reluctantly letting her go, he guided her gently into the chair behind her desk.

"Stay here," he said, voice calm but firm, staring down at the storm clouds swirling in her eyes. "I'm making some calls."

She nodded faintly, still clutching the processors in her hand, hoping they might still come back to life.

Owen brushed one last strand of hair from her face, then stepped aside and around her desk as he pulled out his phone. His tone, when he spoke into it, was steady, cold, and professional.

"Yeah," he said to the person on the other line, jaw tight. "I need Dr. Fleisch. *Now.* Reschedule his appointments for the day. I don't care how much it costs—pay whatever the price is as long as he's here within the hour." He paused, listening to the receptionist on the other end, before growling, *"Put him on the phone now."*

Owen, the charming actor and clown, was gone.

CHAPTER 39

Owen

Owen had been reading everything he could find about cochlear implants.

He'd gone down the rabbit hole weeks ago, watching tutorials, scanning medical journals, even sitting through two online webinars about hearing loss. He'd been on the hunt for a private tutor so he could learn sign language too. But he had been blown away about just how little he knew about it—about the Deaf community in general.

Understanding every part of her world was critical, not as a means to impress her, but because she deserved someone who paid attention. Part of that included having the right support on hand in case of an emergency. For situations exactly like this.

His first meeting with Dr. Fleisch, the best audiologist in Joia City, occurred when he'd shown up for an appointment under the pretense of "research for a role," but ended up spending two hours asking about everything from sound mapping to environmental interference. The man had probably thought he was insane, but Owen hadn't given a shit, leaving that appointment with a confirmation that if Adelen ever needed anything, Dr. Fleisch was the man to call.

Now he was cashing in on that promise.

Owen stepped into the hall, phone still pressed to his ear. His voice came out low and controlled, the way it always did when he switched into problem-solving mode.

“Dr. Fleisch, it’s Owen Voss.”

There was a pause on the other end. “Mr. Voss, this is unexpected—”

“I need you onsite at the POLmArK production studio,” Owen said, pacing as his heart hammered in his chest. “Right now. It’s an emergency. One of the sound engineer’s processors shorted out from a static shock. She can’t hear, and she’s—she’s scared out of her mind.”

“Scaring the wits out of my receptionist was not part of our agreement—”

“Name your price,” Owen cut in. Very rarely did he use his wealth and status like this. It normally made him uncomfortable, but today it was just a tool at his disposal. “Whatever it takes to get you here today. I’ll cover the transport, your time, your equipment, everything. I’ll have a car outside your office in fifteen minutes.”

There was another pause. Then, finally, a resigned sigh. “You realize this isn’t standard procedure.”

“*Obviously*, but I don’t care,” Owen growled. “Bring whatever you need to reprogram them.” He didn’t wait for the doctor to protest again and ended the call.

He needed a car. He texted Ivy.

Then he strode back into Adelen’s office. The despair lingering in her eyes had nearly sent him to his knees. But he kept it together. This wasn’t the time to fall apart, not when she needed someone to lean on for support.

“Someone’s on the way to reprogram them. He’s bringing all the equipment he needs. I’ve got you. I promise.”

A soft, choked noise escaped her. He didn’t even have time to react before she leaped out of the chair and threw her arms around his neck. The force of it nearly knocked him backward.

IVY B. Details

Message
(Today) AM 9:22

URGENT!!! Need the car service sent to 5538 Rua Del Mar Street to pick up Dr. Fleisch at his office in 15 minutes. No questions asked. I will tell you about it later, Adelen needs him here ASAP

Oh shit...I'm on it. I hope she's okay, but give her a big smooch for me and tell her the Shrew Crew misses her

I"ll let her know. Thx

Typing...

She was crying again, but this time it was different—relieved. She buried her face against him, her whole body shaking. And then, without warning, she kissed him.

It was desperate and passionate, filled with every emotion and unspoken word that had been bottled up for days. He froze for half a heartbeat before instinct took over. His hands found her waist, then her back, holding her close, grounding her as much as himself.

He'd been kissed plenty of times in his life...but *never* like this, never by someone who brought both chaos and peace all at once.

When she finally pulled back, tears still streaked her cheeks, but a glimmer of hope shone through the storm in her eyes. He trailed his thumb along her jaw.

"Help's on the way," he said steadily. "You're going to be okay."

She nodded and whispered, "Thank you," as the tension in her shoulders eased, a faint smile ghosting across her lips. Owen leaned in and pressed another gentle kiss to her forehead before guiding her back into her chair.

"Stay put," he instructed, playfully tweaking her nose.

She huffed what sounded like a laugh and nodded, still sniffling, still grasping the devices tightly.

Owen stepped back, pulling out his phone again as he forced out a slow breath. For once, the instinct to step in, to take control, wasn't just him overcompensating—it was necessary. His money, his influence, all the things he tried not to define him, finally had a purpose. He wasn't powerless this time. And he wasn't going to waste it.

For the first time all day, things felt steady again, like maybe the universe had finally decided to give her a break.

But he knew that it was only a matter of time before another curveball would be thrown their way.

CHAPTER 40

Adelen

Her uneasiness had not abated by the time the audiologist arrived, but at least she wasn't alone anymore.

Owen had been a blur of calculated efficiency as he coordinated, paid, and made arrangements to help her. In less than an hour, Dr. Fleisch appeared at the door with a small rolling case and the kind of professional focus that said he'd dropped everything to be here.

Adelen sat across from him at her desk, hands folded in her lap, while he unpacked his equipment: a slim laptop, a cable coil, and a programming interface that looked more like something out of a sci-fi lab than a medical device.

He explained the problem as he faced her, the explanation confirming what she already suspected, but the news didn't quell her fear.

"Static discharge likely corrupted your programming, but you'll need a full remap. Might take a few hours, though."

She nodded. It wasn't the worst outcome. Unbelievably inconvenient and very traumatic, yes—but fixable. Everything was fixable, she reminded herself.

She stayed in the chair, trying to be productive on her computer while the doctor worked. Meanwhile, Owen hovered near the door, pacing like a caged storm. Every time Adelen glanced up, his eyes were trained on her. His handsome face was a thundercloud of worry and anger aimed at the universe for daring to touch her.

The intensity of his fury made her chest ache. He shouldn't care this much, not after how she'd been pushing him away. But she was forever grateful that he did, even if she hadn't earned that loyalty.

Dr. Fleisch adjusted the programming coil against her processor, his eyes flicking to the dual monitors on her left.

He paused and leaned further across the desk for a better look, eyebrows rising, attention snapping back to Adelen's face.

"You're...editing?" he asked, half incredulous.

She read his lips easily. "It's not hard to understand the visual audio wave patterns and tell what's off."

He scratched his head, fascinated. "You can read them? The waves?"

Adelen shrugged, self-conscious. "Sort of. I've always been able to visualize it. The spacing, the shape—it's just math. Voices have distinct rhythms, and words have patterns if you look close enough."

He blinked. "That's...remarkable."

She shifted in her seat, cheeks flushing. "It's practical."

"You're seeing frequencies the way most people hear them," he said softly, almost reverently. "That's not practical, that's genius."

The praise made her stomach twist. She'd spent her life trying not to stand out.

But Owen was silent behind him—utterly still—and when she risked a glance, the look on his face wasn't pity.

It was pride.

Hours later, when Dr. Fleisch finished the final mapping and the sound faded back into her world, the first sliver of relief washed over her. The faint hum of the air conditioner and the soft shuffle of Owen's boots on the floor were nearly overwhelming in their normalcy.

The doctor packed up quietly. "Everything's reprogrammed. You should be good to go."

She thanked him, though the words caught in her throat. When he left, the door clicked shut, and the world felt smaller and different.

Owen stood a few feet away, his eyes unreadable.

Before she could overthink it, she crossed the space between them and kissed him again. It wasn't gratitude; it was primal—an electric rush that had nothing to do with malfunctioning tech.

Her hands fisted in his shirt, pulling him closer until she could feel his breath against her cheek. When she eventually pulled back, Owen simply stared at her, eyes wide and bright.

"Thank you," she whispered. "For everything. And I'm sorry. I have so much to say." She smiled through the tears that threatened again.

He reached for her again, his thumb brushing her jaw—

—and the office door slammed open.

"Adelen!"

Cary filled the doorway, red-faced and fuming, his curls askew. "Do you plan on finishing those edits today, or are we rescheduling the entire production because of a little static shock?"

The icy chill of his words crept through her veins, knocking the air out of her.

Owen turned slowly, his expression shifting from disbelief to fury.

"Wow," he said, voice steady and laced with dangerous warning. "That's how you talk to your team?"

Cary blinked, taken aback. "Excuse me?"

"No," Owen said, stepping forward into Cary's personal space, crowding him in the entry. "You don't get to excuse anything. You have an employee who just had a traumatic experience on the job, and your first instinct is to barge in yelling about deadlines? What kind of manager does that?"

Cary's mouth opened, then closed again. He lifted his chin and sneered, "This is none of your concern—"

"It is when you treat people like shit in front of me."

Owen's tone sharpened, like polished steel. "Here's the deal, Cary: you either start treating Adelen with respect, or I walk and take your job, your pathetic excuse for a career with me. *Today*. And when the press asks why, I'll make sure they know exactly how this set operates."

The silence that followed was suffocating.

Cary's jaw tightened, anger ablaze in his russet eyes, cornered by Owen's imposing frame, knowing there was nothing he could say about it. Not without making it worse.

He slithered away from Owen and stormed down the hall, muttering something under his breath that neither of them cared to hear.

Owen exhaled, shoulders dropping.

When he turned back, Adelen was staring at him, still shaken but with something new behind her eyes—something fierce and unguarded.

CHAPTER 41

Unknown

She wasn't supposed to get hurt.

A simple jolt...enough to shake her, to remind her that she wasn't safe no matter how far she ran or tried to hide. They kept just out of sight around the corner; this section of the building was quiet in the morning.

Though seeing her yelp in pain...that had a different allure to it.

And they'd calculated it *perfectly*. The charge was small, the grounding wire precise and perfectly hidden. Just enough voltage to make her flinch, to rattle her.

But then Owen had to show up.

For one glorious second, everything worked exactly as planned. She stood there shaking, clutching her equipment, completely vulnerable. They could almost feel the fear rolling off her in waves.

And then he appeared.

He always found her. The way he touched her, held her...

Owen didn't understand that she had ruined everything.

And yet there he was, wrapping her up in his arms as if she were something precious instead of a problem.

When the doctor arrived, it was an effort not to laugh.

Naturally, Owen would throw money at the situation. That's what men like him did—tried to buy the world into behaving.

She was supposed to understand that every time she let him in, she put both of them in danger.

But no. She went running to him. Again.

Proving that she'd never learn.

She would regret every look, every touch, every moment she thought she was safe in his arms.

Because she'd made her choice. And now, she'd have to live with the consequences.

Or not.

CHAPTER 42

Owen

Morning arrived bright and deceptively bland, as if the universe were pretending nothing ugly had been brewing beneath the surface.

Filming was almost over, thank god.

Only a few remaining scenes, pickup shots, and promo reels stood between Owen and the first full night of sleep he'd had in weeks. One bright spot was learning that despite discovering the corrupted audio, the ensuing panic, and Cary shouting over her shoulder, Adelen had forgotten the one thing that could've saved her sooner—the local backup copies on her laptop. That one extra step meant the production was only delayed by a couple of days.

Owen only knew that last bit of information because he'd mustered up the courage to ask yesterday while Dr. Fleisch worked. Once Adelen was squared away, he hesitantly left her office, giving her some space to herself and time to get back to work.

But he'd stayed late last night anyway, sequestered in his dressing room, using the time to sort through the pile of unanswered work emails. He'd hoped to catch Adelen on her way out of the building, but she'd slipped out with Kaia, Tessa, and a few other crew members after finishing for the day.

At least she hadn't walked through the dark parking lot alone.

Sitting in his inbox was a short, casual message from Lou confirming his arrival for their next in-person meeting the day after tomorrow. He would be in town for several weeks to focus on the Neuronix project. The news lifted a massive weight off his shoulders.

Part of it was professional relief; the security overhaul had been hanging over him for a while. But if he was honest, most of it was personal.

He actually liked the guy—his dry humor, his easy competence, and especially the fact that he didn't treat Owen like an idiot for once. He'd hired many consultants in the past who behaved like that, promptly ensuring they'd never work with Neuronix again.

...And yeah, maybe he was looking forward to having a friend who didn't mind getting greasy working on motorcycles.

The only problem was Adelen.

When the aftermath of the static shock incident settled—and that kiss that had damn near short-circuited him—she'd pulled away again. Not cold, exactly, just... distant.

That invisible wall of polite efficiency was back, and this time it hurt worse because he'd seen what was behind it.

He'd try to spark a simple conversation, to lighten the air between them, and she'd barely look up from her console. Owen had finally recognized it for what it was: fear.

And it was driving him crazy.

He'd give her one more day to collect herself after what happened yesterday, but then he was done waiting. Habitual line stepper Owen would be tagged in for the assist.

"Dude," Isaac said early that morning when he had quickly popped into the office to meet with his interim successor, Martin, "you're vibrating like a live wire." Owen laughed it off, but he knew what Isaac was talking about. He could feel it too—the edge, the restlessness.

Because every time he looked at Adelen, he saw the tension in her shoulders, the way she constantly scanned her surroundings, how she kept one hand on her keycard like it was a weapon.

She jumped at sudden noises.

Always sat facing the door.

Never lingered anywhere alone.

He couldn't unsee it.

Something wasn't right. She had one more day before he took matters into his own hands. He brooded the entire drive to Starhaven following his meeting.

They were shooting the final scenes that day—the porch epilogue, the heartfelt profession of love, the cheerful small-town wrap. If he could just make it through the day without incident, he would soon be rid of Bertrand *and* Henrietta.

Rita was finally done fussing over his hair and makeup in the stylist's trailer, waggling an assertive finger in his face, warning him not to mess it up. He couldn't escape fast enough.

Stepping outside and onto the grassy field, he surveyed the makeshift farm set up. It still amazed him how quickly they were able to put up a barn and two rustic cabins, and to create a realistic legume field. Despite the unexpected costar issues and the emotional damage, he had to admit that he enjoyed this far more than his work at Neuronix.

The company and its mission were extremely important to him, an integral part of his soul—of his identity, but lately...it wasn't as fulfilling as it used to be. He was a storyteller and romantic at heart, preferring comedic theatrics to the pressure of corporate security. Maybe when everything was settled—and after he met with a few of Henrietta's past co-stars—he'd look at investing in the company.

Or starting his own production company.

The idea lingered as he scanned the gathered crew for a certain dark-haired sound engineer. It was a crisp, cloudless, sunny day, the perfect weather for outdoor filming. Every crew member was relaxed, laughing, and ready to be done too. Everyone except Adelen, who looked more agitated than ever. On a regular day, it would be endearing, but today, it set him on edge.

He was about to walk over to Adelen quickly before they began filming, when a figure appeared at his side.

"Hey there," Tessa said warmly. "You ready to get started? I can't believe how fast time has gone by." She looked at him beneath her lashes as she scanned her clipboard.

Small talk was the last thing Owen felt like dealing with, but being unnecessarily rude wasn't his style either. He kept one eye on Adelen throughout the conversation, shooting a glance here and there at Tessa.

"Me either. I always assumed these films took months to shoot and produce, but having been on the inside, it's fascinating how efficient it is."

"It all depends on the cast—their chemistry and behavior determine how smoothly the filming will go. I think this one was our best run yet, thanks to you," she said shyly. "I'm glad that I followed my instinct the first moment I saw you."

Tessa's arm brushed against Owen's, not enough to cause concern, but there was a purposefulness behind it that made him a bit uncomfortable. Subtly adjusting his stance, he put a smidge of distance between them. He didn't want to give her the wrong impression.

"You're giving this amateur far too much credit. This crew is full of talented individuals who come together to make it happen. The cast would be nothing without them." Anyone off the street could be cast in a leading role in a POLmArK film—hell, that's precisely what happened to him—but the film experts like Adelen milling around the field before them were the foundation.

With pursed lips, her gaze cut to his feet, noticing the movement. An awkward silence blanketed them.

They weren't really in the same social circles back in high school, though he was friendly with everyone, and had gotten to know one another a bit better on the job. Tessa was a lovely woman and had been extremely helpful. She was always there whenever Henrietta had a meltdown or was invading Owen's personal space. Whenever he needed pointers or had a question, she was eager to oblige. And he was very appreciative of her willingness to support him while he navigated the nuances of acting.

But he was only now realizing that she may have a teensy bit of a crush on him. More crew members than he cared to acknowledge had become infatuated with him, but aside from Henrietta, no one had gone out of their way to act on it. Just some casual flirting. That's it. Or at least that's what he'd thought.

Owen didn't have a clue what to say. He almost shuddered with relief when Tessa finally broke the silence. Only to immediately regret it.

"Well, I for one am glad you are here," Tessa purred. Her eyes slowly swept over his body from head to toe and back again. "And I hope this won't be the last we see of one another." Giving him a pointed look and a sultry smile, she added, "Scene starts in five."

Well fuck me, Owen thought dejectedly as he watched Tessa saunter away with a deliberate sway of her hips. This was the *last* thing he needed to deal with.

With one last glance at Adelen, he sighed and made his way over to Dax, and the team huddled together outside of Maggie Bean's cottage.

Please let this day be over quickly, he silently prayed.

This had to be one of the *worst* filming days Owen had experienced to date.

Henrietta was in a foul mood, shrieking at anyone and everyone who so much as breathed the wrong way.

Dax, Gerald, and Altina Pastem—the Producer who helped cast him—were fighting amongst themselves in hushed tones for the last few hours. He hadn't seen Altina much since the casting call, but learned that she always showed up when the film project neared the end.

And then there was Bertrand.

Bertrand, who only had *one* scene, surprised everyone when he appeared. In his Hardware Store Guy attire. Owen tried to be optimistic about the reason behind the visit, to give the living relic the benefit of the doubt, but kept coming up short. He refused to dwell on it, though. They had one last major scene left to shoot, and he was determined to do it in one take.

Especially because it required Henrietta to be in very close proximity.

At long last, Dax began barking orders at everyone, instructing them into their positions. Owen dared a glimpse at Adelen as he ambled over to the cottage porch, and was met with a stoic professional awaiting Dax's next instructions. His heart nearly fell out of his chest when her eyes locked on his. Her lips slowly curved upwards in a tentative smile before the damnedest thing happened.

Adelen *winked* at him.

Owen was so awestruck over the scrap of acknowledgment that it distracted him, causing him to smack right into Henrietta, who went down *hard*.

The screech that came out of that demon's mouth was loud enough to send all the wildlife scattering for miles. It didn't help that the ivory peasant dress she had on was now streaked with dirt. Especially after she spent thirty minutes fighting with Rita to let her wear it today.

He tried to apologize, but Henrietta wasn't listening to anyone, fully immersed in one of her epic meltdowns. Tessa ran over, crouching in front of Henrietta to help calm her down, her soothing words slowly working to pacify Henrietta.

"For all that's unholy, that dress looks like it lost a crappy argument with your backside," Bertrand hollered from the sidelines, doubled over his cane in laughter. The old man parked himself near the sound team, which in hindsight was a bad idea.

Rita slapped a hand over her mouth to prevent her laughter, and Kaia and Lizzie both wore matching expressions of duck lips as their shoulders shook from silent laughter. But it was Adelen's unintentional bark of laughter that sent Owen—and the rest of the crew—over the edge.

The roaring laughter thundered through the group, Bertrand's joke unraveling the team. And the look on Henrietta's face was murderous as she flew up onto her feet and made a beeline for the dressing room trailer, Tessa hot on her heels.

Henrietta was gone for a few minutes at most, having swapped the soiled dress for an emerald tunic, leggings, and cowboy boots—the *original* outfit Rita had selected for her to wear. By the time she emerged, the crew had mostly settled down, though the malevolent gleam in Bertrand's eyes tracking her every movement had yet to dissipate.

Wordlessly, Henrietta plopped herself down on the top step of the cottage's wrap-around farmer's porch, stone-faced and impatient.

That was Owen's cue to get into position.

He trudged up the stairs and settled down beside her. Henrietta scooted closer, leaning her head on his shoulder and placing an arm behind his back. The slightest contact with that woman made his stomach rebel, as did the overpowering and ever-present scent of alcohol. He'd made sure to pack another container of breath mints that morning, but second-guessed if it was enough.

With a heavy sigh, Owen reluctantly placed his arm around her and schooled his features into that of a loving metal band frontman.

"Fantastic!" Dax exclaimed through a mouthful of sour gummy worms. "In three—two—one, *action*!"

"Oh, Dolf!" Maggie/Henrietta sighed, snuggling closer as they both gazed out across the field. "My family's been in the legume business for generations, but if it weren't for you, our lentil crop would've failed! You have a real gift for growing beans."

"Maggie, the only thing I'm interested in growing is our love," Dolf/Owen professed. "I know we didn't get off on the right foot in the beginning, but like the soy beans you ferment, you've melted my silken tofu heart."

"Well, consider my gabbers officially gasted! What a darling couple you two make," twanged the Hardware Store Guy/Bertrand in that awful excuse for a Southern accent...who was *not* in this scene.

Owen had been too busy trying to discreetly breathe through his nose to notice Bertrand shuffling up to the cottage steps. He cut a look at Dax, who merely shrugged and motioned for him to roll with it.

For fuck's sake, why me?

"Hello, sir! What tidings do you bring?" Dolf/Owen asked with a broad smile.

"Why, I simply wanted to congratulate Miss Maggie on her victory at the annual legume festival by delivering some complimentary fertilizer."

"Oh, what a lovely surprise!" Maggie/Henrietta gushed, "You can just leave it behind the barn. I would hate to inconvenience you any further," she added sweetly. There was an added bite to her words, an unmistakable command to get the hell out of the scene.

Owen was unsure whether Bertrand hadn't noticed her tone or simply chose to ignore it when he said, "I apologize for showing up unannounced, but I couldn't help but overhear about your lentil crop."

Where the fuck is he going with this? Owen's patience with this shit stirrer was at its end.

Maggie/Henrietta lifted a quizzical brow, emboldening him to continue.

"Pray tell," Hardware Store Guy/Bertrand twanged. "Do you know what the difference between a lentil and a chickpea is?"

Maggie/Henrietta was at a loss for words, but Dolf/Owen regrettably took the bait.

"Unfortunately, I don't."

Like a rattlesnake biding its time before a strike, Hardware Store Guy/Bertrand crowed, "I've never had a lentil on my face!"

It took a second for his words to sink in before the set erupted into chaos. Bertrand was cackling over his joke while Dax was shouting, "We can't keep that in there! Get that man *off this set*."

"Ya'll need better taste in jokes!" Bertrand yelled over his shoulder as he scurried away as fast as possible, having spotted members of the security team heading in his direction. In a matter of minutes, they carefully led him into the dressing room trailer, where he would be temporarily contained and out of sight.

Owen didn't know what to make of what just happened. Henrietta was equally shocked, still frozen in place at his side. She slowly shook her head in disbelief while he opted to close his eyes for a moment. Her head fell against his shoulder again, ready for a retake.

Apparently, getting through this last scene quickly was too much to hope for.

Owen took a few steadying breaths to quell his rising frustration when it happened.

"The only backside I want to argue with is yours," Henrietta whispered as she confidently slipped a finger down the back of his pants, caressing the top of his ass crack.

"What the fuck is wrong with you?" Owen roared, jumping to his feet.

Henrietta had the audacity to call forth a well of extremely realistic, yet very fake, tears. "Why are you yelling at me?" She wailed.

"Because you stuck your finger in my ass without my consent," he seethed, placing both hands on his ass in a sad attempt to shield it from rogue appendages.

"How could you make up such *lies* like this, and in front of the entire crew!"

Owen was beside himself with rage, hands clenching and unclenching at his sides. He had never felt so violated in his entire life, wondering not for the first time how much worse other men had suffered at her hands.

Needing to look anywhere else but at the foul creature blubbering on the steps, Owen turned his head towards the front of the cottage. Slowly, he shifted his line of vision to the side of the porch, where his eyes locked on the camera operator perched on the other side.

The young man said nothing, and with a carefully blank expression, he gave Owen a single curt nod. A confirmation.

The cameras were still rolling.

Good.

He stalked towards Dax, stripping off his mic along the way.

"I am *done*," Owen rumbled angrily. "Make the first shot work. I don't care what kind of magic your team needs to pull out of their asses to do so. I am *done* being harassed by that vile woman."

He didn't wait for a response. He didn't owe anyone else here another second of his time—except for Adelen.

In the next breath, he was towering over Kaia, asking her where Adelen was.

"Right after the spawn of Satan got up to change out of her dirty dress, she'd mentioned needing to grab her phone from her car and ran off to quickly grab it." Kaia cast a nervous glance behind the barn, wringing her hands together. "That was thirty minutes ago."

Owen glanced toward the large barn structure but saw no sign of her. The makeshift lot was in the field behind it. He told himself she was fine, that she'd probably just taken a quick break in her car or something.

But then that sharp and unmistakable feeling hit deep in his chest.

The same one he'd had when Aurelia disappeared the night of the Harvest Charity Ball. The air shifted, and it felt cold and wrong. So very *wrong*.

The hair on the back of his neck prickled as he scanned the set again, but still no Adelen.

Terror flowed through his veins like ice, sending him sprinting to the parking lot. Rounding the side of the barn, his panic ratcheted up a notch when he saw her car was still there...and she was not.

His pulse spiked, sending him dangerously close to the edge of madness.

"Adelen?" he called out, voice tight but slightly desperate.

No answer.

He started panicking, the same thought hammering into his skull:

Not again. Not her.

CHAPTER 43

Adelen

The set was wild with crew members' uncontrollable laughter. Adelen didn't know how Bertrand managed to slither his way onto the set, but the joke he delivered after Owen accidentally knocked Henrietta down into the dirt...it was *priceless*.

It was her fault.

That damn wink.

She had never winked at anyone in her entire life, once again surprising herself by doing something completely out of character. But how wide Owen's eyes had gotten when she did it was worth it. So was listening to Henrietta's bleating mouth echo across the horizon while she was flopped in the dirt.

These were the kind of moments on set that she was used to. The ones she took joy in. It was a comfortable routine that made everything feel almost normal.

Almost.

She leaned back in her chair, rubbing at her temples. Another headache was forming, and the only thing that could fix it was a decent night's sleep...and waking up next to Owen.

For the first time in months, she'd been thinking about what came after.

After *Metal Love Beans* wrapped. After the long nights, retakes, and endless audio corrections were done.

She actually liked Joia City. Its rhythm, its people, the strange way the sea air always smelled like citrus and electricity had wormed its way under her skin. The breathtaking cliffs and lagoons...She could almost picture herself staying here, settling down, and calling it home.

But the fantasy collapsed under the same weight that always crushed it: the fear.

No matter how far she ran, it followed. It wasn't the danger itself that broke her—it was not knowing when the next incident would strike or who was behind it all.

If someone came at her in an attack, at least she was a confident and extremely skilled fighter.

But this?

This invisible, creeping dread that slithered through her life and stole her sleep and her happiness?

It was a kind of violence she couldn't block or counter, and it was eating her alive.

She caught herself watching Owen again from her position near the barn entrance. He was clutching his side from laughing so hard, hair tied back, sunlight cutting across his jaw in a way that made it hard to breathe.

He looked so at ease. *So alive.*

Maybe...maybe she could tell him everything that had been going on. He wouldn't think she was crazy or overreacting. He worked in security, and after what happened with Aurelia, he definitely understood danger. If anyone could help her make sense of this mess, it was him.

The thought terrified her more than this malevolent being ever had.

Letting Owen in meant risking him, too.

But keeping him out meant watching this thing slowly strip away the parts of herself she was trying to reclaim. She should be part of the group laughing with him, not on the outside looking in.

She paused, a stark truth revealing itself.

That's what it always came back to, wasn't it? In high school, she was always on the outside looking in. The same for after-school clubs, the dating scene, and work groups...

No more. She refused to be relegated to the role of an outsider again. With a deep shaky breath, she decided to do it after wrap—she would tell Owen everything.

She started running through her checklist, preparing to pack up her equipment once this last scene wrapped, when she realized she'd left her phone in her car. Henrietta was still screaming away in a heap on the ground while Tessa tried to calm her down. Which meant Adelen had time to run to her car before they shot the scene.

Tessa offered to carpool again on several occasions, including that morning. Perhaps she should consider it next time. Owen and her other friends weren't the only ones making an effort to connect with her, and she was starting to feel guilty for brushing Tessa's attempts to get to her aside.

Tomorrow, she promised herself. *I'll text her to go grab a coffee or something.*

With a quiet sigh, she slung her bag over her shoulder and turned to Kaia.

"I'll be right back," Adelen said. "I left my phone in the car and since her majesty is prone to prolonged crying fits, I'm going to run and grab it."

"We got this under control, though I'm enjoying every second of that wench's toddler tantrum," Kaia snickered.

Adelen laughed and headed around the barn to the lot.

The late-afternoon light was warm, the air heavy with salt carried on a light breeze. Crew laughter echoed faintly behind her.

She crossed the lot toward her car, already rehearsing what she'd say to Owen later. But as she reached for the handle, something shifted behind her—a shadow.

She started to turn—

—and a cloth pressed against her mouth and nose.

The smell was sharp, chemical, burning her throat before she could even gasp. Her hands shot up to fight, to grab, to do something, but her body betrayed her—knees buckling, vision blurring.

The last thing she saw was the car door glinting in the light.

The last thing she felt before fading into dark oblivion was a pair of hands catching her before she hit the ground.

By the time the lot realized she was gone, the sun had already dipped low enough to turn everything gold and wrong.

CHAPTER 44

Diogo

Diogo had arrived in Joia City only a few hours prior, still running on caffeine, power bars, and curiosity.

He had purposely arrived a day earlier than his scheduled meeting at Neuronix so he could surprise his sister. He'd texted Adelen three times, called twice, and no answer. Every message was left unread.

She *always* responded one way or another, at least to tell him to fuck off because she was working.

No, something was off—*again.* His gut had never steered him wrong. It was a strange sixth sense that he's had ever since he was a little boy.

He'd told himself this particular contract was purely business, a perfect excuse to check in on his little sister. But the truth was that she'd sounded brittle over the phone for weeks, and every instinct in his body screamed that she was hiding something.

He'd built his life around uncovering hidden things, and he was a bit insulted that the person he shared a womb with for nine months had tried to pull one over on him.

So now, standing outside some massive barn built by POLmArK Studios in the middle of a random field, Diogo looked perfectly at home in his black hoodie and combat boots, phone in hand as he pulled up the rental-car tracking data he'd hacked an hour ago.

It made it really easy to spot her car. She should probably just bite the bullet and buy herself a new one at this point anyway.

He circled it once, verifying the plate, scanning for signs of tampering, and leaning casually against the hood as he tried to decide whether to call her again or just barge onto set. Choosing option two, he pushed off the hood and made his way towards the barn, sticking to the cover of the trees.

Suddenly, a figure came sprinting around the other side of the barn like the world was on fire...and was heading directly for Adelen's car. He stood there a moment, frantically calling out her name, the entire scene putting Diogo on high alert.

He headed back towards her car, and who he could now see was Owen.

It was the perfect time to reintroduce himself, as Owen wasn't the only one looking for her.

CHAPTER 45

Owen

Owen's chest heaved, eyes wild, scanning every shadow as he circled her car. That sick déjà vu—that she's-gone-and-it's-my-fault dread—was pounding through his veins. The air felt heavy, the field too still.

Trying to keep his composure and wits about him, Owen willed himself to calm down and *think*.

A flash of movement caught his eye—something near the far side of the barn, by a small cluster of trees and natural bushes that hadn't been cleared away. And then he saw a figure emerge.

A man in dark clothes, hood pulled low enough over his head to partially block his face, drew close to her car.

Owen didn't think. He reacted.

"Hey!" he shouted, closing the distance fast. "Step away from the car!"

The man didn't move, just raised a shadowed eyebrow as Owen barreled forward.

"Listen—"

Owen didn't have a chance to finish his thought. He swung, pure adrenaline driving the motion—

—and the stranger sidestepped effortlessly.

Then a blur of movement, a shift of weight, and suddenly Owen was face-down on the grass with his arm twisted in a hold so precise it barely hurt.

"Easy, Owen," the man said calmly, voice low. "If I wanted to hurt you, you'd already be unconscious. How are we supposed to ride bikes if you're all in the hospital and shit?"

Owen froze. The guy wasn't even breathing hard...and he sounded *very* familiar.

"Who the hell are you?" Owen hissed.

The man released him and stepped back, allowing Owen to flip himself over in time to see the man's jaw clench in irritation. "Is that a serious question?"

That voice niggled at the back of his mind again. "Yeah...and you are?"

He sighed and shook his head, pushing the hood of his sweatshirt back to reveal his face. Owen's eyes widened with recognition. "I can't believe you're the idiot—her words, not mine, by the way—my sister chose to fall for."

Owen just stared at Lou in disbelief. "Your *what*?"

"My twin sister," Lou said flatly. "Adelen."

Owen's pulse sputtered as the words sank in. The shock of the takedown had barely faded before Owen put the pieces together.

He looked at Lou—*really looked*—and suddenly saw the resemblance: the same sharp cheekbones, the same intensity, eyes the same shade of steel...the unimpressed expression that was pure Adelen.

"Oh, shit."

Lou's mouth twitched, halfway between a smirk and a grimace. "Yeah. Oh shit."

"Oh," he blurted, breathing hard. "You're her brother."

Lou's mouth curved faintly. "Yes...We already established that. Are all your conversations with her like this? Because that would make *a lot* more sense..."

The tension bled out of Owen's body in a rush. "You're just as cool as she is," he said without thinking—then instantly regretted it. "I take that back, Lou, this is not the time."

"Actually...my name is Diogo. Lou—Luis—is my middle name."

"Obviously, the *Silver Shadow* gave me a fake name," Owen groused.

The humor vanished a second later as Diogo's gaze swept the lot, expression sharpening. "Now tell me why you're running around here like a man about to have a heart attack. Where is she?"

Owen's gut went cold. "That's the problem," he said somberly. "I don't know."

The panic came roaring back as he, too, glanced around the empty lot. "She went to grab something from her car about a half hour ago," he said, voice trembling. "She never came back."

Diogo's posture stiffened. "She hasn't answered my texts all day," he muttered. "She's been acting off for weeks—jumpy and weirdly evasive. I *knew* she was hiding something."

They both turned toward the car. Owen crouched to look under it, Diogo scanning the ground. The dirt and grass had been flattened, with several blades either broken or pulled up by the roots. Like something had been dragged over it.

Or someone.

Owen's stomach dropped. "Look at this," he said, pointing to the ground, Diogo's gaze shifting to that spot. "There was a struggle."

He was already pulling out his phone before Diogo could stop him.

"Please tell me you have something useful," Diogo said evenly, trying his best to hide his anxiety.

Owen didn't answer right away, focused on opening an app. "Um...maybe?"

Diogo frowned, sensing Owen's hesitation. "Why is that not reassuring?"

"Yeah," Owen said quickly, fingers flying. "So funny story, one we will absolutely laugh about later...I may have given her these super cool new cochlear skins on Valentine's Day. Also, I—uh—*may have* put a small chip in them. Just in case."

Diogo's arms fell listlessly to his sides, his mouth agape. Then Diogo gave a low, incredulous laugh. "You what? Oh my god, this is fucking amazing...you know she's going to murder you, right?"

"It's for safety!" Owen said defensively. "I do it for everyone I care about—friends, family, employees—"

"Oh, I cannot wait for her to find out about how you blatantly invaded her privacy like this," Diogo crooned. "And here I am, no popcorn for the show."

"Really? Please, tell me what legal and *ethical* method you used to track her car down today?"

Crossing his arms defensively, Diogo retorted, "One—she's used to my level of bullshit, and two—we're talking about *your* transgressions, not *mine*."

Owen shot him a glare, but the humor faded fast when the app pinged.

A small blinking dot moved steadily across the screen.

"She's on the move," Owen whispered.

Diogo's smirk vanished instantly. "I'll drive."

Owen was thankful for that small mercy. His hands were shaking too hard to hold the wheel, so Diogo took over without argument. He drove like he hacked—precise, fast, terrifyingly efficient.

"Deep breaths," Diogo said, eyes flicking between the road and the phone map. "You're no good to her if you pass out."

"I can't just sit here!"

"You're sitting here because you're not in the mental state needed to operate heavy machinery," Diogo said calmly. "Let me do the driving."

Owen glared but didn't fight it. "How are you so calm?"

"You obviously don't know my sister as well as you should by now," Diogo replied dryly. "She's tough. Always has been."

He kept talking as he weaved through traffic like a pro racer—part of it was a distraction, the other part a confession.

"She's been trained in jiu-jitsu since she could walk. Tried Krav Maga too, but she didn't love it like I did. Hot-wiring cars? Lock picking? All before high school. Never got caught, though."

Owen's eyebrows shot up. "Wait, what?"

"Yeah," Diogo said, turning another corner. "She didn't take crap from anyone. Especially not the kids who made fun of her. She'd get suspended before she let them think she was weak."

That hit Owen hard because the version of Adelen he'd seen lately—tense, scared, constantly looking over her shoulder—wasn't that person.

"She's been unraveling," he said quietly. "The last few weeks. Things have been happening to her—files corrupted, missing equipment, a serious static shock incident—"

Diogo's jaw clenched. "So it's been escalating."

"Yeah."

The silence that followed was sharp enough to skin him alive.

Then the tracker beeped again.

The dot had stopped moving—frozen in a patch of gray on the map outside city limits.

"Industrial district," Owen said grimly. "We're close to Warehouse Row."

Diogo pressed harder on the gas, tires squealing as they turned onto the main road.

"Hang on, Addy," Owen muttered under his breath. "We're coming."

CHAPTER 46

Adelen

Adelen came back to herself in a wash of perfume and motor oil, the world rocking under a tinny engine thrum.

It took several minutes to sift through the haze so she could think straight. She slowly began to take in her surroundings, each minuscule detail coming together to form a horrifying picture.

She was in the fucking trunk of a car.

For a breath, she panicked—everything was slow, cotton-mouthed, the air tasted like chemicals—then all the involuntary training Diogo subjected her to over the years kicked in gear and overrode her fear like a switch. Adelen's body knew what to do long before her mind finished screaming.

Her wrists and ankles were tightly bound; the cold plastic of cheap zip ties biting into her skin. She tested the bonds with careful, controlled movements, feeling for give, listening to the car's cadence, mapping the space by touch and what she could see. She stayed in shape not just to maintain a healthy lifestyle, but also to keep her body flexible.

Fingers that have knitted thousands of yarn loops, steadied boom poles, and hotwired cars before, found the thin blade hidden inside her favorite pair of boots and pulled it free.

She didn't think about the ethics of it, or anything else really, focused only on the way the metal slid, the quiet snap as she worked at the bindings until the last tight loop fell away.

She waited a beat, chest flaring, because adrenaline without a plan was an invitation for mistakes. The car was still moving; the trunk light a faint rectangle glow in the darkness. She slid her hands along the trunk's interior, taking in every contour. There was a release latch; a fold in the back seat; a handful of plastic ties tossed in a corner, and—

The cables that went missing at the start of the shoot.

A red haze fell over her vision, the need to shatter a bone or two overpowering.

Now it was *really* fucking personal.

But she needed to step back and turn off her emotions. That's how life-threatening mistakes happen, when decisions are made out of anger instead of logic.

She didn't overanalyze. Instead, she improvised, as she always had, and turned the scrap of material into a tool. There was no time to fiddle with theory, only the concise, efficient motions of someone who's done what needs doing before.

Adelen was enraged, and whoever was behind the wheel of this car was about to learn firsthand what that entailed. The hard way. Up to this point, she had been fighting an invisible force, like having her hands tied behind her back.

It was only fitting then that they did, in fact, tie her hands together behind her back...before putting her in the fucking trunk of a car. Her eyes slid to the extra zip ties again, and she grabbed a fistful. Leaving them in the trunk with her was the laziest and stupidest thing her captor could've ever done.

Whoever they were.

But now...that person was tangible, real, and fucking stupid for bringing the lion to their feast. She just had to time it right—one chance to take control.

Shifting back onto her knees, Adelen dropped the backseat a sliver and peeked through it. She took in the shape and size of the interior, the world compressing to one line of sight: the driver's back, the way their hands hovered on the wheel. They were wearing a sweatshirt with the hood up, making it hard to see who it was.

She pulled the backseat back into place and began plotting her attack, her fingers working fast to link several zip ties together. After running through the planned motions twice in her head, she cracked the backseat door hatch and peered through one last time.

Taking a deep breath, Adelen then made her move.

She launched herself through the opening, a hard, controlled weight that took the driver by surprise.

She didn't aim to kill; she aimed to *stop*. Her hands were quick and practiced, finding leverage and pressure points with the finesse of someone who's trained to end a fight before it started.

Those extra zip ties had come in handy. Especially now that she had daisy-chained some of them together, using the improvised restraint around the driver's neck to tie them to the headrest, all without gore or theatrics. It was just enough to force them to comply.

The driver groped for breath and movement, eyes wide and panic-struck, but Adelen didn't give a flying fuck about how they felt. Or if they couldn't breathe. Or if they crashed and exploded in a fiery blaze—which nearly happened as the car swerved hard into the other lane of oncoming traffic, forcing another car to slam on its brakes.

No, it was the *perfect* time to bestow the same courtesy upon this piece of shit gasping for air that they had bestowed upon her.

Simmering rage that had been buried mere minutes earlier boiled over, and Adelen allowed herself to ride that molten wave as she brought her lips close to her assailant's head.

"Pull over," she whispered against their ear, voice measured and lethal as she pulled the zip tie a little tighter for extra measure, eliciting another choked sound. Maybe she was a sadist, but she couldn't deny the deep-seated pleasure she got from hearing that sound.

There would be no pleading or begging from Adelen; she was in command now. Her words cut through the noise of the engine and the driver's flailing thoughts like a blade. They fumbled, then, hands trembling, managed to slow and swing the vehicle to the shoulder.

Adelen kept her body behind them and the seat until the car shuddered to a stop and the engine died. She kept the zip tie restraint tight enough to control but never so tight as to take a life. Her primary focus was extraction. Vengeance would come soon enough.

Her heart hammered against her ribs, but the fury that fueled her was a tool, honed and precise. When the car finally eased to silence, she locked the ties in place around the headrest, jumped into the passenger seat, and made quick work of binding their wrists together with another chain of ties.

Satisfied the driver was immobilized, Adelen looked up at Tessa and let her know—without raising her voice—exactly how small and helpless she was now, and that any sound she made would be the next mistake they pay for. Grabbing Tessa's phone, she poured every ounce of wrath into her eyes as she dialed and called the police.

She didn't need to wait for someone to rescue her. Tessa, on the other hand...Adelen made sure to reiterate to the dispatcher that her abductor's safety was dependent on how quickly officers arrived on scene. She would handle the shock and disappointment of learning it was a friend once everything was over.

Disgusted by the sight of her, Adelen exited the vehicle and parked her ass on the trunk hood, inhaled several gulps of fresh air, and waited for the distant sound of blaring sirens to draw closer.

CHAPTER 47

Owen

Owen had never truly known terror until today.

After the fastest, most blood-curdling ride of his life, they finally caught up to the dot in his app. They were both in fight or flight mode, ready to run Adelen's captor off the road in an epic high-speed chase scene, only to stumble upon a swarm of flashing red and blue lights that painted the blocked-off highway in chaos.

This was...not what he expected. Given the smirk on Diogo's face as he leisurely pulled the car over and cut the engine. He still couldn't believe that Lou—Diogo—was the fucking *Silver Shadow*. After everything that's gone down in the last several months, Owen would be amazed if anything surprised him anymore. He was living in a real-life action movie.

He scowled as he wrestled with his seatbelt, the mechanism not releasing right away. Diogo side-eyed him.

"Do you need rescuing from your safety harness, too?"

"Oh shut up, you fibster! Keeping secrets seems to be a family trait, from what I've learned from your sister. I don't even trust that Diogo is your real name!" Owen was annoyed, frightened, and a million other things he couldn't name right at the moment, and Diogo's answering chuckle only upset him further.

The second the seatbelt released, Owen ungracefully hopped out of the car, already rounding the front as the car door slammed behind him. Diogo easily caught up, and together they approached the crime scene.

Police cars boxed in the foreign vehicle. Officers moved in and out of the scene with purpose. Searching over the sea of lights and officers, Owen's heart pounded as he finally spotted her. He'd been silently praying that she was unharmed, worrying about how scared she must be, how he hadn't been there to protect her...the guilt creeping with deadly force. He examined her from head to toe, ensuring she wasn't hurt.

Except...she wasn't hurt. Not even remotely close.

In fact, she was completely fine, as if it were another day at the office.

Adelen was casually sitting on the back trunk of an unfamiliar black sedan, hair wild, jeans ripped, with what looked like a fresh steaming cup of coffee in her hand. She was chatting animatedly with a small squadron of officers, each of them with stars in their eyes, hanging on her every word.

Owen's mood soured, wondering which of those uniformed pretty boys went out of their way to get her that drink. His mood took another dive when Diogo snickered again.

Don't make a scene, Owen, he chastised himself. *You're not meant to be someone's bitch in prison.*

"Sorry, gentlemen—this is an active crime scene," a middle-aged, stacked cop stepped in their path, holding out a hand to stop them as they neared the threshold of the barricades.

Owen froze, still staring at Adelen. "That's—she's—"

"We know who she is," the officer said, assessing them both with suspicion. "You friends?"

Before Owen could answer, an older man being interviewed by another cop started yelling from the sidelines.

"I'm telling you, officer! The car swerved right into my lane! Nearly clipped me!" Glaring in another squad car's direction, the elderly gentleman put a hand to his mouth and hollered, "Where'd you get your brain, lady—the five and dime store?"

Owen followed the direction of the man's glare, head whipping toward the commotion—a handcuffed woman stood by a squad car, makeup smeared, eyes glassy with shock. It took him a minute to realize that the woman was *Tessa*.

Diogo spoke up smoothly beside him. "We're here for Adelen Mazao. I'm her brother Diogo—twin, actually. We were tracking her after she went missing on suspicion of kidnapping."

He looked at Owen expectantly.

"I'm, uh..." His brain blanked.

What exactly was he to her?

"I'm her boyfriend, Owen Voss."

The words tumbled out before he could stop them.

Shit shit shit.

Diogo shot him a look—brows raised high, mouth twitching—that clearly said, *I can't wait until she hears that you said that.*

Owen glared back. "Shut up."

The cop looked between the two of them for a beat and then sighed. "Alright, fine. Follow me."

As they crossed the lot, the officer remarked, almost admiringly, "I've been doing this job fifteen years, and I've never seen anything quite like what that girl pulled today. She's...kind of intimidating."

Owen stumbled a little, almost face-planting on the asphalt. "Wait, what do you mean?"

With a strange reverence, the officer said, "She choked her kidnapper out with zip ties she found in the trunk. Nearly ran the car off the road herself before using the driver's phone to call us."

Owen stopped dead. "She did what now?"

Diogo laughed darkly. "That's the Addy I know. When we were nine, she once zip-tied my hands and feet together while I was asleep."

Owen only stared at him. “Dude, what kind of childhood did you two *have*? Between the stories she’s told me so far, and now this...this shit isn’t normal.”

Diogo’s smile simply grew wider.

By the time they reached her, Adelen looked tired but fierce, and Owen’s heart finally unclenched. The double take she did when she noticed them was borderline comical.

The officer gestured toward the handcuffed woman and said to Owen. “Listen, we see all sorts of weird love triangle crap in our line of work. The perp is a coworker of hers. Confessed she’s been in love with you, *Owen*, since high school. Something about ‘unrequited love’ and ‘finally having her chance.’”

Owen’s stomach twisted. “I—I barely remembered her until the day I auditioned,” he muttered, dumbfounded. “I stood up for her *once*. Kids were awful back then, and I didn’t tolerate bullying.. My dad had just died, and I—” He cut himself off, jaw tightening. “I thought I was helping. But lately, she’s been acting weird and actually hit on me earlier this afternoon.”

Adelen’s back stiffened at the mention of Tessa making a pass at him.

“It’s more common than you’d think,” the officer said ruefully, slowly beginning to step away. “I’ll give you all a minute. You both need to give statements as well.”

Adelen was silent for a long moment, glancing between him and her brother with narrowed eyes. “Hold on...How did you even find me?”

Looks like Adelen may be going to jail for murder after all.

Owen hesitated, afraid to answer that question in the presence of so many law enforcement officers. “Well...It took you too long to come back from your car, so I went looking. That’s how I came across Diogo—”

“Who you tried to attack,” Diogo interrupted cheerfully. “And then I laid him out without breaking a sweat.”

Owen scowled. “Irrelevant.”

"Completely relevant," Diogo countered, smirking.

Owen pressed on. "We saw signs of a struggle, and—"

"Ask him how we tracked you down," Diogo said gleefully.

Owen shot him a murderous glare. "Can you *shut up* already?"

Diogo cocked his head and simply said, "No."

Adelen's brow furrowed. "Answer my question, Owen."

Owen exhaled, resigned. "Fine. Don't get mad...but remember the Valentine's Day gift I got you? Those *very thoughtful* custom-made cochlear skins?" Adelen's expression flattened. "...I *might* have put a tracking chip in each one."

Her eyes went wide, disbelief sharpening into fury. "You *what*?"

Diogo threw his head back and laughed, shaking his fists up at the sky. "*Yesssss*, this is going to be *amazing*."

CHAPTER 48

Adelen

The drive home dragged on, every mile wound tighter than a violin string about to snap. The air in the car was so thick with tension it practically had teeth, gnawing at her skin, daring someone to make the first move and let all hell break loose.

Owen stared straight ahead, knuckles white on the wheel, while Adelen sat bolt upright, arms clamped across her chest like she was holding herself together by sheer force of will. Her anger was practically a third passenger. The second he'd admitted to sneaking chips into her custom skins, she'd ripped them off and stomped them to pieces—petty, feral, and absolutely unhinged, like a toddler denied candy in the checkout line.

Everything that had happened left her nerves flayed open and buzzing with the kind of violation that made her want to claw out of herself. But Owen's little stunt—his confession—was a deeper betrayal. Rage simmered in her veins, so thick she couldn't look at him without her hands curling into fists. And as for the other pain in her ass lounging in the backseat, he was right up there on her punch list.

Sometimes she wondered if she had a sign on her back inviting people to take over her life.

Her idiot brother was sprawled across the backseat like he'd paid extra for VIP seats to the world's most dysfunctional circus, smirk firmly in place, eyes gleaming with way too much glee for her taste.

"So," Diogo said casually, "do all your girlfriends come with GPS, or is she just special?"

"Do you mind?" Owen snapped, glaring at him in the rearview mirror.

"I'm just saying," Diogo replied, grinning. "It's actually very efficient. Creepy. But efficient."

Adelen ignored Diogo, directing her anger solely at Owen. "We are having a very serious conversation about this when we get back."

Owen returned her glare with one of his own, furious enough for Adelen's rage to momentarily stumble. "Yeah, no shit. You're not the only one who's pissed off."

She let out a low, frustrated growl and slumped back, eyes glued to the smear of scenery outside. The tires hummed, pretending to fill the silence, but all she could hear was her own pulse, thundering in her ears like a war drum at the world's worst parade.

She was tense, every muscle tight. Her thoughts kept circling back to the same thing: Owen had tracked her. He crossed a line she hadn't even realized was there until it was gone.

Without asking.

Without telling her.

Without giving her a choice.

Her processors, the most personal thing she owned, had been used against her. It didn't matter why he did it. Fixing this mess would take time. She still felt unsettled, Tessa's confession about the chloroform clinging to her thoughts. The chemical taste lingered in her mouth. If Owen hadn't found her...*No*. She slammed the door on that thought before it could finish forming.

But that didn't make any of this right.

And then there was Diogo, swooping in out of nowhere, playing the role of self-appointed guardian, making everything ten times worse. She knew exactly what tricks that asshole pulled to track her down. He was just as bad as Owen. Honestly, the two of them deserved each other, both so convinced they knew what was best for her. Maybe they should just date and leave her out of it.

Two pigheaded men.

Two self-appointed protectors.

Zero consent obtained.

It left her feeling like a puppet in her own story, strings yanked by everyone but herself. But if she was honest, had her life ever truly belonged to her in the first place?

No. It hadn't. But she was done letting others pull the strings. That was about to change.

"Do you two not understand what you've done?" she exploded, finally breaking the silence. "You both just decided to do things for me, without asking, without telling me. You both hacked my privacy. You both used your stupid technology to track me. And you both showed up out of nowhere, waltzing in like a weird version of Sherlock and Holmes, like I can't handle my own fucking life!"

"Says the person who's been stalked for months and didn't tell anyone!" Owen shouted back, his voice sharp and exhausted. "You let it escalate and get worse while putting everyone around you literally in danger, too. Not just yourself, but me and everyone important to me. I wasn't given a choice to even discuss how to help you, let alone protect you, because you decided to disappear and shut me out."

His tone fractured at the end, coarse enough to make her chest ache. She really hated how much sense he was making, but she wasn't ready to give ground.

Diogo leaned forward from the backseat, voice firm but edged. "Owen's right. You did the same thing to me. To your family. You packed up and moved across the country with barely a word. No warning, no explanation. Mom and Dad have been losing their minds, Adelen. We knew something was wrong—you just refused to tell us. Do you know what that's like to watch someone you love keep a secret from you while you're forced to sit back and watch them unravel?"

She gripped the door handle, knuckles white.

Every word stung because they weren't wrong.

She had run.

She had hidden.

She had chosen silence because she didn't want anyone else getting hurt because of her, when in reality, there was far more collateral damage than she'd ever imagined. But now...after everything...They both looked at her like she was the one who'd broken their trust.

And maybe she had.

Of everything said, she really hadn't considered the impact it could've had on Aurelia, Ivy, Grace, or Kaia. All amazing women who welcomed her into their fold and treated her like she'd always been a part of their group. Perhaps her decisions were more selfishly driven than she allowed herself to believe.

No one spoke after that.

The only sounds were the faint, rhythmic tapping of Diogo's fingers—a habit as old as childhood and a sure sign he was agitated—and the uneven, ragged breaths Owen tried and failed to steady.

She kept stealing glances at him as the city blurred past, tracing the sharp lines of his jaw, the way his golden hair was pulled back at the nape of his neck. He refused to meet her eyes, not even once, his focus glued to the road ahead as if it was the only thing keeping him from falling apart.

What felt like an eternity later, they finally pulled into the Starhaven set parking lot so Diogo could retrieve her car. His jaw was clenched, shoulders pulled up tight, every inch of him tense.

When he told her to hand over her car and apartment keys, she started to protest—until Diogo leaned in through the window and cut her off.

"The least you can do right now," he said softly but firmly, "is give him five minutes to talk. He earned that much. I'll get my turn later."

His hand remained extended until she dropped the keys into it. Quickly unlocking the doors, Diogo fished her missing phone out of the front seat and tossed it through the window and onto her lap.

He gave Owen a look—something quiet and understanding—and then threw his bag into her car and drove off.

The silence that settled over them was thick enough to touch, pressing in from all sides.

Owen still wouldn't look at her. He didn't speak, barely even moved except to steer, as if any sudden motion might shatter what little control he had left.

She'd seen Owen angry before, but never like this—never so cold, so unreachable. She had no right to complain, not after the way she'd iced him out these past weeks. Still, it stung. She could practically hear the word hypocrite echoing in her head, another unwelcome addition to her growing list of flaws.

This was the worst car ride she'd ever had. Even being stuck in a trunk hadn't felt this bad.

She turned her face to the window, blinking back the sting in her eyes as city lights smeared into streaks of gold and white, the world outside moving too fast to hold onto.

He had every reason to be upset. She knew that.

What truly terrified her wasn't his anger—it was the heartbreak she could feel pulsing beneath it, vast and overwhelming.

He had come for her, risked everything to save her, and somehow she'd still managed to make him feel powerless, like nothing he did would ever be enough.

The thought left her empty. Neither of them had respected the boundaries they so desperately needed.

Underneath it all, she was just as afraid of losing him as she was of being hunted again.

She didn't know which fear was worse.

Adelen had no idea what to expect when the car finally rolled to a stop. She'd assumed they'd head back to his sleek apartment downtown, but instead, Owen had driven them in the opposite direction, away from the city's pulse and into something quieter.

She blinked, surprised. Instead of something dramatic, the house was simple and inviting. Whitewashed walls, blue trim, and terracotta tiles curling along the roof. It looked like it belonged by the ocean, full of memories.

Roses climbed the front of the house and porch columns. Hydrangeas bloomed pink and violet below. A narrow dirt path wound through dahlias, marigolds, daisies, and neat rows of cabbages and tomatoes. The air smelled of earth, flowers, and fruit, with bees humming nearby.

The porch light glowed warm against the soft white exterior, and a single wind chime tinkled in the breeze. It looked nothing like Owen's chaotic, dazzling life, and everything like the kind of place where a kid might ride bikes until dark and come home for dinner at a kitchen table.

It was the kind of house that felt like it might actually breathe, the garden pressing in like it was trying to give the walls a hug, every flower practically screaming about the hands that planted it.

It reminded her of her parents' house...right down to the garden beds.

She had no words.

"This is...your place?" she asked, breaking the long silence for the first time.

Owen didn't answer. He parked, climbed out, and strode toward the front door, his anger still simmering too hot for words.

She followed, steps tentative, letting her eyes drink in every bloom and tangled vine as she made her way up the path.

Stepping inside, she was immediately enveloped by a rush of color and nostalgia, the kind that hit deep and unexpected, tugging at memories she hadn't realized she'd been missing.

The living room walls glowed with a soft yellow, faded by years of sunlight and laughter, warm enough to feel lived-in but still bright enough to chase away shadows. The furniture was a mismatched collection that somehow worked together, each piece worn and inviting, the kind of comfort that only comes from years of use. Framed photos crowded every surface, capturing smiles and moments that seemed to echo through the room.

A small boy with wild blond hair and bright blue eyes grinned from every corner, sometimes perched on his father's shoulders, sometimes buried in his mother's arms.

It took her a moment to realize the little boy in all those photos was Owen with wild blond hair, blue eyes shining with mischief and hope.

Her throat tightened, emotion catching her off guard.

It was heartbreakingly normal, the kind of safe that seeped into your bones and made you want to curl up on a crooked couch and never leave.

It hit her like a sucker punch—this place was her parents' home in Vila Verde all over again. Lemon polish, garden dirt, the echoes of her mother's laugh bouncing off the walls. Homesickness crashed in, sharp and mean, and she had to breathe through it or risk falling apart right there.

She turned back toward him, the question already forming in her head—why here?

But before she could speak, Owen finally looked at her.

"This is the house I grew up in," he said quietly. His voice had softened, stripped of anger, heavy instead with something else—grief, maybe. "I come here when I need to think. Or when I just...need quiet."

Her eyes drifted to another photo on the wall—Owen as a tween beside his father, both laughing, arms around each other.

"I don't know what to do with it now that my mom's in a care facility full-time," he continued, staring past her. "I can't sell it. It's the last tie I have to them. But I can't—" He stopped, pressing a hand to the back of his neck. "I can't bring myself to do anything with it either."

He finally met her gaze again. "It was the most private place I could think of to talk. No press, no crew, no one watching us. I've had enough of that lately."

Her anger started to leak out, dissolving under the weight of all the things neither of them had said. The house still smelled like dust and cinnamon, and everywhere she looked, she could see a younger version of Owen, grinning at her from the corners. Something shifted in her chest,something she hadn't let herself see before.

Maybe this wasn't about control at all. Maybe all his talk about safety was just another flavor of the same fear she carried—losing someone, being helpless, watching the people you love vanish while you stand there, useless.

The thought burrowed in, twisting her anger into something messier—complicated, sticky, impossible to name but impossible to ignore.

He had crossed a line. So had she. Still, she was here, in the place he trusted most.

Adelen ran her fingertips lightly along the edge of one of the photo frames, her reflection merging with the smiling boy inside.

CHAPTER 49

Owen

Owen didn't say a word the whole drive.

He couldn't. If he opened his mouth, everything would come out sideways, and he'd already made a career of that since the moment he met this maddening woman. Anger, fear, guilt—the whole emotional dumpster fire jammed itself in his throat.

So he white-knuckled the steering wheel and stared at the road like it was the last lifeline he had. If he looked at her, he'd unravel right there, and he wasn't about to give her front row seats to that particular meltdown...yet.

Adelen sat next to him, arms crossed, radiating enough fury to choke a horse. The air between them was practically flammable.

He didn't blame her. Not really. But he was still royally pissed she'd kept something this dire under wraps. Owen got the whole independence thing—hell, he practically had it tattooed on his forehead—but the trackers weren't about control. They were his insurance policy for when shit hit the fan, like now.

This was only the second time he'd ever used that app, and both times, someone's life had been dangling over the edge.

He'd crossed a line—no question. He should've asked. But the alternative—never finding her—was unthinkable. Fear made him do many things, most of them questionable.

If he hadn't put that tracker in those skins—

If he hadn't found her—

She'd be gone.

She could have died.

That thought looped in his brain until he felt physically ill. Like a bad song on repeat, except this one came with nausea.

When he finally pulled up to the curb, Adelen looked confused. He could see it in her reflection on the window, her raised brows, and the small crease between them.

If she'd been expecting marble floors and floor-to-ceiling windows, she was about to be sorely disappointed. All she was getting was peeling paint and a porch swing that sounded like it was auditioning for a horror movie.

Good. Let her see the mess.

He didn't need her to see some polished version of him right now. He needed her to see the truth and be honest with herself.

He killed the engine, got out, and headed for the front door without waiting. His boots slipped on the packed dirt, and every muscle in his jaw screamed from holding it all in.

Inside, the air hit him like a memory. Lemon cleaner. The ghost of his mother's favorite candle, the one she'd kept burning even after she forgot what it was for.

The living room was exactly as he'd left it. Warm colors, faded curtains, the wall of family photos still hung slightly crooked. Time had stopped here the day his mom moved into the care facility.

He'd told himself he kept the house for practical reasons—a place to crash, a backup plan. But that was just one of the many hollow lies rattling around in his skull.

He kept it because selling it would've felt like erasing his family, and the half-baked dream of someday raising his own here.

Behind him, Adelen stepped inside, and the air shifted. He could feel her slowing down, soaking it all in—the crooked photos, the battered furniture, the kitchen that always smelled like cinnamon and burnt coffee.

She paused in front of a photo of his dad, younger, laughing with an arm around a towheaded kid who looked like trouble. The old ache flared behind Owen's ribs. Her eyes flicked to him, already asking questions without saying a word.

"This was my childhood home," he said quietly. "I come here when I need a break...when I need to think."

She turned to face him, expression unreadable. He found himself explaining why he kept the place, not sure why he was spilling his guts, but oddly relieved he did.

For the first time since the kidnapping, he let himself really look at her.

Her posture wasn't angry anymore. Not exactly. Just...uncertain. Tired. Like she'd run out of fight for the day.

He couldn't read her mind, but her eyes had softened, the sharp edge dulled by something dangerously close to understanding.

That, somehow, bothered him more than her anger. He didn't deserve her understanding, and he knew it.

He was supposed to be the protector. That was his job, his whole identity, the only thing he'd ever been good at. And today, he'd almost lost the woman he loved because he hadn't seen the danger coming.

He wasn't proud of the tracker move, but standing in this house full of ghosts, he couldn't bring himself to regret it either.

Adelen wandered deeper in, fingers trailing over the photo frames. She paused at a family picture and smiled, wistful and a little sad.

The knot in his chest loosened, just a little.

He'd brought her here because it was his sanctuary. But seeing her in the middle of all his best memories confirmed that maybe she was the safest thing he'd found in years.

The words built up, heavy and hot, until he couldn't hold them back anymore.

He'd brought her here to talk, but now, with her standing in his living room quiet and so damn guarded, he wanted to shake her and pull her close at the same time.

"Why didn't you tell me?" he asked, voice rough, barely holding steady. "Or even your brother? Why did you let this go on for so long?"

Adelen froze where she stood, eyes flicking to him in surprise.

"I'm serious," he pressed. "You were harassed for months. Stalked. And you said nothing. Do you have any idea how lucky you are to be alive right now?"

She flinched slightly at that, enough to make his stomach twist.

He dragged a hand through his hair, trying to find words that didn't sound like yelling but came out that way anyway. "I've spent weeks trying to break through to you, trying to actually know you, and every time I think we're finally getting somewhere, you pull away again."

The memory of their first date, the laughter, the way she'd kissed him first, slammed into him. He swallowed hard.

"I thought we were connecting," he said earnestly. "I thought you were finally letting me in. And then you shut me out, twice. Only to find out you've been living in this nightmare, and it didn't just put you in danger; it put me there. It had put everyone around us there."

He prowled closer, his voice breaking. "You think I don't get it, but I do. I understand wanting to handle everything on your own—to prove you can. That's one of the things I love most about you, Adelen. But you don't have to do this alone anymore."

The last word came out hoarse, like he'd scraped it from somewhere deep inside.

"If you want to set the world on fire, that's fine. Count me in. I'll pour the gasoline and bring the matches. Let me set the world on fire with you. I'm not going anywhere."

CHAPTER 50

Adelen

Owen was a whole new flavor of uncomfortable. So open, stubborn, and unflinchingly honest, it was almost unfair how sexy he looked doing it.

Let me set the world on fire with you.

Those words stuck with her, making the connection between them impossible to ignore.

For once, someone wasn't trying to change her. Owen wasn't angry at her. He was angry *for* her. For every person who'd ever wronged her, whoever had dared to hurt her.

He wasn't trying to change her or tell her to calm down. He was trying to understand her, even the messy parts. Sometimes she wanted to set the world on fire, but having someone willing to stand beside her was new.

The way he looked at her, seeing every flaw and quirk, didn't make her want to run. It made her feel lighter, as if being seen were a relief.

She'd tried every trick in the book to push him away, but he just kept showing up, seeing her exactly as she was. Sure, he'd done it all in the most backward, ridiculous way possible, but she couldn't deny it—he put his whole messy heart into every single moment with her.

The more she replayed it, the more pissed she got—at herself. Letting him in wasn't half as terrifying as she'd built it up to be. Not after today, anyway. Nothing like a near-death experience to slap some perspective into you.

Now came the hard part—figuring out what the hell to say next, and where they were supposed to go from here.

The silence between them stretched so tight it could snap. Her throat burned from swallowing down everything she wanted to say.

Her first instinct was to tell him to quit looking at her like he could handle anything she threw at him, like her mess wouldn't send him running. But when she finally met his eyes, something else tumbled out instead.

"It started a while ago," she said softly, anxiously twirling a lock of hair around her index finger. "Before I even came here."

Owen didn't move, just patiently waited. He stood still, as if one wrong sound might make her retreat again.

"Whoever it was," she went on. "They weren't...obvious about it, not at first. I thought I was imagining it when little things happened at work. But then I started getting messages. At first, they were compliments, things that could've been from anyone. Then they got personal."

She twisted her hands together. "They knew where I lived. What I wore to work. Even what I ate for lunch. They started sending stuff to my desk—flowers, notes, weird little gifts. And when I tried to ignore it, that's when the accidents started."

Her voice went barely above a whisper. "Stuff started breaking—equipment failing, wires cut, sound rigs overheating. I almost needed stitches one time."

Owen's knuckles turned white at his sides, but he didn't interrupt.

"When I reported it to Cary and HR, they said there was no proof. Whoever was doing this was next level—never caught on camera and seemed untraceable. And the more I pushed back, the worse it got. So when this opportunity came up, I jumped on it and left. I moved across the country, thinking it would finally stop. But somehow...they found me. It makes sense now, considering Tessa relocated here along with me. We always had a weird love-hate professional relationship, but I never imagined this."

Adelen shook her head, still trying to piece it all together and coming up empty.

"I thought she was warming up to me out here lately. I'm still not sure I fully understand why she did this either. She didn't meet you until after we relocated here."

She let out a shaky laugh that broke halfway through. "Guess it never really goes away, huh? The fear. You start thinking it's safer to keep everyone at arm's length. If no one gets close, no one gets hurt."

Her eyes stung, but she blinked the tears back, refusing to let them win. "I thought I was doing the right thing. Keeping quiet, protecting everyone. I didn't want to drag you—or Diogo—into my mess."

Her voice broke, and whatever was left of her resolve crumbled. "And now, I almost got everyone hurt anyway. I was going to tell you after wrap today, but I never got the chance."

The man standing in front of her now looked like something split open inside him, too. His blue eyes were wet at the edges, the kind of heartbreak that came from being terrified and powerless. Owen wasn't hiding behind humor or trying to make it easier for her. He was letting himself feel everything, and for the life of her, she couldn't look away.

"I didn't want anyone else to get hurt," she said quietly. "I thought if I ignored it long enough, it would stop." Her voice faltered. "I just needed to keep moving forward."

Owen shook his head, the muscle in his jaw tightening. "That's not moving forward, that's running."

She stared at the floor, cheeks burning with the sting of his words...because he was right.

CHAPTER 51

Owen

He'd pieced together bits of it before, but hearing the whole ugly truth out loud felt like someone reached in and yanked out a chunk of his insides.

He wanted to throttle Tessa until she begged for mercy, maybe even until she regretted ever learning how to breathe. How did one tiny act of kindness from decades ago rot and twist into something this monstrous? It made no sense, but here they were.

But more than anything, he just wanted to reach out and scoop up all the heaviness she'd been lugging around for way too long, toss it out the window, and give her a break. He inched closer, slow and obvious, like approaching a skittish cat, making sure she saw him coming.

"Hey," he murmured, his voice steady where hers trembled. "You did what you thought you had to do to survive. You shouldn't have had to think that way at all."

She finally met his eyes, hers sorrowful and full of regret. "You don't understand, Owen. You couldn't fix this."

"Maybe not," he admitted. "But I could have stood next to you while you figured it out."

Her breath hitched, and that little flash of vulnerability in her eyes just wrecked him. He was done for—total emotional roadkill.

"I get it," he said more softly. "You didn't want to need anyone. Neither did I. After my mom got sick, after my dad died...I decided the safest way to care for people was to protect them from a distance. Trackers. Security systems. Jokes. It's all the same thing."

He gave a small, self-deprecating smile. "So yeah, I crossed a line. And I'm sorry. But I swear it wasn't about control. It was fear...the kind that makes you do stupid things because you can't handle losing someone you love."

Her shoulders sagged, all the fight draining out of her. He could practically see her heart duking it out with her survival instincts, neither one ready to throw in the towel. His Addy was a fighter till the end.

"But the only thing I actually need is your trust," Owen said, voice barely above a whisper. "I'll wipe the tracking app, smash every chip—yours, mine, everyone's. The whole lot." He rubbed the back of his neck, wincing. "Honestly, the tracking was just my emotional security blanket. I need to figure out how to deal with my anxiety like a normal person. Maybe I should finally talk to a therapist or something." He met her eyes, all open regret and hope. "Whatever it takes to make us work. You're it for me."

He reached out an open hand, a silent offer to share burdens as a team, should she be willing to accept it. To put faith in them both.

For a second, Adelen just stared at his hand, afraid it might bite her. Then, slowly, she scooted forward and slipped her fingers into his.

CHAPTER 52

Adelen

His palm was warm and solid against hers.

It shouldn't have felt this right, not after all the fear, the secrets, the shouting matches—but somehow, against all logic, it did. The rightness of it crept in quietly, stubborn and undeniable.

For the first time in what felt like forever, she wasn't carrying the burden alone.

She exhaled shakily. "I know she's in custody now, but I don't know how to stop looking over my shoulder."

Owen's thumb brushed across her knuckles, grounding her. "Then I'll keep looking with you until you can."

That simple promise landed harder than any over-the-top romantic gesture ever could. It swept the wind right out of her.

"Because you love me?" She hadn't missed what he had said. Maybe he hadn't realized it, and it slipped out, but she wasn't letting it go unnoticed.

Owen looked like a deer caught in headlights. A slow, embarrassed flush crept up his neck, blooming across his cheeks.

They stood in the kitchen, the same one where his mother had once baked cookies and kept score of growing-boy appetites on the doorframe.

Something inside her split wide open, like a sprout bursting from its seed, and suddenly she was someone new. Someone who understood what it meant to want, to crave Owen with a shameless hunger she'd never dared to acknowledge before.

Adelen smiled and took a step forward.

"You know, we've had a really weird start to our relationship. The first time I saw you was at Aurelia and Levi's wedding, throwing flower petals down the aisle like an ass."

She closed the distance with another step, watching as Owen's mouth opened, as if he might protest, but the words never came.

"Somehow we went from that first meeting to standing here, in this beautiful house full of warmth, memories, and love."

One last step, and she pressed her hand to Owen's chest, right over his heart, looking up at him with nothing left to hide. "I think it's only right that I add to what this house stands for by admitting I'm falling in love with you, Owen Voss. On our own, we're both a total disaster, but together? Still a mess, but at least it's a mess that feels like home."

Owen stood rooted to the spot, words tangled somewhere behind his lips. When he finally reached for her, it wasn't a reckless impulse but a quiet recognition—two people who had finally run out of reasons to keep their distance.

The lights stayed low, casting a gentle glow that softened every edge of the room. The air was heavy with the scent of cinnamon and the sharp, electric promise of rain, the storm outside rattling the windows with its own restless energy.

She couldn't say who moved first. When their lips finally met, it wasn't desperate or hurried. It was slow, reverent, hungry—the kind of kiss that tasted like relief after a long drought. They lingered, letting hands and mouths wander, every touch feeling impossibly new.

His fingers threaded through her hair, anchoring her as he pressed heated kisses along her cheek, teeth grazing the delicate shell of her ear before trailing down her jaw. Adelen's hands mapped the landscape of his chest and stomach, memorizing every line and hollow, before she caught the hem of his shirt and peeled it away, baring him to the low light. Their mingled breaths filled the space, underscored by the steady rhythm of rain and the low rumble of thunder outside.

Owen's hands settled on her hips, guiding her backward until the cool edge of the kitchen island pressed into her spine. In one smooth motion, he scooped her up, setting her atop the countertop. Piece by piece, he undressed her, leaving her bare and open beneath the golden kitchen lights, legs parted in invitation.

Adelen leaned back on her elbows, feeling the cool countertop beneath her and the heat of Owen's gaze as it swept over her bare skin. His eyes darkened when they found her chest, and she shivered, every nerve ending alive and waiting. As if he could sense her need, he moved between her thighs, lowering his head to draw one aching peak into his mouth. His tongue traced slow, deliberate circles, teasing and tasting, giving each breast the kind of attention that made her toes curl.

Every deliberate lick and gentle pull sent sparks racing through her, leaving her slick and breathless, his name tumbling from her lips. She guided his hand to her other breast, desperate for more, certain that if he kept this up, she would spontaneously combust.

But instead, Owen's mouth traveled lower, leaving a trail of slow, lingering kisses down her stomach, past her navel, until he hovered at her slick center. His breath was hot against her skin as he murmured, "I want to wear you on my tongue."

Adelen's back arched off the counter as he tasted her, his mouth and thumb working in tandem to unravel her completely. Her world narrowed to the heat of his tongue and the relentless pleasure building inside her, until her vision exploded with stars and she shattered around him. She was still floating somewhere above herself when Owen eased inside, slow and careful.

The stretch of him had Adelen gasping, her body adjusting inch by inch. It always felt like the first time, the way he filled her, skin tingling with every slow thrust. Owen gripped her hips, pulling her closer to the edge of the counter, each movement sinking him deeper inside.

It didn't take long before another wave crashed over her, leaving her limp and boneless in his arms. When her scattered thoughts finally settled, she found Owen's eyes on her, and her heart tripped over itself.

Owen looked like some wild, unchained god in the low light, his eyes bright with something fierce and tender all at once. But it was the unspoken words shining there that caught her breath, words that were still new, only spoken for the first time that night.

I love you.

The words remained, weaving themselves into the fragile thread that bound them together. She didn't hesitate, whispering them back as she reached up to cradle Owen's cheek, holding him close as he came undone.

Hours later, they lay tangled together on the living room rug, the world outside forgotten. They whispered confessions into the hush, words neither had dared to say before, letting understanding settle into their bones. It was a quiet beginning, something gentle and new, blooming out of all the chaos and heartbreak that had come before.

CHAPTER 53

Adelen

Adelen crept into her apartment just after sunrise, heart pounding for reasons that had nothing to do with fear. Unless you counted the fear of being caught grinning like an idiot.

Thank god her brother was nowhere to be seen. Hopefully, he was still drooling on a pillow in the guest room. She made a beeline for the shower, got dressed for work, and was this close to freedom when Diogo's voice floated over from the couch. She yelped, nearly launching her keys across the room.

"Morning, sunshine," he chirped. "Nice walk of shame you've got going there." His hair was a disaster, and he looked more comfortable than she'd like in his t-shirt and sweatpants, feet up on her ottoman.

She groaned and shot her pain-in-the-ass brother a look that could curdle milk. "I'm going to pretend you didn't say that."

He smirked in that way that had always annoyed her growing up. "Please do. Makes my job easier. Especially since we are going to be roomies for a while."

Her eyes narrowed as yesterday's puzzle pieces clicked together in her brain. "Wait—ugh, you're the one Owen hired for his company?"

"Maybe," he teased, far too pleased with himself. But that lasted about half a second before agitation took over, his fingers tapping on the cushion. "Anywho, let's not forget, we still need to talk about the stalker situation you neglected to mention. You seem to be super forgetful lately because the Adelen I know would never intentionally omit such a critical thing every time her dear brother had asked what was going on."

The humor vanished. "Diogo—"

"Oh no no. I'm dead serious," he interrupted. "I found myself with time on my hands last night, so I took the liberty of checking the building's surveillance system while we waited for the police to do their investigation. Don't ask how—you already know the answer."

Adelen stared at the ceiling, silently begging the universe for patience before she did something dramatic. Like smothering her brother with a throw pillow. She didn't have time for his nonsense.

"You've got blind spots all over, especially outside your apartment door. It's embarrassingly bad...kind of like the cute little easily hackable security cameras sprinkled around in here." He wiggled his fingers like he was sprinkling pixie dust.

She wanted to slap that stupid, condescending 'aww, you tried' look right off his face. A frying pan would do the trick.

"In more exciting news, I may have...made friends with your building's security guy."

"Oh come on, why?"

"Because Richard is a very nice man who happens to bring his pet iguana Edgar to work with him every night—keeps him in the top desk drawer. You should honestly check it out, Edgar has a pretty sweet setup in there."

Her stomach did a nosedive. "So you made a new friend just to hack the building? Fantastic. Can I go now?"

Diogo's eyes danced with mischief. "I also called mom and dad...and told them *everything*. They are *so* mad at you right now, but are immensely relieved that I'm here keeping an eye on you."

Adelen had a sudden urge to push him down three flights of stairs. "Wasn't being stuffed unconscious into the trunk of a car punishment enough? I didn't deserve you tattling on me to mom and dad like that!"

"They are expecting you to call them bright and early today," he chirped cheerfully.

Fucking hell.

"Anyways...So that coworker of yours who had been leaving you those notes? She had access. You know how? Because she lives in this fucking building and yet you somehow completely missed that."

Adelen's breath caught. "Shit."

"Yeah, shit." He crossed his arms, anger rolling off him in waves. "Guess who also made friends with Richard? Who always made it a point to get into the security room to bring treats for Edgar?"

That was how she got in. No matter how many times Adelen changed the locks, Tessa always found a way to get a new key and peek at the camera feeds as if it were her own personal reality show. Adelen felt like an absolute idiot for not seeing it sooner.

"You worked with her how many times, and didn't notice she was unhinged?"

She rubbed her temples, frustration and guilt mixing together like a bad cocktail. "I should've seen it. I should've..."

"Yeah," Diogo agreed, but his voice had less of a bite to it. "But you didn't. And my job is to make sure it never happens again."

Something in his voice made the hair on the back of her neck stand up. She didn't want to know what he meant, and she definitely wasn't about to ask.

By the time she reached the studio, she had pieced herself back together, at least on the outside. Inside, she was still a mess of nerves and adrenaline.

Especially after dealing with her mother's hysterics and her father's stern lecture about keeping secrets during the drive. She really had to stop taking these kinds of calls on the road. Her mother's wails and scolding would be the reason for a six car pile up one day.

She peeked into the actor's lounge as she walked by and found Owen already there. His hair was still damp from the shower, and he was taking an extraordinary amount of time making a cup of coffee. He was definitely stalling, waiting for her to show up.

When their eyes met, something private passed between them.

It was recognition, like they were seeing each other for the very first time and the hundredth all at once. A pleasant tingle zipped across her skin, equal parts thrill and pure, unfiltered nerves.

She noticed Bertrand was also there for some reason she didn't understand. Maybe security forgot to deactivate his badge. He sat at a table, nursing his coffee, eyes focused on her and Owen, narrowing with suspicion. A sly smirk crept across his weathered face. For the first time since he'd shown up in the building, he didn't say a word, keeping his comments to himself.

It was unsettling.

The rest of the day was a lost cause. They tried to focus on work, but every brush of hands and every stolen glance reminded her of last night. Warmth tangled with restraint, and all she could think about was dragging Owen into a supply closet and making him repeat some of those delicious noises from before.

They managed to keep it professional. Barely. There was no hiding the way their smiles crept out when they thought no one was looking, or the heated looks that promised to continue what they started on the kitchen counter last night.

And on the living room floor.

Adelen felt like a bird finally let out of its cage, soaring above the clouds and breathing in this new taste of freedom.

Not because the danger was gone, but because for the first time, she had someone willing to fly right beside her.

CHAPTER 54

Owen

Last night had been so perfect it almost felt unreal, like a fragile dream he was afraid to wake from.

That was the memory that would cling to him the longest, echoing in the quiet spaces of his mind.

The soft lamp glow in his old house, Adelen's laughter, the way she kissed him after dropping the L-word—every bit of it felt like the universe finally decided to throw him a bone.

Even seeing her again that morning felt impossibly perfect. Adelen had woken up and, with a single smile, managed to chase away every shadow in the room, as if she'd decided the world deserved a little more light.

His phone rang while he was holed up in his dressing room, pretending to care about the endless list of post-editing reshoots.

He almost let it go to voicemail, too busy replaying the moment she'd slipped her hand into his—like they were making some secret pact to take on the world together. It still knocked him sideways that she'd actually picked him. He was grinning like an idiot when he finally picked up.

But the second he heard the voice on the other end, everything changed.

"Mr. Voss...I'm so sorry. This is Bethany from Clear Waters Residences. Your mother—"

Everything after that moment blurred together. His mind filled with the relentless howl of a hurricane, drowning out the world until reality faded to static. He had no memory of pulling his car to the side of the road or of the violent sickness that overtook him as he made his way to the care facility.

He couldn't recall parking either. His car ended up spread across two spaces, as if even it had lost its sense of direction.

He barely registered how he had nearly barreled into an elderly couple in the hallway, his legs carrying him faster than his mind could process, every step a desperate plea not to be too late.

His heart hammered against his throat, the words "Mr. Voss...I'm so sorry" looping endlessly in his mind, drowning out every other sound until the world became nothing but a muffled blur.

By the time he reached her door, he could feel it in the air. The unnatural hush, the eerie calm settled over everything. The sharp scent of disinfectant clung to his skin, cold and sterile.

He burst into her room anyway, lungs burning, clinging to the desperate hope that it was all a mistake—that she'd be there, waiting with that gentle smile, ready to hear more stories about the girl with the dark hair and eyes that sparkled when she laughed.

But it was too late.

The last piece of his family—the brave woman who had loved him fiercely from his very first breath—was gone. Tears blurred his vision as he crossed the room, every step splintering his sense of self until he reached the bed where his mother finally rested.

He sat on the edge of the bed and pulled her into his arms, the same way she had held him countless times in his life. The coldness felt wrong. The air he forced into his lungs felt wrong. Nothing felt right.

If anyone came in or tried to speak to him, Owen didn't notice. He wouldn't have cared if the world ended outside that door.

He stayed there for what felt like hours, cradling his mother and whispering silent wishes that she had found peace, that she was with his dad again. He wished he could pull her back, even as he hated himself for wanting it so badly.

In that moment, he wasn't Owen Voss, the thirty-six-year-old with a career and a life of his own. He was just a little boy again, aching for his parents, realizing with a hollow ache that his whole family was gone.

CHAPTER 55

It didn't arrive like a storm.

Grief crept in as paperwork. Endless phone calls. A mountain of tasks pressed down on his chest, each one a reminder that breathing was suddenly a conscious effort.

People said all the right things, but their words slid right off him, leaving no mark. He wouldn't remember any of it anyway. Their faces blurred together, just more shapes in a world that had lost its focus.

He'd spent years bracing for this, watching her slip away piece by piece, but none of it mattered now. Knowing it was coming hadn't softened the blow. If anything, it left him hollow and numb, as if someone had pressed mute on the world inside his head.

Levi and Aurelia took over the details when he couldn't, gently insisting he step away from filming and everything else. Flowers flooded his penthouse from the crew, Neuronix staff, and even strangers whose names he didn't recognize. He appreciated the gestures, but nothing made sense. He couldn't process any of it.

He just wanted his mom back.

The last few days had been spent sitting at the kitchen table in the house he grew up in, analyzing his role as a son. Could he have been less of a pain in the ass? Could he have done more to help her? Was she in pain?

The more he turned it over in his mind, the more he realized he didn't have many regrets. There was never going to be enough time with someone you loved. He'd spent every moment he could with her, right up until the day she no longer knew his face.

He missed the daily phone calls they used to have and the monthly mother-son Friday lunches where he would spill all the tea he had, and she would be his sounding board when he felt lost. He missed going home to celebrate Christmas Eve and putting out the monstrous collection of ceramic village displays—and her yelling at him and his father for adding giraffes and other zoo animals in the village square.

The truth was, those traditions had faded long before now, but Owen hadn't let himself face it. He could have kept them alive in her memory, but instead he ran from the ache, pretending it didn't matter.

Losing his mom made him miss his dad all over again—the man who'd been taken too soon, but who left behind a lifetime of memories and a quiet blueprint for what it meant to be a good man.

The funeral arrived faster than he was ready for, but dragged on in slow motion. Hundreds of people came. The line spilled out the door and snaked down the street, turning the block into a mess of cars and confusion.

Former colleagues, students, and parents—all people whose lives she'd touched as a special education teacher and advocate for kids with disabilities and special needs. There were thank-you notes, stories, and tears from grown adults who still carried her lessons with them.

Estrella made an appearance and stayed longer than expected; her baleful eyes nearly had Owen collapsing in on himself. Remembering her sage advice that bordered on motherly advice, cleaved his heart into. His knees almost buckled under it all.

Hell, even Bertrand showed up in a rare display of respectful somberness, quietly shuffling through the line. His gnarled fingers gently clasped him on the shoulder in condolence.

Owen remembered almost nothing except the feeling of standing in a suit he didn't remember buying, nodding and smiling on cue. Every gesture felt mechanical, the motions of someone pretending to be whole and silently begging for it all to end.

Then, in the crowd, he saw her.

Adelen.

She wore a simple black dress, her hair pulled back, eyes shining with quiet sympathy. Her brother stood beside her, both of them choosing not to intrude, lingering near the back with Ivy, Grace, Isaac, Levi, Aurelia, and even Kaia. Just knowing she was there, a steady presence in the sea of faces, meant more to him than any words spoken that day.

After the service, when the crowd had thinned to almost nothing, Owen found himself standing in front of an old classmate who'd stayed behind, slouched in a chair in the corner. Auburn hair fell over his face as he leaned forward, arms braced on his knees.

Rhett had his own ghosts to deal with. As a boy, he used to stutter so badly he'd avoided speaking in public altogether. When other teachers were forcing him into reading aloud in class or putting him on the spot to try and "help him," Owen's mother had almost caused a riot in her fury.

Owen approached Rhett and wordlessly fell into the seat next to him. "Hey, man," Rhett said, his voice still carrying that same deliberate rhythm as he remembered. "I'm s-so sorry for your loss. Miss Denise was so amazing, and I w-wanted to tell you...your mom changed my life. She made me believe I wasn't broken. I think about it all the time."

Owen swallowed hard, but that lump still clung to his throat. "She believed that about everyone."

Rhett smiled faintly. "Yeah, she did. Especially you...even when you and Levi were starting shit in school."

He huffed a small laugh and nodded, unable to trust his voice.

Clamping a gentle hand on Owen's shoulder, he said, "Not today, not tomorrow, but when you're ready, give me a shout. I'd love to buy you a beer and catch up."

They both rose from their seats, and Rhett hugged him before walking away.

When the last guest left and Owen stepped through the old front door, the silence inside his childhood home pressed in on him, thick and suffocating. The rooms felt too small, the air too thin. Panic clawed at his chest.

He had to get out of there.

He bolted for his car, hands trembling as he gripped the wheel. His breaths came in short, ragged bursts as he tore out of the driveway, driving on autopilot, the steering wheel slick with sweat.

He didn't realize where he was until the car finally rolled to a stop—King's Miradouro, the overlook perched above the cliffs of the lagoon.

It was the same overlook where lanterns once glowed and Adelen's laughter had softened the jagged edges of his life for the first time in years. The same cliffs where his mom used to bring him for picnics, where he searched for buried treasure in the woods when he was small.

Still dressed in his suit, he trudged up the familiar trail and dropped to the ground, not caring about dirt or grass stains. His breaths came in uneven bursts as he pressed his palms to his eyes, finally letting the tears fall.

CHAPTER 56

Adelen

Aurelia told her the awful news, though it had already spread quickly through the production team. The studio was filled with a different kind of hushed voices this time, with concerned looks and the type of collective somberness that followed good people.

At first, it was because of what happened with Tessa, and the cloud that fell over the studio threatened to dampen the sanctity of their workspace. The entire crew had been on edge. Even Henrietta had been genuinely taken aback by everything.

But a different hush entrenched the building, and when she heard Owen's mother had passed away, her chest tightened painfully.

She'd always known how much his mother meant to him. Her name would light up his face, and stories about her spilled out of him with a kind of pride and gentleness that made you want to know her too. It was obvious where Owen's warmth and loyalty came from, the easy humor that softened even the hardest days. Even his looks were a gift from her: the same golden hair that caught the sunlight, the same mischievous blue eyes that seemed to hold a secret joke just for you.

Meeting her on that second date had felt like a privilege, a rare invitation into the heart of Owen's world. Denise might not have been able to say much, but Adelen liked to think she knew they were there, that she felt the love in the room even if words failed her. It was a small comfort. Adelen clung to it.

The hardest part was not knowing how to help him, not really. She was new to all of this: grief, relationships, the delicate dance of wanting to reach out but not knowing if the gesture would just make things worse. She called, sent messages that felt inadequate the moment she hit send, but Owen had gone silent, unreachable. Aurelia said it was the same for her, which was a strange relief. It wasn't personal.

It was anguish.

She and Diogo went to the service, not out of obligation, but because it felt right. Owen's mother deserved to be remembered, to have her life celebrated by the people who had been touched by her kindness—especially since she'd raised a man like Owen. That alone was reason enough.

She kept to the back with the others, watching Owen from a distance, her heart twisting at the sight of him. He was so still, so silent, as if his core had been carved out and an empty vessel left behind. Each person who came up to him got a polite thank you, but his eyes were far away, and every smile seemed to take something from him, as if he was paying a toll just to keep standing.

It broke her heart.

When he slipped out of the funeral parlor, she stayed put, rooted to the spot by uncertainty. She didn't follow—not yet. Sometimes people needed space more than company, and she didn't want to be another weight pressing down on him.

But as the evening wore on and Owen still wasn't answering calls, the worry started to spread. Levi got anxious enough to check his apartment, then his mother's house, but both were empty. The group's concern grew with every unanswered ring, every minute that ticked by. Adelen, though, had a feeling they were all looking in the wrong places.

There was a tug in her gut, a quiet certainty that told her exactly where he would be.

She changed into warm, comfortable clothes, moving on autopilot as she packed a blanket, a thermos of soup, a couple of water bottles, and a flashlight. The ritual of gathering these things steadied her hands. Then she got in the car and drove, the city lights blurring past as she headed toward the only place that made sense.

By the time she reached the overlook, the sky was a deep, bruised purple, the last traces of daylight fading into night. Lanterns from their date still lined the path, their glow dim but persistent, holding onto the last scraps of solar charge.

At the top, she found him right away—impossible to miss, even in the half-light.

He was sitting on the ground, still in his service suit, knees pulled tight to his chest, head buried in his hands. Seeing him like that, unguarded and broken in a way she had never seen before, nearly knocked the breath out of her. For a moment, she had to steady herself, fighting the urge to fall apart right there with him.

She approached quietly, not trusting her voice to hold steady. Without a word, she unraveled the blanket and spread it out beside him, settling down close enough for him to feel her presence but leaving just enough space so he wouldn't feel crowded. Sometimes, just being there was enough.

He kept his eyes fixed on the horizon, watching the last streaks of light disappear, tears slipping down his cheeks unchecked. When he finally turned to her, his eyes were rimmed red, his voice tattered and scraped thin.

"She was my best friend," he whispered. "The last piece of my family, and she's gone."

Adelen's throat tightened, her own eyes misting. "I know."

He let out a shaky breath. "I don't know what to do without her."

"And that's okay. You're not supposed to know," she said softly. "It's okay to grieve. Remember her. Keep her alive in the way you live.

Write down her story or your favorite memories to one day pass down to your children. It's only the end if you allow it to be."

He drew in a shaky breath and nodded, silent tears tracing new paths down his face, glinting in the lantern light.

Without letting herself think too much, she reached out and took his hand. He clung to her fingers like a lifeline, grounding himself in the simple contact. After a while, he shifted onto the blanket beside her and even let her press the thermos of soup into his hands. He drank, if only because she asked him to.

They sat together in silence, the night wind threading through the trees and carrying the faint scent of pine and distant salt. The quiet between them wasn't empty. It was full of everything they couldn't say, a connection that didn't need words to be real.

Owen would need time—more than anyone could guess—and Adelen was determined to give it to him, to be there for every slow, painful step. If there was one thing she could offer, it was patience and the promise that he wouldn't have to face any of it alone.

CHAPTER 57

Owen

The days bled into each other, a muddled stretch of work and grief, with only the gentle, grounding presence of Adelen anchoring him to the world. Her quiet companionship became the steady rhythm beneath the chaos, a soft reminder that he wasn't drifting alone.

Owen threw himself back into film promotion almost immediately after his mother's funeral, insisting he needed the distraction. Everyone—Levi, Aurelia, even Isaac—told him to take more time off. He wouldn't hear of it.

He kept himself in constant motion because stillness was dangerous. The moment he slowed down, thoughts crowded in, sharp and unbearable, threatening to pull him under.

The interviewers ate it up, oblivious to the difference between a well-rehearsed performance and the stifling pain twisting inside him. His grief seeped into every frame, bleeding through Dolf's agony on screen until the lines between actor and character blurred together.

Director Dax was thrilled. "This is the best film I've ever done!" he said, half-teary after watching one of the final promotional videos, shaking a fist full of licorice triumphantly.

Owen put on the mask, flashing smiles for the camera and feeding Dax the energy he craved, all while something inside him unraveled thread by thread.

But the act was never meant to last. Evidence of unraveling began to show in the smallest ways. A vacant stare in the middle of a conversation, fingers drumming restless tattoos against his thigh, shoulders slumping when he thought no one was looking. Sometimes his hands shook, betraying the storm he tried so hard to hide.

Everyone around him acted as if nothing had changed, as if he hadn't just lost the person who held his world together. That was the cruelest part of grief, the part no one warned you about. The calls and messages of concern faded after a week, replaced by the steady hum of normal life. He was left stranded in the wreckage while everyone else moved on, untouched.

Adelen noticed everything, though.

She started finding small, subtle ways to keep him grounded in this realm. Instead of him leaving her a tea, it was a thermos of his favorite coffee waiting in his dressing room. Short texts throughout the day: You did great today. Breathe. Don't make me drag you to the gym.

It wasn't anything dramatic or showy, but those small gestures kept him tethered to reality, like a lifeline thrown across a chasm.

Their "dates" weren't normal by any stretch. He wasn't sure if they even qualified as dates. One night, she took him to a late-night batting cage and dared him to hit the speed pitch until he finally mustered a smile. Another night, they drove out to the cliffs and just sat in silence, watching the city lights blink far below.

But the silence between them wasn't empty. It had become a hum in the background, a soft song of shared grief and unspoken understanding. The kind that made words unnecessary.

She wasn't trying to fix it or make it better. She was offering him space to sort himself out at his own pace. She created a safe place for him to break.

One evening, however, when he looked more haunted than usual, she finally said, "Come on, you need to hit something that can take it."

He frowned. "What, like Diogo?"

She rolled her eyes. "He would not go easy on you; what I meant was taking it out on a punching bag."

He reluctantly agreed, and the next thing he knew, they were at the same gym where she'd cracked ribs on a mouthy stranger weeks ago. Diogo had decided to join them, inviting himself despite Adelen's protests.

Apparently, Owen didn't know how to throw a punch properly. The twins banded together to show him, correcting his stance, adjusting his balance, and demonstrating proper follow-through. When his first few hits landed wrong, she corrected his form with a hand on his shoulder, a steady guiding touch.

The moment his fist landed solidly against the bag, Owen felt something inside him shift, a tiny fissure that let the pressure escape. For the first time in weeks, he could breathe without feeling like iron bands were cinched around his chest.

It didn't fix anything, not really, but it was a small victory.

Afterward, they collapsed side by side on the gym floor, backs pressed to the cool wall, the air thick with the scent of sweat and the hush of shared exhaustion.

"She was everything," he said after a long pause. "My mom. She was the glue that held everyone together...me, the house, and even Levi. I think I spent my whole life trying to make her proud."

"What makes you think she wasn't proud?" Adelen asked gently.

He stared down at his hands. "I don't know...Maybe I simply never figured out who I was without her. Or my dad, for that matter. I thought I'd already grieved him, but maybe I just...put it somewhere to deal with later and forgot."

Neither Adelen nor Diogo spoke, understanding he needed them to listen.

When he looked at Adelen, he caught a flicker of fear in her eyes—not the kind born from death or loss, but the aching terror of being left behind by someone she cared about.

Maybe that was why he guarded the people he loved so fiercely—so none of them would ever have to feel that kind of loneliness.

A rare smile crossed his lips, the first one since the funeral, as he said, "Alright ladies, let's go grab a pizza."

CHAPTER 58

Adelen

Grief had a sound.

Adelen could hear it in the shallow, uneven way Owen breathed now, like every exhale came with a steep price. The laughter that used to fill every space between them had quieted into long silences and half-smiles that never reached his eyes.

That stubborn fool had gone back to work too soon. Everyone knew it except him. But when she'd tried to tell him that, he'd just said, "I'm fine."

He was anything but fine. He just unraveled at a slower pace, piece by piece, where no one could see.

He poured whatever he had left of himself into the film instead of directly processing his grief. Every ounce of sorrow, guilt, and love he had left was channeled into the project, and the fucking camera ate it up.

Dax was ecstatic. "He's brilliant," he kept saying. "Absolutely brilliant."

But Adelen saw the truth—every take drained him, bleeding him dry each time.

She'd catch him staring off after retakes, fingers twitching against his thigh, lips moving silently as he tried to prepare for interviews. Sometimes he'd get them wrong and laugh it off, but the way his shoulders tightened told her it was far more serious than he was letting on.

When he thought he was alone, he looked utterly lost.

She started showing up early to make sure he had his favorite coffee or send him cringy inspirational messages. He never mentioned them, but he always tried to smile a little on those days.

And when he started skipping meals, she "accidentally" brought extra snacks and food to the set. He'd protest that he wasn't hungry, while simultaneously devouring half a bag of chips before realizing what he was doing.

He never said thank you, but she didn't need the words. She wasn't after gratitude—she just wanted to keep him from folding in on himself and disappearing.

She wanted to see him smile again, but not if it meant pretending. All she wanted was to give him a place where he could breathe, where he could let everything out and just exist. Even when she coaxed a laugh out of him, she could feel the heaviness lingering beneath his skin. It wasn't just his mother he'd lost—it was his anchor, his sense of purpose, the center that held him steady.

She'd watched people fall apart before—rookie actors buckling under pressure, directors unraveling in the chaos of a shoot—but this was different. This was deeper and far more dangerous.

He kept up the charade, channeling every ounce of grief into his work until it threatened to consume him.

Owen was teetering on the edge of burnout, and Adelen's patience had finally worn thin.

In the days that followed, she couldn't stop thinking about that moment, because the way she saw him now was different. He allowed her a glimpse of the man who doubted himself, who carried guilt he didn't deserve, who loved so fiercely it terrified him.

She couldn't even remember why he used to drive her crazy. Looking back, past Adelen must have been an idiot to ever think that way. The more she glimpsed his vulnerabilities, the more she saw herself reflected there. It was enough just to be together, to share the same space in silence and know it was safe.

It was the gentlest kind of intimacy she'd ever known.

But even as they grew closer, she could sense the storm gathering on the horizon. He kept bottling everything up, and the tighter he clung to his pain, the more she dreaded the inevitable moment when it would all break loose.

He'd spent his life being everyone's protector, the guy who lightened the mood, who made things easier for everyone else. But it came at great personal cost in the form of unnecessary pressure, guilt, and the fear of not being enough.

It was a pain she recognized all too well.

She'd spent years feeling like a burden, marked as different and misunderstood, always fighting to prove she didn't need anyone's help. In that way, they were the same: both stubbornly independent, both terrified of what might happen if someone saw the depth of their pain.

Maybe that was why she couldn't keep her distance anymore. His heart recognized hers in a way no one else ever had.

That was what love was about. It wasn't perfect or tidy, but messy and real. They weren't meant to fix each other, just to be the steady light that led the other home.

CHAPTER 59

Adelen

The next couple of weeks slipped by in a strange, uneasy quiet. No threatening messages lurking in her inbox, no cryptic warnings, not even the phantom echo of footsteps trailing her down empty hallways. With Tessa locked away in police custody, Adelen had started to let herself believe, just a little, that the nightmare might finally be over.

Just thinking about her made Adelen's blood run hot, a violent pulse thrumming beneath her skin. The police investigation dragged on, each new detail more gruesome than the last, painting a picture of Tessa's intentions that left Adelen cold. She learned, with a sick twist in her gut, that if she hadn't fought back—if she hadn't been forced to endure the worst invasion of her privacy—she wouldn't have survived that night at all.

Thankfully, the court system had little patience for attempted premeditated murder. That woman would die before she ever saw freedom again—whether it was behind bars or by Adelen's own hands. She knew, without a doubt, that Owen and Diogo would be right there beside her if it ever came to that.

She shook herself, forcing the violent thoughts away, and tried to anchor herself in the present, and on her computer screen, glowing in the early light, cursor blinking expectantly.

That morning, she was curled up on her apartment couch, laptop balanced on her knees as she picked through last-minute edits. The quiet was broken by the sharp buzz of her phone, and when she glanced at the screen, her heart stumbled. The name flashing there was a ghost that should have been exorcised from her life.

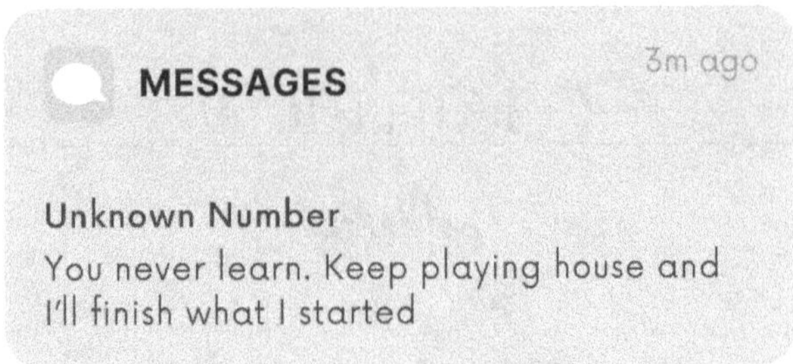

Her stomach lurched so violently she barely made it to the bathroom in time, retching up everything she'd managed to eat that morning. The tremors in her hands were so fierce she had to sink down onto the icy tile floor, pressing her back against the wall just to keep herself upright.

It wasn't just one message. Her phone kept buzzing, relentless, each new ping ratcheting up her anxiety until her hands shook so badly she kept fumbling and dropping the damn thing.

Owen was the first to notice. He had been yapping about motorcycles in the kitchen with her brother—his new best friend, apparently—when she'd rushed to the bathroom. His gentle knocking and increasingly insistent "Addy, are you okay?" brought her back to reality.

Climbing up from the chilly floor, Adelen forced herself to open the bathroom door and face him. With one look at her pale face and trembling fingers, he was at her side, voice tight.

"Addy, what is it? Talk to me."

She almost lied. That natural defense mechanism was screaming to brush it off the way she always did. But the memory of the car trunk, the smell of chloroform, the muffled panic flashed in her mind, putting the brakes on that line of thinking.

Instead, she handed him the phone in silence.

Owen's face went from sunshine to thundercloud in two seconds flat as he read the texts, his knuckles turning white around her phone. He didn't say a word, just started pacing like he was holding himself together with duct tape and pure stubbornness.

Diogo, who'd been stoically watching the situation unfold, peered over Owen's shoulder as he scrolled through.

"Give me that." Diogo scanned the messages more closely, eyes narrowing, jaw flexing. "Whoever this is, they're taunting you, and stupid enough to leave breadcrumbs."

"Diogo—" she pleaded.

"No." His tone cut through the room like a blade. "You're not brushing this off again. I will do whatever needs to be done."

That was the end of the discussion. Diogo stalked off to the guest room to grab his laptop, looking every bit like a bounty hunter on a mission, with Owen trailing behind like his loyal sidekick.

Later that night, the three of them huddled around Adelen's kitchen table, faces bathed in the eerie blue glow of Diogo's laptop, all nerves and caffeine.

"I've already got a firewall up in your apartment," he explained, fingers flying across the keys. "Every incoming text, email, or app ping gets mirrored to my system. Whoever's doing this, they're hitting you from a network that pings local to the studio."

Her heart clenched. "What does that mean—"

"It means they're close."

The words landed like a hammer.

"So," Diogo continued, matter-of-factly. "I'm coming in tomorrow as a guest. You'll get me a visitor pass, and I'll take a 'tour' of the set.

Meanwhile, I'll ghost into the system and see who's been pinging your phone."

Owen frowned. "You think the stalker's someone on set?"

"I think the timing isn't a coincidence."

Adelen didn't sleep a single second that night, tumbling right back into the black pit she'd convinced herself she'd finally escaped.

The next afternoon, Adelen's nerves were buzzing under her skin like she'd mainlined espresso as she led Diogo around the studio on his so-called tour.

They shared the same eye and hair color, but that was where the physical similarities ended. Adelen was a spitting image of their mother and Diogo of their father. Not many people were immediately able to tell they were related.

He was both terrible and weirdly great at pretending to be casual. The tattoos and piercings made him stick out like a neon sign. Kaia and Lizzie dropped everything to meet Adelen's 'special friend,' and her idiot brother soaked up the attention like his ego needed any more fuel.

He turned on his most shameless grin and claimed he was just another tech nerd tagging along, that he'd always dreamed of seeing a real movie set, and had begged her until she finally caved.

The two of them were practically drooling after their brief introduction. Kaia shot her a pointed look that said, We are absolutely talking about your friend later. The idea of talking to anyone about her brother like that made her throw up a little in her mouth.

Adelen knew he was laser-focused under that easy grin, but holy fuck, Diogo was laying it on thick. As they wandered the halls, she could practically see the hamster wheel spinning in his head, his eyes lingering on every spot that screamed 'suspicious.' After the grand tour, they headed back to her office.

Her boss spotted them before she could open the door.

"Adelen," Cary called out, voice too smooth. "Didn't realize we were running a guest tour now."

Her annoyance spiked. Cary had been a royal asshole since day one of his arrival. She shouldn't have to explain Diogo's visit, but here she was, doing it anyway. "He's just visiting for the day. I cleared it with security and HR."

"Of course you did." The man's eyes flicked over Diogo with poorly veiled disdain. "You certainly seem to have a type."

Adelen just stared, stunned, her brain short-circuiting at the comment.

Outwardly, Diogo didn't react, his face a solid wall of cool indifference. But when Adelen glanced at him, he was already signing low and quick: Don't correct him. Friend only. Trust me.

She let the same expression fall over her as she said, "Yeah, he's a friend. What corporate policy does that break exactly?"

The glare Cary shot Diogo could have melted steel. The tension between them was thick enough to cut with a butter knife.

"Nice to meet you," Diogo said pleasantly, extending a hand that went ignored.

Cary only smirked and muttered, "Try not to get in the way," before stalking off.

Diogo's smile stayed plastered on, but his eyes went ice-cold as he watched Cary walk away. Then, in a move so out of character it nearly gave her whiplash, he kissed Adelen's cheek and whispered, 'Go back to work. I've got what I need.'

Then he was gone.

CHAPTER 60

Diogo

By the time he reached his rental car out in the lot, his laptop was already open, tapping into the secure network he'd spoofed inside.

The system hummed to life, data flooding his screen in a blur. This was where the real fun started. Most people thought his job was shady, maybe even a little criminal, like he should be lurking in a dark alley in a trench coat.

In reality, it was basically the same as sitting in a boring corporate IT office. The only difference was that instead of building walls to keep people out, he was the guy looking for a window or a door left just a little too open.

The tattoos and piercings? Pure fun. Sure, he liked how they looked, but the real joy was watching clients' faces the first time he strolled into a Fortune 500 boardroom in business casual, looking like he'd just escaped a rock concert. Never got old.

For hours, Diogo sat in his car looking like a total weirdo, tapping away at his laptop while the screen painted his face ghostly blue, the midday sun having given way to dusk. Finally, the code he'd been chasing settled on a single source—one IP address buried under a mountain of digital nonsense, pinging Adelen's number every time. Same encrypted string, same signal as the one that hit her phone yesterday.

His fingers flew over the keys, chasing down the location and owner, desperate to prove his hunch right. When the info popped up on the screen, he froze, heart pounding as if he'd just run a marathon.

Thank god for GPS apps, it made using satellite data that much more exciting. Except the messages weren't coming from some random cell tower. They were coming from inside the studio—right near Adelen's office. Adrenaline shot through Diogo as he muttered, "Got you."

The answer slammed into him like a freight train. It had been right in front of his face the whole time.

He had to admit that he was momentarily impressed with Cary. It wasn't every day that a regular civilian would even be aware of any programs that masked IPs and delivered anonymous messages. That kind of software was classified and accessible only to a handful of government entities and certain contracting organizations. It was virtually impossible to obtain.

Diogo knew this better than anyone...since he created those programs himself.

He stared at the name on the screen, jaw clenched so tight it hurt. The arrogance of that bastard. The way that piece of shit talked to Adelen—to him. Suddenly, everything snapped into place.

He cursed under his breath and snapped his laptop shut.

"Not tonight, asshole."

He was sprinting across the parking lot before his brain even caught up with his feet, his phone pressed to his ear.

CHAPTER 61

Adelen

Adelen was hunched over her monitor, putting the finishing touches on a few outstanding items, and completely clueless that danger was creeping up behind her.

Cary was standing behind her, way too close and way too quiet, watching her like he always did. She was already jumpy from the last creepy message, but his presence cranked her nerves up to eleven. The promo reel flickered on her screen, and she forced herself to focus on the audio timeline.

The office door creaked open, and her head snapped up. Owen leaned in and opened the door wider so he could fit his body through. His familiar grin eased her for the first time that day. When he acknowledged Cary's existence, the grin disappeared instantly, replaced with blatant hatred.

"Hey," he said in a clipped tone that had nothing to do with her and everything to do with the man standing at her back. "You planning on taking a dinner break at some point? You've been at this for hours, and even the sun decided to call it quits for the day."

She smiled faintly. "Give me twenty minutes. I'll meet you in your dressing room."

"Perfect." He winked at her and stared at Cary like his days were numbered as he backed out of the doorway.

But as soon as he was gone, Cary let out a low, humorless laugh, abruptly stepping back. He rounded the desk in a series of fast, jerky movements and began packing up his belongings.

"It's one thing," he said, voice dripping with something that wasn't quite mockery, "to shack up with the leading actor in a film you're paid to work on, but it is another to bring your second boyfriend onto set as a guest and let him live in your company-paid apartment." He took casual measured steps towards the entrance of their shared studio space.

His words smacked her right across the face.

She'd never told him that. The only person who knew Diogo was staying with her was Owen. She hadn't even told the rest of the Shrew Crew about it since they hadn't gone out together since her abduction.

All the air whooshed out of her lungs like a popped balloon. She stood up slowly. 'What did you just say?'

Cary paused in the doorway, tossing her a smile over his shoulder. A slow, predatory curve of his lips. "You really should be more careful, Adelen. People are always watching."

Something icy prowled through her veins.

Everything snapped into place—the messages, the creepy notes, the power outages, the break-ins back in Vila Verde.

It was him.

It had always been him...Tessa was a more recent development that had Adelen's head spinning with the most obvious question: *why*? None of it made any sense. But there was no time to dwell on it now. Everyone else had already left for the night, and now they were the only ones left in the building.

She shot to her feet, panic flooding her senses, her mind screaming one word: Owen.

Her lungs burned as she tore through the building toward Owen's dressing room, desperate to find him, to warn him. She rounded the corner—and her heart slammed to a stop.

The door was already open.

Cary stood inside, face contorted with rage, and Owen was pressed back against the vanity, hands up in surrender.

"Cary," Owen was saying, calm but tense, "you don't want to do this—"

"Shut up!" Cary hissed, turning at the sound of Adelen's footsteps. His eyes went wild when he saw her. "You ruined everything! They wanted to give you my job when I taught you everything! You're the key to my future!"

Adelen didn't have a chance to process the nonsense that Cary spewed out of his mouth before he lunged toward her.

She barely had time to react before he grabbed her arm and shoved her into the wall next to the vanity, his other hand flashing up—a gun glinting in the light.

"Let her go!" Owen roared, instinctively positioning himself between them.

Cary swung the gun at him. "You stay back! You don't get to take her from me!"

Adelen stepped around Owen to stand at his side. Her mind spun with every self-defense lesson, every move her brother taught her, every instinct screaming for her to act, and not one of them would help them here. One wrong move could end this in blood or death.

She stilled, taking precious seconds they did not have to calculate her options, waiting for Cary to make a mistake that she could leverage. She needed to stay calm and think, or they would both die tonight. And as much as she loved him, she wasn't into a Romeo and Juliet-style ending.

As Cary continued his unhinged tirade with Owen trying to reason with him, she saw a whisper of movement behind him. A shadow hovering in the darkened hallway, just outside the open doorway.

Diogo.

She'd know that shadow anywhere.

An apex predator stalking a lower-level beast as he looked in her eyes and quickly flicked down at his hands, a silent command. His fingers moved quickly: Police coming. Three. Move.

She understood the message loud and clear. There was no room for error, and no time to hesitate; only the element of surprise would help them live to see another sunrise. He began the silent countdown with his hand.

One.

Two.

Three.

With all the strength she could possibly muster, she shoved Owen to the side hard and out of harm's way. There was no time to react, and Owen couldn't maintain his balance.

The moment Adelen moved, Diogo lunged forward, aiming to disarm him. The gun went off in the scuffle.

The gunshot was loud and sharp enough to slice through bone.

Owen gasped and stumbled backward, a burst of red spreading across his chest.

Adelen screamed.

Diogo twisted Cary's wrist with brutal efficiency, the sound of bone snapping loud and distinct, the weapon clattering to the floor as he swept his legs out. Cary hit the ground hard, rage dissolving into pained wails as police sirens screamed outside, answering the call Diogo made when he ran back into the building.

The dark cloud of threats that had been hanging over Adelen for months finally cleared, but she hadn't noticed. Hadn't registered what happened beyond the moment when Owen's entire body snapped back and recoiled.

The world screeched to a halt, everything drowned out by the sight of Owen crumpling to the floor, blood blooming across his shirt.

CHAPTER 62

Owen

Owen woke up squinting into fluorescent lights so blinding they could have moonlighted as police interrogation lamps or the world's most aggressive tanning bed.

His brain felt like it had been stuffed with cheap insulation, and he was slouched on a mattress that had clearly lost a bar fight with comfort sometime in the last decade. The blankets were so thin and scratchy they might as well have been made from recycled sandpaper.

This had to be the worst hotel he'd ever stumbled into. He didn't have sky-high standards, but not sleeping under a sandpaper blanket was one of them. He must have booked this place in a fugue state—or as a prank on himself.

He was already drafting a scathing review in his head, complete with dramatic sighs and at least three exclamation points.

He tilted his head, trying to get his bearings, and immediately clocked an IV taped to his arm.

Must be one of those European spas...when did I book this?

Next, he noticed the hospital gown beneath the sad excuse for a blanket.

This is the ugliest bathrobe I've ever—wait. Hospital?

He peeked down and gingerly prodded the spot on his side that was starting to throb, a not-so-gentle reminder from his body not to get too cozy.

The room and the situation snapped into focus, his most recent memories slamming into him like a Mack truck with no brakes: Cary storming into his dressing room, waving a gun around, Adelen getting shoved into the wall.

That same white-hot rage from before came roaring back, like his insides were trying to start a fire.

He remembered the gunshot, then—pain. Everything after that was a blur: ambulance lights, rapid-fire questions from police and doctors, Adelen shouting somewhere in the chaos.

Owen was alive. Barely. He felt like he'd squeaked by on a technicality, the universe letting him off with a warning this time. The bullet must have grazed his side, tearing through muscle but missing anything vital.

A tidal wave of dread crashed over him, his eyes darting around the room while the heart monitor tried to keep up with his panic. Relief hit him the second he spotted Adelen, curled up in the corner on a chair that looked like it had been designed by a sadist with a vendetta against comfort.

God, he hated hospitals.

Almost like she had a sixth sense for his gaze, her eyes fluttered open and locked onto his. She shot upright so fast she nearly toppled out of the chair, then rushed over, her eyes wild with worry and exhaustion.

He was pale as a ghost, but awake, and his trademark shit-eating grin was already making a comeback.

"Hey," he rasped, his voice dry and scratchy from lack of use. "Guess I've got a badass new scar to show off to people."

Tears burned her eyes as she grabbed his hand. "Don't joke right now. You scared the hell out of me."

"Yeah," he murmured, his thumb brushing her palm. "So did you when I got hip checked out of nowhere. But you're safe. That's all that matters."

She leaned her forehead against his, trembling. "You could have died."

He smiled faintly. "Again, you could have too. I have zero regrets and would do it again in a heartbeat. You're worth it."

Adelen shook her head, trying to blink back tears. "So fucking stubborn."

"I love you," he said simply, the need to say it superseding the pain. "I knew it the second I laid eyes on you at the wedding. I fell for the woman who could silence the world and still make me listen."

Her tears were falling freely as she carefully pressed her lips to his, mindful of his wound.

She was still there when the police showed up for his statement, and when the doctors came in to poke and prod. And when Owen argued with them about getting discharged as soon as possible because he felt "very naked" under his hospital gown and had zero intention of flashing anyone else today.

The simple action of interacting with people had quickly drained his very short well of energy, and the searing pain in his side depleted whatever was left. Tomorrow seemed like a good day to talk about what happened, but for now, Owen needed more sleep.

When he closed his eyes to rest again, Adelen was still there, holding his hand.

CHAPTER 63

Adelen

The relentless beep of Owen's heart monitor had wormed its way into her dreams, echoing through every restless night and refusing to let her forget.

Every time she closed her eyes, the memory replayed itself in brutal clarity: Owen crumpling to the ground, the sharp burst of a gunshot ricocheting off the studio walls, impossible to silence.

Now, standing in the doorway of his childhood home, she felt the weight of guilt settle over her shoulders, heavy and persistent, refusing to let go.

Owen had been discharged two days ago, against the doctor's orders. Because he was stubborn, reckless, and infuriatingly persuasive. He'd insisted he'd recover better here than in a sterile hospital room, nearly causing a riot in the process. The doctor, probably fearing a rise in his own blood pressure, finally caved.

With POLmArK dominating the headlines and news outlets for not one, but *two* separate violent crimes, the press had been relentless.

When Adelen mentioned she was temporarily moving into the house so she could take care of him and escape the crowd of reporters camped outside her apartment building, Diogo gave her a knowing smirk and said, "Of course, '*temporarily*' moving in," using air quotes to emphasize how little he believed her.

That didn't stop him from tagging along, packing all of his clothes and equipment to bring to Owen's house, too. He refused to stay in her apartment alone now that it was swarmed with paparazzi, claiming it would raise too many questions about who he was. The last thing he wanted was for his identity as the *Silver Shadow* to be revealed. And he promised their parents he would stick to her like glue.

Adelen knew it was also because Diogo and Owen's bromance was alive and well, and her brother needed to confirm with his own eyes that Owen was still in one piece.

He was right about the paparazzi problem, though. Owen's public persona on a regular day was enough for news outlets to keep tabs on him, especially after the Neuronix scandal earlier that year. With the promos now running across networks for *Metal Love Beans*, the incident with Tessa, and then Cary, the tabloids were having a field day.

There was public outrage over the incidents, with POLmArK receiving significant backlash for failing to protect its employees and actors. They had begun promotions for the new TV film weeks ago, teasing its upcoming release. The final shots she'd just edited were supposed to roll out this week, but based on the whispers circulating around the studio, it may be in jeopardy.

On the drive over to Owen's house, Adelen had been on the phone with Kaia, who told her the hot gossip being spread amongst the crew and staff: POLmArK may be shutting down the Joia City satellite location.

Adelen's mouth had gone slack at the news. When she pressed for more details about what was being said, Kaia admitted she was the source of the rumors, having overheard a heated meeting between Altina and some POLmArK executives about the back-to-back scandals. And by overheard, Kaia confessed she pressed her ear up against Altina's office door after walking by and hearing angry voices.

The company's stock and public image had taken a beating with the negative publicity. Apparently, their solution was to wipe the troublesome new studio out of existence rather than address how to mitigate this type of behavior in-house. It was the same kind of tactics they had employed when they offered her Cary's position without discussing their performance concerns directly with him.

Henrietta allegedly had the most epic meltdown of her life upon hearing the rumors, threatening anyone who would listen that if her career went down the drain because of all this, she was taking every single one of them with her. Whatever *that* meant.

Adelen didn't know what to make of it. So much had happened in the span of a couple of weeks that would cause stronger people to buckle under its pressure.

Diogo had shot her a quizzical look from behind the wheel, the same questions forming on his face that were forming on her face:

What happens if they shut it down?

Will I still have a job?

Will I have to move back to Vila Verde?

Each silent question crashed over her, a tide of unease and disappointment that left her feeling empty. She'd finally carved out a place in the world that felt like home, a fragile sense of belonging she'd fought so hard to claim. The thought of leaving—of packing up and returning to Vila Verde after clawing her way through homesickness—left a bitter, metallic taste in her mouth. For the first time in ages, Adelen knew exactly what she wanted, and now it felt like the universe was reaching in to snatch it away.

Diogo's grave expression indicated he shared the same feelings and concerns.

The remainder of the drive passed in contemplative silence.

There were bigger and more pressing things to worry about—like Owen's recovery and ensuring both Tessa and Cary could never harm anyone again.

Adelen slipped quietly into the living room, Diogo trailing behind her like a silent shadow. Her eyes were drawn at once to the unmistakable shape stretched across the couch. Even in the dim light, Owen was impossible to miss.

Owen lay half-asleep in a simple white shirt and navy flannel pajama pants, his mother's hand-knit gray blanket thrown haphazardly over his waist, a heating pad pressed to his bandaged side. Even now, bruised and washed-out, he managed to look unfairly beautiful, as if he belonged in a painting rather than a recovery room.

Their footsteps stirred him from the edge of sleep. His lashes fluttered, and that familiar crooked grin tugged at his mouth. When his ocean-blue eyes found hers, the tension in his face melted away.

"Hey, Trouble."

Then he looked at Diogo, who gave him a mock salute, and added, "And Trouble 2.0." His voice was still hoarse and scratchy. "You didn't have to come all the way out here...unless you brought snacks."

She tried for humor, suddenly understanding why it had been Owen's go-to defense mechanism all this time. "You took a bullet for me, Owen. I think the least I can do is bring soup."

"Soup?" He lifted an eyebrow and groaned pitifully. "Please tell me it's not the kind with beans. I've had enough legumes for one lifetime."

She laughed—a small, relaxed sound—and set the container on the coffee table before kneeling down next to him. "Calm down, it's chicken noodle. No beans. I'm not a total monster."

"Okay, I can survive that."

"Although we found a freshly baked lentil loaf sitting on your front steps when we arrived. Courtesy of your buddy Bertrand," she added.

"Feed it to the wildlife. That cartoon character has forever ruined lentils in any shape or form for me after his ridiculous joke. How did he know I was here?" Owen whined.

"No clue," Adelen said as she began unpacking the containers of soup purchased from a local restaurant, "but I think it's cute that he's worried about you. He's adopted you—"

"No, thank you," Owen growled.

"—and probably enjoys your company more than either of you is willing to admit. I think he's lonely." Looking back on the man's behavior, Adelen was confident that every incident stemmed from loneliness.

"Then let's put him in a nursing home where there are tons of other people he can become besties with. Lots of people *who are not me*." Owen's eye caught the second takeout bag in Diogo's hand, shifting his attention away from grousing about Bertrand to curiosity about its contents.

With a wicked gleam in his eye, Diogo held the bag out. "We also brought dessert."

Owen's eyes lit up. "Ooh, what kind?"

"A piece of the best flan you will ever taste!"

"Get out." Owen tried to sit up, yelped in pain, and flopped back down, glaring at Adelen. "Get that abomination of a dessert out of this house right now, or so help me, I'll risk tearing these stitches to do it myself. Which one of my friends betrayed me by sharing this knowledge?"

Diogo snickered and jiggled the bag again. "Just kidding...or am I?"

"You did this to yourself, and I'll never reveal my informant's identity," Adelen said, deadpan.

Owen had never looked more content as he said, "Yeah, I did."

He reached for her hand, and the moment his fingers brushed against hers, something inside her finally loosened. As long as he was here, she could believe, just for tonight, that everything might turn out all right.

CHAPTER 64

Owen

Owen was relieved to discover the bag did not contain flan, but Aurelia's homemade rice pudding.

His strong food-related opinions didn't make him a picky eater. Rather, it fueled a much shorter list of foods that were off the table. Flan was a weird mix of pudding and jello, with a texture that was much to be desired. He'd initially felt the same way upon learning Aurelia actually put real rice in pudding...until trying it.

It was smooth and creamy with hints of vanilla and lemon, topped with cinnamon—not at all what Owen had expected. It tasted like a warm hug and had quickly become a favorite dessert.

That atrocious lentil loaf, however...he wanted to punt it off a cliff into a lagoon.

Fucking Bertrand and his bullshit.

If he were in the mood to examine the gesture more closely, he would have to agree with Adelen. It was the old coot's way of showing affection. Owen supposed he should be flattered by it, but he'd suffered the last few days enough and packed it away to deal with later.

The kitchen was overflowing with flowers and good sentiments from other members of the cast and crew. Kaia and Rita had collected them all and handed them off to Adelen for delivery. She had made sure to toss anything that came directly from Henrietta into the dumpster first, refusing to "bring any demonic forces into this lovely home."

God, he loved this woman.

The freezer and fridge were also packed tightly with prepared meals and other staples, courtesy of his friends. Owen had been thrilled when Grace had paraded through with one of her lasagnas. His small village had rallied in his hour of need—and so many other times before. It was humbling.

Owen cautiously pulled himself up into a sitting position, mindful of pulling his wound open.

Adelen and Diogo were camped out on the living room floor around the coffee table, spreading out the various takeout options they'd brought. She ladled some chicken soup into a large coffee mug and passed it to Owen. Using a mug instead of a bowl was genius—he was still a bit unsteady, and the handle was a blessing.

As he slowly worked through his soup, Owen began running through the mental list of questions that had formed during his periodic moments of consciousness. Quite a bit must've happened while he was resting, if the news stories and tabloid articles he'd seen were any indication.

"So what's the word on the street about *Metal Love Beans*?" Owen asked casually. "POLmArK seems to be taking a beating in every single story I've watched or read so far...Not just about all this, but the sexual harassment allegations and lawsuits filed today."

It was a loaded question, one that would play right into some of his unfinished business. The mix of surprise and trepidation shared by the two siblings, however, was unexpected.

Adelen's brow furrowed. "*What* sexual harassment allegations?"

Diogo cocked his head in silent inquiry, mouth stuffed with buttered bread.

It took Owen a moment to understand their confusion, especially since the on-set sexual harassment story had just gone public earlier that day. And when he finally blew up at Henrietta during the filming of the final scene, Adelen was already in the trunk of Tessa's car.

His stomach clenched painfully at the memory, but he pressed on.

"Ever since our first date, when I shared what creepy shit Henrietta was doing to me, I hadn't stopped thinking about what you'd said that night—that you'd heard rumors about her behaving like this to past co-stars, but no one ever filed a complaint or spoke up."

Adelen slowly nodded in confirmation.

"After she tried to accost me in my dressing room, I put in separate cameras just to be safe. But after validating that cameraman Joe captured the moment she slipped her finger in my ass crack—" he ignored Diogo's sudden choking and Adelen's hard thwacks against her brother's back, "—it got me thinking. And plotting."

Diogo held up a single finger, a request to pause a moment, while he finished his coughing fit. After taking a long drink from his water bottle, Diogo motioned for Owen to continue.

"I tracked down every one of Henrietta's prior co-stars and conducted my own little investigation where I learned two things," Owen stated, holding up two fingers for emphasis.

"One—every single one of them had experienced some form of sexual harassment, with a couple confessing to some non-consensual activities."

He was so dangerously irate when he learned about those incidents. It was why he exploded that day on set when she slipped her finger in the back of his pants. He didn't consent to being her next victim, though he sure as fuck was going to be her last. Judging by the savage expressions on Diogo and Adelen's faces, they agreed.

"And two—my new best friend Joe has noticed this repeated behavior in the past, and has years' worth of footage captured. This superhero has been discreetly letting the cameras roll in between takes for a while now, and the shit he's managed to compile..."

Owen let out a low whistle, "Henrietta will never be in another film again, unless it's a prison documentary. Maybe it'll be a collaborative project with Tessa and Cary!"

Unable to resist the lure of his own joke, Owen winced as the movement pulled at his stitches, but kept laughing anyway.

"I *might* have talked all her victims into filing a class action lawsuit against Henrietta and POLmArK. I also *might* have leaked it all to the press today, including the butt crack escapade." Carefully placing his empty mug on the coffee table, he waited to see which one of them would react first.

Diogo blinked rapidly for several seconds before exploding into a sinister grin. "That's some next-level vigilante shit. I'm actually impressed. I do want to circle back to what the 'butt crack escapade' specifically entailed, though."

Of course, Owen obliged, explaining in great detail and in the most dramatic reenactment he could call forth, beginning with his collision with Henrietta and Bertrand's joke, all the way through to the finger incident. His audience was in tears from laughing so hard.

As an outsider, Owen could see how wild such a tale sounded. He'd probably be laughing just as hard if he were on the other side as a spectator. Perhaps it would become a legend told around campfires, passed down from generation to generation by his children.

His and Adelen's children.

That was another discussion to be had—about their future.

Once they'd calmed down from the story, the smile quickly fell from Diogo's face. He slid Adelen a worried glance and said, "Maybe you should fill him in on what Kaia told you on the way here."

After Adelen recounted her conversation with Kaia, she'd been a little withdrawn.

Understandable given her concerns about the future of her employment.

She and Diogo had then taken the time to clean up the remnants of their soup buffet, while Owen indulged in a little rice pudding. And maybe in a little self-reflection sprinkled with some scheming.

What he hadn't shared yet was how leaking the lawsuit to the press wasn't about creating chaos. It was a strategically calculated move that first came to him as he was being discharged from the hospital. One he learned from Levi when they were publicly fired from Neuronix—and brazenly took the company back.

The move was intended to drive the stock price down while damaging POLmArK's reputation. He'd thought through several potential outcomes and was well aware they would likely shut down the new satellite studio.

Maybe he was an asshole for capitalizing on Adelen's abduction and his near brush with death, but another thing he learned throughout all this was that he couldn't always be the nice guy. The cost of doing business was that there would always be collateral damage in situations like these.

And no way in hell was he going to pass up on this opportunity.

Finished in the kitchen, Adelen entered the living room with a glass of apple juice, gently setting it down on the coffee table within Owen's reach.

He watched her, studying the exhaustion carved beneath her eyes and the way tension seemed to pull her shoulders up toward her ears. The realization that he was just another reason she couldn't sleep twisted his stomach.

"Come here," he murmured, tugging gently until she sat beside him. "You look like you haven't slept in a week."

"Says the guy who whined about flan," she countered, but she leaned into him anyway.

He drew her in under his arm, moving carefully so he didn't pull at his stitches, and pressed a gentle kiss to the crown of her head. His fingers drifted through her hair, slow and soothing.

They sat together in a long, easy silence, letting the house breathe around them. The faint sweetness of his mother's vanilla candles lingered in the air, mixing with the steady hum of the ancient refrigerator. Somewhere in the walls, it felt like laughter from years ago still echoed, memories woven into the place's bones.

She finally whispered, "I should've told you everything from the start."

He understood better than anyone how guilt could twist their thoughts, make them do things that made no sense in the light of day.

Owen brushed her hair back, thumb tracing her jaw. "We've talked about this a million times already, and this is the last time. You don't owe me an apology, Addy. That's not how love works."

Her breath caught at his words. That word. "You never quit, do you?"

He managed a faint, cheeky smile. "Not when it comes to you. And if I were you, I wouldn't spend too much time worrying about your job or what will happen next."

She shifted and peered up at him warily. "Why not?"

With a slight shrug of his shoulders, he breezily replied, "Oh, I don't know. Let's just say these things have a way of working themselves out."

Suspicion intensifying, Adelen opened her mouth to interrogate him further when Diogo leaned against the kitchen doorway and cleared his throat—loudly. They both jumped, having completely forgotten he was still lurking.

"Okay, as sweet as this rom-com hospital recovery special is, I'd like to remind everyone that the last time you two got handsy, bullets started flying."

Owen groaned. “Why are you making it weird? My heroism was wooing your sister.”

Adelen snorted.

Diogo feigned a look of utter disgust. “Because anything involving my sister is weird. Anyway, I brought firewalls and video games. One of those things will save your ass again, and spoiler alert: it’s the firewalls.”

Adelen rolled her eyes at her brother but smiled anyway. “What did you do?”

Diogo strolled back in, dropping his laptop bag on the coffee table. “Upgraded your security. You’re getting some very exciting new cameras, locks, encrypted networks—the works. No one’s getting within ten feet of your house without me knowing about it.”

Owen grinned. “So what you’re saying is, I should feel extremely violated but also grateful.”

“Exactly.” Diogo paused, then added dryly, “Also, I installed GPS in your truck. If you so much as take her on another sunset hike, I’ll know.”

Owen scowled. “You’re kidding, right?”

Diogo didn’t even look up. “Am I? I thought you loved trackers?”

Owen let out a long sigh, but he couldn’t help the warmth that spread through him. This was his family now, quirks and chaos included.

CHAPTER 65

Adelen

Diogo eventually left to finish his setup, muttering about needing caffeine and a break from "grossly inappropriate displays of affection."

Owen drifted in and out of sleep, his head nestled against her shoulder, his hand warm and reassuring over hers. She watched the gentle rise and fall of his chest, counting each breath like it was the only thing anchoring her to the world.

Anything to get her mind off the new set of worries about her future employment running rampant in her head. She knew the whole ordeal with Tessa and Cary wasn't over by a long shot. It would take months for the police to finish their investigations before going to trial. And the sexual harassment lawsuit...

She couldn't bring herself to feel an ounce of pity for that succubus, only fury that it had taken so long for her victims to feel supported enough to take action. She would rather lose her job than allow that vile ghoul to harm another person again. And the two men she took advantage of—she was lucky to be far, far away from Adelen at the moment.

Dragging herself out of the dark pit of her thoughts, Adelen let her gaze wander over the walls and floors around her, searching for something solid to hold onto.

It was a dream she'd barely let herself imagine—what it would feel like to have a home like this, to fill it with laughter and chaos and the kind of love that made the walls feel warm. She pictured living here with someone who made the ordinary feel extraordinary, raising a small pack of hellions who would leave muddy footprints on the floors. The garden beds outside seemed to call her name, promising fresh meals and sun-warmed tomatoes, while the porch swing waited patiently to carry her worries away on a gentle breeze.

Adelen wanted all of it—with Owen.

As if subconsciously aware of where her thoughts had gone, he stirred, eyes opening just enough to meet hers. "You're staring again."

She smiled faintly. "Just making sure you're real."

He chuckled softly. "You can check."

She poked him in the forehead.

"That is not what I meant," Owen sighed.

Adelen laughed, then leaned in and kissed him, slow and deep, feeling his pulse steady under her palm.

For the first time in what felt like forever, the static in her mind faded to nothing. She had everything she'd ever dared to hope for: the man who'd risked it all for her, and the brother who hovered nearby, stubbornly refusing to let her go it alone.

She had no idea what tomorrow would bring, but tonight, she was home. For once, that was more than enough.

EPILOGUE

Owen

Owen was starting to get *hangry*.

His stomach was staging a full-blown protest, and honestly, he was about five minutes away from gnawing on the furniture.

Adelen and her mom, Delia, had kicked him out of the kitchen—his own kitchen—after catching him red-handed with yet another dinner roll. There was a literal mountain of bread in there. Who would even notice if five or six mysteriously disappeared? Apparently, they would.

This was not what he signed up for when he agreed to host Thanksgiving. He pictured himself as the benevolent host, not a starving exile.

He even wore the gold-and-blue sweater Adelen had knitted him. The ache of hunger gnawed at his stomach, so he and Diogo had taken their motorcycles out for a spin. It was a welcome distraction while the women busied themselves in the kitchen.

His hair was still wild from the helmet, strands sticking out in every direction, longer now than it had been in years. The extensions were gone, but he'd let it grow out for real this time, and Adelen seemed to love it. She had a habit of threading her fingers through the tangled mess whenever she passed by, and he found he didn't mind at all. If anything, he welcomed it.

Banished to the living room, Owen sulked on the couch, arms crossed like a petulant child. Diogo, matching his broody energy, lounged on the other couch next to their dad, who was laser-focused on the football game and blissfully ignoring their collective misery.

Delia and Fausto Mazao had arrived in Joia City a week ago for the holiday. Instead of putting them up in a hotel, they were sharing Owen's downtown penthouse apartment, staying in the guest room right down the hallway from Diogo, who was not thrilled to be sharing space with his parents for this long.

After the whirlwind of chaos and criminal activity that dominated their courtship, Adelen had officially moved into Owen's childhood home. The apartment building POLmArK had housed their relocated employees was full of too many bad memories, and they were both lured to this house on a quiet street.

His new favorite hobby was watching Adelen drink her chai tea on the porch swing every morning. That, and watching her try (and fail spectacularly) to keep anything alive in the garden beds. He already knew her coffee was a crime against humanity, but her plant parenting skills were somehow even worse.

It wasn't for lack of effort, either. She tried so hard, but the plants still shriveled up under her care. Owen had actually watched her kill a cactus once. A cactus. He didn't even know that was possible, but she managed to love it to death with too much water.

They'd tackled a bunch of renovations to make the place feel like theirs. Owen was the one who suggested it, but he still dragged his feet at first, worried he'd erase all the memories of his parents. Eventually, he realized they'd want him to fill the house with new laughter and chaos, just like they did.

The only ghosts left haunting the place were his own fears about moving forward.

Most of the changes were just cosmetic—fresh paint, new wallpaper, shiny countertops, and appliances that didn't sound like dying robots. Adelen had brought a few sentimental treasures of her own, like the long, jade-jeweled mirror that rested against the wall in the small foyer.

The biggest change was the addition of a bigger living room, a proper dining room, a couple of extra bedrooms, and a bathroom upstairs. Now they could actually host people. Or perhaps make room for future chaos-makers.

They settled into a routine pretty quickly, even if they were still figuring out the weird quirks of living together. It helped that Tessa and Cary were finally headed to prison, with enough evidence stacked against them to make the jury's job a breeze. That chapter was finally closed, just last week, and it made their new home feel even sweeter.

Sometimes they crashed at his downtown apartment for city events, but honestly, it lost its sparkle after they moved into the new place.

The same went for having Diogo as a roommate. The novelty wore off fast.

Owen didn't really mind if Diogo stuck around, but Adelen definitely had opinions about it.

He actually loved having mini sleepovers in his old room with the bunk beds. The only problem was Levi, who nearly started World War III when he found out someone else had slept in his bunk. The solution? Owen bought *another* set of bunk beds. Now, Isaac could join the party too, if he ever decided to stop being grumpy and have some fun.

He had to admit, every day turned into a competition to see who could out-asshole the other. It always started with an innocent question, then spiraled into the Sarcasm Olympics. Whoever fired off the best comeback got to be the official Torch Bearer of Assholery for the rest of the conversation.

This was their daily ritual. Every. Single. Day.

Diogo was more than happy to move into that apartment, mostly because it was a stone's throw from Neuronix. They were almost done with all the changes Diogo recommended, which meant his contract was nearly up. Lucky for everyone, he just signed on as a consultant to the new Chief Security Officer, Martin Strasburg.

Owen had done some soul-searching and decided to step back from that role to chase a new passion. He still owned a big chunk of the company—everyone did—but he didn't need to be in the trenches anymore. If Martin needed him, he was just a call away. Otherwise, Neuronix was in good hands.

Owen's stomach let out a monstrous growl. Loud enough that Diogo couldn't resist making a comment.

"You sound like you're about to shit your pants," Diogo said darkly. Fausto snorted, but didn't comment.

"No, that's the sound of my stomach eating itself because it's starved for nutrients, because someone," Owen yelled towards the kitchen, "won't let me eat anything!" He needed nutrients to make it through the rest of the evening.

Delia poked her head into the living room from the kitchen. "You can all go sit down now, we are about to bring out the turkey!"

Owen bolted into the dining room with inhuman speed, practically shoving Diogo out of the way like his life depended on it.

The table was a sensory overload—everything looked and smelled incredible. Owen piled his plate high with a bit of everything, then took his first bite. His eyes nearly rolled back in pure bliss. A few more bites and he was almost ready to rejoin the human race.

Adelen and Diogo flanked him at the big, dark wood dining table. He'd picked a round, less traditional table so people could actually talk to each other instead of shouting across a football field of mahogany.

"So Owen," Delia said as she watched him wolf down food with a satisfied smile, "tell me about your new project."

"It's a new double TV romance called *Milk Buds*. It's about two best friends who fall in love with a pair of sisters who own a dairy farm. An old friend from high school is letting us use his farm as the filming location.

Not only were Tessa and Cary behind bars, but Henrietta had finally joined them.

The sexual harassment suit blew up spectacularly with more victims coming out of the woodwork. In a landmark ruling, Henrietta had been found guilty on several counts, including rape. Cameraman Joe had really come through with all the footage he stockpiled. Her defense attorney had been so disgusted that he'd packed up and left in the middle of the trial.

Owen took a weird sort of joy that day, sitting with the other victims and, of all people, right next to Bertrand, who claimed he just "came to watch the show." Owen knew Bertrand was there in his own twisted way to see another scumbag get what was coming.

But the real cherry on top was the millions in out-of-court settlements for everyone's trouble. POLmArK was circling the drain of financial ruin until Owen swooped in and bought the whole mess. Now, their latest adventure was filming *Milk Buds* at Rhett Sousa *Dallingford's* ranch. Ivy had begged to tag along, claiming she needed a "change of pace," though Owen suspected it had more to do with Rhett than anything else.

In another bizarre twist, Owen grabbed a beer with Rhett after his mom's service, only to find out Rhett was Bertrand's grandson. Apparently, he'd kept that little bombshell under wraps all through high school. Now that was a story Owen needed to hear.

It looked like Owen wasn't getting rid of that old man anytime soon.

"That's wonderful to hear! I'm so excited you're both working so closely together! Maybe, soon you'll start talking about getting married and giving me a grandchild or two—"

"Oh my god, Mom, *stop!*" Adelen interjected, mortified by her mother's comment.

Diogo snickered as he sipped his beer.

"What? It's true! I've lost all faith in your brother ever settling down and continuing the family line, you're my closest shot right now!"

"*Hey!* I'm sitting right here, you know!" Diogo complained. "I just haven't met the right girl yet!"

"How about I make this easier for everyone?" Owen said, rising from his seat. Reaching into his pocket, he pulled out a small velvet black jewelry box and dropped to one knee before Adelen. Delia squealed with joy while Fausto remained nonplussed, a small, secretive smile on his face.

Owen had pulled her father aside just a day after they arrived, almost too nervous to ask for permission to propose. When Fausto gave his blessing, he tucked the secret away, holding it close like a precious stone in his pocket. Not even Diogo, who usually caught on to everything, had any inkling of what was coming.

Adelen's eyes went wide, shock blooming across her face as her hand flew to cover her mouth. The fork slipped from her fingers and landed on her plate with a sharp clatter. That morning, she had stood in front of the mirror longer than usual, coaxing her hair into gentle waves that now spilled over her shoulders and softened the edges of her charcoal sweater. Adelen had been insistent about taking a family photo, wanting to capture this new beginning and hang it among the other memories in the living room, a visual promise that their families would stand side by side.

He took a moment to study her, eyes tracing the lines of her face, the way the light caught in her hair, the nervous anticipation in her posture. He wanted to memorize it all, to press every detail of this moment deep into his memory where it would stay untouched by time. With a deep breath, Owen spoke.

"Adelen, the moment I met you, it took me all of two seconds to know that you were the missing piece of my soul, my heart had been searching for. Then you put me through hell for a while and hustled me in curling. You make the worst cup of coffee known to man, and I wouldn't want it any other way. I love everything about you and would set the world on fire with you."

Tears were brimming in those silver eyes he'd come to cherish, falling asleep beside and waking up to in the morning, as he opened the box. Adelen tentatively peeked inside and started to shake, tears streaming down her cheeks. Her mother was stunned silent, which according to what he'd heard from both Adelen and Diogo, was nothing short of a miracle.

The ring was anything but traditional. In the center sat a salt-and-pepper kite-cut diamond, dark and moody, with smoky swirls trapped inside. Smaller diamonds clustered around it, bright white against the shadows, and muted marquise accents fanned out like wings. The band was sleek and dark, lined with tiny pavé diamonds, the whole thing shimmering with a quiet, stubborn intensity. Bold, unconventional, and impossible to ignore.

Just like Adelen.

For what felt like ages, no one said a word, then suddenly everyone exploded with excitement and chaos. Delia was screeching with joy, Diogo was agape, and Fausto quietly laughed to himself as he buttered another dinner roll.

But all Owen could hear was Adelen's sharp intake of breath before she whispered, "Yes!" launching herself into his arms and kissing him soundly before her entire family. By the time they came up for air, her mother was already on the phone with one of Adelen's aunts, spreading the news.

Eventually, when the chaos died down, everyone started clearing dishes to make room for dessert. Owen was still riding the proposal high—until Delia walked in holding a baking dish of flan. Fucking *flan.*

Owen turned slowly to Diogo, who was barely holding back a shit-eating grin.

"I assume this egregious mistake is your doing?" Owen asked evenly.

Delia's eyes darted between the two of them in confusion. "What's wrong, Owen? Diogo said flan was your favorite dessert."

"Oh, did he now? He's been getting awfully forgetful lately—must be a side effect from stepping on one too many *rakes*."

The air got sucked right out of the room. Diogo's smirk vanished, Adelen let out a low, evil chuckle, and Owen just sat back to watch the carnage. He took his sweet time picking out other desserts, stacking his plate with a bit of everything.

"That was a *serious* situation," Diogo retorted. He shot his sister a menacing look. "Which was *your* fault, by the way."

"Except it wasn't, but you're too stubborn to accept that!"

"You were where you weren't supposed to be, and it resulted in what could've been permanent damage to my head," Diogo accused.

"*Permanent damage* is quite the stretch, and I was only in there because mom told me to be!" Adelen snorted derisively.

"No. I told you *not* to go into my room. You asked mom where in my room the lollipops were, then, of your own volition, went into my closet to look for them—*despite* me telling you *several times* not to. I *told you* I would get them when I was done cleaning my truck."

"Incorrect! Mom told me to go look for them so she could replenish the communal candy coffers, and I hesitated *because* you told me not to go in there. She said, 'It's my house, not his,' and instructed me to get them. I tried to warn you about the rake, but you were too blinded by your rage to see it." Adelen was angrily pointing her fork at Diogo.

"Every year," Delia muttered. "They do this every year."

"I told you not to go in my room, it's that simple. If it were the other way around, you would certainly not say mom had the final say if I could go into your room and peruse your belongings for candy." A muscle ticked in Diogo's cheek as he tapped his fingers on the table.

"She *did* have the final say, and so I listened to her when she told me to go to your room! Why in the world would I have opened the window to ask you where they were if I wasn't confident that I had the right and permission to be there?" Adelen threw her hands up in exasperation.

Owen took a massive bite of Delia's strawberry cheesecake, savoring every sweet, creamy second.

"You didn't answer my question. Had the roles been reversed, you would have found it completely acceptable for me to go into your room based on Mom saying it was allowed?"

"I don't think it matters if I found it acceptable because you would've done it anyway, similar to when you took the spare key to my apartment and proceeded to enter it on the basis that our parents owned the building—and my rental unit—to steal my favorite guitar! So the concept of homeownership applied there but not in their actual domicile?" Adelen looked ready to leap across the table.

Diogo scoffed. "I did that as a criminal. So you're the criminal in this case, then as well."

"The only criminal here is *you*!"

As he scraped the last crumbs off his plate, Owen showered Delia with compliments about her cooking and started chatting with Fausto about the football game, leaving the twins to duke it out over their annual lollipop drama.

The Mazaos had taken him in, quirks and all, and Owen finally had everything he ever wanted. He was home.

ACKNOWLEDGEMENTS

Good god, where do I even begin with this one?

This book went absolutely off the rails from the very beginning. When I first announced the release date, my life was pretty normal—we were getting ready for back to school with a third grader and a kindergartener. Summer was coming to an end, but there was still so much fun to be had.

Then my mother-in-law passed away unexpectedly, leaving a massive hole in our family and our hearts. I've heard so many horror stories about the dreaded in-laws which always baffled me, because I had the opposite. The day before the services, my own father sternly said to me, "I hope you realize how lucky you are to have had a mother-in-law like her. Most people don't get that. Most people don't get a parent like that. She is family."

And he was and still is absolutely correct.

Her grandchildren were her joy, but she managed to still make her adult children feel special. She was a former special education teacher who was a tremendous advocate for countless others throughout her career, and a fierce advocate for her grandson (my son) and his special needs.

Wendy was an angel that walked among us, and we were so blessed to have had her in our lives. I know I am not alone in thinking that. Students whose lives she touched attended the services of their former teacher—because that is the impact she made in the lives of others.

The world was made better because she had been in it.

Selfishly, I just wish we had more time.

Grief has a sound, and it looks different for everyone.

For me, I struggled to write this book, because how can someone be funny when all they feel is immense sadness? It was hard, inspiration was fleeting, and I couldn't change the date. So, when I say that it came down to the wire to be published, I quite literally mean it was uploaded with an hour to spare before the account locked and changes could not be made.

This book never would have been possible without my amazing, fantastic, and tolerant developmental editor Melissa McGovern who busted her ass to give me an expedited edit under an impossible timeline. I gave her the most raw first draft and, being the magician that she is (and fantastic friend), she pulled a rabbit out of a hat.

An extra special thanks to Alex, Jen, and author MJ Deck for an equally expedited beta read. Your perspective was so vital in making sure the characters jumped off the page like I had hoped.

But the other star of the show is my husband TJ. He made sure I had time to write when I needed to, was my sounding board for ideas and questions, and the driving force behind the weird shit Henrietta would whisper in Owen's ear.

To my real life MMC...I love you with every ounce of my being and my soul. Writing words is sort of my jam, but there aren't any to adequately describe how much I love you.

Sometimes, it really takes a village to survive and make things happen. Thank you to everyone who played a role in making this miracle happen.

www.ingramcontent.com/pod-product-compliance
Lightning Source LLC
LaVergne TN
LVHW010630110826
845149LV00014B/2819